Acclaim for
THE SECRET WISDOM OF THE EARTH

"A page-turner featuring masculine challenges, bloodshed, and stoic survival...Scotton's prose is colloquial and evocative; the descriptions are sharp, the voice down-to-earth...What [Scotton] should be congratulated on is his willingness to tell a new story in an old neighborhood, to draw characters who are thoroughly human, and to create a story that leads to terror and redemption, love and survival."   —*New York Times Book Review*

"THE SECRET WISDOM OF THE EARTH is a marvelous debut...The setting, in the coal country of Appalachia, is rich in history and lore and tragedy. A young teenager comes of age under the wise counsel of his grandfather. An ugly murder haunts a small town. The story has everything a big, thick novel should have, and I hated to put it down."   —John Grisham

"How marvelous to start the year of reading with Christopher Scotton's big-hearted THE SECRET WISDOM OF THE EARTH...In the world created by Scotton, Appalachia is more than verdant or hardscrabble...Scotton writes with deep understanding about how the mines eventually got played out and the impact of mountaintop removal...Evil may defy understanding, but in that inquiry into evil, this lovely novel brings readers closer."   —*Chicago Tribune*

"Astonishingly confident debut novel...a hugely powerful meditation on the deep cost of change...that will absolutely rivet his readers with a virtuoso combination of uplift and heartbreak. Writing careers don't begin any more promising than this."

—*Christian Science Monitor*

"Solid, sometimes soaring debut...written in taut, propulsive prose...a big, old-fashioned yarn well worth the telling."

—*USA Today*

"Violent and wonderfully tender...bittersweet...full of gorgeously rendered, intricately interwoven story threads...But it's Scotton's clear love of and respect for his subject—and his refusal to rely on clichés when describing Appalachia's humble people, their trials, or their successes—that makes the novel so surprisingly uplifting at times, and profoundly rewarding."

—*San Francisco Gate*

"Marvelous...Scotton writes with deep understanding...with a vivid but light touch." —*News & Observer* (Raleigh, NC)

"A deeply moving story about human cruelty and compassion... wonderful...This book reminded me a little of Harper Lee's *To Kill a Mockingbird*." —*The Oklahoman*

"With its hardscrabble setting and cast of burdened characters hemmed in by seemingly insurmountable circumstances, Scotton's violent and wonderfully tender novel speaks not only to a bevy of America's centuries-old troubles but also to our frustrated yet ardent attempts at fixing them." *San Francisco Gate*

The SECRET WISDOM of the EARTH

CHRISTOPHER SCOTTON

GRAND CENTRAL
PUBLISHING

NEW YORK   BOSTON

Copyright © 2015 by Christopher Scotton
Reading Group Guide Copyright © 2015 by Hachette Book Group, Inc.

Grand Central Publishing
Hachette Book Group
1290 Avenue of the Americas
New York, NY 10104

www.HachetteBookGroup.com

Printed in the United States of America

RRD-C

Originally published in hardcover by Grand Central Publishing.

First Trade Paperback Edition: January 2016
10 9 8 7 6 5 4 3 2 1

Grand Central Publishing is a division of Hachette Book Group, Inc.
The Grand Central Publishing name and logo is a trademark of Hachette Book Group, Inc.

The Hachette Speakers Bureau provides a wide range of authors for speaking events. To find out more, go to www.hachettespeakersbureau.com or call (866) 376-6591.

The publisher is not responsible for websites (or their content) that are not owned by the publisher.

The Library of Congress has cataloged the hardcover edition as follows:

Scotton, Chris.
   The secret wisdom of the earth / Chris Scotton.
      pages cm
   Summary: "After witnessing the death of his younger brother in a terrible home accident, 14-year-old Kevin and his grieving mother are sent for the summer to live with Kevin's grandfather. In this peeled-paint coal town deep in Appalachia, Kevin quickly falls in with a half-wild hollow kid named Buzzy Fink who schools him in the mysteries and magnificence of the woods. The events of this fateful summer will affect the entire town of Medgar, Kentucky. Medgar is beset by a massive Mountaintop Removal operation that is blowing up the hills and back filling the hollows. Kevin's grandfather and others in town attempt to rally the citizens against the 'company' and its powerful owner to stop the plunder of their mountain heritage. When Buzzy witnesses the brutal murder of the opposition leader, a sequence is set in play which tests Buzzy and Kevin to their absolute limits in an epic struggle for survival in the Kentucky mountains. Redemptive and emotionally resonant, The Secret Wisdom of the Earth is narrated by an adult Kevin looking back on the summer when he sloughed the coverings of a boy and took his first faltering steps as a man among a rich cast of characters and an ambitious effort to reclaim a once great community"— Provided by publisher.
      ISBN 978-1-4555-5192-7 (hardback) — ISBN (invalid) 978-1-4789-7975-3 (audio download) — ISBN 978-1-4555-5193-4 (ebook)   1. Mountain life—Appalachian Region—Fiction. 2. Families—Kentucky—Fiction.   3. Bildungsromans.   I. Title.
   PS3619.C698S43 2015
   813'.6—dc23

                                                                                2014012917

ISBN 978-1-4555-5191-0 (pbk.)

For Michael on his fourteenth birthday
... and for Connor on his.

Sweet are the uses of adversity,
Which like the toad, ugly and venomous,
Wears yet a precious jewel in his head;
And this our life exempt from public haunt,
Finds tongues in trees, books in the running brooks,
Sermons in stones, and good in every thing.
I would not change it.

William Shakespeare

The SECRET WISDOM of the EARTH

It was always coal.

Coal filled their pantry and put a sense of purpose in their Monday coffee. Coal was Christmas and the long weekend in Nashville when the Opry offered half-price tickets. Coal was new corduroy slacks and the washboard symphony they played to every step. Coal was a twice-a-month haircut. Coal was a store-bought dress and the excuse to wear it. Coal took them in as teenagers, proud, cocksure, and gave them back fully played out. Withered and silent.

Coal was the double-wide trailer at twenty and the new truck. Coal was the house with the front porch at twenty-eight and the satellite dish. Coal was the bass boat at thirty-five and the fishing cabin at forty.

And then, after they gave their years to the weak light and black sweat, coal killed them.

And began again.

Chapter 1

THE DIAMOND STATE

The Appalachian Mountains rise a darker blue on the washed horizon if you're driving east from Indiana in the morning. The green hills of the piedmont brace the wooded peaks like sandbags against a rising tide. The first settlers were hunters, trappers, and then farmers when the game went west. In between the hills and mountains are long, narrow hollows where farmers and cattle scratch a living with equal frustration. And under them, from the Tug Fork to the Clinch Valley, a thick plate of the purest bituminous coal on the Eastern Seaboard.

June was midway to my fifteenth birthday and I remember the miles between Redhill, Indiana, and Medgar, Kentucky, rolling past the station wagon window on an interminable canvas of cornfields and cow pastures, petty towns and irrelevant truck stops. I remember watching my mother from the backseat as she stared at the telephone poles flishing past us, the reflection of the white highway line in the window strobing her haggard face. It had been two months since my brother, Joshua, was killed, and the invulnerability I had felt as a teenager was only a curl of memory. Mom had folded into herself on the way back from the hospital and had barely spoken since. My father emerged from silent disbelief and was diligently weaving his anger into a smothering blanket for everyone he touched, especially me. My life then was an inventory of eggshells and expectations unmet.

Pops, my maternal grandfather, suggested Mom and I spend the summer with him in the hope that memories of her own invulnerable childhood would help her heal. It was one of the few decisions on which my father and grandfather had ever agreed.

The town was positioned in a narrow valley between three sizable mountains and innumerable hills and shelves and finger hollows that ribboned out from the valley floor like veins.

We had not visited Pops since Josh was born three years before, and as we came over the last hill, down into Medgar on that Saturday, the citizens stared at us like they were watching color TV for the first time. A fat woman in red stretch pants dragging a screaming child stopped suddenly; the child jounced into her back. Two men in eager discussion over an open car hood turned in silence, hands on hips. Booth four at Biddle's Gas and Grub immediately discontinued their debate about proper planting cycles and launched wild speculation about the origin and destination of the blue station wagon with suitcases and a bike bundled onto the luggage rack. People just didn't move *into* eastern Kentucky back then.

Twenty-two Chisold Street sat straight and firm behind the faded white fence that aproned its quarter acre. The front porch was wide and friendly, with an old swing bench at one end, a green wicker sofa and chairs at the other. The house was a three-bedroom Southern Cape Cod with white pillars on the porch, double dormers jutting out of the roof like eyes. One broken blind closed in a perpetual wink. The yard was trim and perfect.

We drew up in the wagon, a thin smile on my mother's face for the first time in months. My father touched her arm gently to tell her she was home.

Pops had been vigiling on the wicker sofa, chewing the end of the long, straight pipe he never lit. He slapped both knees, bellowing an abundant laugh as he raced down the porch steps before the car was even at a full stop. He reached in the window to unlock the door, opened it as the engine cut off, and pulled Mom out of the front seat into a bracing hug. "It's good to have you back home, Annie."

She nodded blankly and hugged back.

I exited the car with my backpack of essentials. "Kevin, I think you've grown six inches in two months," he said, fingering a line from the top of his head to my chin. He bear-hugged me, then gave my shoulder a squeeze. The strength in his grip left me flushed. He spun to Audy Rae, his housekeeper of thirty-seven years, who had come out to the porch. "It's about time we had some life in this old house. The conversation has been wearing thin lately." He turned back to me and winked. She dismissed him with a wave, swept down the steps and over to the car.

Audy Rae Henderson was five feet four and fireplug solid, her face furrowed with wise creases and unmissing eyes that burned brightly from her dark features. She reached up and placed a hand on each of Mom's shoulders and held her at arm's length as if to verify authenticity.

My father came around to the passenger side and stood until Pops acknowledged him. "Edward, how are you?" Pops asked. They shook stiff hands.

The inside of Pops' Chisold Street home was sparkling clean—
Audy Rae saw to that—but to me it smelled old and empty. In
the living room, two matching wing chairs with eagle-claw feet
and brass buttons tacked down the front faced a worn light-blue
sofa with doilied arms. Three of my mother's paintings hung over
it: a man canoeing on a river; wild horses splitting a canyon; the
Chisold Street house sometime in the sixties. The room was alien
and unused, but anything was better than the throttling silence
of our house in Redhill.

Audy Rae led me up to the spare bedroom. "Bet you're glad to
be done with freshman year," she said, helping the bag onto the
bed. I grunted and slumped next to the suitcase.

"High school, my laws. I remember when you was no biggern
my knee and now you're taller than your Pops."

I was silent, examining the way my interlocking fingers roofed
my thumbs.

She came over and sat next to me. "Kevin, you and your mom
been through a bad thing—bout as bad as life gets. I know it's
gonna take a while for her and you to heal."

"He blames me, you know. Says it was all my fault."

She let out a long, slow breath.

A tear dropped down and splashed my hand.

"What happened wasn't your fault, child," she said softly.

"But if I'd..." The sadness and choking anger of the last two
months began to close out the thin light in the room.

She put her hand on my leg. I could feel her eyes peering into
me. "It all may seem black and desperate now, but you gotta just
trust that the Lord's gonna take care of you and your mom."

I pulled at a stray thread from the white cotton bedspread as more tears came. "If he was taking care of us, none of this would have happened in the first place."

She pushed out another long breath, then let it fall away. "Kevin, I can't say why the Lord took Josh and why he took him the way he did. I don't think we'll ever puzzle out the answer. But I'll just keep praying that one day you'll find a peace with it." She stood and moved to the door. "I'll leave you to be putting your own things away."

I finally looked up. She smiled. "It's real good to have you here, child." Her face was filled with fifty-three years of stocked kindnesses. I smiled sadly back.

She held out her hands. "Come to me, honey." I pushed off the bed and took three quick steps into the cradle of her arms. She wrapped them around me tightly and squeezed, as if to try to turn me into a diamond.

⌐⌐⌐

Monongahela Mining Company opened its first mine in 1912 on the gentle shoulders and under the stretching peaks that surround Medgar, Kentucky. Mr. William Beecher Boyd himself drove down in his brand-new automobile to supervise the acquisition of the land after a survey team from Wheeling pulled core samples so thick and pure they made his heart race.

The citizens were roundly suspicious of William Beecher Boyd, seeing as he was from Pennsylvania, and his car caused a considerable disturbance. Story goes, he entered Missiwatchiwie County through Knuckle, and by the time he passed Jukes Hollow, he and his top-down Model T, with its shiny black paint and headlights that looked to folks like the bug eyes of a birth-defected bovine, were trailed by a raggle of shoeless children, eight of the county's laziest farmers, three Negroes, assorted dogs, and seven cattle. Dogs running ahead, barking, and boys fighting for position as each passing farm added to the entourage.

Word spread faster than the Model T, and by the time the car worked itself up the last hill before town, most of Medgar had already changed clothes and assembled outside of Hivey's Farm Supply. Women in their Sunday hats, men with fresh pork fat in their hair.

Boyd parked the car at the hitching post in front of Hivey's, jumped onto the car's red backseat, and stood stock-still, one foot on the spare tire, both hands on his knee, and said nothing. Absolutely nothing.

It was the kind of thirty-second silence that made some men look at their shoes and kick stones. Others rubbed their Adam's apples wondering if they should be the first. Women fanned themselves faster and even the children stopped pushing, everyone silent in suspicious anticipation.

William Beecher Boyd smiled, then cleared his throat. "Friends," he said, "you've a fine town here. A fine town."

William Beecher Boyd's Monongahela Mining Company started first on the north side of Hogsback Mountain with Juliet One driving true into the heart of what came to be known as the Medgar seam. Juliet Two and Three followed hard by, and people after that—like a rock thrown on a lake in the morning, sending out ripples in unstoppable waves.

Lew Chainey was the first to sell, then John van Slyke, then Mrs. Simpson. The surrounding fields suddenly became the town, with bright black asphalt instead of dirt and mud, new pine-board and shingle houses instead of struggling corn. A bank, another church, and two more blacksmiths took Medgar into 1917, all courtesy of William Beecher Boyd and the Monongahela Mining Company.

The 1920s saw Medgar grow to two thousand people in the finger valley between the Hogsback and White Mountain. A school, a jail, traffic.

The Depression came and went like an unfamiliar cousin. Depression or not, people still burned coal and Medgar still dug it because the Monongahela Mining Company made it so.

The opening of Miss Janey's Paris Hair Salon and Notion Shop in 1965 brought Missiwatchiwie County into the modern age. Miss Janey's cousin and partner, Paul Pierce, spent two years of military duty as first tenor in the Army Band and Chorus, culminating with a weekend stint in a muddy tent on the outskirts of Paris, which, when he was back in Medgar, conveyed him instant credibility on all questions of fashion and style and made Miss Janey's an immediate success.

The next decades were Patsy Cline singing on the radio in the afternoon and thick chrome shining on Saturday night. Crew cuts close and tight to the neck and white cement sidewalks too new to spit; television antennae like Easter crocuses breaking through the last mutter of snow. Band concerts and communists and tea dances with the Medgar Women's Club. JFK, Alan Shepard, Bay of Pigs, and a second bank. Negro rights, the Tet Offensive, Martin Luther King, RFK, and Miss Janey's addition. Nixon/Agnew, Walter Cronkite, George Jones, the Apollo moon landing, and an Italian restaurant. Kent State, Gerald Ford, the Statler Brothers, Jimmy Carter, and the mines. Always the mines.

Until 1978, when they extracted the last ton from the Medgar seam and most miners followed the work south, leaving a peeled-paint husk of a place with fewer than seven hundred inhabitants. The once-thriving west side of Medgar, with its Italian restaurant and theater, was shut completely. A strip of businesses still clung to the frayed Main Street: Smith's Ice Cream, Hivey's Farm Supply, Biddle's Gas and Grub, the Monongahela Bank and Trust, Dempsey's General Store, and, of course, Miss Janey's Paris Hair Salon and Notion Shop.

Before the breakfast dishes were cleared my father talked of getting a jump on the highway truck traffic, talked of garage organizing and critical toolshed repairs.

"Let me put these sticky buns in some Tupperware for you," Audy Rae said.

"Nope, I'll just take this one to go." He grabbed the center bun and poured coffee into a travel mug. "Call you when I get home, sport," he said as the screen door creaked and slammed on his exit.

With him gone I immediately began exploring Medgar and the surrounding mountains in expanding circles from my base on the front porch of 22 Chisold Street—a seething, spinning fury in my head and a pack of matches in my pocket.

On the first saddle of mountain outside of town, I gathered up a knee-high pile of tinder-dry leaves and threw a lit match into it. A pencil of smoke rose from the middle, then dissipated as the flames took. A moderate wind fed the fire and I watched impassively as the flames shot up three feet, consumed the fuel, then settled into smoldering embers. I wanted to feel something other than the stifling sadness and rage that had overcome me these past two months—guilt, excitement, brio, embarrassment, anything—but even the heat of the flame failed to penetrate.

I had started with fires in Redhill about a month after Josh died: first a small trash can in the backyard, then a pile of dried grass clippings in the woods behind my house; a stack of deadfall at a construction site, then three tires at the town dump; a few other minor lights around Redhill, until I set an old wooden shed ablaze on city park property. That one brought out fire engines, police cars, crime scene investigators, but nothing from me.

Farther up the mountain I pulled together another pile of leaves, larger this time, and finally felt the heat of the flames as they licked at the low branches of a maple sapling. Then two more fires, each bigger than before.

And so it was my first week in Medgar—a Dumpster fire in back of Hivey's Farm Supply; a grass fire on a clear hillside that got taken by the wind and nearly lost control; an old foam car seat that burned ugly black smoke and stung my lungs when the wind shifted.

It was on one of these burnings that I first met Buzzy Fink.

Chapter 2

WHAT HORSES SMELL LIKE AFTER RAIN

Buzzy Fink's toenail collection, by the time I arrived in town, filled half an old Band-Aid tin. His showpiece was a full big toenail, cracked and yellowed, with tailings of cuticle still attached. Found it on a rock in the middle of Chainey Creek after a summer squall—brown water racing and the big old nail just staring at him like Sunday.

The original owner of the nail was a topic of much debate in the Fink clan. Esmer Fink, Buzzy's grandfather, was sure it came from one of the Deal sisters. Identical twins, the Deal sisters: never married, bitter, lonely. He'd noticed Ethna Deal limping past the closeout bin at Pic-n-Pay the week before the discovery, and he'd seen the sisters down at Chainey Creek with their socks off. It was Ethna's; he was sure of it.

Isak Fink, Buzzy's father, knew Ethna had nothing to do with the toenail. Besides, the Deal sisters always limped. He reasoned, with some support in the family, that the original owner was an old miner named Mose Bleeker who disappeared during the storm and supposedly drowned drunk in Chainey Creek. Buzzy subscribed to this theory because it greatly raised the currency of his find: possessing the only remaining piece of a dead man was something to boast about.

Buzzy's brother, Cleo, boycotted the entire discussion, believing that he was the rightful custodian of the nail. He was with Buzzy at the time of the discovery and thought that as the older brother he should take ownership. He was jealous of the attention Buzzy received and was half-lovesick over Jemma Blatt. Jemma's interest in the toenail only made matters worse.

The only member of the family without an opinion on the nail's origin or its rightful conservator was Buzzy's mother, who believed the big toenail, and indeed his entire collection, would be the undoing of her youngest son. "A boy what keeps parts a people gonna come to a bad end," she predicted into her black soup. "It jus ain't natural."

The debate eventually waned, unresolved, and the toenail remained at the top of Buzzy's collection, brought out like his aunt Pip for special occasions. My first meeting with him was just such an occasion.

⟋⟋⟋

"Tie a slug to that spider bite; it'll stop the swell. Gotta be a gray one, though. Brown ones make it worse."

I was lying on the ground in the hills outside town, prostrate in pain after a red spider had got under my shirt and bit me on the stomach. My feet were against a giant oak tree and I was debating how best to apply my life's remaining hours. I thought of running back to Chisold Street and crawling up to the porch and in my final breath telling Mom not to grieve too deeply; then I would die in her arms. But I was at least two miles from Pops' house and the run back would only rush the venom to my brain. I finally decided to burn an abandoned coal tipple I had seen over the last hill when the voice filtered down from somewhere in the giant tree.

"I'm outta slugs right now, but down the creek there's plenty. An don't try cheatin it with a worm. Gotta be a slug...a gray one."

I gazed up at the gigantic trunk, thirty feet around, branches fostering a great green canopy in every direction. Three limbs up, through the bark and leaves, a boy about my age was smoking a cigarette and reading a dirty magazine. The rippled black soles of his army surplus boots dangled over the tree limb. He threw the naked lady down by my head and quickly worked the forty-foot drop, landing on the ground a few seconds after the magazine. He squatted, knees to ears like a bushman breaking cane, slowly weaving back and forth across the ground in a rhythmic search for something.

"Here she is," he said, pulling the curled carcass of the spider from the leaves. He held it between his thumb and forefinger. "It weren't deadly poisonous, but you'll feel it for a few days less we get you that slug...Name's Buzzy Fink."

"Kevin Gillooly."

Buzzy Fink was a head taller than me and half again as broad, with sandy blond hair cut in a flattop on an already thickening neck. Eyes so blue they made the rest of his face seem freshly washed. A spread of freckles across both cheeks met at his nose; his big white teeth, gapped in the middle, flashed pink tongue when he smiled.

"You're the Peebles kid," he said as a point of fact.

"My grandfather's Arthur Peebles."

Silence.

"Let's you an me get you that slug."

I followed Buzzy close, feeling the expanding numbness around the bite. He strode to the edge of the wooded plateau and plunged straight down the steep, rocky bank to the creek some hundred feet below. I was lagging off, employing saplings as ropes, sliding down the bank on my butt, thankful for finally finding a kid to do stuff with. When I reached the bottom, Buzzy was already under his fourth rock—a few red salamanders, armies of pill bugs, but no gray slugs.

"Here you go," he said after rock five, extracting a gleaming slug twice as big as my thumb. "This'll do you." He stepped over the rocks and slapped the slug into my hand. "I got some duct tape up the tree. We'll make a poultice an tape it up. You'll be jus fine."

He was off again, long, sturdy legs making easy work of the slippery bank. I made after him, trying desperately not to smash such a serviceable specimen. At the tree he took the slug and climbed up one-handed, feet on knobs, hands on bark. Three branches later he was lighting a cigarette in a red pine rocker on the front porch of an impressive tree house. The house nested in the middle branches of the colossal oak at a point where the main trunk divided, providing a perfect platform for the structure. Shingle roof, pane window, plywood walls, and a front porch. A blue door.

I started up the trunk, echoing the nubs and bobs that Buzzy used to earn the first branch, my foot slipping, stomach scraping bloody against the bark.

"What's the matter, Kevin Gillooly, don't you have trees in In-de-anna?" Smoke punctuated each of his laughs.

I finally made it to the first branch and onto the front porch of the tree house, where I could see the whole town, the hollows and the remnants of the old mines on the Hogsback. As I scanned the horizon, something seemed out of place. The silhouette of the mountains over by the Hogsback was strangely malformed, as if some giant had cut off the peaks, leaving a flat gray table. Buzzy was still sitting, enjoying his cigarette. The sound of a massive explosion reached us, muted like distant thunder, but shorter, sharper, and inconsistent with the perfect sky above.

"What was that?

"Big-ass explosion," he said between puffs.

"From what? Do you think anybody's hurt?"

"It's how they mine now. Blow the tops off an dig at it from above." He stood, put out the cigarette carefully on the underarm of the rocker, and flicked it into a dirt-filled coffee can, then went inside, rummaging for duct tape. He reappeared a minute later, tape and slug in hand. He gave me the slug, added a sprinkle of porch dirt, and spat into my hand. He screeched out two feet of duct tape. "Slap the slug on the bite and hold it there." He readied the duct tape for application. "Now take your hand away." I did and Buzzy quickly covered the slug with tape. "Leave it there for a day an you'll be okay."

I could feel the cool slug squirming against my skin and watched its outline in the tape, moving like a puppy under a rug. Buzzy offered me a cigarette.

I sat on the porch deck next to him, trying to look practiced as I lit the end and pulled the first raging drag, holding in a cough with my life.

After a while Buzzy said, "I seen you come into town last week."

"We're living with my grandfather, me and my mom are. My father went back to Indiana because of work. He's a lawyer."

"Heard your momma's gone crazy cause your little brother died," he said, looking hard at me.

"She's taking it kind of bad." I avoided his gaze.

"Is that why you been lightin them fires?"

I froze. "What do you mean?"

"I mean is that why you been lightin them fires?"

"Uhhhhh..." I looked down into the tree-house porch floor at an empty acorn top.

"You don't need to be doin that no more," he said before I could muster even a lame reply.

"I was just bored," I said, eyes still on the acorn top. Finally I looked up.

He was staring straight into me. "You don't need to be doin that no more," he said again—softer this time.

I nodded, then looked out over the town.

"How'd he die?" he asked after a time.

"Hit by a car," I lied.

"That sucks."

"Yeah."

"My brother Cleo coulda died when he was a kid. But he jus broke both legs instead."

"How did he do that?" I was eager to change the subject.

"Fell off the barn roof. Climbed up there to get this airplane he carved."

"Is he older or younger than you?"

"Older; he's seventeen. Gonna be a senior this year. Bad-ass football player. Third-team All-American QB last year. Broke the state passing record again," Buzzy said proudly. His face came alive at the talk of his older brother. "Lets me train with him, most times. Shaggin balls an stuff. Man, he is a machine—probably gonna go pro."

"That's cool," I said and looked back over at the line of lopped-off mountains, hoping to shake thoughts of the brother that Josh would have grown into. Buzzy went on about Cleo's college and pro prospects, and gradually the sad wonderings and guilt about Josh folded back into a dark closet of memory.

We stayed there, in the tree, on the porch, talking about everything all afternoon. The way toenails go hard after they've been clipped; the way dust clings to spiderwebs like dew; spit and the specks that float in your eye when you look at the sun a certain way; scorpions and Hissy Pillsucker, who would strip to her underwear for twenty-five cents; breasts and moles with hair, and Chucky Dingle, who had only one nipple. How wood feels in your hands when it's wet; how to carve a whistle from green willow; what the ocean must look like; what horses smell like after rain.

"My grandaddy's gonna hide me if I'm not home by Clinch Mountain sunset," Buzzy said suddenly and was halfway down the oak in an instant, running off on the whisper of trail. "You help yourself to my smokes and make sure the lock is tight before you leave." His voice threaded the darkened woods.

I stayed another minute, then locked the tree house and shimmied to the ground, tumbling onto a cushion of last year's leaves. I made my way back over the blurred footpaths on the hills outside of town and reached the porch at Chisold Street in full night.

Back in Indiana, arriving home after dark and two hours late for dinner would have won me a half-hour lecture and a weekend pass to my bedroom. But things were different now. As I aired up the steps and onto the dim porch, I could hear the spinning of ice in a glass.

"Evening, Kevin."

I stopped. "Hi, Pops. I'm really, really sorry I'm so late and I missed dinner; I know you and Mom are really mad but I was out in the woods and I got lost and I—"

"Son, relax," my grandfather said in his soothing southern way. "Audy Rae put your dinner in the refrigerator. You know how to work an oven. Heat it up or save it for tomorrow if you're inclined."

"Is Mom really mad?"

"Your mom's still thinking about other things, so I'm gonna be mad for her."

"You don't sound mad."

"Well, I'm only mad for her. If I was mad for myself, your hide would be bright red about now. Go on in and eat your supper."

Just then, Audy Rae pushed quietly through the screen door, summer sweater on her shoulders, walking-home hat in her hands. The hat was rounded and brimless and loaf-bread brown with fabric flowers sewn into the band.

"I see the prodigal come back at last," she said, rolling her eyes over to Pops.

"He has indeed."

"Ummm, umm," she hummed and shook her head. "My day, a child miss supper does without." She affixed the hat to her graying hair, paused for a moment, then readjusted it so the flowers were to the side. "See you gentlemen tomorrow," she said and walked purposefully off the porch, down the stairs, correct and true to the corner of Chisold, her hat flowers captured by the streetlamp light.

I went into the house. Mom was on the wing chair in the dim living room. Her hobbled body followed the slips and contours of the chair as if woven to it. I paused for a moment and looked for any sign of the person I knew from Indiana—the easy laugh that was always the last in the room to quiet; the warm way she would make my childhood tribulations disappear like a late snow; the backbone she showed when standing up to my father about her painting, and about me.

She nodded her head silently to the demons taking tea with her on the sofa. I pushed back out to the porch and slumped next to Pops in the extra wicker chair.

The night was so still we could hear the movement of breath from the living room—every intake a reminder of what I had done; every exhale a calling of my guilt.

Pops leaned forward so his elbows rested on a shelf of knees. "How are you doing?"

"Good." A moth dive-bombed my face; I backhanded it. "Good." I stared at the gray outline of the fence at the hem of the yard.

Pops' sideways gaze stayed on me.

"Doing okay," I said and picked at my fingernails, which still had lines of black ash under the edges. "Everything's pretty good right now."

"Hmmm. I would have thought everything would be pretty crappy right now." He brought both lips into his mouth so that the upper and lower were like a set of bank-rolled dimes. "Cause I'm feeling pretty crappy. It's been an awful two months, and my crappy could use some company."

I looked up. His eyes glistened.

"Yeah. It's pretty crappy," I admitted.

"And being stuck in this left-for-dead town with ancient me doesn't make for better prospects."

I smiled slightly, then shrugged.

"If you want, maybe we can bring that friend of yours out for a visit; Trevor what's his name."

"We're not really friends anymore."

"Why not? I thought he was your best friend."

I shrugged again. "He just got all weird."

"What do you mean?"

"I dunno, you know. Just went weird after Josh. They all did. Like I had some kind of disease or something." I picked at the tail end of a wicker thread, tried to scratch the paint off with my fingernail. "I think it was cause of Mom, not Josh. What happened at the mall and the crying and stuff."

"Friends can sometimes disappoint."

"Yeah."

"You know, when I was about your age I was handed a real turd sandwich. After my father was killed, we were left struggling. But I found a place I could go that would help me forget, at least for a while."

"Where was that?"

"Black Hill Cove, Balnibarbi, Kukuanaland."

"What? Where are they? Was this when you were in the navy?"

"Nope."

"Where are they, then?"

He tapped his temple.

"I don't get it."

"I'll show you." He stood and went inside. He emerged a

moment later with a tattered brown book, two pirates on the cover—cutlass ready, pistols crossed.

"What am I supposed to do with this?"

"Read it, I imagine."

I smirked. "It's just some old book. Don't you have...?"

Pops put his hand up to quiet me and pushed the scuffed copy of *Treasure Island* across the wicker coffee table. "Give Jim Hawkins a chance. I suspect he'll be a better friend than Trevor what's his name."

Chapter 3

THE TELLING CAVE

———

That Saturday I left Chisold Street in the late morning to set fire to an old mine shed I'd found the week before. Audy Rae was off and Pops had office hours, so I stopped into Hivey's Farm Supply to buy a soda and a sandwich for the mission.

Hivey's was a constant in Missiwatchiwie County, a sanctuary for the miners and farmers who would gather at the back by the woodstove. Jesper Jensen was the unofficial leader, four-year pinochle champion, and key opinion former of the men by the back stove. His sons were now running what was left of the farm, which gave him even more time for pinochle and opinions. I went to the cooler case near the back for a turkey sub.

"You really think Tennessee is a better choice, Paitsel?" Jesper asked.

"Cleo's a pure passer and Notre Dame is option heavy," a tall, sinewed man replied. "Irish may be a sentimental favorite, but a bad offense for the boy."

Jesper nodded solicitously; the rest of the men did the same.

Paitsel Meadows was twenty years retired from minor league baseball but still held broad shoulders and forearms muscled and tendoned, veins worming up to his biceps. Short-cropped hair brushed with gray, sparkling eyes, chin enough to hang a Christmas stocking.

Drafted out of Alabama to the Cleveland Indians farm system with a baffling 12-6 curve but little else, he played A ball in North Platte for a season, then went on to Reading. He threw three seasons for Double-A, working his way up the rotation, then finally onto the Mobile Bears. His big break came when two Indians starters blew out UCLs in a late-summer climb out of the cellar and Birdie Tebbetts drove down from Cleveland for a Bears homestand.

He came out against the Washington Senators with the 12-6 on point and his fastball propelled by debut adrenaline. He notched a win, striking out Ken Mullen, Frank Howard, and Don Lock in succession. But as August wore, the 12-6 began to hang, and hitters had at it. Without a fallback fastball, Paitsel was sent down, then down again, eventually drifting out of baseball and into small-engine repair around Missiwatchiwie County. He'd been in Medgar eighteen years, taking the extra room at Paul Pierce's house, but his time in the majors made him an instant celebrity around town and the go-to arbiter on any discussion of sports physiology and practice.

"Got a call from the Tennessee baseball coach, who's an old buddy a mine. Says Johnny Majors wants to come up for a visit."

"He'll have to get in line," Jesper said.

"Yes, he will," Bobby Clinch agreed.

"Long line a folks," someone else said.

"Johnny Majors ain't much of a line waiter," Paitsel said and tipped his Caterpillar hat. "You ladies take care a yourselves."

They all waved and smiled. "You take care, Pait."

"See ya tomorra."

"Bye now."

The door jingled shut. Jesper watched as Paitsel disappeared around the corner, then leaned in to the boys. "Well, I always knowed it to be true bout Paul," he sniffed. "I can tell these things, you know. I been to New York."

"What's New York got to do with anythin?" someone challenged.

"New York's got a pile a them people. Once you seen one, the rest is easy to spot."

"You were up at Niagara Falls, Jesper," someone else reminded him.

"Yeah, but we changed planes in New York City, Bobby. You ain't been there, so you don't know. Airport was full of em."

Bobby Clinch found Jesper's logic hard to argue, so he changed the subject. "Well, I don't think Paitsel's like that. He's jus like one a us. Good pinochle player an all. You sure Paitsel's in on all this?"

"I dunno, Bobby," Jesper said after a long intake of air. "Hilda was in there for the meetin bout how to organize against the blastin. Said that second bedroom is a guest room."

"How would she know?"

"Women can tell a guest bedroom from a regular bedroom, an she said it was most definitely a guest bedroom."

"How can they tell?" someone asked.

Jesper rolled his eyes. "I don't know, Levi. Ask your dang wife."

Bobby shook his head and bladed a hand toward him. "Friends is all, Jesper. Friends is all."

I picked a sub from the top of the pile and started to the cash register.

"Guess we're all gonna have to drive to Glassville for trims now," Jesper announced. "I hear Lark's over to the Pic-n-Pay got him a Wednesday special. Trim an a shave for two dollars an fifty cent."

The men around the stove nodded. "That's a good price," Bobby Clinch agreed.

"Tis," someone else said.

I paid at the register, went out to the sidewalk, and turned down Green Street to head up the saddle toward Buzzy's tree house. The porch was empty and my callings were met with silence. I waited for a while, then hiked over two ridges to the abandoned mine.

At the left of the entrance was the old wooden shed, walls leaning slightly south the way flowers tilt toward the sun, the door hanging from a hinge. Inside were a few dented miners' hats, blackened coveralls with *Monongahela Mining Company* stitched across the chest. A workbench with a row of open glass containers, the dried residue of long-evaporated solvents mucking the bottoms. Under the bench was a nearly full old metal can, its faded *Kerosene* label brushed with rust.

As soon as I saw it, the walls of the shed fell to an infinite horizon and my heart began to push out against my breastbone, as if it was a wrongly accused convict pounding out his innocence on a cell wall. When I picked it up, my feet and the ground under them faded out like a lost television signal blurring to snow. My hands were dead stones, as some other person, some other entity, took control of my limbs and pushed me outside myself to watch the can's contents splash on the old wood wall and watch the way the wood pulled the kerosene into it as dry ground drinks in water.

On the empty, he threw the can into the door and took five steps back and pulled a Redhill match pack from his pocket, struck one, and lifted it to flick into the kerosene puddle at the corner. A hand reached from behind him and grabbed his wrist hard. I spun. It was Buzzy Fink.

He blew out the match.

"So you come to my mountains jus to burn em down."

"No, I'm just, you know."

"No, I don't know."

"I'm . . . never mind." I pulled my wrist free and turned back toward town.

"Hey," he said after a few moments.

I stopped. Turned. "What?"

"I want to show you somethin." The tone in his voice told me it wasn't a request.

"What?"

"Somethin you need to see."

"What is it?"

He walked past me and onto the trail back to the tree house. "You comin?"

I hurried after him, nearly tripping on a jut of granite in the trail.

"Where've you been the last few days, anyway?"

"Watchin you set fires."

I didn't answer.

"Somebody hadta keep it from spreadin."

"They were little fires." Regretted it as soon as the words passed my lips.

He stopped and half turned to me. "You done now?"

I nodded slowly, unconvinced. He went back to the trail and continued on.

At the tree house he scurried apelike up the trunk. I followed slowly to the first limb, remembering the secret handgrabs and footholds, then pulled myself up to the platform. Buzzy had hands on hips, looking out to the mountains that surrounded town.

"See all these." He swept his arm from left to right across the expanse of hills. "I got my own names for em." He motioned to the rightmost mountain. "This first mountain here, grown-ups call Stanley; but I call it Hawk Wing cause I found a baby hawk there that couldn't fly. Took it home to raise it, then brought him back. He still lives up there.

"Next to it is Skull Mountain. I call it that cause me an Cleo found the skull of a cougar or maybe even a sabre-tooth tiger or some other prehistoric thing. Got it hangin on my bedroom wall. Next to it is Buck Head on accounta I got my first deer there. Big-ass twelve-point buck." His hands bragged the rack width. "Me an Cleo was up the stand an the buck was off on a hill bout a hundert yards away. Cle's an expert shot an coulda dropped the buck in a heartbeat, but he let me take it with his rifle cause he's got a scope on it. He's like that, you know, always wants me to be the best at stuff. So I get the buck in the cross-hairs an *blam*—sucker goes down.

"The one next to that is Round Rock. Nothing cool happened there but on the other side it's got these perfectly round rocks size a tractor tires. Over here are Big Tiny an Little Tiny. I call em that on accounta theys the smallest. Next to it is Luck, which has a bunch of old mines cut out of it. I call it Old Cheesey like that cheese with them holes in it. The next two I call Winkin an Blinkin. No real reason; I jus like the bedtime story my momma used to tell me." He stood shoulder-width wide, surveying the range with satisfaction, as if he'd spent the morning molding them all from clay.

"That last one there, the one with the knob on top, that's called Knob Mountain." It was at the end of the eastern line of hills that encircled the town, in opposition to the flat-topped rubble of the excavated mountains. Its majestic reach and perfect shape made the scarred landscape of those dead peaks even more jarring.

"What's its real name?"

"Knob Mountain."

I nodded. "Good name for it."

"It's where the Tellin Cave is," he added.

"What's that?"

"Best cave in the county. Goes on for miles, they say; even gotta river underneath. I've never gone down that far, but Cleo did. Him an Jimmy Pike got all the way down to the river."

"Let's go, then," I said, anxious to explore a potentially dangerous cave.

"Naw, I been there lots a times."

"Come on, man. Let's do something cool."

He sat down in the rocker and lit a cigarette, regarding the ring of hills the way a curator appraises his finest art.

"Look, I want to explore something," I said. "I'm gonna go myself."

"You can't go yourself."

"Why not, too dangerous?"

"Against the rules."

"Whose rules?"

"The Tellin Cave rules, you dumbass. It's why they call it the Tellin Cave in the first place."

"Why's that?"

"Cause everyone who goes in has to tell a secret bout themselves."

I laughed for the first time in months. "What? Who says?"

He frowned. "It ain't nothin to joke bout. You don't tell the Tellin Cave a secret, it'll kill you."

"How can a cave kill you?"

Now it was his turn to laugh. He looked at me like I really was dumb. "Cave can kill you lots a ways. Leighton Buzzard was the first. My grandaddy was with him when it happened. They was up the cave with some friends. This was a long time ago, before my granma an all. They were tellin stories around a fire, an Bicky Wilson, she says to everybody, 'The spirit a the cave wants to know our secrets, we all gots to give it one.' So they went round the fire each givin a secret, an when they get to Leighton he says he ain't gonna tell no secret an that starts a big ruction an he leaves in a huff. Next week he drowns up Glaston Lake. That's how the whole thing started."

I shook my head. "Could've been a coincidence."

"Well, later that year, they was back up the cave, an another one, Rebah Deal, says she ain't tellin nuthin. Then when they went explorin, she gets lost an they never find her. Was like the cave jus swallowed her right up. They say at night, on the anniversary, you can hear her ghost callin from the belly a the cave. I been up twice then but I ain't heard it."

"When's the anniversary?"

"Four weeks. July twenty-third. Once Rebah disappeared the legend a the Tellin Cave stuck. You may not believe, but it's a parcel a bad luck to be hangin over your head. I wouldn't test it."

I was determined to see the Telling Cave. "I'm going anyway.

If the cave kills me, it'll be your fault and I'll come back to haunt *you*."

"It ain't nothin to joke about, I'm tellin you. I'll take you up there but not if you're gonna laugh at the power. The cave might get mad an kill me too, jus outta spite."

"I won't joke, I promise," I said, tightening my lips around a grin.

He went into the tree house, came out with a flashlight and knapsack, and was halfway down the tree before I could blink. I managed to slide down behind him without incident.

Suddenly an object whooshed by our heads and stuck into the oak with a loud thwack. We both whirled to the sound. A twelve-inch metal arrow quivered in the bark.

"What the fuck you faggots doin up here? This is our place."

A large, thick-gutted, zit-stippled teenager with greasy black hair and bad teeth climbed up the rise toward us. Dangling at his right side was a crossbow pistol, drawstring loosed from the shot at our heads. Behind him was a much smaller boy, about the same age, maybe sixteen, but half his mass. The thin boy had enormous buckteeth, thick eyebrows, and bushy brown hair. It all made him seem like he had been raised by impoverished beavers.

"I said, what the fuck you pussies doin in our place?"

"Your place?" Buzzy said calmly. I could tell he was seething inside, but good sense told him to hold his temper in the face of an older, armed teenager. "I thought your place was up Six Holler."

"It's all our place, fuckwad," said beaver boy.

"Well, I'm jus showin Kevin here the mountains, him bein from outta town."

They puff-chested over to us.

"Skeeter, gwon get that arrow out the tree." Skeeter went and put a shoulder into Buzzy as he passed. Buzzy braced and the boy bounced off him like a bird hitting a brick wall. He raised his fist, but Buzzy didn't flinch. "Jus get the fuckin arrow, Skeeter," the boy said. Skeeter went to the tree and pulled the bolt out of the bark.

"Where'd you get that crossbow, Tilroy?" Buzzy asked. "That's badass." He knew flattery would ease the situation.

"My uncle give it to me for my birthday. Sucker is deadly." He brought it up to show us. The handle was burled wood and lacquer, the bolt guide and bow were gunmetal gray, the bowstring a hundred fibers tightly woven into a single high-tensile filament. "Already got a possum an a coon," he said proudly.

Buzzy whistled. "That is seriously cool." Tilroy was lost for the moment, just gazing at his new weapon.

Skeeter looked up at the tree house. "Where's the ladder at?"

Buzzy started moving away. "We gotta get on home. Chores an stuff." He walked past me, grabbed my shirtsleeve, and pulled. I followed.

"Fuckwad. Where's the ladder at?"

"I ain't seen no ladder. It's Cleo's tree house. He don't let no one up there."

At the mention of Buzzy's brother, Tilroy and Skeeter went silent, looking up at the nested structure. While they whispered and pointed up, we walked down the trail.

"Hey, faggots!"

I stopped and turned. Tilroy lowered the crossbow to me.

"Jus keep walkin," Buzzy hissed.

Tilroy and Skeeter laughed. I turned to catch up. Once down the slope I grabbed Buzzy. "Let's get out of here." I started to run.

He shook me off. "I ain't runnin from that asswipe." Buzzy's forehead was hunkered, lips pushed out in a scowl. "I swear, I hate that mutherfucker."

"Is he a big bully in school?"

"He's the one who gets bullied cause he's so fat. Seniors mostly. Then he goes an takes it out on the freshmen. I seen him do some crazy shit in the parkin lot. Doesn't mess with me, though. He knows Cleo would kick his ass."

By the time we got to the trail fork, afternoon was closing out. We said our good-byes and agreed to meet up again the next day, maybe for a trip to the Telling Cave. I made my way down the mountain, over the train tracks, and up Green Street to Main.

Chapter 4

THE AERODYNAMICS
OF FLYROCK

Arthur Bradley Peebles was born to Missiwatchiwie County on January 3, 1919, in sideways snow and wind that flailed Jukes Hollow for three days, cresting and spilling frozen waves against the southern edge of the timber cabin his father, Oriel Peebles, had built ten years before. The Peebles clan had been scraping a life from the dirt and rock and walled sunlight of the hollow for sixty-five years by the time Arthur was born. The Peebleses were broadaxed and sure. Drum chested and stubborn, with thick hands cut for hard work; laughter like the crack of bowling ball on pin.

Jeb and Hershel, two years apart, followed their father into the mines at fifteen. Arthur Bradley, however, was a thinker and a questioner and a reader. His mother, who could read and write better than most of the county, taught him his letters from the book of Genesis, spelling out words on a pine board with elderberry chalk. Within eight months, Arthur was into Exodus, reading aloud to his mother, following her ponylike as she labored to run the house in Jukes Hollow.

At eight, Arthur was walking five miles every other Tuesday to Mrs. Robert J. Taylor's in Glassville to borrow a book from her considerable collection of eighty-five volumes. He was Robinson Crusoe sneaking through the jungle, scouting for ambush. He was Gulliver negotiating the fleshy landscapes of the Brobdingnags. He was Ahab, substituting green moss boulders for the white whale and losing his leg a thousand times. For Arthur, the words gathered in waterfall thoughts that spilled off the page into the pools of imagination collecting in his head.

Oriel was concerned about his idleness and Jeb thought he was weak and yellow. He entered the University of Kentucky to study philosophy the year his father was killed by a fertilizer bomb in the back of the union offices in downtown Medgar. The murder in 1936 touched off the bloodiest union uprising in the region, the Sadler Mountain Wars, which lasted nine months, until federal marshals took control of the town and the mines, gradually restoring the peace.

(Oriel's funeral service was a caution. The union wanted a full casket despite the fact that the only piece of Oriel available for burial was his left hand. His wife, a clear thinker even in grief, thought it a shameful waste of timber and opted for a foot-square polished wood box with a gold handle on top. It made for a sight as half of Missi County followed the family up the hollow from the church, a single pallbearer in the lead carrying the gilded box as if they were burying the most popular hamster in the county.)

After the Sadler Mountain Wars, Hershel returned to the mines and Jeb bought a farm on the other side of Cheek Mountain. Arthur went back to school on tuition earned selling shoes door-to-door in Lexington for the Emory Grove Shoe Company.

It was on his third call of the morning that he met Miss Sarah Ryder Winthorpe.

"Hello, my name is Arthur Bradley Peebles representing the Emory Grove Shoe Company; we make the most comfortable shoes in the entire South," he announced. "So comfortable, in fact, that if you ever get a blister or a bunion as a result of our shoes, we will gladly give you double your money back. You see, each shoe is custom-made to the exact measurement of your foot so our shoes feel as comfortable as your stocking feet."

The woman at the door, granite faced, severe dress, and graying hair screwed to a bun, looked him over dismissively. "Young man, we don't need new shoes," she said, beginning to close the door.

Then footsteps down the stairs and a voice in the hall. "Just a minute, Gertrude. I would like to hear more about the gentleman's shoes."

Gertrude glared at Arthur and wordlessly ushered him into the sitting room—red velvet and mahogany, tasseled and warm.

Miss Sarah Ryder Winthorpe swept into the room on air and light that dissolved Arthur's practiced speech into fragments.

"Um, I sell shoes, and uh, they are very much like your stocking feet, these shoes . . . because they are comfortable and . . . uh . . . if you get bunions we will gladly give your money back because we make the most comfortable shoes in the entire South . . . uh, miss."

"Is that a fact, then—the most comfortable shoes in the entire South?" She gave him a half smile.

Arthur brightened, remembering his lines now. "Absolutely, Miss . . . ?"

"Winthorpe, Sarah Winthorpe."

She extended her soft, exceptional hand, and its warmth made Arthur want to run. Her long chestnut hair played against her neck and shoulders, taking the tired sunlight from the front window and turning it electric. He forgot his speech again. Gertrude stood in the doorway, arms across her chest, eyes folded in a shriveling stare.

If proper Emory Grove Shoe Company procedure had been followed, Miss Sarah Ryder Winthorpe's shoes would have been delivered via post within three weeks; however, Arthur felt that special handling was required in this particular case and delivered them himself. Special handling was also required for the next four pairs of size-seven shoes he delivered to the Winthorpe residence.

Arthur's sales for the following six months fell precipitously; however, the waves that spiked through him every time he saw Sarah did not. They married on June 18, 1940, to the shattering disappointment of Mr. Winthorpe, who believed "if Jesus Christ himself came from Missiwatchiwie County he wouldn't be good enough for my Sarah." (The fact that Jesus was Jewish would have eliminated him from contention in Mr. Winthorpe's mind long before county of origin was ever discussed.)

After a weekend at Glaston Lake, they moved into Arthur's one-room apartment above Stack's Butchery half a block from campus. Arthur went back to his school and his shoes; Sarah went back to her particular state of effortless grace.

He spent six more months at the University of Kentucky, then started as assistant professor of philosophy at Maryville College in Tennessee, when the war broke. He joined the navy and soon was oiling the Bofors antiaircraft guns of port broadside turret number two on the carrier USS *Enterprise* in the Pacific.

It would begin with the low, airy rumble of distant engines, the frantic scouring of the horizon, then contact. The kamikaze always arrived in proud formation and, as if from the hand of some phantom conductor, broke off expertly in threes and fours. Fascinating and terrible. Once kamikaze entered the kill zone, the gunners had exactly seventeen seconds to down the plane.

The May morning in 1945 burned clear, as the sun flushed from a following sea. Arthur was hitting baseballs to the *Enterprise*'s star shortstop when the alarm started slow and shrill against the nearing drone of the kamikaze.

The attackers swarmed like sweat bees. Eight to a ship. Three on the middle portside. Two high, one low. Guns screaming. Seventeen seconds. First kill immediately. Swinging right, middle portside number one down, fourteen seconds, second kill. Twelve seconds left.

The third bomber flew true off the churning water. Arthur turned the guns, firing immediately. Tracers spinning soundlessly past. Closer. Nine seconds. Arthur spraying the air with shot, each one missing the plane. Five seconds. The face of the pilot coming into focus now. Three seconds. His plane parting the chaff like a car through morning mist. Closer. Two seconds. Salt and sweat in Arthur's eyes. As the plane flew under his sight line in the last half second before it slammed into the hull, the pilot looked up at him. Their eyes locked in a terrible instant. The pilot was smiling.

Everything erupted in thunder and death, shaking the thirty-two-thousand-ton carrier to its bolts. He left the gun to his partner and ran down three flights into the aircraft elevator, where the plane had struck the ship. Heat from the firestorm blistering his face. Screams and burning flesh. Into the hold and out with the first man. Black smoke. Up the stairs and onto the deck. Back again four times until the hold exploded, sending flames through the wooden deck, showering burning splinters and steel around them.

For his bravery, Arthur was awarded the Navy Cross, the service's highest honor. The ceremony in Washington, D.C., four months later was the proudest his mother had ever been. She took the bus to Lexington and bought a dress for the occasion—the first store dress she'd ever owned.

There wasn't much work in the county for war-hero philosophers, unless they happened to be miners, so Arthur took a full military scholarship to the veterinary college at Auburn. After three years he was in Ned Pike's old barbershop in downtown Medgar listening to the palpitations of Mrs. Biddle's nervous cat.

Sarah was determined to bring Lexington zest to small-time Missiwatchiwic County. She started the Medgar Women's Club and Literary Society, organized the county's first-ever rendition of a Shakespeare play, *A Midsummer Night's Dream*, gave up her Lexington bus seat to a pregnant colored woman, let their maid eat with the family.

After years of trying, Sarah finally became pregnant and the trouble started. The difficult pregnancy became a harrowing birth, with the baby breeched and Sarah losing blood fast. The infant survived, but Sarah died three hours after delivery.

Then weeks of darkness and garroted sobs. Months in smothered sadness. A year of black guilt and dimly lit rooms. And from it, in the ash of death and broken expectations, came a little girl on air and light with chestnut hair named Anna Ryder Peebles.

My mother.

Every morning that second week I rose early, shoveled in cereal, and lit out for Kinder Mountain and the tree house, determined to arrive before Buzzy Fink came and went. The prospect of actually finding a friend in this forsaken place began to wash the stain of anger and hopelessness that had attached itself to my recent past. I would wait for him there, in the tree-house porch rocker, looking out over the mountains and conjuring my own names for them from the future adventures we would have. Sometime after ten o'clock his head would pop up over the porch platform. "Ha...Indiana!" And off we would go.

But back at Chisold, evenings slid into a routine of awkward dinners in the kitchen and strained conversation on the porch afterward. Pops in his worn wicker chair with his never-lit pipe and a glass of Clinch Mountain sour mash whiskey over ice. Mom in one of the wing chairs in the living room soundlessly replaying the horrifying memory loop of Josh's last moments. Me lying on the edge of the porch, mute and brooding.

To combat my numb boredom, I took up Pops' copy of *Treasure Island* and found myself transported to a new world with Billy Bones, John Trelawney, and Long John Silver—a place of buried treasure and murderous pirates, of desert islands and mutinied ships, plunder and mendacity, adventure and deliverance. A world without the weight of judgment, the sting of reproach, the crush of blame.

Some nights an old friend of Pops' would wander by to sip mash and offer snips of argument that were either taken or not. Other nights Pops and I would just sit by ourselves, sometimes in silence, sometimes in one-way conversation, watching the evening fold over itself. Evenings so still, even small winds teasing the old hickory by the front porch sounded like brushfire. And the easy spinning of ice and sour mash whiskey in a low glass with *SWP* etched into it like a flower. He would hold the glass from the top and swirl the mash and ice until a random thought revealed itself like the white ball of a roulette wheel settling on a number.

"Lead pipes...that's why the Roman Empire collapsed...they all went insane from lead poisoning."

And so it would begin.

—=——

"It jus ain't fair is what I'm sayin. They dint invite us into this country, we jus took it," Lo Gilvens argued one evening. Lothario Gilvens was a regular visitor to the porch at 22 Chisold Street, primarily due to sloth, since it was twice as far for him to walk into town as it was to sit on Arthur Bradley Peebles' front porch drinking the man's sour mash whiskey. Pops didn't begrudge Lo the whiskey, although it was widely known that Lo Gilvens couldn't carry his half of an interesting argument.

"I'm not defending it, Lo. All I'm saying is what the whites did to the Indians was no different than what the Indians had been doing to each other for five thousand years before we came. Coveting is one of the three basic human emotions, right behind love and fear."

"You left out hate," Lo corrected.

Pops shook his head. "Hate is overrated. People only hate if they can't attain what they covet." I could tell Pops felt the conversation unchallenging so he changed the subject.

"Kevin, I'm going out on calls Monday morning to dehorn

and castrate some yearlings and inoculate some pigs. I'd like your help."

Pops was still a practicing large animal veterinarian, usually making several calls a day around the county. Recently, however, he had turned over much of the office business, the dog and cat stuff, to Mrs. Quell's nephew, whom he held in slight regard. "Couldn't pull the prick off a parrot," he said when Lo asked why he wouldn't bring Dr. Quell instead.

"Dint know parrots had pricks," Lo said.

"Well, Lo, I confess that parrots are not my area of speciality, but I can assure you that they do indeed have penises, albeit not particularly large ones."

That seemed to satisfy Lo, who knew better than to test an argument with Pops on anything related to the veterinary sciences.

I was secretly excited about going on a call with him, but the last four years of my father's missed ball games and broken promises had left me expecting little.

"So, how about it Kevin?" Pops asked.

"I guess," I said sullenly and looked off at the abandoned house across the street and studied how it seemed to be brushed in alternating shades of black.

Two gray forms accumulated from the vapors of the evening and took the porch steps. "Kevin, could you please get Mr. Skill and Mr. Meadows a glass of sour mash with no ice?"

I had graduated to official bartender on the porch, which didn't require much expertise since the only thing Pops and his friends ever drank was sour mash whiskey. I poured the drinks and brought them to the men on a tray.

"Thank you, son," they said.

"Arthur, the standard of service on this porch has improved substantially since Kevin arrived—I commend you," Chester said and raised the mash. Pops grunted agreement and began spinning his mash and ice in the low glass with the *SWP* monogram.

Chester Skill and Pops had been friends for most of their lives. They attended the University of Kentucky together, and after a thirty-year career in newspapers in New York and Chicago, Chester retired back home to Medgar. For him, investigation and argument were as essential as air and water, so after a year of penetrating boredom, he acquired the *Missiwatchiwie County Register* and was now its publisher and editor in chief.

"You boys hear about Simp Dodger?"

Pops and Lo shook their heads.

"Killed by flyrock this afternoon. That's why I'm late. Wanted to get it into tomorrow's paper. Everybody's talking about it."

Pops sat up in his chair. "Where did this happen?"

"In his own damn backyard," Paitsel said, measuring out the syllables like they were bitter medicine.

"What's flyrock?"

Pops looked over at me. "Flyrock is what comes off the mountain when they're blasting."

"I heard this huge explosion last week."

"We are becoming a regular war zone the way they are blowing up everything." He frowned and shook his head. "Back when the mines were underground they would use just a bit of explosives to loosen things up; you could barely hear it. With this new way, they blast through four hundred feet of rock and dirt to get to the seam from the top. That takes some ordnance, let me tell you."

"Why don't they just do it the old way?"

"Greed, mostly. They can get twice as much coal out with half as many men by coming in from the top. Plus, some of the seams are thin or unstable; on those you really can't be tunneling."

"I saw three mountains the other day when I was exploring that had the entire tops taken off. It looked weird."

Pops harrumphed. "It's a crime, if you ask me."

We were all silent with our thoughts until Pops took a sip and shifted. "How's Betty? I'll go on up tomorrow."

"Not good," said Paitsel. "She was home when it happened. Rock was the size of a basketball an took off most a Simp's skull. Paul says he's going up Frankfort to meet with the regulators."

Pops sat back in his chair. "We've got to put a stop to this."

"Now you're soundin like Paul," Lo said. "He's a regular one-man ruction. Says he's gonna chain hisself to the dragline." He chuckled and shook his head.

Paitsel unwrapped a long, powerful arm and chopped the air with his hand. "Don't underestimate him, Lo. The man's got no back-down."

"An Bubba Boyd don't neither."

"That's a fact."

"His boys been sayin some things bout Paul. Disgustin things."

Paitsel opened his mouth to reply, but Pops beat him to it. "That's when I knew Paul was onto something." He pointed his pipe end at Lo. "Bubba wouldn't be spreading all these rumors if Paul wasn't a threat."

"Heard Bubba's pushin hard for the Mitchell place," said Lo. "Next, he'll be comin here to buy Jukes."

I sat up on the mention of Pops' boyhood home in the mountains. Mom had told me so many stories about Jukes Hollow—the unimaginable beauty, the waterfall, the natural swimming pool, the centuries-old trees—I felt possessive of the place even though I'd never seen it.

"Who's this Bubba Boyd man?"

"He's the one taking the tops off all these mountains. He owns the mines and most of the town," Paitsel said. "Not a man I want in my foxhole."

"And he wants to buy Jukes Hollow?"

"He'll have to pry the deed from my cold, dead hands," Pops replied, staring out into the darkness.

In the bountiful plenty, when the mines were fat with fuel and the soil gave back its best, they passed with shoulders set high and arms working like pistons pushed and pulled by the rods of their legs. Always forward. Relentlessly forward, hard hewn to task and actualized on effort. The talk, when had, was tricked trucks and new ATVs; rear-projection televisions and football prognostications; animal husbandry triumphs and county fair ribbons. In the bountiful plenty, usefulness was their province, their simple singularity.

But now, in the staggering lean, they lay by on make-work and unrequired errands; they passed to no place in particular with shoulders slumped and eyes averted, with a discourse that ran to foreclosures and fully played-out seams, meager harvests and disappearing trout streams. It was as if everything they had set store by—the fields, the mines, the consistent means—was all turned about, leaving truck repossessions and canceled Florida vacations; idle squeeze chutes and farm store credit; questioning wives and hard kitchen table talk.

Chapter 5

BULL TESTICLES

———

I was up Monday morning before Pops, just as the sky was beginning its run to purple and blue. I put on a full pot of coffee for him and sat at the kitchen table until he woke—coffeepot dripping and spitting as the first yellow light from the east fired the tops of the Medgar mountains. Then stirrings from upstairs and the creaking of floorboards under weight.

"Morning, Kevin," he said as he entered the kitchen. "Are you early for work or late to bed?"

"Early. I wanted to get a head start on things."

"That's a fine habit. We won't be leaving for about a half hour, but better to be ahead of schedule than behind, I say."

"I made you coffee."

"I see that. Thank you." He poured two cups, sat at the table opposite me, and pushed the extra cup across the white painted wood. "Anyone gets up this early is deserving of a cup."

"Thanks. Mom lets me sometimes when my dad is away."

"How's your dad doing? He and I didn't get to talk much when he was here."

I shrugged. Watched an air bubble sail across the brown sea of coffee. After a while I said, "He thinks it's my fault, you know."

"That's ridiculous. What makes you say that?"

"Because he told me."

Pops' lips became a single line and he dropped his chin as he stared into me. "When did he tell you this?"

"About a month after it happened. He was driving me to band practice. We were in the car, not talking or playing the radio or anything; just riding, me and him silent. After Josh died it was like that—never talking." I took a sip of coffee and pushed the cup around in a circle. "We come to this stoplight and he turns to me and says, 'None of this would have happened if you'd just done as you were told.' Then the light goes green and he turns back to the road and goes all silent again and we just keep driving as if we had been talking about a school project."

Pops exhaled slowly and brought his right hand up to his eyes, rubbed the sleep from them, then ran his fingers down across his cheek to his chin in time with the last remnant of air expelling from his lungs.

"What happened was not your fault. You know that, right?"

I nodded. Could feel approaching tears.

"But being blamed for a tragedy like this by someone you count on is about as hard a thing as a man can handle."

I blinked into my coffee until I could swallow again. "I just don't know why he blames me. He never told me to—"

Pops cut me off. "Kevin, people deal with grief in different ways. Some folks turn inside themselves like your mom, and others need to blame like your dad is doing. He'll come around—in the meantime, you stick with me." He put his hand on my arm and squeezed. His grip was strong and warm. I looked up and he smiled.

"It wasn't your fault," he said again, softly this time.

"I'm afraid she's always gonna be like this."

"Unlikely, but I suspect it'll take her a while. What you both saw would rip the head from the shoulders of most people. I'm real proud of the way you've handled it. You've acted like a man and you've been a big help to me and Audy Rae—and to your mom."

We were silent for what seemed like a quarter hour, Pops with his hand on my arm, eyes into me; me moving my coffee cup around the table, drawing circular patterns with the drippings.

"Let's start thinking about breakfast."

After dishes, I followed Pops out to the shed where he kept his veterinary supplies. The outside of the structure was weathered gray wood—thick of the grain brought out by the elements—topped with a corrugated tin ceiling and a weather vane stuck on west. Inside was immaculate and organized, with row upon row of polished wooden drawers, brass knobbed and wearing unrecognizable names: *Amitraz, Bacitracin, Clindamycin, Dexamethasone*, and on.

The ceiling was stocked with gleaming metal veterinary accessories—several sizes of forceps, polished spreader bars, clippers, clamps, shears, syringe guns—all dangling from overhead racks the way a chef hangs pots and pans.

"Castration is usually a simple cut-and-snip affair, but dehorning adult bulls is a bloody business. Usually we do it when they're a few weeks old, but Grubby Mitchell waited too long, so we'll give them a quick anesthetic. Let's see…" He opened and closed several drawers. "Here we go." He pulled out a small glass bottle that read *Lidocaine HCL.* "This will take the sting out."

He loaded his satchel with several other veterinary accessories, latched it, and locked the shed. In the kitchen he poured us each another cup of coffee in travel mugs. Mine read:

Bacitracin
for Ulcerative Posthitis
Merck Animal Health

"What's ulcerative posthitis?" I asked. I figured any additional knowledge would serve me well as Junior Veterinarian.

Pops laughed. "Something you don't want to get."

"What is it?"

"Pizzle rot."

"Pizzle rot?"

"A nasty fungus that affects ram penises. A ram with pizzle rot is an unhappy ram, let me tell you. For that matter, a man with pizzle rot is pretty unhappy too."

"We can catch pizzle rot?"

"We can, but not from sheep." He winked and put his hand on the back of my neck to direct me toward the door. A fragment of a smile tried to find its way up from the last two months.

Pops' truck was a twenty-year-old green Ford F-150 with thick tires at the back and a history of dents and dings from a generation of calls around the county. He put the satchel in the back and I slid onto the passenger-side bench seat. He reversed out to Chisold and took a right on Watford.

We headed through the west side of town to Route 17, passing storefronts abandoned like October cornstalks—*X*s taped across windows, a crack in one. Edwina's Discount Apparel. Diffley's Taxidermy. Kathy's Kustom Kurtains. A deserted gas station on the corner—naked islands stripped of pump hardware, weeds breeding in the pavement fissures. A still-open liquor store.

We came to the intersection of Routes 17 and 32. A four-story structure sat abandoned on a cut-in on the corner. Small windows frosted over, some boarded, some broken. Ten-foot chain-link with concertina wire on top.

"What's this old building?"

"This used to be the plant for Lux Industries, a chemical company that employed just about everyone in town who wasn't a miner. They made urinal mints, splash guards, and other things for public toilets."

"What are urinal mints?"

"You know, those little round perfumey things in the bottom of urinals."

"Why do they call them mints? They don't taste like mints, do they?"

"Well, I've never tried one, Kevin, but I imagine they don't taste like mints. Anyway, the Medgar plant was one of the leading producers of urinal mints in the entire country. Just about every urinal mint east of the Mississippi and south of Maryland came from Medgar."

I thought about all those men, holding their penises and staring down at a urinal mint from Medgar, tearing the rinds off cigarette butts with their piss streams. *Lux Industries, Medgar, Kentucky* emblazoned on the splash guard. It made me proud.

"What happened to it?"

"They moved production to Mexico and closed it the same

year the mines shut." He looked over at me. "It wasn't a good year for us."

We took a right on 17 and followed the edge of the valley floor. The Mitchell farm occupied a prime funnel-shaped valley between two rolling hills of Rag Mountain that eased out of her like inviting legs. Next to Rag was the flat gray wound from the strip-mine operation, running across three stubbed hills and hollows.

We dusted up the dirt road, past a company of steer enjoying a morning cud, to the barns and pens and the slight incline of the lane, which signaled the business end of the farm. Farther up the hill, the Mitchell house, with its two stone chimneys, one at either end, watched old and proud.

Despite the name, Grubby Mitchell wasn't a particularly messy farmer. In fact it was generally held that he ran the farm better than his father, or even his grandfather, Clovis Mitchell, who had the original misfortune to acquire the nickname "Grubby" in 1922. In Medgar, nicknames did tend to stick.

As the story goes, Grubby's father, Liam, dug and built Clovis a private outhouse for his fiftieth birthday. One with a fancy metal toilet-paper holder, a hand-laid parquet floor, and a real porcelain toilet and seat (first one in the county). Clovis, a proud man, assiduous in appearance, lorded the toilet over the other farmers and miners who played cards at the back of Hivey's Farm Supply, allowing everyone a look but denying all, even family, the opportunity to try the smooth, inviting seat.

One spring night six years later, with the toilet seat in full use by Clovis, the floorboards gave way, and he and the toilet splashed into the effluvium ten feet below. His shouts went unheard for a day and a half and the search was in high rash when he was discovered and retrieved from the black muck, clutching the broken halves of the toilet seat in both hands, mumbling incoherently.

The men at Hivey's, all of whom participated in the search and were present when Clovis was hoisted from the hole, gut laughed uncontrollably when Dell Hitchens, a Negro who worked the farm, said loudly, "Das da grubbiest I ever seen Mr. Mitchell." Clovis was never particularly well liked at Hivey's, even before he got the porcelain toilet, and the name Grubby stuck like gum on a summer sidewalk.

When he died, the farm and the nickname passed to Liam, then to his son, Raymond, who was standing with Paitsel Meadows in the barn door examining the carburetor they had just pulled from his deep-red Massey Ferguson tractor when we rattled up into the barnyard.

"Morning, Grub, Paitsel," Pops said as he eased himself down from the worn front seat of the truck and reached into the back for his brown veterinary satchel.

"Mornin," they returned, staying fixed on the suspect carburetor.

I exited on the other side and followed Pops close behind.

"Grubby, this is my grandson, Kevin."

They looked up from the engine piece.

"Heard you was livin here now, pleased," Mr. Mitchell said and nodded.

Paitsel smiled. "Good to see you again, son."

"Engine's been leanin out so I thought I'd have Pait up to pull the carb and see."

"Well, that's sensible, Grub. While you're doing that we'll have a look at those bulls. Where are they?"

"Pen behind the pen barn."

We walked to the back of the pen barn, which held two petulant bulls with proud horns and swaying testicles, who looked as if they wouldn't relinquish them without a discussion.

"How are we going to do these bulls without getting kicked?"

"Getting kicked is the last thing we should worry about… Look at those horns."

I leaned on the fence. Pops opened the double doors of a large barn and began assembling a run of portable fencing from the pen gate to the barn.

"Pops, really, how are we gonna do this?" I worried.

"Well, Kevin, I don't rightly know; I've never done it before."

"You've never done this before?"

"Nope, that's why I asked you to come."

"I've never done this before either, you know that."

"Well, we're just gonna have to learn as we go, I guess—do you want to hold the bull or do the cutting?"

I thought about my options for a moment. "Uh, I guess I'll hold the bull."

We moved inside the barn. It was kept as the rest of the Mitchell spread, well used and well placed, with five stalls, a wood ladder to a hay-stacked loft, honed farm tools of various utility shining the walls. The farm was fifty acres of pasture, feed corn, and steer, except for eight sheep, four goats, two horses, and a pig. Pops said that after the Mitchells' only child, Ray Jr., was killed in Vietnam, Grubby threw himself into the place to stop from thinking about it. The farm was his pride now, and it showed.

"Well, Kevin, I think you're off the hook. Mr. Mitchell has a squeeze chute for just such delicate procedures." He gestured to a narrow aluminium-sided gauntlet with stocks attached to the exit gate for holding an animal's head.

Grubby and Paitsel walked around the corner wiping their hands on a greasy towel.

"Bad float," Paitsel said and moved to help Pops finish the run to the squeeze chute.

"You're eight months late on these yearlings, Grubby. Why the delay?"

"Was hopin to stud em with Earl's stock, but all they want to do is fight. Shem nearly got gored last week."

"Where is he, anyway? You seem short of hands today."

"Lazy sumbitch quit on me."

"What are you going to do for hands?"

Grubby put out his and splayed his fingers like he was showing the years in a decade.

"I'll stay an help," Paitsel said.

"Appreciate it, Pait." Never one for fence-post chat, Grubby opened the pen gate, split the bulls, and began sheepdogging the smaller one toward the squeeze chute.

"Gwan, bull, hep...hep gip, gya ha gwan."

The bull responded immediately, sprinting out of the pen, into the run, and into the squeeze chute as if he couldn't wait to be rid of the annoying protrusions from his head and the danglings between his legs.

Paitsel immobilized the bull's head and shoulders in the stocks. Pops quickly loaded a syringe with lidocaine and began feeling the space between the bull's ear and eye. "There's a nerve called the cornual that snakes up into the horn. It's easier on the animal if we take that out." He tapped a spot on the bull's skull and injected the lidocaine. Same on the other side.

"Son, hand me the dehorner. It's the one that looks like a mini post-hole digger."

I gave him the tool, hand grip first, and he slid the cup over the bull's horn and pulled the handles apart like he was trimming an errant tree branch. The horn popped off and a spurt of blood pulsed from the bull. Pops reached into the cavity with forceps and pulled out the bleeding stump of artery, then switched the apparatus to the other horn and repeated the procedure. He sprayed both stumps with antiseptic.

Next Pops went to the animal's husky testicles. "The key to a successful castration," he explained as he removed a long, thin knife and a syringe from his bag, "is to act with dispatch, before the bull knows what you're up to … and to use copious amounts of lidocaine so you don't get your head kicked in." He shot the bull's scrotum full of the anesthesia and stood for a moment while it took effect. After a few minutes, he quickly cut off the bottom third of the sac, reached in and snipped the bull's balls, and dropped the gonads in a nearby metal bowl. It took about four seconds. Blood and fluid ran from the hollowed sac. My hand went instinctively to my crotch. Pops sutured the blood vessels and sprayed antiseptic onto the wound. Through it all the young bull happily chewed his cud and gaped at the gardening tools on the other side of the barn. Pops opened the stocks and pushed the head of the bull out the gate and into the exit run that led back to the holding pen.

The second bull stood in the corner of the pen facing us. Grubby started toward it, waving his hands wildly. "Hep, ha bull piyow ha hep ha bull."

The bull regarded us contemptuously. As Grubby neared, it jerked away to the other side of the pen and stopped, facing us again.

"Hep now, ha bull yipe hiya."

Grubby closed and the bull jerked away and ran to the other side, facing us once more.

"Ho bull, ho hep bull hya."

Same result.

And again.

"I think he's on to us, Grub," Pops deadpanned after Grubby's sixth unsuccessful attempt to herd the animal. "That's an uncommonly smart bull."

"Well, he ain't smarter than me...hep, hya bull now."

Same result.

"Normally I wouldn't argue the point, Grubby, but he's still got his oysters attached and all you've herded so far is wind."

"Lemme show you how it's done, Grub." Paitsel hopped the fence in a single easy motion and sauntered toward the bull. As he approached, arms flailing, the bull put his horns in gear and chased him around the pen—it made for a sight as Paitsel, running as if hard to home plate, streaked to the gauntlet and one-stepped over the fence with the athleticism of a professional rodeo clown. We all collapsed in laughter as the bull speared the fence post.

"Paitsel, that bull almost herded *you* into the stocks. If he had, I'm afraid I might've done my business on you."

"Well, I wouldn't a paid you then," Grubby responded. If nothing else, Grubby Mitchell was a practical man.

Pops reached into his bag and removed a syringe gun, then loaded it with brown liquid.

"Keep him occupied."

He walked around the outside as Grubby eased off the fence

into the pen. While the bull was distracted by the flapping human, Pops quickly stepped over the fence and shot the solution into the bull's flank, then rejoined us by the squeeze chute.

The bull was stationary, watching us with engaged horns. After about two minutes he snorted and jerked toward us, leaving his four hooves in place, falling chin first into the dirt.

"Jus bout had him," mumbled Grubby to nobody in particular. He was embarrassed at not being able to control his own farm animals and still angry at Shem Glick for quitting the place.

"Kevin, my dehorner, please," Pops said, already at the bull's head. "And the chloroxylenol; I don't want such a clever bull to get an infection."

I came back with the instrument and the disinfectant and watched him go to work. Within one minute he had the bull dehorned and deballed.

Grubby took the bowl, turned to the house, and yelled, "Maynaaaaaa. Oysters is up." After a few moments, Mayna Mitchell banged out the side kitchen screen door and walked toward us, full frontal apron dusted with flour. She was an ample woman with small eyes sunk deep into an oversize head. She wore stern, square-toe shoes holding up ankles run over by the fat in her calves. Titanic, slung-low breasts that lolled from side to side and seemed ready to rip from their moorings on a single misstep. She wordlessly took the metal bowl, turned, and walked back up to the house.

We washed up and exited into the yard just as the bleeding bull made his first awkward steps. Paitsel went off to repair the siding on a grain shed, and Grubby Mitchell stood with his abnormally long arms wrapped around his thin frame, hands tucked so far behind him he could swat a fly on his right buttock with his left hand. He took a step toward Pops and whispered, "Been wonderin your take on this Paul thing." He unwrapped an arm to scratch a place on his cheek.

"It's a damn molehill, in my opinion. Everybody needs to just untwist their girdles and get back to living their own life. What Paul does is his own business."

Just then, a piercing explosion broke across the valley and a plume of smoke and debris rose from the hauled-off mountaintop at the back of Grubby's farm. We all turned to it as if we were watching fireworks on the Fourth. A clump of cows charged to the other end of their field. A horse bolted and kicked at the air. "That ain't no dang molehill."

"Betty Dodger would agree with you."

"Goddamn Bubba Boyd. All that blastin is makin my herd nervous. I think that's why the rut went so poorly."

"No doubt. That'll put any animal off of conjugal activities."

"Says he wants to meet with me. Think he wants to buy me out."

"Who, Bubba?"

Grubby nodded.

"Don't do it, Grub. This land here is who you are."

He shrugged and looked over at the lopped-off mountain that used to tower over the farm.

Pops frowned and placed his satchel in the truck bed. "We'll see you in a month for the blowfly."

He backed up the truck and we headed down the road, dust eddies swirling in our wake. I kept thinking about all that blood and how the bulls didn't even flinch or cry out. "Don't they even feel it when you cut them like that? I mean, it's like they don't feel a thing," I said as we turned onto Route 17.

Pops thought for a moment. "Well, I did give them a local, but that's the one thing the bovine community has over us humans. God gave us the power to reason, but he made them pretty much impervious to pain. To be honest, I'm not sure who got the better deal."

That evening Pops brought Mom out to join us on the porch. She folded her arms around herself and sat like we were strangers at a bus stop in a bad town.

"Kevin, you did real well today," Pops announced with one eye on Mom. "I'm proud of you."

"I didn't do much," I mumbled and turned to the street so I wouldn't have to look at her.

"That's precisely my point. You stayed out of my way and didn't get gored by one of those bulls. A splendid first day as a veterinary assistant, in my book."

"What do you mean, 'first day'?"

"I mean I'm hiring you to be my personal veterinary assistant. Pay you ten dollars a week; all the Appalachian mountain oysters you can eat."

I nodded and said nothing, but a secret smile climbed within me.

"Great news, Annie," Pops said hopefully to Mom, who was staring at the great hickory tree in Pops' front yard as if a primer on loss and heartbreak had been written into the bark. "Kevin's graciously agreed to join the Peebles Veterinary Practice. We may have to get a new sign, 'Peebles and Grandson.' What do you think, Kevin?"

"Why not 'Grandson and Peebles'?" I said, too loud to sound natural.

Both of us looked eagerly for a response. She put her hand to her mouth and went at the thumb quick.

"Not until you do your first solo castration," Pops said, his voice trailing to a whisper when he realized we would get no answer.

I inspected a divot of paint that had been chipped from the porch floor, revealing years of alternating white and gray coats, seven in all, as Pops regarded his silent, broken daughter and the ice in his sour mash glass shifted.

That week was calls in the morning with Pops and afternoons with Buzzy learning the mystic ways of the mountains: a sheep dipping on Tuesday and a dammed-up creek; a hoof clipping on Wednesday and a home-strung zip line; blue tongue shots on Thursday and a found fox pelt and bones on Friday. Each time I mentioned the Telling Cave, Buzzy waved the notion away. "Got somethin better." And off we'd go, breaknecking the hills and plundering the hollows where the compounded guilt and grief I felt would fall away like original sin at a baptismal.

Chapter 6

THE RIFLE-SHOT SLAP

One thing you need to know about *Lord of the Flies*, it's a classic study in human nature—not particularly flattering but accurate nonetheless," Pops said as Thursday evening settled into one of the wicker chairs. He handed me the dusty volume, its jacket cover yellowed and cracked in places. "This is a first edition, mind you, so read it, enjoy it, but treat it with respect. There aren't many out there. Golding only sold a few thousand copies in the States before it went out of print."

"What does it teach you about human nature?"

"Almost everything."

"Like what?"

"Oh...the tension between civilization and anarchy, between good and evil—and the fact that both can live within us. Understanding that will serve you well in this valley." He chuckled shrewdly, took a sip of mash, and spun the ice clockwise slowly.

"Is there evil around here? It seems pretty quiet."

"Evil doesn't have to be loud, son. In fact, it reserves that for the merely boorish. Evil is quiet, stealthy—it sneaks up on you, smiles, and pats you on the back while pissing down your leg. Take Bubba Boyd, for example. He goes about his business of blowing up the mountains and destroying folks' lives without so much as a raised voice. He throws around money at Christmas and Easter so people love him. He's got a smile as wide as this valley, but the most soulless eyes I've ever seen. Owns most of the town but is content to keep us hobbled."

"If he owns everything, how is anybody going to stop him?"

Pops thought for a moment. "I don't know yet, to be honest."

"And if he owns the land, can't he just do what he wants with it?"

"Think of it this way. Just because a river runs through my property, do I have the right to pollute it for the people living downstream? Suppose they get sick and die because of my mess; should I be held to account?"

"I guess so."

"I guess so too. But folks are so used to taking Bubba's money, they're afraid if they oppose him, he'll shut off that big fat teat of his."

"That's gross."

"Not half as gross as what he's doing up there. And the only person in this town with the cojones to oppose him is Paul Pierce."

"That's some talk coming from Missi County's resident war hero." It was Chester Skill at the bottom porch step. He eased into the wicker chair with an exhale as if he and his old bones had called a temporary truce. I got up to pour him a sour mash whiskey and delivered it on a silver tray.

"What did you do to be a war hero, Pops?"

"What any man would have done. I survived."

Chester smiled and shook his head. "Son, your grandfather single-handedly saved the lives of five men."

"What? Mom never told me that. Tell me the story."

Pops shifted in his chair and grimaced as if the thought of talking about himself had triggered back pain.

"His bravery that day won him the Navy Cross—got nominated for the Medal of Honor—bastards wouldn't give it to him, though."

I looked over at Pops, who was in the middle of an extended eye roll. "Why didn't you ever tell me?"

He took a sip of mash and watched as the ice in his glass slowly rotated with the careful movement of his wrist; then he looked over at me with a barely discernible smile. "It's not our way."

Our eyes locked for a few moments more, and the porch fell into silence until Chester finally said, "Well, if you won't tell, I will. Boy needs to understand his stock, Arthur."

Pops raised his glass. "Have at it, then. I seem to get braver each telling."

Chester put his glass on the table and squared to me. "It was toward the end of the War in the Pacific and the Japs were taking a beating..."

"...Once the ship limped back to Pearl Harbor they sent him home and had a big ceremony in Washington, D.C., with all the brass there. Whole Peebles family drove up for it. I came in from Chicago."

"That was a sight." Pops laughed. "Caravan of hillbillies roasting deer meat in the Pentagon parking lot."

"Your momma was proud, though," Chester said, pointing.

"She was indeed." Pops raised his glass and looked into the ice at the patterns they drew on their devolution to water. "She was indeed."

"So, Kevin, I'm afraid I have to disagree with your grandfather's assertion that no one in the county other than Paul Pierce has balls. Arthur Bradley Peebles is the bravest man I know."

Pops waved away the compliment. "Bravery is when you have time to weigh out the peril and you act anyway at great personal risk. I just acted without thinking. Now, what Paul is doing—standing up to Bubba Boyd—that's bravery."

"Who's this Paul person?"

"You'll meet him tomorrow after calls. I arranged for Audy Rae to take your mother for a new hairdo with Paul at Miss Janey's salon. I imagine you could use a summer cut as well—unless you're going for that *Lord of the Flies* look."

⌐⌐⌐

"So I says to Toomey, I says, 'I'm...not...puttin...thaaaat thing in me!' This water too hot for you? If it is, jus say so. So he looks at me an says, 'It would be nice if we tried somethin different for a change.' So I says, 'Yeah, it sure would be nice if we tried somethin different, like a movie an some presents or somethin. That would certainly be different for a change.'"

"So what'd it look like, then?"

"What do think it looked like, you fool girl?"

"What I mean is, did it look like a real one?"

"No, it looked like a giant flesh lipstick. He said he stole it from his sister, who stole it from Bubby Allison's momma. So I says to Toomey, I says, 'Least you could do is get me my own one.' I says,

'If you get me my own one I might try it.' An you know what?...
He did!...An man, Levona, you wouldn't believe..."

"Levona!" Mr. Paul spurred from the storeroom at the back
of the Paris Hair Salon. "I'm not paying you to gab all day with
Petunia. She's got work and so do you. Mrs. Gillooly's ready to be
shampooed; please see to it...now!"

"Yes, Mr. Paul." Levona slunk away and Mr. Paul went back
into the storeroom, leaving me and Petunia to fill the empty
spaces with conversation.

Upside down in the trough of the sink in the washing department at Miss Janey's Paris Hair Salon and Notion Shop, I knew
for certain that Petunia Wickle was the most beautiful creature
on earth. She lathered a palmful of Breathless Body shampoo
into my scalp with fingers that felt like a thousand giant flesh
lipsticks. I cleared my throat to let her know I was capable of continuing the conversation.

"Would you like conditioner?"

I nodded.

"Okay, you got it."

Petunia's ink-black hair hung straight down from the sides of
her face, turning in just below her grapefruit-size breasts, which
were rudely constrained in a yellow midriff top. Tight button-fly
jeans and burgeoning hips budding to full promise. Between the
bottom of her midriff and the top of her jeans was a sanctuary of
bare flesh. Light pink, like the new skin under an old scab.

She leaned over to the counter for conditioner and her stomach
touched my cheek, sending slashes of electricity to my feet. She
leaned again to put it back. The brass buttons of her jeans were
dry ice against my face and made her easy skin seem torrid. The
elastic band at the bottom of her yellow midriff was stretched

well past the point of serviceability, which afforded me full view of the top's contents.

"So how you like it here in the dust pit a the universe?"

The question startled me from my fantasy. "Fine," I said, instantly regretting my lack of wit. She worked the conditioner into my scalp expertly. My eyes were three-quarters closed so I could watch the vast expanse of skin and breast in private. She rinsed me one last time and narrowed the water from my hair with her hands.

"Sit up now so's I can dry you."

My face met her stomach, which smelled of still-warm laundry.

"Mr. Paul's gonna do you an your mom special."

She led me to the first chair, smiled, and swished back to the washing department. I scrutinized her every step in the old mirrors that lined both sides of the room.

Miss Janey's Paris Hair Salon and Notion Shop was not weathering the downturn in the Medgar economy well. At its peak, the salon boasted eight cutting stations, a washing department with four new sinks, and two full-time manicurists. Miss Janey's partner, Paul Pierce, ran the hair operation and Miss Janey spent most of her time with the beauty school they had opened in 1974. The beauty market was tough now, especially in Medgar.

The cutting stations lined up like ghost-town soldiers at attention. Only the first three showed signs of any life. A crush of black combs in a white plastic jar. Yellowed beautician licenses framed in yellowed Scotch tape. Fossiled chrome blow dryers with frayed cloth cords and cracked oblong black plugs. Gray-patched mirrors reflecting faithfully every day since opening, but now as weak as old flashlights. Beige and brown tile, pocked with bare concrete where tiles had broken. The walls were light yellow at the ceiling, fading to a dull beige at the bottom. Years of forgotten hair clippings gathered in every corner. An orange vinyl settee in the waiting room with ten-year-old style books faded from the morning sun. The Notion Shop had closed two years ago; a dusty sheet hung in the open doorway that linked the two.

In Petunia's department were four yellow porcelain sinks, two black-and-chrome reclining chairs bettered with duct tape. The eight bays hadn't been full since senior prom morning years ago, and the staff had been whittled from twelve to just four, including Miss Janey, who came in only twice a week. Paul Pierce now performed all the colorings and perms and most of the manicures himself. Hadn't held an elocution class in eighteen months. He whisked out from the back, blade thin and posture perfect, with soft blue eyes and a welcoming smile.

Before she died, Paul's mother would always thrust herself between them and their father, sweet-talking the old man down or taking the brunt when life put hard upon him. Back then, it was only open hands, or maybe a fist when he was up with shine. On nights when the blocking and the sweet-talk failed them, she would gather up the hurt, usually just Paul because he was small and slow and lacking in guile, and hold him close for hours, drawing out the pain like a madstone for poison.

With her gone, the rage came sure as thunder, delivered from a hickory stave instead of hands. Afterward, Paul would walk up Cheek Mountain, high above the cabin, to a quiet place that looked out across the hollow toward Indian Head. He would dig out a shallow dint in the cool loam, just long enough for his ten-year-old body, strip to underwear, and lay down in the wallow, covering himself with the soothing dirt and leaves the way kids in a wholly different universe sometimes bury themselves in beach sand.

Once he was interred, the mountain became his new madstone, extracting the hurt of beatings or the sting of schoolyard spites until he was cleansed and healed and delivered back pure. After the earth had done its work, he would sing up at the sky, in a voice that church folks said was gifted from God.

His brothers, Jacob and Wagner, lit out on their eighteenth birthdays: Jacob for West Texas and Wagner for whatever wind. But by then, the old man was stooped and Paul was large enough to fight back. He distinctly remembered the last time his father beat him, when the seventeen-year cicadas emerged that spring, bedlamming the woods with a shrill that cloaked the cabin shouts.

In his teen years, after the beatings stopped, he would go to the mountain hoping the cool earth would draw out the strange, disturbing desires he felt. But as the years passed, the stirrings became robust, then relentless, as he stopped trying to blunt them or even understand them; he just pushed them down inside the mantle of his soul.

Paul joined the army at eighteen, thinking it would merit some respect from his father, but when the service deemed him unsuited for infantry, the old man just laughed. He was billeted to the administrative pool at the Pentagon in Washington, D.C., and soon won a spot with the newly formed U.S. Army Chorus as first tenor. The Army Band and Chorus toured the U.S. and most of Europe west of the Iron Curtain: London, Stockholm, Madrid, Brussels, and, of course, Paris.

But the burning desires continued and the unslaking made

them compound on themselves until they took him dizzy and fixated to the dark corners of parks in Paris, to right-angle alleys in Earls Court, and to the murky edges of monuments in Washington, D.C., furtive in the dark with the other nervous shadows. One night in the bushes by the Iwo Jima memorial, the police swooped and Paul pleaded to indecent exposure and a general discharge.

In shame, he drifted down to Nashville, bunking with an Army Band buddy who had just gotten a session gig with Decca. Paul sat openmouthed in the corner of the studio watching Patsy Cline and Owen Bradley fight over the thirteenth take of "Crazy." When the backing tenor took sick, Paul pushed himself to audition. He opened with "Wings of a Dove," and after the first bar, the great Owen Bradley himself looked up from the soundboard with a smile broad as the twelve-track console.

~~~

"Hello, young man, I'm Mr. Paul, how are you? Just fine? That's nice. What sort of haircut would you like today?"

I mumbled something and he went straight to work, scissors and syllables flashing with equal pace and precision.

"So how are you finding Medgar so far? Good? Well, don't you listen to what people may be telling you about this town. I've lived here nearly all my life and it's a fine town. Ask your grandaddy what a fine town this is. How is he, by the way? I hear you're helping him with the vet business now. That's a fine thing. You know, I've known him since I was a boy. It seems he's as much a part of this town as the mountains. And your granmomma Miss Sarah, now, there's a lady who had class. I first saw her when I was thirteen and she and your grandaddy had just moved back into town. One day she walked into church, tall as timber, with this big red hat that she took off and laid on the pew next to her. Took up two places, that hat did. Lands…the way she used to go into town so pretty and straight like an ad in *Look* magazine. All the girls took to walking like her and wearing their hair like her, and one time when I was in Dempsey's with Jane she came in, smiling as ever, and says to us, 'Good morning, Master Paul, Miss Jane,' like we were best friends, and I say, 'Good morning, Miss Sarah,' back to her, and then Jane says, 'That's a might pretty hair ribbon, Miss Sarah'—she had this bright red ribbon in her hair—and she says to Jane, 'Oh, do you think so?' and she takes the ribbon out and sits Jane down and ties it in her hair and gives both her shoulders a squeeze and says, 'Miss Jane, you have such exceptional hair, will you do me the honor of wearing my ribbon?' "

Mr. Paul paused with his scissors for a few seconds as if to consider the memory, then continued cutting and talking.

"…'such exceptional hair,' she told us. When she died, a bit of this town died with her. Is this part too high for you? Okay? But you know, she did get some people's backs up. Some ladies sniffed at her, and she made a mortal enemy of a few men."

Mr. Paul looked toward the lobby and lowered his voice. "I tell you, I remember her ruction with some local bullyboys like it was this morning. Two of those boys were out front of Hivey's giving a black girl the business, you know, touching her and so forth and saying rude things. I was sitting on the bench out front of Smith's Ice Cream and this poor girl didn't know what to do because back then black folks didn't give sass to whites, especially young men like these. One of them grabs her and starts pulling her into their truck. And she just keeps saying, 'Please, sir, just stop it, please, sir.'

"I go on up and tell them to quit. But they just laughed at me and called me rude names. So I grab the girl's arm and try to pull her back to the sidewalk. But they were too strong. We were in a tug-of-war for that girl and I was losing. Then your granmomma, she walks out of Dempsey's, arms fulled up with parcels, and sees what's going on, and she knew what those boys were gonna do. So she sets everything down, your granmomma does, and walks over to the one boy and slaps him across the face so hard it sounded like a rifle shot. And she says, real quiet, 'Don't you ever touch a woman against her will again, do you understand?' And they were so surprised they all just stood there like a bunch of dumb stones. She took the black girl by the arm—she was shaking like sixty that black girl—and Miss Sarah calmly led her off like they were going to a party. And those boys just skunked away, but you know they never did anything like that again. Jane wore that ribbon to her funeral. She still has it."

Mr. Paul was silent for half a minute, reflecting on the ribbon and the rifle-shot slap. Fingers working so fast it looked like he was trimming air.

I imagined what my grandmother must have been like: a quiet confidence that marked every gesture, a bounding laugh, the simple joy she took in even the most mundane chores. I looked over at Mom sitting in the waiting room and tried to imagine what her mother would say to her to set things right, but my mind went empty. I took a deep breath to try and crowd out the despair tightening me.

"You know, in the years after she passed, your grandaddy was a prime catch among the single ladies in Medgar. He even caught Jane's fancy for a time, once she became a successful business-woman, but he wouldn't have none of it."

I thought about Pops' pain and sadness on losing my grand-mother and tried to measure it against my own. But mine was shot through with guilt and anger built on blame rather than lost love.

"There aren't many like your grandaddy," Mr. Paul continued. "Don't tell him I know this, but for the last four Christmases he's been secretly delivering toys and turkeys to about forty of the poorest families. He doesn't think anybody knows, but most of us do." There was a moment of quiet while Mr. Paul searched for another topic. "This is a fine town, you know. Best folks in the world live here." From outside the salon came the sound of a muffled explosion. Mr. Paul's face darkened. He stopped cut-ting and closed his eyes and gathered in a deep breath. "I will *not* abide what they are doing up there," he said in precisely measured syllables. His eyes shot open, anger flaring them out. "Do you know what Bubba Boyd's done to the streams and the wells around here? Poisoned. The water from the taps up Corbin Hollow comes out gray now. Everyone up there is getting sick from it. Their slurry pond is all filled up and we think they're pumping the slurry into one of the abandoned mines, which is totally illegal."

"What's slurry?" I asked, although I knew it didn't sound like a good thing.

He paused and put down his scissors, folded his hands across his chest. "When they bring the coal up it's all dirty and dusty so they have to wash it before it can go on the train. The slurry is what comes off the chunks of coal—dust, dirt, nasty chemicals, all mixed in water. If he's pumping it into the mines, guess where it ends up?"

"Uhhhmm, in the drinking water?"

"That's exactly correct." His picked up his scissors and began cutting again, faster, purposeful, his mouth a single taut line. After a while he softened. "I'm sorry, I just get so angry at that Bubba Boyd...what he's doing to this place.

"Well now, let's just see," he said, holding up a hand mirror so I could see the clown smile of white skin at the nape of my neck. "I think you're ready for the prom, young sir." He dusted off the snips of hair clinging to my shirt and escorted me to one of the orange vinyl chairs in reception next to Audy Rae and Mom.

"You just have a seat while I do your mom special. Normally Mary Alice does the cuts and I do the perms and posture, but seeing as you're Arthur's kin and Mary Alice just quit, I thought I'd do you both special." He went to my mother, freshly combed out by Levona and sitting calmly in a blue pastel dress, fingers shuffled into Audy Rae's right hand. Lips set to flat, neither frowning nor smiling.

"Annie, I'm Mr. Paul, remember me?" Mr. Paul said loudly, as if Mom's trauma had left her deaf as well. "I'm gonna do you special today." Mom looked to Audy Rae for consent. Audy Rae nodded. Mom offered a tired smile as she gave Mr. Paul her arm and was led to the first station.

Mr. Paul parted her hair, pinned the left side, and began cutting and combing, checking the mirror as if he expected a wince of pain with each snip. He saw none and began speaking in bromides.

"Is this weather too hot for you? They say it's gonna cool soon."

Mr. Paul had a habit of asking questions and never waiting for the answers. "Personally, I like the hot weather. Is it hot like this in Indiana? I heard in Texas it's gonna be a hundred and eight degrees today." And so it went.

"...well, since Jane's been poorly, I just threw myself into this place, but with most of the mines closed, business is off a fair patch. And Mary Alice, she just got tired of cutting hair, I suppose, but me, I love it."

Petunia Wickle, who had been idled in the washing department, breezed past Mr. Paul and announced, "I'm goin to Biddle's for lunch." She opened the door with a ring of the synthetic bell and was halfway across the street by the time it closed, vertebrae in the small of her back actioning with every step.

Mr. Paul finished cutting and wrapped my mother's hair in chrome curlers and led her to a bank of ancient floor-standing silver-domed hair dryers. He fired one to a vacuum whirl, carefully fitting the half-egg-shaped dome on my mother's head.

Two ladies, freshly washed by Levona and ready for service, were sitting on the vinyl chairs opposite Audy Rae and me.

"That's her," the first whispered.

"Who?" the other said, not looking up from *Soap Opera Digest*.

"You know, the lady that's gone nuts cause her little boy died. That's Dr. Peebles' daughter."

The other looked up from the magazine and squinted to focus. Audy Rae darted up from her book and fixed the women with a withering glare.

"That's her, then? Heard about her; they say she's gone plumb crazy," the second lady said, returning to her magazine. "What her little boy die of?"

"Shish, Lorraine, don't be ignorant; she'll hear you."

I shrank in my seat on the embarrassment of it and took up a *Ladies' Home Journal* to hide behind.

Lorraine put her magazine down. "Under that dryer? She couldn't hear a hammer to pavement."

Audy Rae cleared her throat loudly—gave them butcher knives.

They both regarded her coolly; then the first lady continued. "Well, the family says he got hit by a car, but I heard it warn't no such thing."

"What then?"

"I don't know exactly what, but Lida Wickle said she heard it was some real bad accident at home, poor woman saw the whole thing happen. Imagine, seein your child get kilt. It's no wonder she's crazy."

"Where's her husband, then? He die too?"

"No, he sent her to live with Dr. Peebles. Lida said Dr. Peebles an him had a bust-up ten years ago an barely spoken since."

"What was the bust-up?"

"Lida didn't know. That's the thing about these Peebles—they don't tell you their business. My friend Deloris is friends with Jeb Peebles' wife and when Jeb died Deloris didn't even know he had the cancer, never even tole her. Suffer in silence, them Peebles do." They were quiet for a moment. "How bout Simp?"

"Flyrock size a basketball come down from number two. My friend Kitsy's husband is a volunteer fireman, second truck on the scene, an she said Simp didn't have much of a head left."

"That's awful. Poor Betty."

"You don't know the half. When them trucks pulled up she was out there with him jus holdin his hand. Kitsy said she had gathered up all the broken skull pieces an brain pieces an tried to fit them all back together on top a Simp's head."

I closed my eyes on the scene in Simp Dodger's backyard only to be greeted by the visual of Josh dying in our driveway in Redhill. I shook my head and looked out the window for anything to pull me away from the reliving of that scene.

"You goin to Paul's meetin tonight?"

"I don't know, Bebe...more minin means more jobs. That's a good thing. Ain't like nobody's usin them mountains."

"You seen what they done to Corbin Holler. It ain't there no more. Gone like it never was."

"That ain't a bad thing. Ain't nuthin good ever come outta Corbin."

"They say all the water round there is cancer water. I'm goin to the meetin to see what it's all bout."

Mr. Paul pulled the silver hair dryer off my mother and led her back to the number one chair, unwinding the curlers and poking her hair with the sharp end of a black comb, then fogging everything with hair spray.

The final result was spectacular given the steady decline Mom had allowed herself in the last three months. Even Mr. Paul was proud as he held the hand mirror for her to see all the angles. Mom nodded impassively. Mr. Paul led her to the chair next to Audy Rae. The *Soap Opera Digest* lady and her friend watched Mom, returning to their magazines only when they were met with Mr. Paul's disapproving glare.

"Annie," he said, squatting to face her, "I swear, you are surely as beautiful as your mother."

Mom smiled, this time from her eyes. "What a lovely thing to say, thank you."

Mr. Paul stood for an awkward instant, then turned to the magazine ladies with a sigh. "Hello, Miss Lorraine, Miss Bebe… Miss Lorraine, if you please." Miss Bebe peeked over the top of her periodical until the bell on the front door jingled and Pops walked in, arms full of veterinary supplies, followed by Paitsel Meadows with a scoop of ice cream in a cup—mint sprinkles trailing from the top—and Petunia Wickle, fresh from her lunch break at Biddle's.

"Well now, don't you girls look pretty as peaches," Pops said to us with a chuckle. Petunia looked at me and laughed. Mr. Paul brightened at the sight of my grandfather.

"Paul, you are an artist."

Mr. Paul just smiled into Miss Lorraine's thinning hair. Paitsel put the ice cream cup on the cutting-station counter. "They was out a chocolate, so I got you strawberry."

Paul grinned and took the cup. "What a lovely surprise. I thought you had to go to Knuckle today."

"He don't got the part. There's a place near Johnson City with a ton a Chevy blocks. He'll have it."

Paul moved to the trash can and began gently sloughing the sprinkles off the scoop with the spoon. We all watched as he cleared the ice cream of every mint piece. He must have felt all our eyes on him. He looked up and smiled. "I'm gonna just take a few of these off… such a nice surprise."

Paitsel shook his head and smirked over to Pops. "Some people there ain't no pleasin."

Pops laughed. "I don't even try."

"You two hush up now," Mr. Paul said and loaded a spoonful of sprinkleless ice cream. "Hits the spot on a hot day like today." He offered the next spoon to Paitsel.

"Nah, I take mine with sprinkles."

Pops chuckled and took the spoon.

"I guess I'll get on down to Johnson City," Paitsel said as he pushed open the door. We said good-byes and followed him out to the sidewalk.

I turned to sneak a last look at Petunia, but she was gone. All I could see was Mr. Paul, ice cream put to the side, looking into the gray double mirror in front of him, pondering the red ribbon, the exceptional hair. And the rifle-shot slap.

Chapter 7

THE NEW BEST KINGS OF THE EARTH

I left Pops and Paitsel talking about a tapping valve and walked up to the tree house, where Buzzy was plugging a bee-dug hole on a roof truss with chewing gum.

"Bout time."

"Had to get a haircut."

"You look like a dork." He flashed a gap-toothed grin. "Come on. With a lame-ass cut like that, you're gonna need the Treatment." He was limb to limb before I could ask or argue. I got to the ground as quickly as I could and ran to catch up.

"What's the Treatment?"

He stopped, turned back to me and laughed, then kept on down the trail, pacing faster than before. We crossed the valley, through cow fields and corn, until we came to Route 17 and the entrance to Grubby Mitchell's farm.

"This is Runnin Creek. We follow it past the farm to the hollow where Mr. Mitchell dams it all up. The Treatment is in there."

"What exactly is this Treatment thing?"

"It ain't really a thing you can describe." He took off up the creek.

A quarter mile into the hollow we came to a wooden dam and a wide pool held back by it. On the left edge of the pool was a tarn of black loamy mud, smooth and glistening like freshly poured black concrete. A twisted old hickory clung to the high bank, a big branch hanging over part of the mud pit. Thrown over the branch was a rope with a simple noose at the end. The bark on the branch had been worn smooth from use.

"This used to be called the *Nigger* Treatment, but my grandaddy hides us if we use that word, so now we jus call it the Treatment."

I had read about the lynchings of blacks in the South, but I thought it all ended in the sixties. "Buzzy, why did you bring me here?" I asked, confused that he would speak so lightheartedly of murder.

He looked at me quizzically. "I thought you would like it."

"Why would I like a place where they *killed* black people?"

"What are you talkin bout?"

"The noose...the *Nigger* Treatment! This is where they lynched black people, isn't it?"

He looked over at it and started laughing. "It ain't for hangin people."

"What's it for, then?" I said defensively. The noose, the tree, the name—it all added up to me.

"I'll show you," he said and stripped completely naked, hanging his clothes on a thick root jutting out from the bank.

The end of the noose rope was tied to another root. He untied it and handed it to me. "Tie this tight round your waist. When I swing out over the mud, you walk up the bank to lower me into the Treatment. Once my hands disappear into the muck, jump off the bank an your weight will pull me out."

"Uhhhh...Buzzy, I don't think this is such a good idea."

"I done it a hundert times."

"What if I can't pull you back up?"

"Then pull harder," he said and climbed halfway up the bank. I wrapped the end of the rope twice around my waist, tied it, positioning it low on my hips, under my butt. He pulled the noose in with a long stick, grabbed hold, and tugged it tight. "Now I'm gonna swing on out over the mud. My weight's gonna make you able to walk straight up the bank to the top. That'll lower me in the Treatment. When the rope goes slack, jump back down the bank and it'll pull me out."

"But what if I can't pull you out?" I said again. Buzzy outweighed me by at least thirty pounds.

He looked at me with a raised eyebrow. "The Treatment ain't a place you want to get stuck in. Best you pull harder."

"I'm serious, man. You weigh a lot more than me."

He looked down on me with mock seriousness. "Then I'm in deep shit." He laughed and swung out over the expanse of mud. The rope tightened and I braced against the bank.

"Walk it!" he screamed, and I took a step up the bank, then another and another. I felt weightless, like Batman scaling the side of a building. With each step Buzzy sank deeper into the mud—up to his knees, his waist, his chest. I hesitated. "Keep goin," he shouted. I took three more steps and his head disappeared into the black mud, then his arms and hands—nothing but the rope sticking out of the pit like the new wick out of a black candle. The rope went slack as I reached the top of the bank. I pushed off to rappel down. The rope tightened but the weight of him held me fast. I just dangled in the air, my feet against the bankside. I jumped up, pushed off again, but the rope made no movement. I jumped again with force, and the rope unstuck, lowering me to mudside. As I went down, up came onyx arms, a black head, an obsidian chest, coal legs. The watery mud was just thick enough to cling to him, leaving a thin black film on his entire body. He looked as if he'd just been plucked from the rendering vat at an India-ink factory. He smiled and his white teeth were pearls against the dark of it all. He swung his legs up and back to maneuver the rope onto solid ground, then let go and jumped to safety.

I fell back onto the ground at the loss of counterbalance, laughing hysterically. "Buzzy, you look straight out of the jungle."

He picked up a spear-like stick and climbed to the top of a large rock overlooking the pool. Black and naked, he reached both arms up to the blue-cotton sky. "I claim this land in the name a the new best kings a the earth." His voice boomed across the swimming hole. "Whoever chooses to be like marked will join me on the throne. You, young prince." He pointed the spear at me. I stood. "Got you the makins of a king?"

"Uhhhh. I think." I grabbed the noose and Buzzy wrapped the rope around his waist.

I climbed halfway up the bank and looked at the expanse of mud, glistening in the sun. It looked harmless, no deeper than a few inches, but I knew it was a treacherous bottomless pit.

"White-skinned prince, you must rid yourself of your princely clothes to become a king."

I had never been naked outdoors before and hesitated. The king put his spear down and resumed his previous persona. "You don't want to be gettin the Treatment with your clothes on. It ain't a good idea. My brother Cleo did it and momma never got the mud outta em."

I balanced on the root and slowly took off my shirt and stripped down to my underwear. I pulled my boxer shorts down and stepped out of them and threw them down to Buzzy. I gripped the noose tightly and pulled the rope tight. Buzzy wrapped the other end twice around his waist. "I got you now—jus swing on out like I done."

I picked my legs up and Tarzanned out over the flat. Buzzy stepped up on the bank face and my toes hit the mud, then my feet. It was cold. The chill crept up my legs as I sank into the pool.

"Whatever you do, man, do not let go a the rope," he said from the bank. "There's ain't no bottom to it."

I tightened my grip on the noose.

The mud was like watered-down pudding as I sank deeper into the pit—past my navel, up to my shoulders. I took a deep breath and went under. It was black, probably blacker and colder than the deepest unexplored corner of the Telling Cave. I kept sinking, like I was being sucked down into a cold, black death, unable to move my limbs. I felt the rope go slack, and my upstretched hands sank below the surface. A stripe of panic seized me; I tried to kick to the surface, but the mud held me under. I couldn't bring my arms down to swim to the top, and the more I struggled the deeper I seemed to sink. My lungs began to sear and my legs and arms thrashed around in the wet concrete–like encasement. In panic I dropped the rope. I groped frantically for it, but it was gone.

I turned myself around, sweeping the black expanse in front of me with my arms, lungs bursting, head ringing, frantic fingers feeling for the rope. It brushed against my cheek. I caught the end of the loop just as it was pulling away from me. The rope went tight and I started rising to the surface. My hands broke the mud expanse, just as dizziness from lack of air started to take me. Finally my head broke the surface and I felt the cool air fill my lungs. I opened my eyes to the bright new world. The colors on the trees, the blackness of the mud, and the blueness of the sky all seemed new and wonderful, like I had died and been pulled back to life. My mouth was full of gritty, loamy mud, but I didn't care. I was alive and everything was right again with the world.

I swung my legs up and over to the edge of the mud pit and dropped next to Buzzy. I put my hands on my knees and panted, searching for breath. "Man...I thought...you were never going to pull me up."

"Works best if you soak in it for a few seconds," he said and laughed. He jumped down from the rock. "Come, my brother king. Let us lay in the light an give homage to the sun god." I followed him across, out to the sunbathed far bank, and lay in the sand to let the sun dry the black mud. I stretched out with my hands behind my head, as content as I thought I would ever be.

We were silent then, feeling the wet mud congeal on our bodies, the new best kings of the earth, black and naked with the sun baking us dry and me wishing a way to stop the world from spinning so that this singular moment in my life would never end.

Chapter 8

THE PRICE OF FUTURE MEMORIES

That evening, the porch seemed to meld into dusk slower than usual. Lo and Paitsel stopped by at six o'clock, and at six twenty Chester Skill eased up the worn steps and into one of the faded green wicker chairs.

Paitsel launched the night's discussion. "The Company is tryin to buy the Mitchell place. Looks like they're goin to create a second slurry pond down mountain. The one on top is definitely at capacity."

Pops nodded. "Grubby said Bubba was courting him. Don't think he's going to sell out, though."

"With that kind a acreage, Bubba'll be expandin," Lo offered.

Chester sighed. "We are talking mountains that have been here for ten thousand years. Mountains that have defined us for generations. We all went to bed soon after the sun set over them, and when we got up every morning, they were there. They were the one constant in this scratch-a-living life of ours, and now three are gone. Just gone. And nobody but Paul is raising a stink about it." He shook his head. "But you know what pains me to my soul? The fact that they are not coming back. Indian Head ain't coming back. Ever."

"Greed is a vice to be reckoned with," Pops said.

"So is Bubba Boyd," Lo piped in.

"You can't just blame Bubba and his crowd. You've got the folks who sold him the land or the rights, the miners working the mountain, and everyone else who likes the money it brings." Pops shook his head and took a sip of mash.

"I'm happy just to blame that fat-ass Bubba. He and his kin have been raping the mountains since we were kids. It's just gotta stop," Chester said.

"As a member of the fourth estate, you have a tool to rile the masses," Pops replied with a wink over to me.

Chester nodded purposefully. "I do, and I intend to use it. Been working with Paul and his people at the Appalachian Project up in Washington—doing a major feature on surface mining and its effect on the environment and the towns. Coming out in two weeks. They even have a new name for it, you know."

"What's that? Cutting off your mountains to spite your future? Redneck plunder?"

"Mountaintop removal is what they call it now," Paitsel cut in.

Pops whistled. "That is catchy, if not precise. More malevolent than surface mining and more descriptive than strip mining. I like it."

"Boys from Washington are comin to Paul's meetin tonight with all their facts and figures. We get enough folks takin a stand, I reckon we can stop em."

Pops was skeptical. One of his eyes closed to a slit. "Facts and figures don't mean spit, Paitsel, and you know it, especially coming from some Washington do-gooder come down trying to help the ignorant hillbillies."

"He is an expert on strip minin, apparently."

"People don't care about experts; they care about Betty Dodger being a widow." Pops pointed the end of his never-lit pipe at Paitsel for emphasis. "They care about black water coming out of the faucets up in Corbin Hollow. They care about their neighbors getting sick from all this crap in the water."

"They've done an exhaustive study of the environmental impact in West Virginia," Chester defended.

Pops shook his head. "Focus on the local, Chester. What folks know and can see and touch."

Chester sat back and nodded, contemplating the advice. Lo was feeling left out of the conversation and piped in. "I ain't been sick yet this year."

Pops smiled. "That's a blessing, Lo. We would miss your scintillating wit on this porch."

"My cousin Rafus says he caught hives from them new T-shirts theys sellin at Pic-n-Pay. Says the Chinese put something in the cotton to make us all itch."

"Dang Chinese never came up with an original idea in their lives. Stole that one from the British," Chester said, chuckling.

"Paper and printing were pretty original, if you ask me, Mr. Newspaperman," Pops said with a laugh.

Chester grinned and raised his glass. "Touché."

Pops slapped his thighs and stood to stretch. "Well, we'd better get on over so we can get the good seats before the selfish people take em."

"Red rashes on their back an legs. They all got it up Corbin, most up Pigeon an Goat Leg got it too."

"Does it itch? I heard it's a powerful itch."

"Itches like they been poxed with sumac."

"I bet my soda poultice take that itch right away."

"No, ma'am. Soda don't work on it."

The other lady sniffed. "My poultice works on everthin."

Other snips of conversation were floating around the crowded hall. Two laid-off miners were arguing the merits of goat manure over horse manure in tomato cultivation. A handful of women were leaning in to each other, whispering quilting-party protocol. Others were worrying on which casserole to bring Betty Dodger. Two men were turned around in the front row listening to another describe the gray water that had been coming out of his faucets. Grubby Mitchell, Jesper Jensen, Bobby Clinch, and other men from the back of Hivey's were standing in the fifth row, bent down in a huddle.

The place was filling up fast as Pops, Chester, Lo, and I settled into seats in the middle. Paitsel walked to the front row, removed an International Harvester hat that had been placed on the seat, and sat.

Mr. Paul, crisp in brown pants, white shirt, and blue tie, was speaking to a young man with tussled black hair, jeans, and a gray sport coat. The man was listening intently as Mr. Paul chopped a flat hand into his palm to emphasize some point.

I turned around and saw that every seat in the place had been taken—people lining the walls as if it was Easter service. In the middle of the aisle on a chair was a projector with a half-filled carousel of slides. A bedsheet screen hung from pipe-strung twine. Mr. Paul looked at his watch, nodded to the stranger, then moved to the middle.

"With the PA system broke, I'm going to have to speak loudly, so if any of y'all in the back can't hear me, just give a shout." Folks nodded. "Thanks to all of you for coming tonight. And thanks also to Mayor Smith for letting us use the hall. Mayor, are you here? Mayor?" Mr. Paul scanned the audience. "Well, anyway, I think this is probably one of the most important meetings we are ever going to have in this town. I've lived here nearly all my life, just like all of you, and these beautiful mountains and hills that surround us are as much a part of this town as each and every one of us. They were here before us, and they should be here long after we are gone. But Bubba Boyd and the Company want to change all that. They already have blown the tops off Indian Head, Sadler, and Cheek, and completely filled in Corbin Hollow. It is unrecognizable from what it once was. The Company thinks they have dominion over the mountains, but I say that is wrong. The only one who has dominion over these mountains is God himself." Most folks nodded at the invocation. "The Company has been taking wealth from this land all our lives. They have been taking and taking and giving nothing back. Think about it. What have we ever got from the Company?"

"A job," someone said from the back.

"I will give you that," Mr. Paul replied. "They've paid us well for our efforts. Until they don't need us anymore, then they discard us like old shoes. They've been taking and taking from the start, and now they want to take away the mountains themselves. I say...*enough*!" He stamped his foot on the tile floor; the sound banged across the silent room. "*Enough*," he shouted and pounded his foot again. Several folks nodded. "Do you know what mountaintop removal has done? That's what it's called now, mountaintop removal. Do you know what mountaintop removal has done to other communities? Devastated them. Destroyed them."

People were sitting forward in their seats now. Men were scratching at their stubble, ladies fidgeting with their bracelets.

"I have with me tonight a very distinguished gentleman from Washington, D.C., who works for the Appalachian Project, which helps small towns like ours fight for our rights. He's going to show you a slideshow of what mountaintop removal has done to other towns. I would like to introduce you to Mr. Jonathan Pendrick from the Appalachian Project." Mr. Paul clapped his hands enthusiastically, and most in the crowd followed, albeit less so. Jon Pendrick walked fervently to the middle of the stage. He took off his jacket to sweat blooms under his arms; his five-o'clock shadow seemed a black smear against his white skin. He picked up the projector remote and clicked it. Nothing happened. He clicked again, then again. Still nothing. Mr. Paul moved quickly to the projector and turned it on. A white light square flashed on the bedsheet screen. "I think we are ready, Mr. Pendrick," Mr. Paul said. Pendrick clicked the remote and a slide appeared on the screen:

The Residual Effect of Mountaintop Removal
on Constituent Towns in
Bituminous Coalfields in West Virginia

A Pictorial Study by The Appalachian Project

© Copyright 1985 The Appalachian Project

"Hello, everybody. I'm from Washington, D.C., and I'm here to help," he said and chuckled. No one laughed. The single standing oscillating fan moved its head from right to left and back again across the room as if it was counting the crowd. He cleared his throat. "That's . . . that's a joke we tell sometimes when we go out into the field. Cause, you see, most folks don't think much help ever comes from Washington, D.C., you see." Silence. Staring. He cleared his throat. "Right, well, let's start, then." He clicked the slide projector. A beautiful row of mountains, fourteen by my count, and green with trees. A light mist rose from one of the hollows to a sparkling sky that held up a few cloud wisps. "This is an aerial view of the Dawson Range in Wayson County, central West Virginia. This picture was taken in 1980, when all of the mining activity in the county was underground. Beginning in 1982, Jayco Energy started a massive mountaintop removal operation once the underground seams ceased to be productive. Now, here's the same Dawson Range in 1984." He pointed the remote at the projector and thumbed the button. The slide advanced to an unrecognizable moonscape of gray rock and flattened land. Seven of the mountains in the middle of the range had been hauled away, leaving a flat, bleak expanse of rock and erosion completely devoid of vegetation.

A few folks in the audience gasped.

"They jus cut the tops right off," someone said.

"That's what theys done to Indian Head an Sadler," another said.

Pendrick picked up a pointer and moved to the bedsheet screen. "You see this slurry pond right here?" He circled a black lake with the pointer. "Six months after this photo was taken, the dam here burst and two hundred million gallons of coal slurry flowed down the hollow into the Clemet River." He pressed the advance and the picture changed to a hollow swamped in black water; a double-wide askew and half submerged; two pickups pressed against a tree as black water swirled around them; a family on the roof of their house, watching forlornly as their steer fought the force of the black flood. "Eleven people drowned that day." He paused so the import could settle. "The Environmental Protection Agency has called the Dawson flood the worst environmental disaster east of the Mississippi."

"I seen it on the news," someone said. Others nodded.

"My sister's ex-husband grew up in Dawson. Had kin kilt that day," someone else volunteered.

"Indeed, slurry ponds are a toxic cocktail of heavy metals, chemicals, and all kinds of harmful contaminants," Pendrick added. "And if you think Dawson was bad, the horror continues." Pendrick clicked the remote and the slide advanced to another bucolic set of flowing mountains, then the same mountains butchered and shorn of themselves. Each image more jarring and disturbing than the last. Spivey's Corner. Keller's Run. Big Wayson's Gap. All denuded, removed, smoothed over and planted to meager grassland. "This one is the Shiloh Run range, where Deeds Energy has..."

Suddenly the double doors at the back burst open and banged against their stops. One of the largest men I had ever seen waddled into the room. Heads swiveled and folks murmured as he strode down the center aisle. He had the bearing and the belly of a retired football lineman. His thick arms hung low at his sides and his palms faced backward as he walked. His buttocks were boulders as they drew in the seam of his gabardine pants tight to the space between them. Tree-trunk thighs swishing friction on every step. His face seemed pulled taut, as if adipose tissue was stretching his skin to its natural limits. His neck fell directly down from his jaw, tongue hung languidly on the edge of his mouth. Lips better fit for fish.

A younger, smaller duplicate followed four steps behind, matching his father's duck gait, arms swinging in time. A third man, face cut to a practiced frown, moved to the far corner of the room, arms crossed.

"Sir," Pendrick said. "The seats up front are all taken, but I'm sure we can find you one somewhere." The men kept walking down the center aisle, footsteps clicking linoleum. Other than their tapping heels, which worked as one, the only sound was the harmonized whoosh of the fan and the projector. The larger man went to the projector cord and snatched it out of the wall socket, plunging the hall into twilight. "Excuse me," said Pendrick. The man ignored Pendrick, brushed past him to a bank of light switches on the wall. He flicked all of them on. Everyone looked around, blinking in the new bright. He went to the bedsheet screen and, with a sharp tug, pulled it down. He balled it up and threw it aside.

"Bubba Boyd, what the heck you think you are doing? I reserved this time with the mayor and you've no right to burst in here like this." Mr. Paul's hands were on his hips and his face was building to crimson.

"Yeah, well, I own this goddamn building, so I reckon I can do as I please."

Folks were silent, some mouths open.

"You may own it, but the town leases it from you, so you can't just come in here and disrupt our meeting."

"Oh yeah? You got a copy a the lease on you? Dint think so."

He turned to the audience, then licked his lips and smacked them together to spread the moisture. "Hey there, Hep. How's Margie an the boys doin?"

A man in the fourth row nodded. "Doin fine."

"Frank, how's Eric's knee healing up? Cleo Fink's gonna need him hundert percent come September. Dang kids an their minibikes." He chuckled, then moved to the center. Paul and Pendrick were beside him and seemed inconsequential by comparison. "Hey, Wade, Joe Bob," Bubba said and waved, smiling.

He turned to face the crowd. "Y'all know me. Know my family. Know I've lived in this town all of my life. An y'all know how much I love this town an I ain't about to lay around an watch it die. But the mines is all played out, an if we don't find a way to get jobs back in this town, it will die. I don't want that. Do you want that?"

Most in the audience shook their heads. Pops' face was red with anger.

"I dint think so." Bubba licked his lips. His son, off to the side now, did the same. "But there is still coal up there in the hills. And there are still coal jobs to be had on these mountains. Right now, today, I got a hundert twenny-five men workin up Sadler. Paul, how many folks you hired at the Notion Shop this month?" Paul glowered straight on and crossed his arms. Bubba put a thick hand to his ear. "How many was that? I dint think so." Another lip licking.

"You are raping the mountains," Pendrick yelled. The arteries and veins in his neck were pulsing with indignation. "It's an abomination."

Bubba whirled around and regarded Pendrick with a dismissive half smile. "Are you the Jew boy come down from Washington, D.C., to save us poor ignorant hillbillies?"

"I'm not Jewish."

"I heard you was Jewish."

"I'm Lutheran."

"You look like a Jew boy to me."

"My mother is Italian," he replied defensively.

Bubba sniffed, turned to the crowd, and confided. "That's what all them Jews do, try to pass themselves off as Eye-talians." He adjusted his belt buckle, licked his lips again, and continued. "Friends, you know that my family has brought jobs to this valley for years. Good jobs. Jobs that pay a fair wage for a fair day's work. But now the only way to keep those jobs is to go at the coal from the top. The seams are too thin an unstable. The only way to get at it is from the top. All the other digs is played out—y'all know that. So if we are gonna create jobs for Medgar folks, we gotta dig at it from the top. You want work, it's gotta come out the mountain. That's the choice." He looked from face to face. Men were looking down at their shoes, pulling at their ears. Some were feeling the back of their scalps. Bubba continued. "I love this town more than anything in the world. But you know what gets me riled. Is when some Jew boy from Washington, D.C., comes down here an tells us how to run ourselves."

Pendrick shook his head and said again. "I'm not Jewish; I'm Lutheran."

Bubba ignored him and continued. "He talks about abomination. I'll tell you what's an abomination that will not abide. An that's a sodomite abomination destroyin this town. I will not allow a homosexual abomination to take jobs away from all a you." At the mention of Sodom, heads shot up. On *homosexual* the place went all atwitter. "That's right, folks. I heard the rumors jus like you did, an I found out that they are *true*! Paul Pierce and his homosexual lover, who ain't even from here, are living in an unholy an debauched union right here in our town." His voice raised to a shout. He turned to Mr. Paul and pointed. "You are an abomination to the Lord with your homosexual goins-on in that house." Mr. Paul's face was chalk, mouth opening and closing. Bubba Boyd looked back to the audience and lowered his voice to a level that implied reason. "I'm sayin it now, friends, cause it needs to be said."

Pops stood and brushed past us to the aisle. "Bubba, you crossed..."

"Arthur, you sit yourself right down, now." It was Mr. Paul. Pops paused, folded his arms, and stood astride the aisle. Mr. Paul moved off the low stage, took two steps down to the audience level. "Look, you all have known me since I was a kid. I've lived in this town most of my life too, and you all know what it means to me. Paitsel and me have lived on Green Street in our place for eighteen years. And now folks have been spreading talk about me being homosexual. So what if I am? Is that gonna change what's happening up on that mountain? It's not gonna make the water up Corbin Hollow clear. It's not gonna bring Simp back for Betty. We all need to decide—"

"We ain't decidin nothin—" Bubba Boyd broke in and started to continue before Pops cut him off.

"*Let...him...finish!*" Pops yelled with a booming voice that rebounded off the walls and carried outside. He had slowly worked his way to the back of the hall, and the admonition seemed like a calling from the heavens above. A few heads turned, but everyone recognized the voice; knew of the bad blood between Pops and Bubba Boyd; knew the history. Bubba opened his mouth to speak, then closed it. Like all bullies, he was flummoxed when challenged. Bubba's man in the back corner took a step toward Pops, but Bubba waved him off with a subtle shake of his head.

"Like I said," Paul repeated. "This isn't about me. It's about the kind of people we want to be. I, for one, will live here poor with my mountains and hollers and streams rather than take the Company's blood money."

Grubby Mitchell raised his hand and spoke before being called. "Yeah, but, Paul, the Company ain't offerin for Miss Janey's. Bubba says he'll pay me seventy-five thousand dollars for my place."

"Raymond, your family's lived on that farm for generations. That land is who you are. Every summer you, and your daddy before you, dam up Running Creek and make the best swimming hole in the county—been doing that for sixty years. I remember swimming there when I was a kid. Well, when the Company pushes all that overburden into Running Hollow, what do you think is gonna happen to Running Creek? There isn't gonna be a creek, is what. Raymond, if you decide to sell, you're not just selling your farm and Running Creek, you're selling all the memories still to be had there. How much is that worth to you?"

Folks nodded. Grubby's Adam's apple bobbed as the inequity of the deal was laid bare.

Jesper Jensen raised his hand. "I hear what you're sayin, Paul, but Bubba does raise an important point. We been hearin all kinds a things bout you an Paitsel. So I gotta ask you, an you know I respect you, Paul, but I gotta ask you: Is you or ain't you homosexual?"

Pops opened his mouth again to speak, but Paul looked at him and gently put his hand up.

"Yes, Jesper, I am homosexual."

"Paitsel too?"

Mr. Paul paused and looked to the front row. Paitsel nodded slightly, a nearly imperceptible smile.

"Paitsel too."

Whispers and head shakings. Several men blew out long sighs.

Bubba Boyd smiled and licked his lips. He stepped in front of Mr. Paul. "I think we are done here, friends. Let's all get on home." He started shooing folks out of their seats the way shepherds drive sheep.

Mr. Paul pushed to the side of him. "We are most assuredly *not* done here," he said loudly. "Mr. Pendrick has already been in touch with the Environmental Protection Agency and I have a meeting next week with the Department of Natural Resources. Your slurry pond is over capacity. We're gonna shut you down."

Bubba pretended not to hear him and started walking slowly down the aisle, his doppelganger son, Billy, a step behind. They paused here and there to shake hands and talk of fishing lures, the fall rutting season, Cleo Fink's college prospects.

They had chanced upon each other when Paitsel, recently sent down to his last minor league team, was flat-tired on the side of Highway 81 on the outskirts of Johnson City. Paul pulled over and drove him and his holed-out wheel into town and back again, tire plugged and aired and occupying the backseat. Paitsel insisted on beers and Paul followed him warily to Duke's Bull & Billiards in Elizabethton.

Life and place had helped Paul construct a masculine veneer, applied when conditions required, and so they talked of Sandy Koufax's recent perfect game and Ned Jarett's Grand National win, but all the while Paul was drawn to Paitsel's hands, which were sizable yet somehow delicate, with flawless cuticles and long, courtly fingers that seemed to be exquisitely carved from alabaster marble.

Paul took in the Johnson City Yankees game the next day, on a ticket Paitsel left at will-call—Paul and his popcorn in the front row and Paitsel glancing over at him before each pitch, as if Paul was a runner ready to steal home.

Paul became a fixture in the front row when Paitsel pitched home games, and at season's end, Paitsel drove north to help him rehab the newly bought Runyon place on the corner of Watford and Green. They were stripping a generation of wallpaper to the bares when Paitsel burned his index finger on the steamer and Paul grabbed ice and held it to the burn with both hands. Paitsel reached out with his good fingers and touched Paul's cheek.

After the town meeting, Pops and I, along with Lo and Chester, walked back to 22 Chisold and settled back into the porch. I poured mash for all.

"Bunch of dang cowards the way they suck up to him," Chester complained.

"What did you think we have in this town, superheroes?" Pops replied. "Most folks can be astoundingly brave or dog cowards depending on the circumstances."

"That's easy for you to say; you're one of the brave ones."

Pops shook his head. "You want pure brave? I give you Paul Pierce. Probably the most courageous man I know."

Lo shifted, clearly uncomfortable at the topic. "Where you gettin brave from that? It's disgustin, you ask me."

"I'm not talking about his *being* homosexual. I'm talking about standing up to Bubba Boyd. I'm talking about admitting to the whole town that he and Paitsel *are* homosexual. *That* took guts, let me tell you. I have tremendous respect for both those men."

"I kind of thought he was, you know, a homo and stuff when I met him," I said. "How come no one else knew that?"

Chester laughed and brought his arms wide. "That's the absurdity of it all—everybody knew! He and Paitsel have been living together in town for eighteen years! And here he comes tonight, finally admitting to the pink elephant in the room."

"That ain't true, Chester. Not everyone knew," Lo mumbled. His forehead tacked up in rolls.

Chester snorted. Pops waved him away. "You're right, Lo. Not everyone knew. But lots of people suspected."

"I don't get it." I was on the edge of my chair now. "You say a lot of people suspected—then why the big shock?"

"We all . . . *some* of us knew it, but nobody talked about it. Paul was born and bred here, which makes him one of us. He and Paitsel were politely referred to as 'bachelor gentlemen.' It was our awkward truth—our dirty secret. And Medgar has a way of trussing up its awkward truths and putting them on a shelf in the attic, never to be spoken of again."

Lo seemed anxious to change the subject. "I ain't got a attic," he said. "Got a basement, though." Basements were rare in Medgar, and he was boastful of his good fortune.

"A basement's a fine thing," Chester allowed.

"'Tis," Pops agreed.

"But Mr. Meadows…" I struggled to put my thoughts to the correct words. "…he seems normal. Like he's one of us." I instinctively knew my phrasing was set to the completely wrong pitch. "Do you know what I mean?"

Lo nodded vigorously.

Pops smiled. "Son, the more people I meet, the less good I get at labeling them. That's a wisdom I hope you acquire."

Chester brought his hand to his chin; Lo seemed confused.

We all went silent for a moment; then I asked about the story Mr. Paul had told me that morning about my grandmother and the rifle-shot slap. The more I heard of her, the more I wanted to know, if only to attach Pops' loss to my own. At the mention of Sarah Winthorpe Peebles, Lo and Chester immediately began searching for interesting items in their sour mash. Pops adjusted himself in the chair until he found a position that let the memory of his one true love sit in comfort.

"Your grandmother was quite a lady," he said quietly, spinning the sour mash and looking off to his left at nothing in particular. "And saving that girl was one of her finer moments."

No one spoke for a while; we just listened to the night sounds around us. A large figure materialized out of the darkness at the bottom of the porch. It was Bubba Boyd. In the street, just out of the lamplight, Billy Boyd and the frowning man from the town meeting stood, arms crossed.

Bubba took deliberate steps up to the porch and paused in front of us for a moment. "Lo, Chester, Arthur." He nodded. "How are you boys this evenin?"

"We're just fine, Bubba," Chester answered.

"To what do we owe this pleasure?" Pops asked.

"Jus come to talk, Arthur."

"Okay, let's talk. Pull up that chair there." He motioned to an extra green wicker chair on the other side of the porch. "Kevin, can you please get Mr. Boyd a glass of mash. On the rocks, if I recall."

Bubba walked to the other end of the porch and brought over the chair. As he sat in it, the old legs pushed out several inches under the unaccustomed strain. I went to the bar table, poured mash on ice, and took it to him. "Thanks, son," he said. He wet his lips, sipped, and toasted Pops. "Arthur, you always did have the good stuff. Clinch Mountain?"

Pops nodded, but said nothing. Chester was staring intently at Bubba Boyd. Lo was digging mud out of the waffle sole of his boot with a pocket knife.

"Do you remember when we was kids? All the crap we used to get into? I'm surprised our families dint disown us or ship us off to the formatory. Those were some good times." He chuckled, licked his lips, and took a sip of mash. "Good times, indeed." He brought the glass to eye level and inspected the brew. "This is some fine mash, Arthur. Reminds me a the time we broke into the Company Store to get at the liquor in there. Tenth grade I think we were. This hadta been thirty-three, thirty-four. Me an Bump, an Jesper, one a your brothers, I think it was Hersh, and a few of my boys, even little Gov Budget was taggin along, I think.

You were there too, as I recall. Do you remember how we all snuck out an met up at the old trash dump? It was so long ago, I can understand if the memory has faded."

"I remember it," Pops said.

"Chester, you weren't there, as I recall. And, Lo, you was jus a weeun." He paused and looked up at the porch ceiling. "Whose idea was it to break into that place, anyways?"

"It was yours."

Bubba chuckled. "I guess it was my idea. I remember we all snuck down there like we was World War One spies. But the place was locked up tightern a drum. How'd we get in there, anyway? I can't remember."

"You stole the key from your daddy's man who ran the store. Wasn't much of a break-in. More of a door unlocking."

He chuckled again. "You are right, I did have the key. Made things a whole lot easier. But once I opened up that door, you dint come in. You said somethin like 'I ain't doin this' an went on home. Hersh stayed an helped out, but you went on home."

"Stealing wasn't one of my sports."

"Well it warn't really stealin since my daddy owned it all, now, was it?" Bubba smiled and licked his lips. He took a sip of mash. "The police thought otherwise, though, dint they? Arrested us all an took us to Glassville. I always wondered how they knew who done it. Cause I know none a my boys woulda tole. You were the only other one who knew. I always wanted to ask you, jus never did—was it you who tole the police what we did? Was it you who ratted out his own brother?" The humor had left Bubba Boyd, edged out by simmering malevolence.

Pops' mouth was a paper edge. "Hersh lived his own life, made his own mistakes. He didn't need my help of it. As to you, Bubba.

You weren't worth the ratting. A year or two up juvie wouldn't have changed a thing about you. That would be like putting new rings on a bad piston."

Bubba's neck went red and he drew his tongue into his mouth. "I dint come here to talk engine repair."

"No doubt."

"Come here to talk bidness."

"Business? Your Rotties having trouble? They do have some questionable hips."

"Not vet bidness, land bidness. Been out to see Hersh last week."

"He mentioned that."

"Then you know I come to talk bout Jukes."

"Okay. Talk."

"The Company jus bought Bridger Mountain and I want to make you an offer for Jukes. Best way in and outta there is on your old road. You ain't usin it no more, an I will make you a fair offer."

"So make it."

"Fifty thousand dollars for the whole two-twenty."

Pops nodded and sat back calmly. "Why do you want to buy the whole parcel? A smarter play is to just lease the road from me."

"I guess I jus like ownin things."

"Of that we are all well assured. But I suspect you'll need somewhere to push all that overburden. The other side of Bridger is all Old Blue National Forest. The park boys will never let you hollow fill Blue. Jukes is the only option you've got."

Bubba didn't react. He just stared intently at Pops. "Got lots a options. Truck it out to Hogsback."

Pops crossed his legs. "I'm no expert of coal economics, but I do know the cost of dump trucking…you're not trucking it out. But it's all moot if Paul gets the feds involved. Says he's going to shut you down."

"That ain't gonna happen."

"You think he's gonna back down after tonight?"

Bubba blew out of his nostrils with certainty—the way a whale knows it's reached the good air. He sucked at a piece of pork barbecue that had lodged in his teeth from dinner.

"I've made you a fair price an Hersh wants to sell."

"Hersh and I have been known to disagree."

"It ain't nothin but weeds up there."

"Bubba, you can be dumb as a stone. How long have you known me? Fifty-five, sixty years? Jukes ain't for sale. Not for fifty thousand or five hundred thousand. Those weeds up there happen to be quite important to me."

"Think about your family, Arthur. Think about what you an Hersh could do with all that money."

Pops regarded him coldly. "Answer is no. Now, kindly leave my porch so I can get back to the important business of enjoying the evening."

Bubba sat for a moment, staring quietly at Pops. He stood slowly and walked over to the mash serving table and carefully placed the glass down, holding it from the top and lowering it gently so it made no sound when the glass met wood. He turned, heels clicking on the porch, and paused at the top of the steps looking out over Pops' quarter acre. He picked his head up and sniffed at the air, as if he could read the future in the vagaries of night scent. He adjusted the lay of waistband on hip and strode casually off the porch steps, out to the lamp, and down the street until darkness bled over all the places he had been.

⟿

I remember it as a staccato rumble, down the hill from Main Street, rattling the glass in Biddle's window, then the plates and the coffee cups as the throttle unwound. We had just finished breakfast and pushed outside to the curb corner as it edged onto Green Street and up the hill to Main. It was massive, obstructing everything it passed, blocking everything behind as it crept slowly to hillcrest—and once so achieved it shrouded the sun like some errant thunderhead sidling in from the North.

Its front bumper was six feet high and spanned sidewalk to sidewalk across Green, with four enormous headlights that looked to be the giant dead eyes of a birth-defected leviathan. The top of the haul bed overhung the tiny cab, and the driver, twenty-five feet above us, seemed like a monkey riding herd on a blue-ribbon bull. The monstrosity cleared the stoplight at Green and Main by two inches and turned slowly to nurse itself into position.

It had arrived in twenty-seven pieces, laid down in the train offload parking lot at the bottom of Green Street. The six wheels came first, each on its own train car, chains crisscrossed to keep them upright. The engine appeared next, on a wide-load semi from the plant in Peoria, and the dump bed came in five trailered sections, butt welded together in the north corner of the parking lot. The frame arrived on two side-by-side semis with state police escort that had to let air out of the semis' tires to clear the 402 underpass outside of Lexington. The assembly men came soon after and took up the SleepEZ Motel in Glassville and the Woodsman Bar on the way to Big Spoon. It all amassed in ten days and nights of welding, craning, bolting, pounding industry—cinders arcing out like sparklers on a Fourth of July evening.

The spec sheet for the 650H 1-Q talked of a ladder frame with omnidirectional bolsters and a duo-max canopy. Rear-wheel rock ejectors and variable-rate hydropneumatic suspension with accumulator-assisted twin double-acting cylinders to provide constant-rate steering. A sophisticated operator environment with integral four-post ROPS/FOPS structure and an adjustable air-float seat w/lumbar support and retractable armrests. But to me, it was simply the biggest truck I had ever seen—twenty-one feet tall, twenty-eight feet wide, and forty-five feet long, with a bed capacity of 195 tons.

As it rumbled to a stop in front of Miss Janey's, the shops along Main Street seemed inconsequential next to the colossus. I could see Mr. Paul in his front window, eyes like dinner plates. He rushed out of the salon, arms waving, mouth jawing. He kicked a ten-foot tire, then came to the front, shouting up to the driver, voice blanketed by the bass-drum rumble of the truck's engine.

The state police had blockaded traffic into town since the truck took up both sides of the street. The Company had arranged a ceremony on Main with the mayor and Bubba Boyd at court. The driver cut the engine and folks closed in around the front. Bubba climbed the four steps to the top of the bumper. He put one foot on the red railing and both hands on his knee and said absolutely nothing. It was the kind of thirty-second silence that made some men rub at stubble, made others examine palm creases. Petunia

Wickle fanned herself faster, and even children stopped pushing, everyone silent in weary resignation.

Bubba Boyd smiled, then cleared his throat. "Friends," he said, "we've a fine town here. A fine town." Mr. Paul's arms were crossed, hands jammed hard under opposite arms. Jesper Jensen looked down and kicked at a stone.

It's the eyes you notice first.

Deep-sunk sockets ringed gray against candle-wax skin. Skin like the grass that labors thin and white under a freshly turned rock, wincing in the unfamiliar sunlight. Thick hands, a ready cough, and fingers like great stubs carved from sallow stone; nails cracked, with black coal lines tattooed under them.

But this new way sets a different mien. Same hands, same cough. But now ruddy paint has replaced candle-wax skin, dragline callouses instead of tattooed coal lines, deep sockets traded for tan crow's-feet.

The sun is their burden now as it drums down on them, sourcing the gray sweat and warming the dust to float long and high in the noon stifle.

But if you look, some of the old muckmen are still around. You see them stalled in an aisle at the Pic-n-Pay. Or on a slow traverse of the Main Street crosswalk. The light turns and they are there still. One foot forward, then the other. You inch, they look up, and it's the eyes you notice first.

Miner's eyes.

Chapter 9

THE DEAD MULE

Kevin, out of bed," Pops yelled that Friday from the bottom step. "We've got two calls today and only half a morning to do them." I rolled onto the worn pine floor Pops had laid himself years ago; washed, dressed, and hustled down the hall, stopping quietly at my mother's door. We had been in Medgar exactly four weeks and she had made no progress, standing, as she was, alone in the room, in her robe, mulling over the faded Glassville Rotary Club banner on the wall and the ballerina music box that had belonged to her mother, the hair ribbon holder and the ribbons washed by the years into a sepia rainbow, the ceramic bowl she made in pottery class and the three dried rose heads it held. These, and the many other favors and trifles a girl keeps to hand, all of it suspended in the room like a box of time. She reached for one of her old charcoals of Main Street, then pulled back as if it was electrified. I couldn't look at her anymore and continued to the kitchen.

"We've got a full schedule, so eat some cereal quick and meet me in the truck," Pops said and disappeared out the kitchen door and into the vet shed. I gulped my Cheerios and was in the cab before him.

For three weeks Pops had been taking me on calls around the county, and I was beginning to feel a confidence that only comes from doing—a familiarity of task that allowed me to assist without being asked.

I knew to hand him the pick instead of the nippers when examining pony hoof; I instinctively reached for the antiseptic spray after suture tie-off; I automatically locked my legs around a goat head when he was checking for blowfly. It seemed Pops was actually starting to depend on me, actually starting to need me.

"First stop, Beaver Hollow," he said as he backed carefully into the deserted street. We drove through town, then after a few miles, turned left on Route 27, then onto a dirt road that snaked through a thick hollow.

The woods were empty for the first mile, until we began passing disturbing signs of life: the hood of an ancient truck, holes buckshot through it; sculptures of rusted metal tubes from an old swing set; a naked baby doll with an arm missing; a discarded washer with the wringers still attached; an old four-footed tub filled with rusted chains; kitchen trash everywhere; someone's dirty underwear.

"Who are we seeing up here?"

"Senator Budget's lame mule."

The road suddenly became a cul-de-sac servicing seven houses in competing degrees of disrepair. Chickens guarded the apron to the first three houses and skittered a safe distance as we rolled past. Dogs and goats ambled about, eyeing us and offering lackadaisical barks and bleats. The houses were a throw of mobile homes, trailers, double-wides, and prefabs. Dotted between them was a collection of cars and tractors that seemed arrayed in order of breakdown. Rusted burn barrels smoldered with yesterday's garbage. Four satellite dishes, like giant meadow spoor, brought the world to Beaver Hollow. A mob of dirty, half-naked children ran shoeless into the road.

"It doesn't look like a senator lives here."

Pops laughed. "Senator is only his first name. One of his brothers is named Governor. I guess I can't fault his father for having high expectations."

We pulled into the driveway of a blockish, one-story prefab, too square to be called a mobile home, too simple to be called anything else. Broken wrought-iron rail around the front porch. Rusted chain-link fence, fencing nothing in particular. Behind his house by the barn were two decayed cars from the sixties. An engine rusted on the ground; milkweed and a sapling grew through one of the engine voids. A huge sycamore tree shaded most of the backyard. A brown wirehaired hound was tied to a poplar out front.

Pops put his arm on the seat top and turned to me. "One thing you have to understand about the Budgets; they aren't like the rest of us. Most people in Missi County are simple country folk—hardworking, some education, God-fearing. The Budget clan is different."

"How are they different? Don't they work hard?"

"How can I explain this?" Pops thought for a moment. "The Budgets generally don't go to school past the tenth grade; they live off the land, get handouts, and work the mines and odd jobs to make up the rest. They've been living in this hollow for almost one hundred years, marrying each other and having each other's babies. The gene pool is getting a bit shallow."

We exited the truck and walked up to the house. An obese woman in a dirty pink tank top and light blue stretch polyester shorts sat shoeless on the front porch reading the *Weekly World News* and straining an aluminum lawn chair to its absolute limits. Her upper arms were the size of salted hams, her head like a pumpkin on a stump.

The porch was choked with old appliances: a broken air-conditioning unit; the shell of an old TV; a cracked cooler; a refrigerator without a door, everything stacked inside it.

"Morning, Lucille," Pops said on the second step. "Sen asked me to come by and look at your mule."

She considered us for a moment and turned to the open front window as much as her considerable neck would allow, cigarette clenched safely in the right side of her mouth. "Sen," she yelled, "Dr. Peebles's here," and went back to her magazine. No response from the house. She pulled the cigarette out of her mouth, turned even farther. "Sen! Git out here." Still no response. "Damn him," she said to herself and threw the magazine on the floor, slowly pushing up from the chair. It rose with her, sticking to her skin for the first ten inches, then clattered back to the porch. She turned and waddled into the house mumbling, the back of her cordwood thighs crosshatched in red welts from the chair. Knees rubbing soundlessly together with each step, lubricated by sweat. Pops leaned against the wrought-iron rail as I looked over at the dog under the tree.

"I'm comin, woman...you watch your lip," came a menacing aside from Sen Budget before he burst through the screen door and into the morning sunshine, closing one eye to the light.

He was small. A head shorter than Pops, with pallid skin, highlighted by black, greasy hair, freshly combed for company.

His high pockmarked cheeks and hard-cut chin dissolved into dingy gray from relentless stubble. A jutting Adam's apple. Pops said Sen's older brothers had bullied the humor from him long ago, leaving runt bones covered in thin skin. Eyes as warm as the black glass in a stuffed buck head.

"Mornin, Dr. Peebles."

"Morning, Sen, how's your mule?"

"Poorly. Broke her leg in a gopher hole haulin trees over Hintons Creek. Almost had to shoot her right there."

"Well, let's see what we can do." We walked around to the back of the house near a squat barn where the mule was sitting forlornly on its hindquarters, broken foot held slightly off the ground. Two naked girls no older than four were playing in the dirty water of an inflatable wading pool under the sycamore. Pops felt the break. The mule jerked its foot away.

"Mr. Budget, may I use your bathroom?" I said, suddenly realizing I had forgotten to pee in the morning's rush.

His black eyes considered me for the first time. "Down the hall past the livin room," he said. I ran up the back steps and into the filthy kitchen. Stacks of dishes competed for sink space. The overflow covered the faded Formica countertop, crisscrossed with knife cuts. A ring of garbage spilled around a fifty-gallon trash can.

I hurried through the brown-paneled living room, down the brown-paneled hall, and pushed into the first brown door on the left.

It was the smell that hit me first. Even before I realized that I was in the wrong room, it was the smell. Old. Unwashed and unwanted as dog-pissed newspaper brought up from a damp basement.

An emaciated man with sunken cheeks and chiseled eyes lay on the narrow bed in the room, a patchwork throw pulled up to his chest, arms pinned beneath, edges tucked tight under the mattress. A tube ran from each nostril. Oxygen bottle and a soiled bedpan on the floor by the bed. His eyes were closed, mouth half-open in a terrible gape. Chest laboring infantlike breaths, quiet and quick. He opened his eyes slowly and turned to me, mouth still ajar.

He was tired. I could tell just breathing made him tired. His collarbones competed with his Adam's apple for unnatural distinction. Sen Budget's Adam's apple.

I was statued, unable to back out of the room or even explain my mistake. He continued watching me. Plastic flowers in a beer pitcher on the windowsill; Rorschach-stained window shade pulled down behind it. Peeling wallpaper in the corner and a worn maroon shag carpet, the shags burring like clotted blood.

"Um . . . the bathroom. I . . . I thought it was in here."

He continued to stare at me, breathing small and soft so as not to waste his dwindling allotment of air. I backed slowly out of the room; his eyes followed me in a helpless gaze until they were gently closed by the door. I found the bathroom with its old toilet. Rust ring in the bowl and sink. I peed, flushed, and tiptoed past the mistaken door, feeling his eyes on me still.

Miner's eyes.

"What the fuck you doin here, homo?" It was Tilroy, the fat bully from two weeks ago at the tree house. He was shirtless in his bedroom doorframe, pink stretch marks feathering the sides of his dough belly.

I froze, felt like I'd been caught rifling a secret closet. "Nothing, I was just going to the bathroom," I stammered. "What are you doing here?"

"I live here, fuckface."

"I'm just helping my grandfather; he's looking at a hurt mule," I added. That seemed to soften Tilroy just a little.

"Agnes?"

"Who?"

"The mule, dipshit. Agnes. You're here to fix her?"

"Uh, yeah. My grandfather does the fixing—I'm his assistant, though," I said proudly.

His black eyes seemed to gather up light, his face relaxed, and his voice became plaintive, hopeful. "She broke her leg an it's all kinds a painful. Your grandaddy's gotta fix her. He's good, ain't he?"

"He's the absolute best."

Tilroy's smile was a nearly imperceptible upward twitch. "You wanna see my crossbow pistol?" He motioned for me to follow him into his bedroom.

I hesitated. "I think I'd better get back outside. My grandfather may need my help."

"It'll jus take a second. I ain't gonna shoot you or nuthin." He chuckled in a way that offered me no assurance.

I looked down the brown-paneled hall to see if Pops had come looking for me, then followed him into the bedroom. The room was Spartan, with a simple single bed pushed against the wall, a dirty coiled rug on gray particle-board floor. A work desk at the foot of the bed fashioned from cut plywood laid across two sawhorses. The walls were covered in black-and-white heavy-metal music posters: Slayer, Metallica, Dokken. As I moved closer I could see that the posters were charcoal and pencil drawings, not photographs.

"Where did you get all these drawings?"

"You like Slayer?"

"Sure," I lied.

"I copied that one from a picture I saw in *Metal Head*." He pointed to the Metallica drawing. "That's from the album with 'The Four Horsemen.' "

"You drew all these?"

He nodded. The workmanship and detail in the drawings were truly spectacular. It was hard to tell them from a photograph.

"Who taught you how to draw like this?" I asked with a half laugh. I was amazed and perplexed that such talent was housed in the same mind as the bully I knew.

"Nobody taught me nuthin. I jus do it."

"Seriously, these are really, really good."

"These ain't even the best. Hang on."

He moved to the closet and pulled back the curtain, then knelt, digging into the far corner under a pile of clothes. He stood and turned slowly around. He was holding a long, thin metal box, the size of two briefcases. He put it on the worktable, unbuckled the hasps, and gently opened the lid. Inside was a full array of pencils, brushes, pastels, paints, every bit of art gear imaginable, perfectly ordered in row upon row. The bounty of art supplies seemed completely out of place among the meager surroundings. In a sleeve in the top he gingerly pulled out a large pencil drawing. It was a picture-perfect rendition of the inside of Miss Janey's, with Mr. Paul standing in front of the bank of cutting stations, arms crossed, smiling wide.

"Wow, it looks exactly like him."

Tilroy was beaming now, his face inviting. "He got me this artist set so I tole him I'd draw him up. Gonna make it all color an stuff. Maybe he'll hang it up the shop. That would be cool... professional sorta." He gently brushed a cluster of dust off the drawing.

"Man, you should go to art school or something."

"That's what Mr. Paul says. He even talked to my daddy bout it." Tilroy looked down at the drawing again and the smile left him; his eyes went cold. "I ain't gonna go, though. Art school is for pussies."

We were awkwardly silent now. Finally I said, "Look, I really gotta get back to my grandfather. He probably needs my help." I started to drift out of the room. Tilroy was still standing at the table running his fingers gently down the line of colored pencils. "I'm gonna go outside now," I said again. But he was already off somewhere to a world where art supply suitcases were celebrated and husky, awkward kids didn't have to kill deer or race cars or say *nigger* or get whipped. "I'm gonna..." I stepped through the door and ran down the hall out into the thick morning.

Pops was explaining the mule's prognosis to Sen Budget. His hand chopped at the air for emphasis. "The cast would stay on for eight weeks, then just a splint for another four. She'll be able to walk, but her hauling days are over."

Sen rubbed the back of his neck. The mule was still on its hind-quarters, holding the broken foot in the air like a begging dog.

"That ain't gonna do. A mule what can't haul ain't much good, now, is she?"

"No, Sen, I don't suppose she is."

He grabbed the halter rope from the dirt and pulled the mule toward the barn. The mule refused. He pulled again and the mule dug deeper. A third time, with muscle. The mule didn't move. Sen threw the rope down, mumbled something to himself, and walked purposefully toward the house and into the kitchen door. Pops watched him, puzzled. Thirty seconds later, he bounded from the door, walking stiffly toward us, his right arm taut as wire, big-barreled handgun hanging down past his knee. Lucille banged out after him, leaning against the iron rail, arm slabs taking the bright sun. Tilroy came out right after her. The two girls stopped playing in the pool and turned to see what was going on.

I stood frozen as Sen clipped up to the crippled mule and put the long gun to her temple. Pops acted fast, grabbing me by the collar suddenly and jerking me from the line of the shot just as Sen pulled the trigger. The boom of the gun sent us both jumping. The bullet passed through the mule's head, sending it sideways and breaking the only windowpane left in the barn. The gun recoiled past his right ear.

Agnes shook her head as if a fly was buzzing it; blood fauceted from both holes. She placed her hooves on the ground for balance, then jerked her broken foot up, causing the good leg to slide slowly forward until she was prone in the dirt with the good leg splayed out front and the bad leg tucked under her body. Chin in a spreading blood pool; dust floating on the blood like miniature sailboats.

The girls, standing now, held each other and wailed. I looked over at Tilroy, whose mouth was an O, eyes popped, hands on his shaking head. His face went scarlet.

It was the first time I had ever seen any animal killed; it fascinated and frightened me at once. The air had taken on the consistency of water, and everyone's movements seemed checked by the new aerodynamics.

Sen watched the mule bleed, gun still at his ear. He brought the barrel down slowly, readying for another shot, when Pops stepped forward and wrenched it from his hand.

"I think we've had enough gunplay for one morning." Pops was in a boiling rage, his ears red. He pushed Sen back and emptied the remaining bullets from the gun and tucked the weapon into his waistband.

"Hey, you can't just take a man's gun like that. It's my mule an I'll do as I please."

Pops' ears went white. "You goddamn idiot, you almost shot my grandson. Now you will do as I please. Go tend to your daughters."

"Don't you be lettin that stand, Sen Budget," Lucille bellowed from the back porch. She huffed off the steps into the dirt and wombled toward us. "Who the hell you think you is anyway, comin in here takin my husbin's gun like that?" The girls began crying a fresh chorus.

"Lucille, this is my bidness," Sen barked.

"Like hell it's your bidness—my daddy give you that gun." She turned to Pops. "Give me the gun, now." Left hand planted on her substantial hip, the other held palm up to Pops.

"Ma'am, you'll get no such thing. You can pick the gun up at Sheriff Binner's tomorrow. Kevin, let's go." Pops turned and strode to the truck. I followed quickly. Lucille stalked after us. The wirehaired hound yapped disapproval at the commotion.

Tilroy came running over to his father, his face still flecked with scarlet, tears freshly wiped on his shirt. "Whoa, Daddy, that was cool." His voice was a pitch higher than usual. "I ain't never seen nuthin drop like that."

His father regarded him coolly, then smiled and gave him a high five. "I thought you were gonna be a pussy again."

Tilroy shook his head and blinked back tears, then shook his head again.

Mrs. Budget began to rail into Pops. "You think you're bettern everybody else; well, I'm callin the sheriff, is what I'm doin. That's right, you get the hell outta here. This ain't Russia—we got us rights."

Pops was silent and angry as we pulled onto the dirt road that led out of the Hollow with Lucille Budget's tirade fading into the trees.

"Pops, I mean, he just shot her! Right there in front of us. Shouldn't we call the police or something? I mean, he shouldn't be allowed to just do that. Should he?"

"It's his mule, his gun, and his property," Pops replied. "I don't have much say in how Sen Budget lives his life, but I can't respect any man who's careless with a firearm."

The shock of the incident made my throat feel crowded with cotton. And today, as I think about that morning in Beaver Hollow and lay it alongside the rest of the summer, it accords to a deeper and necessary understanding of the whys and hows of everything that came after.

Chapter 10

THE PARADOX OF PENNING CATS

~~~

We rode out to Route 27 and back toward town. "All five of the Budget brothers were laid off from the mines," Pop explained. They've been getting by cutting wood, doing odd jobs, and taking charity. Sen wasn't prepared to carry a lame mule on the family income. Besides, that mule will feed them for a month. I don't spite him for killing the animal; I just objected to him endangering you and subjecting his family to it. Tilroy raised that mule from a colt. It was like a family pet."

I thought about how the mule seemed to take death in a plodding, deliberate way; how the shot broke the window across the yard; how Pops confronted Budget with a rage I'd never seen in him; and how the dying man in the room looked at me, pleading for something to interrupt his own plodding, deliberate death. I shook my head, like the shot mule, to rid my mind of death thoughts. "Is mule meat any good?" I asked.

"Let's hope we never have to find out."

We followed the road around Medgar toward the opposing line of mountains on the eastern side of town. Abandoned mine shafts spotted the hill grades, and the rusted remains of the underground economy were laid out in front like the rejected toys from a family of giants—a four-foot-high electric locomotive attached to a line of low-slung hopper cars, its tracks worming down into a mine shaft; ventilating fans the size of jet engines next to two thick iron hoops of a rotary dumper; a dead Joy loader with one arm missing; idled conveyors running to rusted corrugated structures, then snaking up to the hillside shafts like felled dominoes.

After a while Pops broke the silence. "Next stop, Fink's Hollow."

"Fink's Hollow? I know a kid named Buzzy Fink. Think he lives up there?"

"I know he does. Buzzy's grandfather is who we're seeing. We've got to vaccinate some animals against rabies. A rabid fox attacked a cat and the cat tried to bring down a horse at full trot. The cat's dead, but the horse and the rest of the barn animals need shots. How do you know Buzzy Fink?" He glanced from the road.

"I met him in the woods couple weeks ago. I got bit by a spider and he made me a poultice."

"Really?" Pops said, looking at me with bemused eyebrows.

We rumbled along Route 27, then turned right, then left on Route 32. Soon after, Pops took a sudden left onto an unmarked dirt road that disappeared into the thick woods.

We followed the slow grade up the hollow, occasionally crossing the bolting creek that split the middle. Unlike in Beaver Hollow, the woods and gullies were clean of hillbilly garbage. I asked Pops about it.

"The Finks are poor, but they're proud poor. Esmer runs the hollow hard. Kids stay in school; they truck their garbage out once a week. These are solid people."

We pulled into a semicircle of twelve trim, self-built houses, some with siding, some with plywood, set around a large old log cabin as points are placed around a compass. Behind the log cabin was a rank of barns, pens, and miscellaneous farm equipment. An idle pig nursed an old corn husk, claiming acceptable shade under an old piece of plywood stacked against the side of the house. In the corner of the low-ceilinged porch, smoking a cob pipe and rocking in his homemade rocker, was Esmer Fink, patriarch of the hollow, pushing onto his toes and back down gently onto his heels.

Pops and I got out of the truck. He pulled his leather case from behind the cab. "Afternoon, Esmer," he said as we climbed the worn wooden steps, fitting our feet into the scooped runners.

"Taint afternoon yet," Esmer said.

"Morning, then."

"Mornin back," Esmer responded, rocking onto his toes and back down gently onto his heels. His face was pleated and pinched from eighty-three years in Fink's Hollow. According to Pops, he was born in one of the ruined cabins on the hill, lived for most of his life in one of the hollow's plywood houses, then moved to the main cabin—"Giggins Hoo," the Finks called it—fifteen years ago after his uncle Thurlow died of lung and he became patriarch of the family.

Esmer Fink was a man of simple desires. His only vanity was his teeth, which he had proudly kept until age seventy-six (a record in Fink's Hollow). Since then he had been losing them at a precipitous rate, and with every lost cuspid, the entire hollow walked on eggshells.

"Giiaaddaaamnmmisserabblesonsabitches," it would start from the bowels of Giggins Hoo. Esmer would storm for a week in a black funk, kicking chickens and treating the goats unnecessarily rough, until he settled back to his old self.

By now, Esmer was down to a few molars and a single incisor, which gave his cheeks extraordinary height and his chin unusual prominence.

"Esmer, this is my grandson, Kevin, says he knows Buzzy."

Esmer raised his eyes slightly to look me over and exhaled wispy pipe smoke. "I suppose he does."

"Is Buzzy here today?" I asked.

"He's here." Rocking onto his toes and back down gently onto his heels.

"Well, I guess we'll get started," Pops said.

"Cleo an the boys herded the propriate beasts into pens at the back. Let em loose when you're done. Couldn't round the cats, though. Cats is hard to pen."

"That was thoughtful, Esmer. We'll do our best with the cats."

Esmer nodded.

"How is Cleo doing?" Pops asked. "Gonna be hard to have another year like last year."

"He's workin it ever day. Makes me tired jus watchin. Coach from Ohio State come up last week. Dint impress me." Esmer sniffed. "Cle's got his heart set on Notre Dame, anyway."

"Notre Dame's a fine choice. I'd like to talk more about it after we inoculate your herd."

We walked down the steps and around the side of the house.

The two pens held five ragged dogs of suspicious pedigree, one about to give birth. Four were sleeping, and the nervous yelp of the pregnant one brought them to their feet, barking excitedly. The other pen held miscellaneous farm animals of varying social order. Four goats, seven sheep, an old swayback horse, and assorted lower barn life. The sheep tufted like lint, eyeing the goats and us with equal mistrust. Other than the cats, the only animal not penned was the pig in the shade out front. Penning him would have seemed redundant.

"Kevin, I'll handle the dogs, you see if you can round up the cats, then we'll do the others together."

I was off to the front of the house, where a large mottled tabby lazed on the porch. I brought him to Pops, and after a quick shot he was back in the only sunny spot on the porch, annoyed at the intrusion. I spied two more on the hood of an early sixties Rambler station wagon that some years ago had suffered an arc welder conversion to pickup. They came peacefully and I replaced them on the hood in the sun. "How many cats do they have, Pops?" I asked as he was finishing the last of the dogs.

"Eighteen," he said, loading a new syringe. I stood for a moment, unsure if he was joking. "You're fifteen short." He wasn't joking.

The barn. Had to be cats in the barn. I walked toward the gray and red barn, which sat on the slight hill behind the houses. I crept into the darkened door but didn't see any cats. Suddenly, from the top of the haystack in the corner, a six-foot blue-yellow flame, like the blast from a hot-air balloon, lit up the barn. I could see someone's profile in the flame. It switched off abruptly, leaving the echo burning in my retina. "What was that?" I said to anybody, still blinded. I heard the haystack person jump to the ground and walk toward me, silhouetted against streaming sunlight through the barn slats. A lighter flicked and the flame returned, swallowing air in a whoosh, licking inches from my face. I fell back into a hay bale, then scrambled up to run. Buzzy Fink walked into the sunlight, laughing. A can of hair spray in one hand, a lighter in the other.

"Hope you brought more hair spray," he said. "This can's bout beat."

"What the hell are you doing?" I demanded, still frazzled from my close encounter with the hair spray flame.

"Fryin spiders. What the hell you doin?"

"My grandfather's here to give your animals rabies shots and I'm trying to find all your cats."

"The cats are gonna have to wait: I got two more spiders left and they're gettin nervous. Come on."

We climbed up hay bale steps to the sweltering top of the barn. In the corner, strung between a wood beam and the siding, was a perfectly formed spiderweb, a huge brown-and-black spider in the middle. The height, the spider, and the potential for an explosion made me tingle nervously.

"Lighter, flamethrower," he yelled and handed me the can and the Bic. "Sergeant, take out that gook bunker—now." I hesitated, not knowing whether to start the spray first or the lighter or whether the whole thing would combust in my face. "Sergeant, what is the delay? The enemy will be on us; burn em—now." I lit the lighter and pointed the can at the web and pressed. A thick flame rushed out, engulfing the spider. It tried frantically to escape Armageddon, making it only an inch before curling and dropping twenty feet to the floor. Very cool.

"Aren't you afraid of catching the barn on fire?" I asked, breathing heavily from the excitement.

"Yep, but if I wasn't, this wouldn't be nearly as much fun. An I figure the only way the barn'll catch fire is if the can blows up, which'll kill me so I won't get into any trouble for burnin down the barn." It made sense.

We crawled over the tower of hay to a Vietcong safe house on the other side of the barn. Buzzy slaughtered them all with a wide swath of the aerosol flame.

"Kevin!" Pops called from the house.

I looked at Buzzy and we jumped off the hay and ran out of the barn to Giggins Hoo, where Pops and Esmer were talking.

"You're still fifteen cats short and making little progress."

"I found Buzzy. He was in the barn."

"Hello, Buzzy. How are you at herding cats?"

"Cats is hard to pen," he said. Esmer nodded agreement and pushed up onto his toes and back down gently onto his heels. Buzzy went into the house and came out with a jug of milk and a discarded tuna-fish tin.

"That's quick thinking, Buzz," Pops said and grabbed his bag as Buzzy led us back to the barn. He poured the milk into an upside-down pail lid and offered the tuna to an immense cat with a tattered left ear. Soon the trough had eleven cats drinking.

Pops loaded a syringe. We looked for the remaining four cats but gave up after about ten minutes, all agreeing that the stragglers would have to risk rabies.

"Them others ain't barn cats," Esmer instructed later on the porch. "They come an go as they please." Pops and Esmer rocked and talked for half an hour about Cleo's college prospects while

Buzzy and I built a fort in the hay bales. Pops finally called me down and we walked back to the house slowly.

"Can Buzzy sleep over tonight?" I was craving some younger conversation and companionship.

"Not this weekend; your dad is visiting. Maybe Monday. Esmer?"

Esmer shrugged. Buzzy and I swapped excited grins.

"Monday it is. Esmer, you take care of yourself, call me if you need me," Pops said. I nodded good-bye and walked to the truck with Buzzy.

"See you up at the tree house tomorrow?"

"I'll be there," he replied.

I climbed into the cab and Pops turned the truck around. As we pulled away, Cleo Fink was jogging up the road, turning sideways every twenty feet, then jogging backward, then to the front. I looked back at him as we passed with Giggins Hoo shrinking in the distance—Esmer Fink on the porch watching his pride work the Fink's Hollow Road.

My father arrived with evening, and after dinner I walked to Smith's Ice Cream with a fist of quarters he had given me Judasing my pocket. It was dark when I returned, and I could see him and Pops on the porch. I hid in the shadow of the hickory and listened to the anger in Pops' voice seething and popping like fresh fire, dressing the air with disgust, disappointment.

"I don't think this is the time to be placing blame, Edward." The words came slow and measured. "In fact, what you just said may qualify as the most asinine statement ever uttered on this porch. No, I take that back; it's the second-most asinine statement. You probably remember the first."

"I'm not blaming the boy, Arthur. I'm just saying that this whole thing could've been prevented if he'd just done as I taught him."

The words came to me as a blistering spear. A picket-fence post driven into my chest by a hurricane. I knew that my father blamed me for Josh, but actually hearing him say the words to Pops bludgeoned me, making my knees so weak I had to brace myself against the back of the old hickory in a half squat. My hands were shaking and I think at that moment I actually felt my heart tear.

"Oh, for Christ's sake, Edward, when has a kid always done what his parents taught him? If Annie did what I taught her, she never would have married you."

"Very funny."

Pops didn't respond.

"It didn't have to happen, is all I'm saying."

The comment caused an immediate stir in Pops. "But it did . . . it did happen," he urged. "You can't get yesterday back, and all the could'ves, should'ves, and would'ves aren't gonna make your boy heal and your wife whole again. You've got a woman almost broken from what she saw and a boy carrying enough guilt for five religions and all you can do is point a finger and say, 'This is who caused it; this is who we'll blame.' For once in your life, Edward, put the needs of your family before your own goddamn self-centered desires."

"You don't know what I've been through."

"I don't know what *you've* been through? You idiot, for the last four weeks I've been living with what *you've* been through."

My father was quiet, then ventured a new line of discussion. "She seems better."

Pops calmed himself. "She's eating now. Audy Rae took her to Paul's for a new hairdo, but it's like she's on horse tranquilizer. Comes in and out of touch. I'm still looking for that one spark that will bring her back to us, that one hook that will start to make her heal. I know it's there somewhere. Audy Rae's been a big help, doting on her and talking with her until she's talked out. We need that spark, though."

"How's Kevin doing?"

"Ask him yourself."

"I'm planning to, but I wanted to talk to you first. How is he dealing with it?"

From the hickory I could hear the sour mash spinning in the glass. The quicker cadence of the ice matched the piercing sarcasm in Pops' voice. "Well, let's see, he saw his brother die in a terrible accident, he's watched his mother go crazy, and his father blames him for it all. Just the kind of character-building exercise every fourteen-year-old should experience. But, in spite of your every effort to separate his head from his shoulders, he's doing great, making me real proud." They were silent for a moment; then my father changed the subject again.

"I've tried to talk with her, but she just looks at me like one of those Stepford wives."

"It's gonna take her some more time to heal, but fortunately time's something we have in abundance around here."

I had to quit, had to get away from there. I traced the tree's shadow toward the street, well past the possibility of detection, and ran around to the back kitchen door. The light from the kitchen's single bulb spilled insolently into the backyard, broken by the slow turning of the ceiling fan. Up the steps and into the kitchen. I let the screen door slam to announce my return. Mom was at the table worrying a cup of tea, and the sound of the door made her jump.

"You startled me," she said. The words drew out of her slowly, as if they were the last water in an old well.

"Sorry, Mom. I'm going to bed, good night." All I wanted was my room and the quiet cocoon of Pops' books, where I could lose myself for hours on end and not think about the past three months—or the last five minutes.

I was halfway up the steps when my father called. "Kevin, how was the ice cream?"

"Fine," I said, continuing to the top.

"Come on out here, son. We'd like to talk to you."

"I'm real tired. I'm going to bed."

"Won't take a minute."

"I said I'm going to bed."

Pops interjected, "Kevin, your father wants to talk to you. Please come out to the porch...*now.*"

I shuffled down the steps and poked my face against the screen door.

"What?"

"Come on out here, son."

I pushed open the door.

"Pops tells me that you're his assistant now. How are you liking it?"

"Fine."

"Just fine?"

"Yeah, it's fine."

"Well, have you made any friends since you've been here?"

"No." Didn't look at him, couldn't look at him. "Can I go to bed now? I'm really tired," I said to Pops.

"Sure, Kevin," he replied after a moment.

My father was fixed on me, and I could feel him scowling into my soul, searching for fodder to criticize. I looked up and scowled right back into his lies and selfishness and blame. I turned and pushed back through the screen. Halfway up the steps, I heard him say in muffled tones, "He doesn't seem normal like you say."

I crawled into bed, shelled and numb.

I had run through *Treasure Island, Lord of the Flies, Last of the Mohicans*, and took up the ancient copy of *Gulliver's Travels* that Pops had given me from his bookcase full of first and second editions. The leather spine rasped as I opened the thick cover. The brittle pages smelled like cellar and the leather was warm to the touch.

"My Father had a small Estate in Nottinghamshire; I was the Third of five Sons. He sent me to Emanuel-College in Cambridge, at Fourteen Years old where I resided..."

Lost.

Chapter 11

THE DRAWING UP OF IT ALL

My daddy says to me, he says, 'You ain't gonna be workin there no more no how.' An I says to him, I says, 'You ain't gonna tell me what's what, you ain't nuthin but a pothead drunk.' I called him that, girl. Do you believe I actually called him a pothead drunk?"

"No way, what he do?"

"He raises up his hand like he's gonna hit on me an I says to him, I says, 'You hit on me an I'll tell Uncle Floyd an he's gonna kick your ass again.' So he puts his hand down an cusses at me an walks out the front door," she said with a giggle.

On Sunday I was upside down in Petunia Wickle's washbasin again, trying in vain to peek up the open space of her shirt bottom. I really didn't need another haircut, but Mr. Paul's telling of my grandmother and the rifle-shot slap left me yearning for more details, more stories. I felt that if I could gather up all that was known about her, I could somehow draw on her strength and wisdom and fearlessness. The opportunity to view Petunia's breasts was a collateral benefit. She leaned over to reach for the conditioner and the bottom of her midriff shirt bent open; a flash of nipple jolted my stomach.

"My momma ain't said nuthin," Levona said. "She don't care what I do. All she said was she ain't comin in here no more, even with the discount."

"I think it's kinda cool, knowin one a them," Petunia said. "Like it's gonna put us on the map or somethin. In the beauty trade it ain't a bad thing, you know. I may get one a them when I get my own place." The front door chimed open and Petunia said, "Speakin a queer boys, look what jus come in."

"Stop talkin smack, girl; you don't know shit bout what went on."

"Hissy seen him," she said with certainty.

I picked my head up and could see straight through to the waiting room. Tilroy Budget was fidgeting at the front with his art supply case. Mr. Paul came out from the back and smiled. "Hello, Tilroy. How's the future famous artist of Medgar, Kentucky, doing?"

"Good, I guess." He seemed nervous, looked behind him, out the window, and back at us. Petunia pulled my head back into the basin.

"Well, that's just dandy," Mr. Paul replied.

"Well, that's jus dandy," Petunia mimicked. She puffed her cheeks and pushed out her tongue in faux vomit.

"Got somethin I drew I wanna show you."

"Let's see, then. I thought that rock poster you made was exceedingly good."

Petunia was working conditioner into my hair, and the feel of her fingers on my scalp made it hard to concentrate on the conversation at the front. I heard the metal case click open and Mr.

Paul take a breath. "My lands," he said. "Son, I just don't know what to say. I just don't know what to say."

"You can hang it up, you know."

"Not only will I hang it up, Tilroy. I am going to have it framed. This is one of the nicest presents I believe I have ever received."

"It was jus cause, you know, you got me this art set an stuff. I thought it would be cool to do you a picture a your place. Somethin you could hang up somewheres."

"What is that loser kissin Mr. Paul's ass for?" Petunia hissed. "I swear I'm right about him, girl. Hissy says she seen him an that skinny boy."

"Then you can hire Tilroy for your place," Levona shot back and chortled at her clever retort.

"Not a chance. My fag's gonna be one a them French fags that all the girls fall in love with an can cut hair like nobody's bidness."

She washed the conditioner out of my hair and tapped the back of my head. "Go on an sit up sos I can dry you." They were the first words she had spoken to me since I had arrived. I felt the awkwardness between us evaporate, her play at conversation giving me confidence.

"He drew a picture of this place for Mr. Paul," I ventured, smug on my inside knowledge.

"What are you talkin bout?"

"Tilroy, he's really good at drawing stuff. I saw the picture he drew of this place. It looks amazing."

Petunia got excited now. She came to the front and positioned herself between my legs and leaned forward with her hands on both my arms. I was shot through with lightning. I couldn't decide to where to focus: her breasts or her bright red lips.

"Am I in it?" she asked. "I ain't never had no one draw me up before." I opened my mouth to speak but really didn't want to answer, didn't want to change the mood. "He dint do me fat, did he?" she asked.

"Uh..."

"What? Am I in it or not?"

"Umm..."

"Stop lookin at my tits an answer me!"

"I think it's only of the shop and Mr. Paul," I finally said.

"What you mean you 'think'—you seen it or ain't you?"

"No, I've definitely seen it," I said. The last thing I wanted Petunia thinking me was a liar.

"Then am I in it or ain't I?"

"You're not, sorry." I could feel the air slipping out of our balloon end; the temperature around us dropped several degrees. She took her hands away from my arms as if I had been suddenly poxed. A towel hit my head as she marched into the back room. "Dry his ass, Levona."

⸺

"Is your daddy still in town?" Mr. Paul asked.

"Uhh, yeah. He's leaving today."

"I don't think I've ever met him."

I didn't answer and focused instead on three framed photographs hung next to his faded beautician's license. The first was Paul as a young man standing crisp with two rows of army singers, mouths open in frozen harmony. The second was him singing to a microphone with *DECCA* emblazoned on the capsule. In the third, he was standing in front of a wide table arrayed with knobs and meters and wires in and out. He was flanked by a man and a woman smiling broadly.

"What are those pictures of?" I asked to shift the discussion.

"Oh, they're from my singing days. The one on the bottom is me, Patsy Cline, and Owen Bradley." He stood straight up as he said it, and a rush of memory from those days brought a smile to his face and palpable wist to the moment.

"Who are they?"

"Patsy Cline was one of the greatest singers who ever lived. Owen Bradley was her producer. I sang for her a little back then. Took me under her wing, she did. One of the nicest ladies you could ever meet. You never woulda known what a big star she was. Took me around Nashville to auditions and such."

"Did you ever make a record?"

His lips rolled into his mouth and he shook his head. "I was getting close. Patsy even got her friend Harlan Howard to write a song for me, but then my daddy got real sick and needed care. My brothers were out west somewhere, and with my momma dead, there wasn't anyone to do for him. Patsy said to call her as soon as I got back to Nashville, but then she died in a plane crash later that year. Nineteen sixty-three it was. So I stayed for my daddy until he died; then I opened up this place with Miss Janey."

"Do you still sing?"

"In the church choir and such." He stopped cutting and took in a deep breath and began with a clear voice that filled up the old salon like it was Carnegie Hall.

This old mountain lives inside me
Always has and always will.

The hollows and the lonesome hard rock
Beating in my body still.

Even Petunia and Levona stopped gossiping in the back and turned to listen.

And though I'm far away from home now
Riding out a city chill
That old mountain still abides me
Always has and always will.

He smiled sadly and began cutting—scissors flashing under the fluorescent glare.

"What song is that? I've never heard it before."

"That's the song Mr. Howard wrote for me. It's called 'This Old Mountain.' Marty Robbins ended up recording it." He shook his head and shoulders quickly as if taken by a chill. He grabbed the hand mirror and held it up to my neck. "Enough of those old times. Let's see how you look, young sir."

Just then, the door jingled and Paitsel ambled in with a brown lunch bag. Mr. Paul's back was to the door, and as Paitsel's reflection moved into the faded mirror, he beamed. "I'm sorry, sir, we're booked solid today," he said with mock seriousness. "We'll have to schedule you for later in the week."

"Ha! You think I'd trust my good looks to this overpriced barbershop?"

Mr. Paul waved him away and grinned into the back of my head. Paitsel raised the lunch bag. "Made us BLTs an some a my spicy coleslaw. Thought we could picnic in the park today if your schedule allows."

"After Kevin, I'm wide open for the rest of the week."

"You mean the town meetin ain't brungt the customers like we thought." His eyes twinkled sarcasm and shared consequence.

"Six cancellations this week." Paul sighed.

"It'll pass." He leaned his elbows on the counter. "More time for picnics."

Paul took up a soft hand broom and began whisking cut hairs from my shoulders and back. Paitsel's arm brushed the new drawing of Paul and the salon left by Tilroy. His face darkened. "He was here?"

Paul stiffened. "He was. I think the portrait is astonishingly good. Don't you think?"

"What I think clearly don't matter." Paitsel's mouth went to taut wire, hands to his back pockets.

"Pait, don't be starting in with this again."

"P, the boy's a bad seed, an you helpin him ain't gonna bring nothin good for him or us."

Mr. Paul put his head down and kept at my now clean neck, brushing faster and with stubborn resolve. I started to chafe.

"Look, I get how you see yourself in him an his daddy in your daddy an all that stuff, but we need—"

Mr. Paul whirled. "Enough! This ain't the time or place."

Paitsel opened his mouth to reply but said nothing; he grabbed both sides of the counter and focused on the thread that had recently unthreaded from the vamp of his shoe. I paid and hurried out the door as he brought his head back up into the breach.

Chapter 12

THE OCCASIONAL SHIFTING OF BOOT SOLE ON PINE

~

The next day, on my way to meet Buzzy at the tree house, I took an inexplicable detour down a game trail into a thickly wooded basin. Two dead pine trees had blown down into each other, and the combined crowns created a house of perfect dry tinder—pinecones piled invitingly amid a thick of combustible pine needles. My hand went instinctively to pocket and fingered the old match pack I'd been carrying around since Redhill. I brought it out and turned it over in my hand, examined the worn flap edges, bent down one of the three remaining matches. I turned a circle, half expecting Buzzy to be watching me from a rock outcropping, but the woods were quiet.

I thought about my father's betrayal and blame from two nights ago and how Pops had stood for me; thought of my developing friendship with Buzzy Fink and how his history was so deeply written in these hills with mine. How real friendship in Redhill had been only a curious concept and how Buzzy seemed to actually like me without any preconditions of cool—seemed to want to hang out with me regardless of my awkwardness. I put the matches back in my pocket and backtracked the trail to meet him.

—

Lo Gilvens tramped up the steps at six ten that evening and eased into a rocking chair with an overly loud exhale. Pops checked his watch. "Lo, you're late tonight. I was starting to worry that you'd found a better offer."

"No better offers," he said. He went silent and unblinking, staring intently at the great hickory as if the patterns on the trunk could help him untangle his thoughts. The creases on his forehead rolled together like poorly installed carpet. He tugged at an eyebrow hair, then dug an index finger into his ear, moving it in a circular motion, the way one cores an apple.

"What's the rub, Lo? You seem out of sorts tonight."

He shook his head slowly. "Arthur, it's...you know..." His eyes darted to me; then he whispered, "This whole Paul an Paitsel thing." He opened his mouth for further comment, but nothing came out.

"What whole Paul and Paitsel thing?"

Lo mouthed something to Pops, then gave two sideways head jerks toward me.

"Oh, you mean the whole homosexual thing," Pops said. Lo waved him off with both hands as if the mere mention of such depravity would ruin an impressionable boy.

"It's okay, Lo. Kevin knows what homosexuality is. I don't think talking about it will turn him"—he lowered his voice—"to the dark side." He chuckled and winked at me.

"It ain't to be played at, Arthur," Lo said, clearly exasperated. "You jus don't get it. The Budgets are gettin everybody all riled, sayin all kinds a things. Bad things." Lo paused and leaned forward. "Like theys gonna teach him a lesson for bringing sin into the town."

Chester walked up the steps and eased into a chair. I went to get him a glass of mash.

"Gotta be talking about the Paul scandal," he said with an eye roll.

"Yup, we're living in a regular Garden of Eden, aren't we? That dang Paul and his queer apple ruining paradise for everybody," Pops said and let out a belly laugh.

"It ain't to be played at, Arthur, I'm tellin you. Them Budgets can get nasty. Say they gonna run him an Paitsel outta town."

"Where did you hear this drivel... Hivey's?"

Lo nodded quickly, lips tight.

Pops let out a breath and wiped his hand down across his mouth, then scratched his chin.

"They're just big talking is all. This whole Paul thing will blow over and the Budgets will all get back to the important business of being hillbillies." Pops took his pipe out of his mouth and pointed the tip at Lo. "You can bank that."

"I don't know. They're all havin a meet-up tonight to decide what to do about it. I think it's more'n big talk."

That got Pops to sit up in his chair. "Who's they?" His sharpened tone made Lo flinch.

"Jesper, Bump, Andy, an them... Gov Budget called it."

"Bump? I thought he had more damn sense."

"Well, it's Gov what called the meetin."

"What time?"

"Eight."

"Gov Budget," Pops said under his breath.

Hivey's was buzzing when we arrived, fifteen or so men standing in clumps of twos and threes around the cold woodstove at the back. Bump Hivey, holding court with Bobby Clinch and several other men, was predicting the quantity of autumn rain.

Grubby Mitchell walked in and up to the group, shifting foot to foot, crossing and uncrossing his hands, nodding in agreement at the slightest declaration. Finally Bump acknowledged him. "Grub."

"Best call me Raymond now, what with the farm nearly solt."

Bump snorted; Bobby eye-rolled over to Andy Teel.

Jesper Jensen was with another group, waxing on the deficiencies of British culture. "You can't get baked beans with dinner over there...they refuse to sell em." A group of three others were complaining about the price of feed corn. I saw Sen Budget on the other side of the stove and froze; the memory of that horrific barnyard mule kill came forward. He was in close conversation with a taller, older version of himself. The older man had Sen's same jutting Adam's apple, same brush of stubble, but the frown lines and creases in his face cut deeper and to harsher angles, as if his was the tally board for every injustice the entire Budget clan had suffered at the hands of others.

I found an empty corner in the back of the store where I thought I could go unnoticed. Pops nodded to some of the men, shook hands with a few others, then sat in one of the rocking chairs around the circle. He crossed his legs and began chewing on his pipe end. Lo came over, sat down, and started whispering, gesturing toward the cluster of Budgets. Standing just outside the family clump was Tilroy. He looked over. I awkwardly half waved. He frowned and went back to the group discussion.

The men began drifting over to the circle, taking chairs or occupying standing room. Finally, Bump stood up. "Seein as this is my place, uh, Gov asked me to spread the word about all of us meetin up an talkin bout this Paul thing." He moved from foot to foot, as if the shift would help him configure his words. "An, well, we're all here now, I guess. So…I guess…maybe…" He looked over at Gov Budget, who was standing rigid. "Gov, you wanna have your say?"

Gov Budget nodded slowly to acknowledge the seriousness of the topic before them. He walked purposefully to the center of the room, gaze moving from face to face, letting the silence around the room gather up until he spoke in an almost whisper.

"We got us a devil cancer right here, right now, in this town. A devil cancer it is!" The words *devil cancer* came out as a hiss. "Y'all know who I'm talkin bout." Some folks nodded; most were looking at the floor. Pops was staring straight into Gov Budget, teeth clamped hard on his pipe.

Gov rambled on for about ten minutes, recounting the proud and virtuous history of Medgar, sprinkling in Bible quotes at appropriate intervals. Finally, in summation, with his voice rising to a high fever, he shouted, "We can't be havin this kinda sick, Satan, devil cancer in our town. The Bible says it's…it's"—voice notching up—"it's abomidational," he shouted with a finger in the air. Then he lowered his voice to a whisper. "An it jus ain't natural…it's gainst the natural order a things."

Sen Budget was mesmerized, staring proudly at his brother with unfettered awe, but the rest of the men seemed bored. Elrod Henry was testing the flexibility of his left thumb. Wade Wickle had taken his shoe off and was digging a splinter out of his heel. Bump Hivey was counting stock in the tool aisle.

Gov looked from man to man and frowned. He closed his eyes for a moment, put his fingers in the shape of a church steeple, then continued. "An people be talkin all over," he said, arms swinging back and forth across his audience. "This queer boy an his queer boyfriend have made us a laughinstock. Big Spoon, Glassville, Knuckle, theys all talkin." He paused to gauge the reaction of the group. Wade stopped digging after the splinter and looked up. Bump came around the aisle with hands on hips; the others were all staring at Gov now.

"Who's talkin?" someone asked.

"Everybody in Big Spoon."

"Everybody who?" someone else asked.

"Hill Watson for one. All the boys at Shanky's. Bobby Joe an them."

"What's that Bobby Joe been sayin?" Wade asked.

"Sayin that if we don't do nuthin bout Paul bein queer, then we must be all queer too. I don't know bout you, but I ain't havin no Bobby Joe Blemish call me no faggot."

The boys at Hivey's were in a rash now. The very idea of Bobby Joe Blemish and the boys at Shanky's, which they all regarded as a white trash version of Hivey's, calling their manhood into question was a slight of grievous consequence. (Big Spoon and Medgar had been bitter rivals ever since 1963, when Medgar and not Big Spoon was chosen to receive the first stoplight in the county. The ill will deepened two weeks later when the mayor of Big Spoon, a notorious drunkard named Winton Blight, facing certain defeat in the upcoming election, rammed his car into the new stoplight pole, toppling the light and shattering it into a hundred pieces. His landslide victory two weeks later only cemented the municipal tensions.)

Gov gained confidence and his voice rose and took on the quality of a preacher in the highest possible fever. "Are we gonna be men again? Or are we gonna let these faggots ruin our town? I want to know what we're gonna do bout it."

Bobby Clinch nodded. Jesper Jensen stood. "We gotta take care a this."

Someone else said, "You got that right."

Sen Budget couldn't hold back any longer and burst into the circle with the enthusiasm of a puppy who has just learned his first trick. "I say we go over there right now...all a us together, right now...an run em right outta town. Make em leave right now." He looked at his brother to make sure he approved. Gov Budget smiled, and Sen Budget stood up a little straighter. "We need to do this."

Andy Teel said, "Let's run em out!" There was general har-rumphing and nodding all around.

Pops rose slowly from the chair. As he did, the talk quieted as everyone turned to him. He walked over to a display holding wood-splitting tools and accessories. He picked up an ax handle, felt its weight, swung it once, then tossed it to Jesper. "Here you go, Jesper; this may come in handy if Paul and Paitsel put up a fight."

He grabbed two more and tossed one to Andy Teel, then another to the general circle of men. Grubby reached up and caught it before it clocked Webster Flen in the head. Next he picked up a double-bladed broadax, checked the blade for true, and threw it to Bobby Clinch. "What's a mob without a broadax man?" he said. Sen Budget smirked enviously at Bobby's good fortune, then went over to pick out his own broadax. He looked over at Bump Hivey, eyebrows arched. "We ain't gotta pay for these if we bring em back clean, do we Bump?"

A few in the crowd tittered. Gov Budget was scowling next to the cold stove, arms wrapped around his thin body. "Shut up, Sen," he said out of the side of his mouth.

"We're doin community work here, Gov." Sen's voice took on a reedy, plaintive quality. "I'm thinkin we bring em back clean, Bump can still sell em."

"Bring them back clean?" Pops shouted. "No, sir, I think we're in for a fight." He made like a boxer, ducking and weaving. "Paul and Paitsel may have all manner of weapons in their house— scissors, razors, electric shears, baseballs." More men sniggered; Sen Budget looked puzzled.

"It's community business is all I'm . . ."

"Sen, sit your ass down and shut your goddamn mouth," Gov Budget finally said.

Sen's mouth was still open but no words came out, his shoulders slumped, his jaw quivered; then he closed it slowly and slunk over to the wall behind the woodstove, hands jammed in his pockets, face screwed down in a mix of embarrassment, hatred, and confusion. Tilroy's face, however, had no such mix—he was shooting pure hatred at Pops. It was a look I had never seen on a kid before.

"Now, where were we?" Pops said, looking around the room. Andy and Jesper had quietly put their ax handles behind them. Bobby's broadax was lying across a stack of goat feed. "Oh yeah, we are going to run Paul and Paitsel out of town. That's right."

Bump stood, feeling a need to defend the group since they were in *his* place. "Now, Arthur, no one's talkin bout doin no violence. It's jus some a the boys think this kinda thing shouldn't be happenin in our town. Kinda makes us look foolish, some think."

Pops was standing with his hands on his hips now. He looked down and rubbed the stubble on his jaw. "Boys, most of us have known Paul since we were kids; we all grew up together, for God's sake—family was up on Cheek Mountain for eighty years. And we've known that Paul was a little different from the get-go, but we didn't care because he was one of us. He *still* is one of us. When he moved back here eighteen years ago with Paitsel, we all knew, deep down, they were together, and no one raised a stink; we all just went about our business." He whirled around and caught as many eyes as he could. "You all know that to be the truth."

"But it's all out in the open now," Bump argued. "That's the difference. Come football when we're playin Mingo . . . I jus don't know."

"Out in the open? The whole goddamn county has known about Paul and Paitsel for years."

Jesper stood to make his argument. "But us knowin is fine. An Paul an Paitsel knowin we know is fine. But now all a Big Spoon knows that we know, an that ain't fine, not by a wide space."

Pops tried to hide a half smile without much success. "Okay, let me see if I understand your position, Jesper. Them being homosexual was okay as long as no one else in the county knew that we knew."

"That's right."

"But *everybody's* always known is my point—us, Big Spoon, Knuckle."

"They knew, but they didn't know that we knew."

Pops put both hands up. "Okay, I think I got it now. You are okay with Paul being homosexual. You just don't want anyone to know that you've known about it all these years?"

Most of the men nodded.

"And now that the jig is up on our town's little secret and some fools in Big Spoon and Knuckle are talking, we're gonna run Paul and Paitsel right out of town." Pops looked around. "Did I get that right? Because Bobby Joe Blemish is big talking, we are gonna run Paul and Paitsel out of town?" Everyone was looking into the floor now.

Pops took up one of the ax handles and leaned on it like a walking stick. Then he looked at Bump. "When Ida had her cancer years back, who started that fund-raiser so you could go with her to Atlanta for treatment? Who took your girls in for three weeks while you were gone?"

Bump looked over at the poster of the new John Deere grain header but said nothing.

"Andy, was it Paitsel who lent you the down payment for that new tractor when the suits at Glassville Bank said your credit was bad?" Andy Teel rubbed his chin and bit part of the inside of his cheek.

"Who started the food pantry to help out folks laid off from the Company?"

"Paul done it," Jesper mumbled.

Pops nodded. "When my Sarah passed, I had a black time, as you all know. I couldn't even feed myself, let alone care for a baby. Who was it came over every day to spell Audy Rae so she could care for her own family? Who did all the house shopping?"

There was silence in the room as Pops looked from face to face. After a while he spoke again, softer. "Run Paul and Paitsel outta town? Boys, that's just not who we are." He said it again, almost in a whisper. "That's just not who we are." The only sound in the room was the low hum of the double-door soda refrigerator at the front and the occasional shifting of boot sole on pine. After a full minute Pops continued in the same tone. "I think we've had enough talk about this for one day. Let's all just get on home to our families."

One by one the men stood and walked wordlessly up the aisle and out of Hivey's. Sen Budget followed the men out the door, still holding the broadax.

"Don't be leavin without payin for that, Sen," Bump said.

Sen looked down at his hand and dropped the ax on the floor as if it had been electrified. Gov Budget was the last to leave. He moved in front of Pops and squared himself. "Who the hell you think you is, anyway?"

Pops stood a little straighter. "I think you know exactly who I am, Gov."

Gov Budget looked him up and down and said under his breath, "This ain't gonna stand…you an me…this ain't gonna stand." Then he sniffed, walked down the aisle and out the front door.

Pops put his hand on the back of my head and directed me toward the exit. Bump was standing sheepishly behind the counter. He opened his mouth to talk but couldn't fathom what to say. Pops filled the awkward silence for him. "I think that was a good thing, you organizing this, Bump. Good to get all the talk on the table, don't you think?"

Bump nodded, then adjusted the bee pollen display on the counter so it was square to the register.

We walked out into the heavy night air, down Main Street and Watford, then onto Chisold in silence. Pops put his arm around my shoulder. Back in Redhill whenever my father would try that I would flinch, feeling the weight of it on me like it was a cold, wet towel. Pops' arm felt warm and sincere and soothing.

"What you said back there. That was really good."

"Thank you, Kevin."

We were silent for a while more.

"Is that why you wanted me to come?"

"What, to listen to me talk?" He smiled and shook his head. "Noooo, you hear enough of that as it is."

"Why then?"

"Let me ask you a question. Did you learn anything tonight?"

"I think so."

"Good...care to share it?"

"Well, that you stand up for people—that you don't like it when people get pushed around. Good people like Mr. Paul."

"But you already knew that about me. What did you *learn* tonight?"

I paused, thinking about the scene in Hivey's and trying to parse what it all meant. "I guess I learned that even though most people are good, they can be talked into doing bad things by one or two jerks, like that Budget man."

Pops nodded, but was silent.

I thought some more. "And I guess, people sometimes need someone who can stand up and remind them that they are good people and they know what's right."

Pops nodded and smiled slightly. He seemed satisfied, but said nothing. As we opened the gate to number twenty-two, I could see the light from the living room and my mother sitting frozen in Pops' big wing chair. Her head was pushed hard against the high back of it, her hands and arms were heavy on the rests, her thinning body flattened into the cushions as if grief had written some new law of gravity just for her.

Chapter 13

THE HIDING

On Monday, after a full day of calls around the county, I followed Pops up the pulldown stairs into the attic to find his old fishing tent for Buzzy's sleepover. "Haven't used it since Glaston Lake last summer," he said. "Put Lo and Chester to shame, me catching everything." He turned on the top step and whispered, "I've got a honey hole away from camp where the big boys linger. We probably would have starved to death if I hadn't."

"Come on, Pops. You guys would have just hiked back to town or something. You wouldn't have starved."

Pops stopped, caught his breath, put his hand on my shoulder, and leaned in. "Son, Chester would've happily starved rather than admit to Hivey's that he couldn't catch a dang fish. He's a humble man, except when it comes to his fishing. Now, let see where I put the tent."

We were both in the attic now. The air was thick with dust and heat and the history that seemed to be seeping out of the trunks, valises, and boxes stacked neatly against the gable walls. Old slip-covered furniture, brushed tan by dust, was pushed up against the inside slope of the roof—shapes of dining room chairs, a desk, a table on its side, two matching bookcases, all seemed to be sad old ghosts pining for the opportunity to live once again. In the middle of the room, standing vigil over all the timeworn history, was a large, dark oak wardrobe—the only piece in the attic without a cover. As I moved closer, I could see the intricacies of its woodwork—feet fashioned into eagle claws clutching balls. Each claw became a spiral twist of rose vines, which grew flowers and leaves all the way to the top of the wardrobe, where they curled into a bouquet arch at the top. One side of the wardrobe was a carved relief of a mountain ridge and valley, a rising sun sending beams out of a cloudless sky. The other side was a crescent moon and a star-filled sky over the same slumbering dale. On the doors was a family crest, a coat of arms in four quadrants: a lion on haunches, a stand of tall trees, a bunching of wheat and corn, and a man at a plow. Over top of the doors under the rose bouquet was a beautiful hollow with a waterfall at one end, a small barn in the middle, and a cabin on the right. Beyond the house were tiny fields of corn, then mountainside. Pops was behind me now. "That's Jukes Hollow, where I was born."

"Is there really a waterfall up there? Mom said there was."

"Indeed. It empties into the best swimming hole in eastern Kentucky." Then Pops chuckled. "We were the only hollow folk with an in-ground pool."

"It's beautiful."

"That it is. One of the most beautiful places on this earth. And I've seen some nice places in my travels." Pops reached up and brushed a few dust specks from the arch at the top.

"He was something, my dad was—a big drum-chested man and stubborn as hell. But when he laughed, which was often, it was like a roll of thunder." The memory made Pops smile.

"When did he die?"

"In thirty-six trying to organize the mines—ours was one of the last in Kentucky to unionize, and William Beecher Boyd, the owner, was hell-bent to stop it, so he had my daddy killed."

"Wait a second." I put my hands up as if to take better hold of this new information. "You mean that Bubba Boyd man...his father killed your father?"

"Well, he didn't kill him directly, but he had him killed, yes. One of his men planted a huge bomb in the union office, and Dad was meeting there to plan the strike. He died along with seven others."

I finally started to understand the bad blood between Bubba Boyd and Pops—the history was all falling into place for me.

"Did you make this?" I asked after a while, staring at the workmanship and detail of the armoire.

"No, my talents are elsewhere. Jeb carved it for your grandmother as a wedding present. Did it all by hand—we didn't have much in the way of power tools in the hollow. Quite a piece, isn't it?" He ran his hand across the top and sides like he was assessing the workmanship for the first time. Amid all the dust in the attic, the wardrobe was sparkling clean, as if Jeb had just delivered it for their wedding.

Pops pulled lightly on the double doors. They swung open silently. Inside was a row of dresses, hung neatly on wooden hangers. Bright blues and reds and yellows that made the rest of the dingy attic seem like sepia tone. He gently picked a speck of dust off the red dress and moved the blue one another a few inches to the right to give it more breathing space. He was elsewhere now, running his hand lightly across the shoulders of the dresses, lost in the memory of a time and of the person who once filled them. Seeing her dresses made my grandmother seem so real that I could almost remember her too: walking to church on an Easter Sunday in the bright blue dress, chestnut hair tied back with a wide ribbon and Pops stealing glances at her, marveling all the while at his great fortune. And I could almost see her alive today, at the stove downstairs baking something delicious and saving me the batter-filled spoon. I could almost hear what she would say to my mother to put things right—to make the withering heartbreak of losing Josh just a little easier to bear. But deep inside me I knew that those words had yet to be invented.

"I just can't part with em." Pops sighed to himself as much as to me. He put one hand on each of the doors and stood there for a moment, eyes filling up, staring into the wardrobe as if reading an instruction manual on exactly how to close it. After a time he eased the doors shut, ever so gently, so that movement of the attic air wouldn't strain the creases from her last ironing.

We walked over to a corner piled with fishing rods, discarded creels, an old baseball bat, and various retired sporting equipment: Pops' high school football helmet, an ancient leather fielder's glove with none of the fingers linked. I tried to put it on, but the leather was unforgiving. Pops began digging in boxes and trunks, and I wandered over to a light-blue and yellow trunk with *ARP* written in gold lettering under the hasp. Inside was my mother's high school career. Her yearbook from senior year, a prom picture, sheaves of A-plus papers, class president certificate, first copy of the school newspaper she started, founding president of the Student Volunteers. All of her teenage accomplishments compiled before me like an old newsreel. I had never thought of her as a kid, or a teenager; she was only a mom to me. And now with her half-broken from grief and guilt, it seemed like that high school girl, so full of promise and purpose, was from some other planet. I closed the trunk.

Pops moved to a large green box and opened it. "Here we are." He pulled out a brown ball of nylon and tossed it to me. I caught it with both hands. It smelled of old grass clippings, smelled of rain.

We set the tent up in the backyard and after dinner waited on the porch for Buzzy. Pops was twirling his first sour mash of the night and I was breaking a twig into small pieces and flicking them out into the yard. "What if he doesn't come?" I complained. I was eager to see Buzzy again—eager for some teenage company and conversation. Each time we got together seemed easier than the last, as if the shared adventures of summer were fusing us into blood kin.

"He'll come," Pops assured me.

"Maybe his grandfather has work for him or something." After years of my father's no-shows, expectation management had become second nature for me.

"He'll come . . . it's no small walk from his hollow, you know."

The worry in my stomach that Buzzy wouldn't show for the campout reached a boiling point. "He probably had to stay home and do extra chores," I said to no one in particular.

"He'll—"

"Dr. Peebles!" a voice yelled from the dark street. I recognized it as Buzzy's. We both stood and turned to it.

He was bolting down Chisold empty-handed. Running as if chased by a pack of pit bulls. Pops was on the bottom step as Buzzy threw the front gate open.

"He's hurt real bad, Dr. Peebles. You gotta get someone quick."

"Who, son?"

Buzzy was bent over, hands on his knees, gasping for breath. He threw up.

Audy Rae came out from the kitchen.

"Who's hurt, son?" Pops asked urgently.

"Mr. Paul…out backa…his place." He panted. He leaned over and heaved again.

Pops looked up to Audy Rae, who immediately disappeared into the house.

"You boys wait right here," he said and took off running toward downtown. Buzzy stood up and looked at me; we both ran after Pops. He was thirty steps ahead of us as we chased him past the stop sign at Chisold and Watford, past the spray of double-wides on Madison, past the bank on Main. In a flash we were at the row of shops—Hivey's, Smith's, and Ms. Janey's on the end. Pops dashed down Green Street, paused, then disappeared into the alley behind the shops.

Mr. Paul was lying on his side, curled into the fetal position, a spreading pool of blood at his head—white fluid oozing out of his ear. His head had an abnormal shape to it, like a reject melon. His slight breathing came out as a gurgle, and his face was a mass of blood and cartilage. A piece of bone stuck out of his nose. One eye socket was smashed in. His other eye was staring off at an odd angle.

Pops worked furiously, checking his pulse, clearing blood and matter from his mouth so he could breathe. On the concrete, in the bloody pool, were seven small white stones; it took me several seconds to realize that they were Mr. Paul's teeth. At his head were Buzzy's bedroll and a cloth bag of belongings. I moved around and picked them up to get them out of the way.

"Go out to the front to wait on the ambulance." The tone in Pops' voice left no room for argument.

We backed out of the alley to the corner. I handed Buzzy his blanket and bag. He was silent and fidgety, looking every which way for the ambulance. "Man, where the fuck is they?"

"They're coming. I know Audy Rae called them."

"He can't die...he jus can't die."

"Buzz, what happened, man? How did he get like that?"

Buzzy just shook his head and looked down the road again for the ambulance.

"I mean, he was beat up or something. Had to have been beat up. Don't you think so?"

Buzzy wrapped his arms around his chest and jockeyed foot to foot. The night was still and we heard the low wail of the ambulance from far off. "Bout fuckin time," he said and started running in the general direction of the sound.

"They're coming right here, Buzz. Let's just wait like Pops said." The sound grew and the red and white lights of the ambulance reflected off Biddle's as it turned the corner onto Green. Buzzy ran out to the middle of the road, waving his arms wildly. The ambulance approached and he directed it to the alley opening. Soon after, Sheriff Binner arrived, trailed by two state police cars. The front porches on Green Street were filling up. People began walking down to the alley. Two state policemen established a perimeter across the road; one of them said to us, "Hey, you kids, get back over here." We obeyed and joined the thickening crowd on the other side of Green.

"They ain't gonna bring out the amblance for a break-in, Bernice," someone said.

"Dorlees says it's a suicide. Ain't that what you said, Dorlees?"

"Yes'um. The state boys only come for the suicides."

"That's what I know."

I felt a hand on my shoulder, which made me jump. I turned and relaxed when I saw it was Audy Rae.

"He's real bad, Audy Rae."

She squeezed my shoulder. "Been praying."

A fat lady looked over at me. "Who's real bad? You know who kilt themselves in there?"

"No one's killed themselves, Ms. Bandy," Audy Rae answered patiently.

Ms. Bandy looked at her as if she had told her that the sun wasn't going to make the sky in the morning. "How the hell you know? Dorlees says it's a suicide." Audy Rae ignored her and gently moved us out of the crowd to the corner of Green and Main.

She stood between us with a hand on each of our shoulders; as the ambulance gurney came out of the alley, the hands rushed to her mouth. "Oh my Lord."

Two technicians were working furiously on Mr. Paul, one forcing air into his lungs with a ball attached to a mask. A sheriff's deputy pushed the stretcher. Another held an IV bottle. Two more police came out of the alley, then Pops. They hoisted Mr. Paul into the back of the ambulance and it pulled away silently. Once it was out of town we heard the wail of the siren. Pops was standing just outside the alley talking with the sheriff, who nodded his head and looked over to Buzzy. Pops walked out to the front of the shops, then crossed toward us. There were creases in his forehead that I'd never seen before, and his lips were a straight white line. "Audy Rae, take these boys home, immediately. I'm going over to Paitsel's."

Chapter 14

How Bad Dreams Happen

What the fuck is going on? I'm serious. Someone tried to kill him. I mean, they knocked out all his teeth. Did you see that? Did you see all the teeth on the sidewalk in all that blood? Those were teeth... *teeth*! What is the deal?"

"Dunno."

"Did you see who did it? I mean, they beat the living shit out of him."

"Dint see nuthin."

"No one running out of the alley or anything like that?"

"Nope."

We were lying half out of the tent in the backyard. He rolled over and put his back to me and closed his eyes. Soon he was breathing long, slow breaths. I couldn't believe he was able to sleep after what we saw. I had absolutely no hope of sleep anytime soon, with my mind reeling from the alley scene. I sat up and peeked over his shoulder, watching him for a minute. One eye opened and peered up at me.

"Don't be starin at people when theys sleepin. It's how bad dreams happen."

"You're not sleeping."

"You dint know that."

"Whatever. Buzzy, I gotta talk to you about this. I mean, he had a *bone* coming out of his *nose*, white stuff coming out of his ears. I think they killed him and you're all ready to go to sleep."

"He ain't gonna die."

"How the hell do you know?"

Buzzy flipped over on his back. "He just ain't is all."

I was sitting up now. "All right, tell me everything that happened."

He exhaled an annoyed sigh. "I came down over Kinder Mountain an was walkin up Green Street by the alley an heard a moan, saw Mr. Paul all hurt, an then ran here to get your Pops. That's all I know."

"And you didn't see anybody around in the alley or on the street?"

"No, man, it was deserted."

"Who do you think did it?"

"I can't even take a guess on it."

"I think it was that Budget man."

He looked down. "Dunno."

I told him about the meeting at Hivey's. "...and I saw one of the Budgets shoot their own mule last week. Killed it right there in front of his whole family. At the meeting he was talking about running Mr. Paul out of town. Do you think he did it?"

"I got no earthly idea."

I started to catalog all the reasons why the Budgets were guilty when Buzzy cut me off. "Look, man, I really don't want to talk bout this. Let's jus lay here an go to sleep. I been pullin hay all afternoon an I'm beat."

"Sure, Buzz."

He turned his back to me again and soon his breaths were slow and even. I lay there and looked up at the stars. All the blood and teeth and bone that were the wreckage of Mr. Paul carried the memories of Joshua forward. Memories I had pushed so far into the shadows that when I drew them out again, they were still as raw and unprocessed as before. The numbness I had felt for so long after he died began to creep back into my legs and arms and lungs on Mr. Paul's blood and broken teeth.

Buzzy's breathing became rhythmic, and I could tell this time he really was asleep. But for me, any hope of reasonable slumber was gone. I stayed half out of the tent that night, watching the travel of the stars and thinking about Josh, replaying everything I did and failed to do on April 11 over and over and over until the east began to muddle the night sky with purple and light blue.

I didn't remember Pops coming home that night, but he was at the kitchen table drinking black coffee, talking in low tones with Audy Rae, when Buzzy and I opened the back screen door. "Morning, boys," he said quietly.

"Hey," I said as barely a whisper. Buzzy nodded to them, then went over to the refrigerator, examining the cluster of family pictures magnetized to the door: my mom, my cousins and uncles, a spread of me.

"How is Mr. Paul?"

"Not good, Kevin."

"Is he gonna die?"

"They don't know yet," Pops replied grimly. Buzzy acted as if he hadn't heard the report. Audy Rae was busy at the stove, pouring pancakes.

"Can I have a cup of coffee?"

"Okay," he said. "Buzzy?"

"Sure," Buzzy replied, not taking his eyes off the photos.

Audy Rae brought over two cups overloaded with cream. It tasted bitter, tasted appropriate.

"Where's Mom?"

"She's upstairs in her room. Probably going to sleep in today."

I smirked. Mom had slept in past noon just about every single day since Josh's funeral. By now Pops had perfected the art of casual understatement whenever anyone asked about her condition.

"Did you tell her about Mr. Paul?"

"No, and I'll likely hold off on that for a while. I think she's got enough on her mind right now."

Audy Rae delivered the pancakes. Buzzy dug in as if it was a last meal, but I couldn't eat.

After a while Pops spoke. "Buzzy, Sheriff Binner is going to come by after breakfast to talk to you about what you saw last night. I called your mom and she said it was fine as long as I was there with you."

Buzzy looked up from his pancakes, nodded, then went back to stuffing a three-stack triangle into his mouth.

"He told me he didn't see anything, Pops," I said, although I wasn't sure why.

"Then he can tell that to Sherriff Binner. It's what sheriffs do after things like this."

I pushed the pancakes around on my plate.

―――

Sheriff Binner pulled up at ten o'clock. Zebulon Binner was a large man, even by Missiwatchiwie County standards. His arms hung from his body at forty-five degree angles; the fat on his biceps pushed out the edges of his tight short shirtsleeves like a hand-squeezed balloon. Wrists the size of my thighs, head like an overinflated beach ball. His most impressive feature, however, was his belly, which hung long and low and looked as if an undigested boulder had lodged in his gizzard. His colossal thighs forced a duck-like gait that made his arms and belly swing in opposition.

"Zeb, how are you this morning?" Pops asked.

"Same as last night. Dang hip jus creaks when it gets humid like this."

"You'll be creaking all week, then. They say weather's not gonna break until Friday."

Sheriff Binner grunted.

"How're Floreese and the kids?"

"Floreese's runnin things in the bridge club now, so she pretty much leaves me alone," he said with a chuckle. "Boys are great, cuttin wood all summer for walkin money."

"You can put me down for a half cord," Pops said, then turned to Buzzy. "Zeb, I don't believe you've met Elrod Fink." Buzzy visibly flinched at the sound of his real name. "He goes by Buzzy, though."

Zeb Binner stuck out a meaty hand and Buzzy shook it. "How are you, son? I've known your daddy an grandaddy for years." He paused to catch his breath and mop his brow with a handkerchief. "My boy Jake blocks for your brother."

Buzzy nodded and tried to smile. Sheriff Binner pulled up a wicker chair, sat, and put both his elbows on his knees. "Can you tell me what you saw last night, Buzzy? Start from the beginnin."

Buzzy shifted in his chair. "Well, I was walkin from home to Kevin's house for a campout. He an his grandaddy was helpin out my grandaddy an he asked if I wanted to camp out so I said yeah. I walked over Kinder Mountain and down into town cause it's quicker than the highway. I came out down by the old railroad wayside, then came up Green Street. So I'm walkin up Green when I hear this moan come out the alley. I thought it was a cat or somethin, so I kept walkin; then I heard someone say, 'Help me,' an I turned back an saw him there on the ground."

"What did you do next, son?"

"I jus ran to Dr. Peebles to get help."

"Did you go in the alley at all?"

Buzzy paused and looked Sheriff Binner straight in his eyes. "No, sir."

My head shot up. Pops noticed my reaction, but said nothing.

"That alley was awful dark, son. How could you know it was Mr. Paul, as bad as he was beat up?"

"Maybe I went in a little bit, but I was scared whoever done it to him would still be there."

"So you went in just enough to see who it was an then ran to Dr. Peebles?"

"Yes, sir."

"Okay…was there anyone in or around the alley? Anyone on the street that you saw?"

"No, sir, there warn't nobody nowhere."

"And you're sure bout that?"

"Yes, sir."

Zeb Binner sat back in his chair with his hands on his knees, paused for a few seconds as he appraised Buzzy, then said, "That's all I need, son. Thanks for your help." He patted Buzzy's shoulder.

"Why don't you boys go out back and take the tent down," Pops said.

Buzzy got up quickly and opened the screen door. I followed deliberately. We went through the house and out the kitchen door. "Come on," I said and started to run to the front of the house to eavesdrop.

Buzzy didn't move. "No, man, let's jus get the tent," he said.

"Buzzy, we gotta hear what he's saying." I continued on and he tailed me reluctantly. We plastered ourselves against the wall of the house and inched our way toward the front of the porch. Near the porch edge we got on our stomachs and made like marine recruits crawling under barbed wire. We lay flat on our backs, looking up at the clouds and listening. The sky was summer blue and empty except for a few crisscrosses of jet stream and an errant cloud wisp.

"…gotta drain in his head tryin to relieve the pressure—that's the most important thing—brain's so swelled up. They gonna take him to Louisville tomorrow night. Got some Indian surgeon guy who's best in the world at this kinda stuff. Beside the skull, he's got a broken nose, five broken ribs, one punctured lung, a busted eye socket, and not a lot a teeth left. With all that, bein in a coma probably ain't a bad thing right now."

There was silence for a while; then Pops said, "Paitsel's a mess. I was up with him til don't know when last night. What did you get from the scene?"

"Not a damn thing, not even a bloody footprint or anythin."

"You been out to the Budgets? This has Budget written all over it."

"I'm headin out there right now. We'll see what comes of it."

"I'm going with you, Zeb."

"Now, Art, you know that ain't gonna be helpful. Let me do my job an see where things lay."

"You heard about that meeting the other night."

"I did . . . don't mean nuthin other than a motive."

"I'm telling you, Gov Budget's got his hands in this."

"That may be . . . it's jus too early to say what's what. You look like a rabid dog pissed on your head . . . go on an get some sleep. I'll come by tonight and let you know what we got."

We heard him walk down the stairs, then the sound of a car door closing, an engine starting, and tires pulling away— then footsteps on the porch. Suddenly the streaky clouds were obscured by Pops' face looking down at us.

"How's the tent coming?" he asked without a hint of amusement.

"Not too good," I replied.

"I can see that."

"Umm, we'll just do that right now," I said and started digging my heels in the dirt, slinking away on my back.

"I imagine you'll make better progress if you get up and run."

And that's exactly what we did.

We folded up the tent in silence. I kept staring at Buzzy, but he wouldn't meet my eye. Finally, I couldn't hold my thoughts in any longer. "Buzzy, why did you lie to the sheriff? You didn't do anything. It just makes you look guilty or something."

"I dint lie an I dint do nuthin."

Anger that I didn't quite understand boiled up in me, and I threw down the tent. "Bullshit. I found all your stuff right up by Mr. Paul's head and you told the sheriff that you didn't go into the alley."

"I tole him I went in a little."

"But you went in all the way. Why did you lie?"

"I'm jus scared."

"Scared of what? You didn't beat him up. In fact, you probably saved his life."

"Just scared a the cops. I mean, I'm thinkin maybe they think I did it or somethin."

"That's stupid. Why would you beat up Mr. Paul?"

"I'm jus sayin you never know what the cops is gonna do, is all. Better off sayin as little as possible."

I picked up the tent and wrapped the pole lines around it and led him into the kitchen.

"I'm headin back now, I guess," Buzzy said.

Audy Rae smiled and brought out a huge bag of leftovers from our last three dinners. "Take these to your momma," she said.

He nodded thanks.

"Let me go wake up Dr. Peebles so he can drive you."

"No, ma'am. I'm gonna walk."

Audy Rae didn't press the issue; she just smiled and went back to her kitchen work.

I showed him out to the empty front porch. "I guess I'll be seeing you around."

"Yup," he replied and walked quickly off the porch steps. About halfway down Chisold Street he turned and looked at me. I raised my hand to a wave. He gave back a halting half wave that seemed to be pulled right back down to his side by the weight of what he had seen. He turned, broke into a run, and was gone.

Chapter 15

INTO RICH AND SPLENDID WINGS

I was dozing on the porch a few hours later when Audy Rae came out of the door carrying flowers and a foil-covered casserole dish. "I'm off on an errand, be back in a few hours," she said.

"Where are you going?"

"I'm off to see Paul in the hospital and give Paitsel this shepherd's pie . . . he loves my shepherd's pie."

"Can I come?"

She nodded. "Just tell your Pops what you're doing."

Pops had been sleeping all morning, and it was now well past noon. I ran into the house and up the stairs. His room was all the way at the end of the hall. I tiptoed past my mother's closed door. The wood floor creaked under my weight. Pops' door was slightly ajar. I pushed it open just enough to slip inside.

He was there on the four-poster bed, stripped down to boxer shorts and T-shirt—one arm over his eyes to shield the day, mouth slightly agape. I watched as his chest rose and fell ever so slowly. The headboard of the bed had the same intricate carvings as the wardrobe in the attic. On his nightstand was an old photo of my grandmother by a lakeside with a handful of sand ready to throw at the picture taker.

On the other nightstand was their wedding picture—Pops dashing in his Lexington store suit, Sarah Winthorpe dazzling in a white satin dress.

I stood at the side of the bed, just watching him breathe; a slight smile came to his face and I backed away slowly, so as not to disturb the dream that was producing it. I found a notepad and a pencil on his dresser, jotted my plans, and left the note on the bed.

Audy Rae was already in Pops' truck with the engine started. She had put the seat as far up as it could go, and I pulled myself into the cab with my legs pushed sideways. "Sorry about the tight squeeze, Kevin. I seem to be shrinking with the years." She sighed and backed out of the driveway slowly, looking both directions twice before gingering into the street. We passed Green Street and I couldn't help but look down to the alley, now covered with police tape, a sheriff's car still parked on the road. We picked up speed after the abandoned stores in town and shot over the last hill before the highway. The cab was quiet except for the sound of the old engine firing. We passed an abandoned church and Audy Rae began softly humming.

"What's that song you're humming?" I asked to break my silence.

"Oh, it's just an old gospel song my daddy taught me years ago. When I drive out this way I think of him and sing it." She broke into an abounding voice that sounded like a track from an old movie.

Hail, Brother Jesus, send me hope and grace
Make me a brilliant angel to lead them from this place

Make these simple shoulders, in an effortless embrace
Into rich and splendid wings

"He's buried out at the church we just passed," she said. "It's closed now, but all the graves are still there. I go out once a week and tend to it and the others."

"How old were you when he died?" I asked, not wanting to stir up sad memories but curious about her life.

"A little older than you, sixteen. Left me and my momma struggling, but we managed. She's still going strong, probably live to be a hundred."

"How did he die?" I asked tentatively.

"He was killed in the mines. It was dangerous work back then, especially for black folk. Our men had to do all the jobs that the white folks refused. My daddy's job was setting explosives deep in the shaft, and one day his charge exploded before he could get out."

"I'm really sorry, Audy Rae."

She looked over at me and smiled, then gave my knee a squeeze.

We were silent for a few minutes. "I can't believe what they did to Mr. Paul," I said to myself as much as to Audy Rae. I looked over at her.

She shook her head and let out a resigned breath. "It is an evil as big as I've ever seen. There ain't nobody I know more gentle and caring than Mr. Paul. It's a tragic day for this town . . . a tragic day indeed." Her eyes were welling.

"He's been telling me stories about Grandma, Mr. Paul has," I said after some silence.

"Has he now," she replied. "Paul and Miss Sarah were good friends. When she first moved into town, he was one of the few who took to her right away."

"Did the other people not like her at first?"

"It wasn't that . . . She was just different than any other woman in town. Didn't take sass from nobody. Spoke her mind to the men." Audy Rae laughed at the memory. "She was a handful, I will tell you that, but she won folks over pretty quick."

We drove past the shuttered urinal-mint factory, then onto Route 17 toward Glassville.

"He told me about the time that she slapped that man and saved that girl."

"Oh, I remember that one very well."

"You saw it too?" I said with surprise.

She hesitated. "I did indeed."

"I mean, that took guts just walking up and slapping the guy."

"She had nerve, your grandmother—couldn't abide injustice of any kind." Audy Rae shook her head slowly, "Mmm, mmm, mmm . . . I remember that day like it happened yesterday. Must be nigh on thirty-eight, thirty-nine years. She saved a life that day."

"How did she save a life?"

"Cause those men were gonna kill that girl."

"He didn't say that." I was skeptical that anyone in a town like Medgar would do such a thing to a kid, but after Mr. Paul, I wasn't so sure.

"Those men were taking that girl away and were gonna kill her for sure."

"How do you know?"

"Some things you just know and you can't explain why you know em," she said, and turned back to the road and began humming again. I was silent for a while thinking of Mr. Paul and my grandmother. At the rise of the next hill was an old redbrick building. A sign announced, *Glassville General Hospital*.

"I wish I could have known her . . . my grandmother," I said as we pulled into a parking space.

Audy Rae put the car in park and turned sideways to face me. She reached out and put her rough hand on my cheek and let out a long slow breath. "It's a nice thing to think about, child, but don't spend all your wishings on things that can't ever be."

⸻

As we walked into the hospital, my mind jolted to my father rushing into the emergency room holding Josh's limp body in his arms—me right behind him negotiating the wake of death smells. My father screaming for help and a nurse intern dropping a metal tray and bringing her hands to her face. "Oh my God," she said when she saw his destroyed bundle. Him screaming again when no doctor or nurse appeared. The toddlers in the waiting room who started crying from his shouts. Mom wandering in behind us, her quintessence taken in flames.

Mr. Paul was unrecognizable in the bed of the intensive care unit at Glassville General—face a swollen mass of purple flesh and blood-soaked bandages; drain hole drilled into the top of his head to relieve pressure from a bruised and swollen brain. A ventilator hissed and groaned and his chest heaved with it in a terrible death rhythm.

Paitsel was sitting next to his bed speaking gently as we entered. ". . . said she's gonna open the salon for you tomorra and is gonna do all your appointments til you come back." His voice was deep and steady. Audy Rae knocked gently on the open door. "Oh, look who it is, Paul. Audy Rae and Kevin. Please come on in. I was just tellin Paul that Mary Alice is gonna take over the salon til he gets back. He's true bout keepin appointments, you know."

I stood awkwardly in the room, not quite knowing what to do next. He stretched out a hand. "It's good to see you again, Kevin." I took it silently.

"How's he doing, Paitsel?" asked Audy Rae.

"Well, Paul's workin hard to get that darn swellin down. Aren't you, Paul?" Paul's eyes were shut tight, chest rising with each thrust of the ventilator. He didn't seem to be working on much of anything, except dying.

Audy Rae went to the bathroom to fill an extra plastic water pitcher. She placed the flowers she had brought in it, then put the pitcher on the empty windowsill.

"We're takin a trip to Louisville tomorra, aren't we, Paul? The doctor there is gonna fix us up right, get all that swellin down, he is."

Pops and I were alone on the porch that night. It had rained in the early evening for the first time in a month, and the air smelled like sweet asphalt.

"Napoléon was not a large man, you know," he said to start the night's conversation. "Barely stood five-six." Despite the events of yesterday, I think Pops was determined to continue our routine so that some trace of normalcy came back into our lives.

"How did he get on his horse, then?" I asked, thinking he must have ridden a pony.

"He had wooden steps that his assistants brought with them everywhere. But his problem wasn't the size of his body; it was the size of his ego. Like most tyrants he didn't take advice from anybody. Kept pushing on to Waterloo."

"Why did he always have his hand in his shirt?"

Pops sniffed. "Dirty fingernail, I suspect. People never bathed back then."

"He must have stunk."

"Well, everybody stunk in those days, so it was okay. Body odor is only a problem if you're the only one who has it."

Audy Rae opened the screen door, affixed her walking-home hat, and pulled her summer sweater tight around her shoulders. "See you gentlemen tomorrow," she said sadly and padded down the stairs, out past the streetlamp. We watched her disappear around the corner.

"Have you ever met Audy Rae's family?" I asked after a while.

Pops stopped spinning his sour mash. "Of course I have. Audy Rae and her family are almost like my own."

"Is she married? Does she have any kids?"

"She and Frank have been married for over thirty years. He works over at the printing plant in Glassville. They raised four great kids. Tilly is in school in Raleigh and the boys are all spread out. Raymond's a lawyer in Atlanta; Frank Jr. lives in Baltimore—sells insurance, I think—Curtis teaches school in New York City. As solid a family as you'll ever know."

"We were talking about that black girl that Grandma saved, Audy Rae and I."

"Were you now," he said, spinning mash.

"She said they were going to kill her. Is that true? Did Grandma really save her life?"

"That's an open question. I don't think so, but Audy Rae is convinced of it."

"Why? What did she ever do to them?"

"Absolutely nothing."

"Why would they try and kill her? Were they ex-cons or something?"

"No, they were from old-time Missi County families."

"They just must be evil."

"Evil? I don't think I'd go that far. However, what they tried to do to that girl was certainly evil. I'd classify them as just scared, insecure, uneducated rednecks raised by scared, insecure, uneducated rednecks. It's kind of a pattern in these parts."

"But if they'd killed that girl they would've gone to prison, right?"

"Probably not."

"Why?"

"Well, you gotta know the history. That girl's daddy was one of Medgar's leading black citizens, respected by blacks and whites alike. He was also the former Kentucky heavyweight boxing champion seven years running. A big, powerful man. About a year before the slapping incident a few of those men had attacked that girl. She was walking home alone through the woods and they must have seen her. They tore off most of her clothes, probably were gonna rape her, but she fought back like a panther as they beat on her. Somehow she managed to escape and ran home to her daddy. Now, Lucas was a proud, decent man, but he had a crazy temper. When he saw what those men did to his daughter, he went wild. He had had run-ins with a couple of them before and he knew the law wasn't going to do much about it. Three white men beating up a black girl with no witnesses—forget it. A few nights later he lay for two of them and beat them to a bloody pulp. They arrested Lucas but couldn't prove anything since it was at night and neither man could remember much anyway. Besides, most folks in town thought those two had it coming, so the whole thing just blew over. Six months after that, Lucas Steptoe was killed in the mines. Whether he was murdered or died accidentally, we'll never know. But after he passed, those men—boys really, barely out of their teens—started getting bolder, following the girl around and saying rude things, strutting round town like fighting cocks. I don't doubt they would have raped her, but I don't think they've got killing in them. Anyway, they were trying to force her into their truck right out in front of Hivey's when Sarah saved her with that slap."

"Whatever happened to him? The one she slapped."

"Oh, he's still around causing trouble. You met him the other night. Gov Budget's his name."

"What?" I exclaimed. "He's the one?"

"Indeed he is," Pops said and took a sip of his sour mash.

"He's the one that beat up Mr. Paul."

"We *think* he is . . . or put someone up to it."

"But you told the sheriff that. I heard you."

"Me saying it and Zeb proving it are two different things."

I was silent for a while thinking about my grandmother and how Gov Budget's face must have shot sideways at impact. "Audy Rae said she saw the whole thing," I said, as much to fill in the silence as anything else.

Pops paused and leaned toward me with his sour mash cradled in both hands, fingers interlocked under the glass. "Kevin, that black girl Sarah saved *was* Audy Rae."

I sat back in my chair, stunned. Why hadn't she told me?

Pops continued, "After the 'slap heard round the county,' Sarah gave Audy Rae a job working for us. Did all the cleaning and sewing, just about anything else she could."

"Weren't you afraid that Gov and the others would try to hurt her again or do something to Grandma?"

"No...those men are classic cowards and bullies. Besides, that slap set the whole town talking for months; if they had tried anything, they would've probably been jailed out of respect for Sarah."

We were silent for most of the next hour as I let the revelation about Audy Rae and Gov Budget sink in. At eight thirty, Sheriff Binner's car pulled to the curb. He worked his way up to the steps, took them one at a time, then eased into one of the wicker chairs. He pulled a white handkerchief from his pocket and mopped the new sweat around his neck.

"What do we know?" Pops asked after he settled himself.

"We know that Gov Budget's outta town. Down in Johnson City—Rachel's brother is racing on the dirt down there. Whole family went down for it. Sen too."

"Sen went with him?"

"He did. No one's up the holler cept Lucille an that whole raggle a kids."

"When did they leave?"

"Two days ago. It'll be easy to check out."

Pops was chewing furiously on his pipe end. After a while he said, "Had to have put someone up to it."

Zeb Binner took a cigar out of his breast pocket and lit it. "Thinkin is easy; it's the provin what's hard. An on that score we got a lick a nuthin."

Chapter 16

TWO HEARTS BEATING
EACH TO EACH

The next morning was driving rain and a chill that spoke of late fall rather than midsummer. Audy Rae had taken the morning off to clean Mr. Paul's house, so Pops and I decided to stop into Biddle's for breakfast before a morning of calls around the county.

We rattled onto Main Street, the old wipers on Pops' truck leaving a frowning streak of water on every cycle. There were two cars in Biddle's parking lot as we pulled in.

Hank Biddle bought the place in 1965, two months after Miss Janey's opened. Pops said he was semiretired now, which wasn't difficult, since business was off by two-thirds. Charlie Swanson, the cook, leaned on the counter. "What's the latest with Paul? It's all everybody's been talking about this morning. How bad is it?"

"Bad. They are taking him to Louisville today to a brain specialist."

"Who the hell would want to hurt Paul? Nicest man in the county, I think."

"Been thinking about that all night. Don't have any answers, but I've got some ideas."

I excused myself to find the toilet and caught snippets of similar conversations in the few filled booths as I walked to the bathroom.

"...his brain so swelled up they hadda drill a hole in the top a his head," from booth three. "Heard he's gonna be fine, though."

"...brungt me the eggs in a nice basket ever mornin. He an Paitsel got eight in the roost back there...," from booth five.

"...I seen the Budget boy settin on the porch with him ever Saturday. Paul helpin him learn to draw is what," from booth seven.

And in the bathroom, "...lent me the money with no interest so I could get that backhoe...," said a man at the urinal to another. It was Andy Teel with Jesper Jensen on their breakfast break from loafing at the back of Hivey's.

"Uncommon generous. No better man in town, I say," Jesper said solemnly.

Breakfast came steaming on plates, and we gulped it down with two milks. We paid the bill and went out the door just as Petunia Wickle was coming in. She had on a short yellow skirt and a tight-fitting top. She smiled at me and I almost lost breakfast.

We drove out to the morning calls: first to Mrs. Tainey's near Knuckle, where we clipped horse hooves, vaccinated sheep for blue tongue, and stitched up her dog's barbed-wire-cut ear. Word of Mr. Paul's beating had spread before us like a new tide. "Who would hurt such a gentle man?" Eloise Tainey asked to the morning.

John Gumm, her foreman, was off under cover of the barn eaves talking to the Garvin brothers. "Pait's a top hand. I don't see him messing with that queer bidness, regardless a what Paul says."

Ned Garvin agreed. "Fixed the rings on my tractor engine—man that handy round engines can't be that way. Paul I can see, but not Pait—play poker with him ever Monday, for Christsake."

"Paul come out with needfuls last winter. Wouldn't even take no tip money," someone else said.

Similar sentiments were expressed on all of our calls that morning. Headshaking disbelief, speculation on the perpetrators, and vows to help Paul heal.

When we returned home for a late lunch, Audy Rae was in the kitchen working up cabbage-and-ham soup. "How are we doing?" Pops asked Audy Rae under his breath. "Have we emerged yet?" Each week it seemed Mom would sleep later and later into the day, only to stay up most of the night in her mother's old wing chair, staring off at a place somewhere in her past.

"Not a peep. I went up to check and she's just lying in today."

"I'm going to go see her," I said and trudged upstairs. Up until Mr. Paul's beating, I had felt the grip of Josh's death begin to loosen its hold on me. A month and a half in the warm surround of Pops and Audy Rae and my growing friendship with Buzzy Fink had started me on a slow path to healing. I wanted to parcel out some of that to her.

I was on the landing when the phone rang. Audy Rae answered in the kitchen. After a few seconds she took in a sharp breath. "Oh, Paitsel, I am so very sorry. I am so, so sorry."

Pops' quick footsteps into the kitchen from his den. "What's the story? Is he gone?"

"Do you need someone there? Just a second. Dr. Peebles would like to talk with you."

"Paitsel, Art here." Silence. "When was this?" More silence. "What can we do, Pait? Just tell me what we can do." He listened for another minute, then said, "I understand. We'll just keep you in our prayers, Pait." Pops hung up the phone and, without a word to Audy Rae, went into his den and closed the door. I came down the steps.

Audy Rae's eyes were red and brimming, tears streaming down her cheeks. "I suppose you heard that Mr. Paul has passed."

I nodded.

"He was one of the finest men I have ever known. I can't believe he's gone. I can't believe someone would do that to him." She put a hand on the stove to steady herself. I went over and took her other worn hand in mine, then brought her into an enveloping hug. She wrapped her arms around me and sobbed. All of the Josh thoughts that had been easing since my arrival came rushing back. The guilt and the grief and the wishing it all away suddenly became fresh and raw again. "He was such a fine man...such a fine man." I held her and she cried into my shoulder so deeply that I could feel the sorrow from her soul blending completely and profoundly with my own.

The afternoon sun, flooding through the Baptist church window, hit off the polished burled-wood casket and created a quadrangle of light on the ceiling that eased to the altar, shifting shape as the casket moved down the center aisle, pushed solemnly by two black-suited men. Folks were levered into every pew, shoulder tight on shoulder, hands folded on laps.

Pastor Barnes rose when the caisson reached its destination. He brought his hands wide as if to caress the congregation's collective sorrow. "Friends," he said, smiling sadly, "we are brought together today in this most tragic of circumstances to say goodbye to one who has touched our hearts and filled up our souls with friendship, love, and kindness." Pastor spoke on of a merciful but perplexing God who sometimes allowed awful things to happen to wonderful people and how we were to unquestioningly accept his actions and decisions as part of his larger plan. He finished with a few relevant Bible quotes on loss and belief, then moved to an appropriately severe wooden chair at the side of the altar.

Paitsel rose from the front row and walked slowly past the coffin, up the two stairs, and over to the lectern. He gripped both sides and lowered his head. He looked up with reddened eyes that stood out from his chalked face, opened his mouth to speak, but nothing came. Everyone in the church was silent; there were no cars on the roads, no rustle to the trees; it seemed as though even the birds had taken respectful wing. Breathing itself had stopped. I looked over at Pops, who was staring straight ahead, eyes fixed on a day thirty-six years earlier in the selfsame church when he had tried to articulate a selfsame loss.

Arthur Bradley Peebles regarded the casket of Sarah Winthorpe Peebles on a swell of memory as fresh as morning. "I will never forget the moment I first saw her," he began haltingly, holding the sides of the pulpit to counter the draw of his knees to the floor. "Standing in the foyer of her parents' house in Lexington. She had on this bright blue skirt and a white blouse and a matching wide blue ribbon in her hair. Can't believe it was ten years ago. Seems like it was just yesterday to me, and yet it also feels like a lifetime ago, we've done so much living in between. Sarah was, quite simply, the most beautiful girl I had ever seen. The instant I saw her, I was shot through with an electricity I'd never felt before." He paused and looked to the left wall. "She was the most beautiful girl I had ever seen." He shifted and looked back into the congregation. Jeb and Hersh were there in the front row with their fresh wives, watching their younger brother with recently acquired respect—Arthur's mother thin between them, her hard hollow years hanging on her like a worn-out dress. In the pew behind, Sarah's parents, choked with grief and anger at the blunder of their daughter's mate choice. "But it wasn't her beauty that won me. It wasn't her beauty that won me. It was the way she smiled from her eyes. You all know it because you've seen it too. The way she smiled from her eyes. It was a warmth and inner beauty that came up from her heart, spilled out from her soul, and touched everybody in its path. That was her gift to all of us." He looked up as if to find some special understanding of her death Sistine Chapeled on the ceiling. His voice rose to near shout and cracked. "My God...how I love her so." He looked down again, then locked on the assembled, tears streaming. He gazed over at the church window and on out into the morning. "She lived for days like this, you know. The first nod of spring when she could walk outside in a sleeveless dress and get some color on her arms. She'd start planning her vegetable garden on days like this. Loved her vegetable garden...and she loved me. Lord how she loved me." He chuckled through tears. "That I never really understood.

"I used to say to her, back in the early days, back before we were married, 'Why do you want to be with a backwoods hill-billy when you could have the pick of men in Lexington?' And she would just laugh and take up my hand and say, 'There are no men in Lexington.' Sometimes when she was feeling serious, she would say, 'Because I love who you are and I believe in who you will become.'" He paused and repeated the words slowly. "I believe in who you will become. Good God, if that wasn't something to live up to.

"You know, I've never told anyone this, but she was the one who said 'I love you' first. I fell in love with her almost instantly, but I was too damn chicken to say it. I just could not believe someone so beautiful and smart and refined could love a holler kid like me. We had been courting about three months. I took her that Saturday rowboating on Reservoir Two, and she stands up in the boat with her hands on her hips, steam just about blowing out of her ears, and she says to me, 'How come you haven't told me that you love me yet?' And I started stammering and hawing, and she says, 'You imbecile, don't you realize that I am madly in love with you.'" Pops laughed through tears, and many in the pews smiled at her brazenness. "So here I am still stuttering some excuse about timing and proper moments and trying to keep the boat from capsizing, and she just says, 'Oh, shut up,' and leans down and kisses me for the first time." More smiles and chuckles from the pews.

He looked out the window again. "On spring days like this we used to walk down to Chainey Creek and sit on a rock and take turns reading each other poetry. I'd read her something from Robert Browning and she would read me something out of *Songs from the Portuguese*, which was written by Browning's wife, Elizabeth Barrett. Her favorite was called 'Meeting at Night.' I read it to her so many times, I've got it memorized." He looked up to collect the words, to sequence them properly, then fixed wistfully on the casket and began:

The gray sea and the long black land;
And the yellow half-moon large and low;
And the startled little waves that leap
In fiery ringlets from their sleep,
As I gain the cove with pushing prow,
And quench its speed i' the slushy sand.

Then a mile of warm sea-scented beach;
Three fields to cross till a farm appears;
A tap at the pane, the quick sharp scratch
And blue spurt of a lighted match,
And a voice less loud, through its joys and fears,
Than the two hearts beating each to each.

He went silent, transfixed on the gleaming casket that held the remains of his one true love. He slowly stepped away from the lectern and down to the aisle end where Sarah reposed. He stood for a moment, placed his hand ever so gently on the casket, then leaned down and whispered something to her. Whispered something to her for the ages.

The round silver pier caps of the catafalque reflected the crisp of blue sky as we stood with clasped hands at the graveside. The green of the overhanging branch melded with the blue, making four discriminant earths that adorned the corners of the casket and seemed a fitting send-off to the heavens.

Most mourners had drifted away after interment prayers, leaving just Pops, Mom, me, Audy Rae, and Paitsel, who was staring intently out over top the coffin at eighteen years of small joys and boundless treasures, unspoken gifts and finished sentences, shared disappointments and pooled support.

The Tingley brothers were off to the side, allowing us time with our grief, but after a while the oldest stepped and whispered to Paitsel, who nodded. The brothers took up the lowering straps and on a somber count began feeding him down. As the coffin top came level with the four earths, Billy Tingley faltered, the casket tipped, and Paitsel rushed forward, took the straps, and matched the pace of the lowering. Pops stepped up and took the other straps, and together they lowered him into the cool earth.

As Paul came to rest on the dark loam and shovelfuls rained down, the earth became his madstone once more, extracting the pain of this last beating, as it had so many times in his youth. Each ladle of dirt drawing out whatever remained from the alley on Green Street and the childhood of hurt and loathing until he was cleansed and healed and rendered up pure.

We walked slowly back to 22 Chisold after the burial. The entire town had come out in grief and guilt, and Paitsel delivered a simple, beautiful eulogy that spoke of their love and respect and the bond that started when they met on the side of Highway 81 and only deepened as Paitsel's baseball dreams slipped away with every hung curveball.

Audy Rae put her arm around me and squeezed. Pops and Mom were walking with her arm hooked in his. She had insisted on attending the funeral, against Pops' strong dissent, and I watched during the eulogy as a single tear gathered at the corner of her eye and rolled slowly down her cheek. We took the porch steps and Audy Rae and Mom went inside to talk in the kitchen. The sun was starting to fall in the west and the trees were quiet. I sat in the wicker chair and Pops went inside to pour himself a glass of sour mash, even though it was only four o'clock in the afternoon. "There are some days, Kevin, that allow for early mash drinking. Today would be one of them," he said and eased down into the chair next to me.

"Mr. Paitsel really did love him," I said. "I didn't think gay people could be like that."

"They just want to love and be loved like the rest of us. Not much difference, really."

"I guess...I guess I didn't really understand it. I always thought of them as something bad. You know...kids call other kids fags and all, and I just thought that they all were bad."

"They're just like the rest of us—some are good, some are bad, but a whole lot are somewhere in the middle. I'll tell you this: Paitsel and Paul had an uncommon love that was no less worthy than any other."

"But why would anyone want to be, you know, gay like that? With all the teasing and meanness they go through."

"I don't think they can choose—I think they just are."

We were silent with our individual thoughts for the next hour—me with Josh, Pops with Sarah Winthorpe Peebles. As evening washed over us, he began spinning his sour mash in the low glass with *SWP* etched into it.

"I'll never forget the first time I took your grandmother up to

Jukes Hollow. We had been courting for about six months. I was almost shaking I was so nervous for her to see where I came from."

"Why did that make you nervous?"

"Hers was one of the wealthiest families in Lexington, and I was foolish enough to think that mattered to her. But she embraced my family like we were Vanderbilts."

"What's it like, Jukes Hollow?"

"Kevin, I've traveled the world, and it is truly one of the most beautiful places I have ever seen. I'm not saying it cause I grew up there. I'm saying it cause it is the bald truth."

"When can I see it? I've been here a month and a half and you haven't taken me yet."

"Very soon. In two weeks you and I are going on the Tramp. You'll see it then."

"What's the Tramp?"

"Every year in August, I hike up into the mountains for a few weeks, deep into Old Blue National Forest, which is on the other side of Bridger Mountain." He pointed to one of the mountains ringing the town. "About twenty miles into Blue, on a plateau, is the best fishing east of the Mississippi, place called Glaston Lake. That's where I took your grandmother for our honeymoon. I couldn't afford a real honeymoon and she couldn't have cared less... another reason I loved her. Jukes Hollow is at the trailhead that goes up there. So we can spend the morning at Jukes, then head up into Old Blue."

"You mean hike up there?"

"I do. Little walk in the woods never hurt a boy."

My camping experience consisted of a pup-tent blanket in the living room and my recent backyard foray. The idea of two weeks in the woods excited and scared me.

"That's a lot of food to be bringing up there."

"We won't be bringing much food. Only enough to get us there."

"How are we going to eat?"

"You obviously have never been fishing with me," he said with a tired smile. "I know all the secret honey holes. We are gonna fish, trap, and live off the land like mountain men. Bout time you learned how to do that, don't you think?"

"I guess. It sounds cool, like we're pioneers or something." I was still brooding over Paul's funeral and the thoughts that attended it. Escaping into the mountains was appealing. With death all around, it seemed like the last, best chance for peace of mind.

Evening finally came with an uncharacteristic bite to the air. I looked out to the streetlamp and a form materialized. I was expecting Lo or Chester, but the shadow grew with each stride. He stayed at the bottom step watching us as if looking through a window opened on a living room. "I was . . . I was out walkin an I saw the light from the road."

"I'm glad you did. Please come on up and join us."

He took the steps and eased himself slowly and silently into a wicker chair. I brought him a straight-up whiskey and a glass of ice. He took the whiskey with both hands, the way a child holds milk in a grown-up glass. He sipped and brought the glass back to the cradle of hands.

Pops didn't try to soothe him with words of a life well lived or fill the silence with eulogy platitudes, for he, above all, knew there was simply nothing to say. So there they sat in silence, sipping mash and leaving each to his own memories.

Pops with Sarah moving into the new Chisold house and trying to push the Lexington-bought mattress up the stairs with little success. They finally collapsed in laughter and spent that first night on the mattress in the living room laid out before a dancing fire.

Paitsel up a ladder in July scooping gutter sludge and Paul matching him muck for muck, but geared out like he was handling radioactive waste—rubber kitchen gloves to his elbows, head swaddled in a white towel, a surgical mask. Paitsel chuckled, which brought Pops out of his rememberings and back to the porch.

"He was a fussbudget, warn't he?"

Pops laughed. "He was indeed persnickety—but always with a smile. One of his greater charms, I think."

Paitsel sipped, held the glass from the bottom. "Took me five years to get the dang coffee makin right. Hadta be fresh ground. Hadta be exactly the right mix a coffee an water." He shook his head, smiling. "I'm always the early riser, so coffee was one a my jobs. I'd always bring him up a waker." He went silent and staring, as if another memory had come forward that appropriated all of his faculties. Pops abided. After about five minutes, Paitsel spoke again.

"Goin home's the thing."

Pops shifted; the wicker creaked.

Another long silence.

"I don't think I can." More silence. "He's everywhere in that place...in the walls, the floors, the bricks an the blocks...then suddenly he ain't. Tonight I think I hear him callin me downstairs, so I rush down...I rush down cause I swear I heard him"—his voice hushed—"but it's all empty."

Pops was leaning forward now, elbows on his knees. His eyes were red and moist. "I wish I could tell you that it gets better, Pait, but it don't. It just gets less bad."

Paitsel nodded with hard-bought understanding and finished his glass and stood. "I don't know where this chill come from. Feels like September instead a July."

"They say it's the jet stream, dipping down from Canada."

He turned, hands in his pockets, and looked out over the night, then slowly took the steps down to the walkway and off into the darkness.

He stood half in Paul's closet, brought two shirtsleeves to his face, and breathed in slowly, deeply. When his lungs were filled, he closed his eyes so that the essence would take him back to the archive of their life together. He held the scent like he was holding Paul one last time, afraid that if he let him go, let his essence go, he would never capture this moment again. This and the moment Paul exited his car on Highway 81 with a smile that obliterated flat-tire frustration; or the first time he thrashed violently in his sleep against the old tormentors until Paitsel slayed them by simply holding him tight and whispering into his ear; or the moment Paitsel's brother surprised them at the Kaymore place and Paul covered, sleeping the weekend at the Notion Shop. And town hall, the moment ten days fresh, when he had never been so proud. Never been so proud.

Finally he exhaled slowly, closed the doors, and went down to the kitchen to start coffee for one.

Chapter 17

THE SECRET LIFE OF
THE EMPTY PACKHORSE

Pops and I drove up the Mitchell farm road in the morning to spend the day examining and certifying Grubby's animals for sale. Bubba Boyd had increased his offer to eighty-seven thousand dollars and all auction proceeds. Grubby signed the papers without consulting Mayna. Now it was a matter of inspecting the beasts, cataloging the equipment, and readying everything for public sale the next day at noon.

Grubby was with the Went & Went Auctions man in the cul-de-sac, tagging three generations of gear as it was brought out from the barns—a sprayer, manure spreader, bed tiller, three drag harrows, bale wrappers, hay rakes, front loader and back-hoe attachments, an ancient mechanical scythe, a rusted reaper-binder with broken tines—all of it power washed and prepped and laid out like casualties of a lost battle.

We parked and exited the truck. Grubby had herded his animals into various pens at barn side and in the back. Sheep and goats in one, steer in another, the single stud bull tied to a tree.

Pops introduced himself to George Went but didn't linger.

"We've got a full day, so best get at it. Anything I need to know, Grubby?"

"Gotta bit a hard bag on one a the ewes. You'll see."

Pops nodded and we went to the sheep pen. I set up the squeeze chute to the stocks and a return chute to an empty holding pen. By lunch the sheep had been inspected, vaccinated, and turned out.

Pops and I ate on the open bed gate of his truck and watched silently as piece after piece of Grubby's equipment inventory was brought out from the barns or up from the outfields. It seemed as if the entire history and evolution of farming apparatus in eastern Kentucky was located, cleaned, tagged, and ledgered—waiting expectantly for new employment. I told Pops I had to pee and he pointed to the house. I knocked on the side kitchen door and after no answer I pushed in.

Mayna Mitchell's kitchen was old and childless. A small table of red-speckled Formica and shining chrome legs. A butcher block by the stove, scooped and pitted from generations of Mitchell carvings. Heavy oak cabinets on the walls, so thick it appeared as if the rest of the house had been built around them.

A crowded knickknack shelf hung by the stove holding Mayna Mitchell's life in miniature. A black speckled cow with a tiny blue ribbon; a pewter church; a carved farmer and his wife bending over to kiss; a tiny lock-top box for her mother's wedding ring; a ceramic Magic Kingdom from their trip to Florida; the silver medal from the Tri-County Spelling Championship in 1955; a miniature Bible with words too small to read; carved letter blocks spelling *Bless This Kitchen*; Ray Jr.'s combat ribbons; next to it a photo of him in his dress whites and an army-issue scowl; another of him on a mountain somewhere, dogtagged and shirtless.

I found the bathroom, peed, and returned to the yard. The auction van had left, and Pops and Grubby were standing alone in the driveway. Pops' arms were crossed. Grubby's hands were jammed into his back pockets.

"...gettin out from the bank's the thing."

"How behind are you?"

"Enough. It's wearin on Mayna."

"Where is she today?"

"Visitin Ray. This is the week when..."

"I know, Grub. Not an easy time."

I could see Grubby begin to well up. "I think they mighta left the other sprayer in the barn." He took off, head down.

"Let's see to these steer and get out of here," Pops said to me, hard edges of disappointment and disgust in his voice.

We set up the squeeze chute at the steer pen and began herding the animals into the stocks, including the recently castrated and dehorned yearling bulls, which were docile and compliant. By six o'clock we had finished and walked up to the Mitchell house.

Grubby was alone at the kitchen table. The screen door diffused the weak kitchen light into a gray halo that hung over him. We knocked, then eased into the room.

Grubby had taken Ray Jr.'s photo from the knickknack shelf. The table was empty except for the picture and a rounded plate of clay with a child's handprint pushed into the middle. The clay had been kilned and shellacked to sienna, then painted *Happy Father's Day, Love Ray 6-17-59* at the bottom in blue.

Grubby held the hardened handprint like a holy tablet. Brushing the edges and brailling the indented fingers; feeling the young creases at each knuckle and outlining the innocent folds of his boy's palm; tracing his lifeline as if drawing out memories of those first eight years, memories as raw and lush as if they had come in from morning.

"Um, Grubby, we're heading out. I left all the paperwork on the workbench in the barn."

Grubby was lost in the handprint and said nothing.

"Grub?"

We left him drowning in thoughts of his only son, the recollections flooding back in a levee break of sadness. He stood and walked slowly out of the kitchen, all the old rememberings stooping him like bagged sand.

When Bobby Clinch's thumb began to throb, it was a sure barometer of coming weather. Usually, the boys at Hivey's would spend a day tracking the regularity of the thumb twitches and vigorously debating their relationship to probable rain. But peculiarities of climate just seemed less important now. They ringed the cold woodstove, blowing down on fresh coffee, trying unsuccessfully to fill the morning with normal.

"She's goin again," Bobby offered and held his thumb to the light.

"Hmm," Jesper said.

"Comin regular now," Andy Teel assessed.

"Twice this hour," someone else said.

"Nevmind, she done stop," Bobby reported, lowering his hand.

The conversation hawed again.

They barely noticed Grubby Mitchell come in, freshly washed and shaved, with a press on his shirt. He paraded to the back by the stove, stood awkwardly with his new tool belt waisted, until the boys nodded. None of them were in the mood for Grubby Mitchell.

Grubby shifted foot to foot, waiting for a conversation thread with which to spool. Bump rearranged the Captain Earl's Bug Buster display and moved it two aisles to the right. Andy Teel picked up a wayward kernel of feed corn and tossed it into the open door of the stove.

"Way Uplander says he thinks his hip replacement wasn't greased right or something," Grubby finally offered. "Says that Indian doctor cut corners on him."

"Hmm," Jesper said.

"Doctors," Bobby replied.

"Yup."

Grubby and Mayna Mitchell bought one of the old houses on Kaymore Street for thirty-five thousand dollars cash. She soon adjusted to town living, walking to Dempsey's, walking to Hilda Jensen's and the Deal sisters', walking to her women's club meetings. Sometimes she missed the old place, but town living had so many advantages. There wasn't that constant track of dirt throughout the house, for one, or that incessant farm smell, which she had only really noticed once they had moved and the smell went. It was Raymond who was having difficulty.

Grubby Mitchell was a man who needed to be doing, and for forty-five years of his life, doing is exactly what he did. Now, with some money in the bank and time on his hands, he kicked around the county like an empty packhorse. Paid cash for a new Ford truck with a chrome step bar and double tires at the back and drove proudly up and down Main Street to break the engine in ahead of schedule; he accomplished that in two weeks and was idle again.

He raked all the leftover leaves in the deserted yards on Kaymore, then was idle again. He went out to Bobby Buford's to talk farming, but Bobby had never taken Grubby's advice before and certainly wasn't going to now. He visited other farms around the county, but his suggestions were met with polite silence. Now that he was a town man, his farming experience, regardless of its length and quality, just wasn't valued.

He soon settled into a plodding existence that made even the long summer days seem perpetual. He would lie in bed each dawn searching for any subtle change in the ceiling as everything about the morning glaciered to another interminable afternoon.

Chapter 18

STONES OF A RUINED CASTLE

Each day for the next week, after my morning calls with Pops, I went up to the tree house expecting to see Buzzy rocking on the porch, reading a dirty magazine or planning some other dangerous adventure—we still hadn't been to the Telling Cave, and any diversion from thinking about Mr. Paul's murder would have been welcome.

However, the rocker stayed empty and the tree house remained deserted. Finally, on a hazy, torpid Saturday, I decided to walk over Kinder Mountain into Fink's Hollow to find him.

I left Chisold Street after lunch, passed through town, and paused at the alley behind Miss Janey's. It had been scrubbed clean, as if the town wanted to remove all traces of what had happened there only a week ago. The old rack of empty hangers had been hauled away; the desk with missing drawers had been taken to a dump. Mr. Paul's blood had been sprayed off the cement, his teeth swept into the gutter to be taken by the next rain.

I continued down Green Street, across the railroad tracks, and up the hill toward the tree house. "Hey, Buzzy," I called when I got within shouting range. No reply. "Hey, tree house." Nothing. This time I decided to climb up to the porch in case he had left a message or some sign for me. The front door was locked up tight and the porch was covered with a week of acorns and squirrel droppings, a spiderweb in the seat of the rocker. I cleared the web and sat down to ponder Buzzy's whereabouts. Was he busy helping out in the hollow? Was he angry at me for accusing him of lying? It had been so long since I'd had a real friendship, the idea of it slipping away made me feel more alone than ever. I had to find out why he was avoiding me. I worked my way down the tree and followed the slight trail up the ridge of Kinder Mountain. A half hour later I was inching my way down the steep track that led into Fink's Hollow.

The place was quiet as the collection of barnyard animals lazed in the early afternoon heat. Two cats were languidly batting paws; the big pig was eating the tongue out of an abandoned shoe. On the porch of Giggins Hoo sat Esmer Fink rocking back and forth in his hand-hewn rocker. His one tooth glistening white against his darkened gums and the darker porch shade.

"Excuse me, sir, I'm—"

"I know who y'are, I ain't senile yet," he said, not breaking stride on his rocking.

"Is Buzzy here? I just came by to say hi."

"He ain't here."

"Is he out of town or something?"

"He's there," Esmer said, pointing at Buzzy's father's house on the other side of the compound. He grinned at his ready wit and kept on rocking.

I walked over to the house, a simple one-story rectangular structure with gray siding chipped and patched in places. It was the second-largest of the twelve houses in the hollow and appeared as old as Giggins Hoo itself. The front porch was poured concrete with a wrought-iron railing.

I knocked and Mrs. Fink emerged from the darkened room, peering suspiciously through the screen door. The silvery haze of the screen seemed to smooth her hard years in the hollow. She opened the door and aged a generation before my eyes, her face reading like old newsprint: sideways quotations around her eyes, double parentheses enclosing her mouth, and an exclamation point in the folds of her forehead.

"You're the Peebles boy," she said in her hollow clip. "Come on in . . . Buzzy's in the bedroom with his daddy. You go on back." She returned to the kitchen.

It is always strange going to a friend's house for the first time, as if you are invading a secret world they try to keep apart from you. Buzzy's world was simple and clean. Three old, handmade coil rugs covered the unvarnished pinewood floor. Two tattered sofas, one covered with a patch quilt, the other naked and thin, squared the room. Black-and-white photos of the family and the hollow storied the off-white walls. A large stuffed buck head with a crown of antlers watched the room from its position over the cast-iron woodstove; under it hung a large rifle with a black scope. The buck's dead eyes seemed to follow me across the room.

Next to the woodstove was an old brown La-Z-Boy recliner. I followed voices into the back room. Buzzy's father was sitting on the edge of the bed, back straight, collarbones at attention. His skin hung on him like someone else's suit, as if the pith and marrow of his once powerful frame had been sucked out, leaving a haggard, poorly fitted husk. His blond hair was striped with occasional gray, which made his miner-white skin seem almost transparent. His breathing was ragged, urgent. He looked up at me with miner's eyes.

Buzzy was clearly taken aback by my arrival. "What are you doin here?" he asked. His usual friendly tone was suspicious, questioning.

"I haven't seen you around and I was up at the tree house, so I thought I'd just walk over the mountain and see how you are doing."

"I'm helpin my daddy to his sick chair is how I'm doin," he said and carefully held his father's thin upper arms as he tried to stand. Mr. Fink was wearing worn-out blue pajamas; on his long, thin feet were dirty white hospital slippers. He shuffled one foot forward, then another. Buzzy grabbed the handle of an oxygen trolley and pulled it forward—one wheel squealed and shuddered like a bad shopping cart.

I backed out of the room to give them space. Isak Fink's condition stunned me to silence. I imagined the way he must have been before—the way Buzzy surely would be. Tall and thick; jagged face, powerful arms and shoulders; sturdy legs and a purposeful stride. I saw it all in that single instant the way you can sometimes see the past in the stones of a ruined castle—the glorious battles, the inexhaustible feasts, the confident knights. Now he just seemed old and rubbled. His hands were chiseled and cracked as if years in the dim mines had layered on a translucent yellow film, like old surgical gloves, over his white bones.

Mr. Fink watched each foot slide forward as if walking was some new form of transport requiring extreme powers of concentration. "We're almost there, Daddy," Buzzy said gently. "Jus a few more steps is all."

He paused after every other step and breathed in long and slow through the hose attached to his nostrils. Buzzy attended his father patiently, mirroring his small steps and waiting as he caught his breath. Finally they arrived at the La-Z-Boy. Buzzy positioned the oxygen bottle at the side of his chair, then held both arms as Isak eased his back to the seat. Slowly, with Buzzy guiding him, he lowered himself into the recliner and let out a long, labored breath as he settled into it.

Buzzy's brother, Cleo, came out of another bedroom holding a football. "Hey, Peebles kid," he said when he saw me.

"His name is Kevin," Buzzy said with a splash of anger.

Cleo laughed. "Easy, my man, I'm jus jokin. How are you this fine mornin, *Kevin*?" he said with an exaggerated bow.

"Good. Just came over to see Buzzy." For some reason I felt like an intruder who needed to explain his presence.

"Hey, Buzz," Cleo said and tossed the football to him. "Shag some balls for me?"

"Can't, man. Kevin an me are doin somethin."

"Come on, Buzz, I need you to shag. I'll let you throw some."

"Why don't you get Tilroy to shag. Looks like you an him is tight now."

Cleo stood silent for a moment, looking at his brother quizzically.

Suddenly from the chair came a raspy voice, almost a whisper. "Buzz, you be helpin your brother train, now." A wheezing cough. "Only thirteen days to camp."

Buzzy's face hardened and he followed Cleo wordlessly out to the yard.

In a forty-yard space behind the house, Cleo had set up a

makeshift football training ground with white spray-painted lines, old tires hanging from trees, a single lashed sapling goal post. He had fashioned a zip line across the end zone with a pulley system that whizzed an old tire along the line like a crossing receiver. He positioned me on the sideline and put a rope in my hand. "Kevin," he said. "You pull the line in quick an Buzz'll shag. You ready?"

"Ready," I said.

Buzzy nodded unenthusiastically.

Cleo made like he was crouching behind an imaginary center; he barked some numbers and smacked the football with a loud "Hike." He backpedaled five paces; I pulled on the rope furiously to bring the tire across the space. He cocked and fired a perfect spiral right through the middle of it. Buzzy caught the ball and threw a wobbly pass right back to him. "Bring it over your ear, Buzz," Cleo said, demonstrating proper technique in slow motion. He turned to me. "Kevin, you gotta pull like you got a world-record jimmy on the line." He set up at center again. "Y'all ready? Sixteen, sixteen, blue thirty-two, hike." He backpedaled exactly five steps. I pulled the rope with newly found pace; the tire whipped across the wire at running-back speed. He stepped up and threw another perfect pass through the opening. Buzzy caught the ball and tossed it back, careful to follow Cleo's passing instructions. "Great throw, Buzzy. Way to get your hip into it. Kevin, that was good pullin. Our guys can't run that fast, but in college they all do." Buzzy and I switched places. Cleo fired another pass, this time missing the tire. I brought my hands up to catch it, but it came so hard and fast that it bounced off my chest, nearly knocking the wind out of me. I picked it up and threw a wobbly pass back to Cleo. He laughed and said, "Who taught you how to throw?"

"No one," I said. "I taught myself."

"I can see that. You stink," he said with a grin. "Come here for a minute."

I walked over to him. He put the ball in my hands. "First thing, you're holdin the ball too close to the middle; hold it toward the back like this." He showed me how to properly grip the ball. "Then bring it back with a straight arm and swing your hips toward the target. Go on and try that." I did, and the result was measurably better, though still quite lame. Buzzy caught the ball and zipped it straight back to Cleo. "Good try, but you've got to bring your arm down to your ear and move your hips to the target at the same time." I tried it again, this time almost a perfect spiral. "That's it," Cleo said. "Great try." He gave me a high five. I smiled, my first real one since April. We worked with Cleo for another hour in the stifling heat, throwing footballs and doing all manner of drills and exercises.

"Time for road work. Anybody wanna run with me?" he said with a grin.

Buzzy shook his head. "Naw, we got stuff to do."

"Whatever." He started off down the road, then stopped. "Hey, hang on jus a second." He ran into the house, then came out a few moments later carrying a two-foot-long thick black plastic box. He put it at Buzzy's feet. "This is for you."

Buzzy knelt, unclipped the hasps, and opened it. Inside, nestled in gray foam, was a gleaming crossbow pistol.

"That asswipe Tilroy give it to me. An now I'm givin it to you."

Buzzy pulled it out slowly, reverently. "Whoa, this thing is cool." He raised it, closed an eye, and took aim at a squirrel on a branch.

"Thought you'd like it," Cleo said proudly. He patted Buzzy on the back, then took off running down the gravel lane that led out of the hollow to the highway.

"Man, Buzzy. Cleo is really cool. I can't believe he just gave it to you. It's like he doesn't treat you like a pissant younger brother or anything. It's like he's your friend or something."

"Yeah, he's an awesome brother," Buzzy said. There seemed to be a doleful tone in his voice that I'd not heard before. "Come on, let's head up the tree house an shoot it."

We walked over Kinder Mountain to the tree house. I was curious about Buzzy's father's illness but decided not to pry.

We took a piece of plywood and made an *X* in the middle with dirt and propped it against the tree. Buzzy cocked the bowstring and loaded the heavy metal arrow into the groove at the top of the gun. He closed one eye for aim and pulled the trigger. The gun made a whoosh sound and the bolt flew out and hit the dirt *X* exactly in the middle. The bolt drove through the plywood and lodged in the tree behind it.

"Dude, that thing is powerful. Let me try."

Buzzy cocked the string and loaded the second bolt. I aimed, hands shaking slightly, and fired, hitting the upper left of the target. "Ain't bad for city," he said and laughed. We collected the bolts and tried again. For the next three hours we practiced with the crossbow pistol—once Buzzy missed a squirrel by a whisker. After a while we went back up to the tree house and sat on the front porch.

Buzzy lit a cigarette and handed me one.

"No, thanks, man." I knew Pops would disapprove and I didn't want to do anything that would cause reproach.

"We oughta camp up the Tellin Cave tomorrow night. It's Rebah Deal night."

"What's that?"

"That's the night when all the ghosts a people killed there come hauntin up from the bottom a the cave."

"You don't believe that old legend, do you? I mean, seriously, how can a cave kill you?"

"You can ask Rebah Deal herself when she comes ghostin tomorra."

I looked for a smile to betray the joke, but there was none. "I don't know. I don't think Pops will let me spend the night in a cave."

"Of course he won't; that's what makes it fun. Tell him you're campin with me up the tree house. I owe you a campout."

We said good-byes and I walked back over the mountain into town just as dusk was settling. Pops was on the porch with the mustering night.

"He is back from his travels at last," he said when I opened the gate. I walked up the steps and collapsed into the chair next to him. "I assume you either caught up with Buzzy Fink or found an abandoned coal mine to explore. Best stay out of them, mind you."

"I went all the way over to Fink's Hollow. He was there helping his father."

"That's a lot of walking for a single day."

"His dad seems really sick. Like he's got cancer or something."

Pops nodded. "He's very ill. It's sad for Buzzy and Cleo."

"What's wrong with him?"

"Pneumoconiosis."

"Cancer?"

"Black lung. It's what some miners get after breathing in all that coal dust for years."

"Is he going to die?"

"I'm afraid so. This last year has been bad for him."

I picked at a paint chip in the porch floor and thought about Buzzy and his father and the coming loss. Thought about my father and everything we lost when Josh died. Finally understanding our common trial somehow brought me closer to Buzzy—as if tragedy, or the prospect of it, had inducted us into some secret society of the baned.

"He invited me over to camp out tomorrow night," I said after a while.

Pops scratched his chin. "Tomorrow night, eh?"

I looked up at him.

"And where exactly will you be camping?"

"Probably up on the mountain somewhere." It wasn't a complete lie.

He looked at me with concern. "Just be careful wherever you boys decide to camp."

"I will," I said and ran into the kitchen to call Buzzy.

Mom was sitting at the kitchen table with both hands around a hot cup of tea. Audy Rae was working dough by the sink.

Mom looked up to me when I entered the room. She smiled for the first time in months. It was a small, almost indiscernible upturn of the lips, but a smile nonetheless. "Hey," I said.

"Hi, Kevin," was all she could manage, then back to staring at the residue on the bottom of her teacup, as if studying the meaning of loss in the leaves.

"My friend Buzzy invited me to camp out tomorrow night," I said to fill the vast silence.

"That will be fun," said Audy Rae. Mom opened her mouth to reply, but nothing came. It seemed she had lost her capacity for regular conversation and was able to speak only in grief and salutation.

"Do you know Buzzy's mom—from when you were growing up?"

She took in a breath and looked up at the corner of the room where the ceiling joined two walls. "I do know Isak Fink and his sister Velva. We were in high school together; Isak was a senior when we were freshmen." She let out several short sharp breaths.

"I saw your high school stuff upstairs," I said, hoping the remembrance of her accomplishments past would somehow bring her spirits up. "You were running everything."

Mom didn't respond. She continued staring at the corner of the kitchen.

Audy Rae finally broke the awkward silence. "She's got her mom's organizational skills and her daddy's bossiness."

Pops and I were alone on the porch that night. Chester was off working on the Paul Pierce murder investigation special edition, and Lo was at a Rotary Club meeting in Knuckle.

A Cadillac pulled up to the curb and a large man got out of the back. I knew instantly it was Bubba Boyd. He opened the fence gate like he owned it and strode to the bottom porch step, his son, Billy, a few steps behind. The driver was the man from the town hall meeting and stood under the streetlamp, arms crossed in the same posture of malevolence.

"Bubba, you picked an inauspicious time to come calling. I'm not in fine humor this evening."

"We need to talk bidness," he said and trudged up the steps.

"I didn't think we had any business."

"We got the bidness a Jukes."

"Not for sale, Bubba."

"You ain't heard my offer."

"Okay, make it."

He sat down in one of the wicker chairs, its legs flaring on the load; Billy Boyd stood a pace back. The girth of Bubba's thighs forced his legs wide. He wore thick gold rings on each of the fat fingers of his right hand, the gold seemingly embedded in the expanding flesh around it. He licked his lips and regarded Pops for a moment. Billy did the same.

"Hundert thousand cash money."

Pops regarded him coolly. "That's a fair offer."

"I thought you would like it." He leaned forward, elbows on thighs.

"Didn't see you at the funeral last week."

"I was otherwise engaged."

"You missed quite a tribute. Paitsel's eulogy touched everyone in the place. That was a special love those two had."

"Special? What the hell you talkin bout special? That was disgustin, unholy, an sick is what it was. Paul coulda been big-time with his singing, but he chose the path of iniquity."

Pops laughed. "So says the righteous man. You really think anyone would choose that life?"

"I do. We hold our destiny in our own hands."

"So you think it was Paul's destiny to wind up beat to death in an alley in his own town?"

Bubba licked his lips and looked straight at Pops. "He had it comin."

Pops nodded like he understood. "You think he had it coming. So who do you reckon did that to him?"

"I don't have any idea."

"When they catch them it'll be murder, now. That's a whole different kettle."

"Zeb ain't got a lick to go on. Without witnesses, it ain't likely to go nowhere."

"How would you know that? Did you talk to Zeb?"

"Somethin happens in this town, I know bout it."

Pops leaned forward in his chair. Bubba did the same so that they were almost nose on nose. "I think you put some of your boys up to it. Just like that time you put Gov Budget up to accosting Audy Rae. You sat there in the truck and let him do your dirty work like the coward you are. Let me tell you something, you're lucky you stayed in that truck, or Sarah would have humiliated you just like she humiliated Gov."

"I don't reckon she woulda slapped me." He grinned and his yellowed teeth showed for the first time. "She had, I woulda taken her behind Hivey's an made her pay. Hell, she probly woulda liked that little ride." He chuckled deep and darkly, then cut himself off when he saw the look on Pops' face. It was a fusion of burgundy and purple with red-tipped ears. Pops' eyes opened wide and seemed ready to burst out of their sockets. The skin on his forehead crumpled up into ridges and rolls of anger that made the mule-shot scene at Sen Budget's seem like Christmas morning.

Pops lunged at Bubba Boyd, and his momentum pushed the bigger man back until the chair tipped and he fell to the porch boards with a heavy thump. Billy Boyd moved to help his father, then took a step back. He turned to the streetlight man. "Harlan!" Harlan came on a run.

Pops grabbed Bubba's ear and twisted him up and off the floor. Blood trickled down Bubba's jaw, and he leaned down to the pain and yowled.

"You will never speak of her that way again, you understand me?"

Harlan was at the bottom step now.

"Do *not* even think of coming up here," Pops shouted and pointed with his free hand. Harlan paused, then stopped.

Bubba was still yowling. Pops twisted the ear again, and a fresh rivulet of blood washed Bubba's neck.

"You understand me?"

"I got it, I got it," he said through gritted teeth.

Pops dragged him to standing and down the steps by his ear, throwing him in a heap at Harlan's feet. Billy Boyd's mouth was moving, but no words came out. It was the first time he had ever seen his father at submission and it perplexed and unnerved him. He and Harlan helped Bubba to his feet and out to the car, a hand cupping the serrated ear. Pops turned wordlessly, chest heaving, and strode back up to the porch.

He paused at the top and turned to the road as Bubba Boyd's Cadillac peeled off. Normal color returned to his cheeks and ears as he sat down in his chair and settled himself.

I was wide-eyed and openmouthed. The fury that exploded and the speed with which it arrived frightened me—it was as if a raging magma, held down for so long by rearing and position, ruptured its vessel and spewed forth in an overpowering surge. Then, just as quickly, the rage drew back into itself or dissipated to the night.

Pops picked up his mash, regarded the *SWP* etching, and said with surprising calm, "I won't tolerate a man who speaks so rudely of my Sarah."

Chapter 19

How to Carve a Whistle Out of Green Willow

$\smile$

I packed my knapsack the next day, tied a sleeping bag to the side of it, and set out for the tree house at four o'clock. Buzzy was already there when I arrived, leaning against the tree smoking a cigarette.

"Got the new *Playboy*," he announced proudly. "Found it under Cleo's mattress."

"Let's see."

He pulled out the thick magazine and we sat against the tree parsing every inch of Miss August as if we were archaeologists and she was a Dead Sea scroll. After a half hour deciphering the secrets of female flesh, we set out for the Telling Cave.

We covered the five miles to the cave in two hours over an abandoned mining road and a well-used hunting trail, stopping occasionally for Buzzy to instruct me in the ways of the woods. We scrambled up the side of Knob Mountain to a small clearing on a shelf near the top. At the end of the clearing, abutting the granite face of the knob, was the car-size opening to the Telling Cave. As I stood just outside it, I could feel the warm air around me convecting into the cave. Inside was dark and exciting.

"This is cool—I've never been in a cave before. Looks like people come up here all the time," I said, gesturing to an old campfire ring riddled with melted bottles, broken glass, and other detritus from previous visitors.

"Teenagers, mostly."

"How does it work?" I asked, trying to take the legend seriously. "Do we tell the secrets before we go in or after?"

"You tell the secrets inside, an once you're in you can't leave without tellin."

The cave was wet and washcloth cool from the dank air, a menacing smell that shot tingles of excitement through my body. The chamber expanded from the opening to a thirty-foot ceiling glistening with moisture and blackened with soot from the fire ring in the middle. Around the ring were sitting rocks and some tree stumps with seats worn in from years of telling. On a four-foot ledge against the south wall was an old hay mattress and another fire pit.

The walls were smooth in places and covered in years of graffiti that read like a history book of Missiwatchiwie County. *Janey Beverage was here 1945. Cleatus and Sharon '54. Ethna Deal loves Billy Winwell. B.G. Hivey + E. Fink '62. Sharon + ? in 74. Class of 1984 rocks! Petunia ain't got no secrets.*

Buzzy set up camp inside while I scouted firewood, collecting enough to last a week—if Rebah Deal actually did arrive, I didn't want to be caught without a flame.

As I arrayed our fuel, Buzzy went off into the woods. He came back ten minutes later dragging a long willow branch with green leaves still attached.

"What did you bring that back for? It'll never burn."

"Ain't for burnin; it's for carvin." He took a shiny hatchet from his knapsack and, working on an old stump, cut three eight-inch pieces of willow wood from the straightest part of the branch. He sunk the hatchet in the stump and motioned for me to follow.

We climbed the rocks above the cave to a ledge that jutted out from the summit about a thousand feet above the valley below. We sat on the edge with our feet dangling over the side. The previous evening's rain had cleared the mid-July haze and the view extended into forever.

"What are we carving?"

"Whistles."

"I don't know how to carve a whistle."

"Bout time you learned, ain't it?"

He handed me Cleo's best wood-carving knife, which he had filched from their bedroom, and one of the willow blanks. I followed his lead and carefully stripped the bark from the wood until my piece was like his: clean, wet, and almost perfectly cylindrical.

I watched him as he fashioned the mouthpiece from the green wood; watched as shavings helicoptered to the ground like maple seeds. I copied his technique and soon had a cruder version of his delicately shaped mouthpiece. He examined my work and pronounced it satisfactory—for a beginner. We hollowed the insides, taking care not to make the walls too thin or too thick. Cleo always made his walls too thick, Buzzy informed me, which flattened all the notes.

We punched through the space between the hollowed core and the mouthpiece and cleaned the hole to make a smooth tube. He inspected my work; again it passed his whittler's eye.

The reed is the most important part of the whistle, he instructed. If it's not right, it will ruin everything. He showed me how to make a triangular cut for the reed opening and how to fashion the reed from the remaining willow in the hole. He cut the reed hole and shaved the piece to near perfection. He examined it closely, shaved off a ribbon more, cleaned the cut, and blew into the mouthpiece. A perfect whistle came from the willow wood. Still, he wasn't satisfied and made almost imperceptible adjustments here and there: a hair off the reed, a snub from the core. He tried it again and pronounced it fit.

Now it was my turn. With Buzzy coaching over my shoulder, I made the delicate triangular cut into the willow stick and lifted out the piece of wood. I cleaned out the cut and put the whistle to my lips. A shrill sound, like winter wind, blew out of the willow stick. "You cut it too shallow," he said. "Take a bit off the top."

I removed a paper-thin shaving from the reed and tried again. A little better. I rived off another layer and blew. A clear whistle burst from the wood. Warbly and unsure, but a whistle still. "Not a bad effort, Indiana," he told me with a smile.

Next, we cut four note holes into each whistle stem with the pointed blades of our knives. We doctored the reed and note holes ever so slightly, and when Buzzy was finally satisfied with his work, he blew a clear, strong note that resonated off the rocks around us. His fingers danced on the note holes as he played a slow, mournful song that perfectly scored Mr. Paul's death and my last three months.

"That was great," I said when he finished. "What song was that?"

"Warnt no song; I jus made it up."

"Come on! When? Just now?" I couldn't believe he could create such beautiful music on the spot.

"Sure, listen," he said and put the whistle to his lips. He launched into a slow, lilting reel that soared and tumbled and ascended again like a sad foundling bird on first wing. I watched him closely, watched a talent in him I never knew existed. He held the final note in an arcing vibrato, then slowly pulled the mouthpiece from his lips. I was speechless.

"Your turn."

I laughed and licked my lips. "I'm gonna suck at this." I blew into the whistle, and out came a shrill, off-key, out-of-time screech as my unsure fingers searched for an agreeable tune. I finished with an atonal salute and looked to Buzzy for assessment.

"I've heard better music out the ass of a coonhound," he said grimly. We dissolved into laughter and spent the next hour on the ledge overlooking the Kentucky hills, inventing songs and discovering the affiliations of the notes. It was the first time since Josh's death that I felt truly at ease, as each song we wrote erased some of the hurtful past. It gave me a first peek into new way, a bloom of belief that the nightmare of the past three months was finally ending. On the edge of everything, with the wet, cool willow whistle at my lips and the tired sun newly buried in the west, I had little idea how wrong I was.

Chapter 20

WHEN HIGH EXPECTATIONS AND LOW EXPECTATIONS ARE DEVASTATINGLY UNMET

Before we realized it, evening had drifted in from the east. "Let's start thinkin bout food," Buzzy said after the sun disappeared somewhere over Missouri. We climbed down the rocks into the cool of the Telling Cave. I had taken a large bag of Doritos from Pops' pantry and Buzzy pulled out four hot dogs, some mustard, and bread. He built a fire. I cut two roasting sticks from what was left of the willow branch.

The smoke from the expanding flames rose to the top of the room and conveyed out an unseen opening at the ceiling. I laced the dogs onto the sticks and we cooked them to tar and ate them thick with mustard. The light of the fire and Buzzy's kerosene lamp was enough to give the dark cave a warming glow. It actually wasn't such a gloomy place after all, Rebah Deal notwithstanding.

We finished the hot dogs and chips and lay down on our

sleeping bags, watching the circle of coals as the fire died to a single flame. The blue evening light at the cave mouth bruised to purple, then black, as night extended. Mr. Paul and the alley hung in the air with smoke from the fire, but both of us seemed reluctant to bring it up. Instead we talked about Petunia Wickle's breasts, my friends back in Indiana, his friends at Missiwatchiwie High School. After a while we floated into a comfortable silence, which great friends seem to share so easily. But I could tell his mind was roiling, as it had been since the alley. Finally, his smile vanished and he looked into the fire as if searching for the right words to match his thoughts.

He knocked some dirt into the flames with his heel, then turned and looked at me, face in a half grimace.

"I know who done Mr. Paul," he said to the dying coals in a voice barely above a whisper.

I popped up off my elbow and turned to face him. "How do you know? Was it that Budget man?"

He shook his head, plowed more dirt and ash with his heel. "I seen it—seen it all."

"Why didn't you tell me?" I felt a little betrayed that he'd been carrying this secret for so many days and it took the Telling Cave to wrestle it free. "Have you told anybody? Told the sheriff?"

Buzzy shook his head violently. "Ain't tellin no sheriff. No way."

"You gotta tell me, Buzzy," I implored. "You know I won't tell anyone."

The dirt and ash he had been heeling now formed a small wall between him and the flame, either to keep the fire out or to keep the truth in.

After a few minutes of silence, punctured occasionally by a popping coal, he spoke. "I was walkin down Green like I tole you, when I saw a man run out the back a Miss Janey's, then some others. I thought they was robbin the place, so I hid behind the Dumpster to watch em. Then I see it's Mr. Paul an someone comes out an throws him down on the pavement an they all start laughin. It was Tilroy fuckin Budget, smilin like he's the king shit."

"What? It was Tilroy? Jesus Christ, I can't believe it." I knew Tilroy was a punk and a bully, but I couldn't believe he had it in him to kill.

Buzzy just kept staring into the fire and continued. "And the others are all laughin an sayin stuff to Mr. Paul. Rude stuff. An Mr. Paul starts to get up, he's up on his knees facin Tilroy an says, 'Tilroy, leave me be or I'm gonna tell your father.'

"An someone says, 'Oh, Tilroy, *what's* he gonna tell your daddy?' An everybody cracks up. Someone else says, 'Yeah, we all been hearin you two was *special* friends.' The boys all laugh an Tilroy gets this look about him like I never seen. Then he jus runs at Mr. Paul an kicks him square in the face. You know he's got them boots he wears, an Mr. Paul's face jus crumbles an he falls back an hits his head on the pavement. An the others are all laughin an sayin, 'Ohoooooo, look at Tilroy the badass,' an stuff. An Tilroy's jus heavin an puffin an standin over Mr. Paul, who's got blood comin out his nose like a gusher. Finally Mr. Paul sits up, blood down his shirt, nose all broken, an says, 'Tilroy, I won't tell. I promise I won't tell.' He starts to say it a third time, an before he can even get the words out, Tilroy is on him, this time kickin him square in the mouth, an Mr. Paul goes down, an Tilroy keeps kickin an stompin, an I close my eyes cause I can't even watch at this point. But it was the sound, man. The sound a that boot hittin his head an hittin his head. I close my eyes but I can't stop the sound a that boot hittin his head.

"An all the others go silent, mouths hangin open, while Tilroy jus keeps kickin him, until one a them screams '*Stop it!*' an tackles Tilroy, who starts to fight him, so he pounds him good an calls him a fuckin idiot an stuff. Then the one that stopped it all goes up to Mr. Paul an tries to help him, but I guess he got scared an says, 'Let's get the fuck outta here,' an they all run off.

"Then I go up to Mr. Paul, he's still breathin, but jus barely, so I run as fast as I can to your house to get your Pops."

Remembering the scene in the alley, the blood and broken teeth, made me want to vomit. Buzzy sat staring into the fire, arms wrapped around his knees. Finally, after a few minutes of silence, I said gently, "Buzz, man, you gotta tell. You can't let that prick get away with this."

He shook his head.

"Dude, you have to tell."

"No way." Tears started streaming down his cheeks, and he started rocking back and forth. He made no attempt to wipe the tears away and soon they mixed with the ash on his face from fire building to form streaky gray lines.

"He killed Mr. Paul!" My voice broke with grief as I said it, as much for Buzzy's pain as for Paitsel's.

"Cleo was one a them," he said softly.

"What? He hates Tilroy!" I replied, almost shouting. Buzzy winced on my volume.

"I can't be tellin."

Like some valley fog lifting with the sun, it all became clear why Buzzy had been so different since the alley—I finally understood the crushing load he had been carrying all these weeks. I sat back, stunned. "Damn, Buzz," was all I could think of to say.

The fire was popping and the black walls of the cave were slick with sweat. I could hear the trickle of water from somewhere down in the crag opening. After some more time—it could have been two minutes, could have been thirty—I was finally able to speak. "Does Cleo know you know?"

Buzzy shook his head.

"You've got to talk to Cleo about it. You've got to tell him you know."

Buzzy was silent still.

"Why would Cleo beat up Mr. Paul?" I wondered out loud. "Was it the fag thing?"

"Cleo dint do nuthin," Buzzy retorted. "He's the one that pulled Tilroy offa him . . . had to beat on him to make him stop."

"Then all the more reason to talk to him. He probably didn't know that Tilroy was gonna do that. Get him to go to the sheriff."

"That ain't gonna happen."

"Just talk to him—see what he says."

"He's got senior year comin up. By the end a last season he had Kentucky, North Carolina, *and* Notre Dame comin to his games. This is his ticket year; I ain't gonna fuck that up."

"What do you mean?"

"His ticket outta here. He does well this year, he'll get a full ride somewheres. Get the fuck out the hollow."

I gave Buzzy a quizzical look, for I truly didn't understand. For me Medgar was sanctuary; I had never felt more at home—or more loved. "Why does he want to leave . . . ? This place is awesome; I could live here forever."

Buzzy laughed and just shook his head. "Kevin, you're the smartest kid I know, but sometimes you're so frickin stupid." He looked at me now and smiled. The tears on his face had dried with the ashes and given him the look of a half-ready circus clown.

I laughed and told him to wipe his face. "Why am I being stupid? I don't get it."

"You love it here 'cause you don't live here. You can leave anytime you want. Where's Cleo gonna go?" His face became pained. "Where am I gonna go?" he said as a whisper.

"To college, man! Do good in school, get good grades." I just couldn't grasp why this was a difficult plan for him, for Cleo.

"I ain't like you, Kevin. It don't come easy for me."

"You think it's easy for me? I study my ass off. My father kills me if I bring home a C. And if I get an A he bitches because it wasn't an A-plus."

"Maybe he jus wants you to do your best. That ain't a bad thing."

Now it was my turn with silence. Buzzy had no idea what it was like to live in Redhill with my father.

"I got an A once," he said sadly. "Know what my daddy did?"

"What?"

"He laughed. Jus laughed an walked around the holler for a week, sayin, 'Buzzy the Brain, gonna live above his rearin.'" He shook his head and said again, this time in a bitter hush, "Gonna live above his rearin."

Now we both went silent, staring into the fire at the dancing light of the single flame and at the flame's reflection on the sweating walls; listening to the slow drip of water somewhere down in the cave and the irregular popping of dying coals; fresh friends from completely different worlds faced with the hard shapings of truth and deceit, of right and wrong, and of the equivalent damage when high expectations and low expectations are devastatingly unmet.

Chapter 21

THE HAINT

I am the phasim of Rebah Deal…help me find my way home." The ghostly howl jolted us awake. The fire had died completely, and the only light in the cave was the weak flicker of the kerosene lamp shining off the wide whites of Buzzy's eyes.

"Did you hear that?" I asked, unsure if it was my imagination. "Shhhhhh!"

It came again from the woods outside the cave. *"I am the phasim of Rebah Deal…help me find my way home."* It was a sad, half-human voice trailing off at the last syllable to a spectral wail.

"We gotta get outta here," Buzzy said, panic binding his voice.

"We can't go out the front—that's where she is."

"I am the phasim of Rebah Deal…help me find my way home." It was right outside the cave now. I was terrified, ready to bolt like a frenzied horse.

"Follow me," he hissed. We grabbed our knapsacks, sleeping bags, and lantern. I followed him to the back corner of the chamber and into the craggy opening that led to the rest of the cave. From our spot down in the crag hole we could see the entire room and the yawning entrance. A nearly full moon backlit the opening, spilling weak light around it.

Suddenly she was there, an elephantine figure silhouetted at the cave entrance. "*I am the phasim of Rebah Deal . . . help me find my way home.*" She raised her arms over her head and shrieked a forlorn howl that made us nearly shed our skins.

From outside the cave came another voice. "Levona, if you don't shut the fuck up, *I'm* gonna take your ass home." It was Petunia Wickle. Her flashlight cut the blackness of the room as she stepped around Levona and entered the Telling Cave like she owned it.

"It smells like smoke in here. Hey, who's in here?" she called and shined her light around the room. Flashlightless Levona was a step behind.

Buzzy moved to climb out of the crag, but I held him back.

"What are you doin?" he implored. "This is our lucky night. They might leave if they think it's deserted."

"Just wait a second."

Petunia shined her light on the fire ring and stopped suddenly; Levona rammed into her back. "Quit crowdin on me, Levona, I swear."

"But I can't see nuthin. Why do you get to hold the flashlight anyways? It's my flashlight."

"I get to hold it cause I'm holdin it," Petunia said through clenched teeth. Her reply either confused or satisfied Levona; either way, she didn't respond.

Two other silhouettes appeared at the cave entrance, a tall, big-bellied shadow and a thinner, smaller shape, each with a flashlight. "Where'd them girls get off to?" the smaller one said. His voice was familiar. They entered the cave, the big one carrying a paper bag filled with bottles that clinked every step. The thin one carried two blankets.

"Look, Tilroy, someone was kind enough to leave us a pile a wood. Ain't that nice?"

Tilroy chuckled dumbly. I looked over at Buzzy's fallen face, slumped shoulders—I think we both would have preferred the ghost of Rebah Deal to the flesh and menace of Tilroy Budget.

"Why don't you get the fire goin while I make sure them girls ain't had the pants scared off em," the thin one said.

Tilroy put the bag next to the fire ring and grabbed his sleeve. "Don't you be givin no orders, Skeeter," he hissed.

Skeeter instantly lost a notch of bravado and assumed his proper bearing. "I'm jus sayin we need a fire, is all. Ain't gotta go all mental on me, Til. You can build a fire bettern anybody I know—that's a true fact."

The compliment soothed Tilroy, and he began to assemble a tent of twigs over the few remaining coals. Skeeter sidled over to Petunia, who was standing ten yards from our hiding place. He circled his arms around her and kissed her neck, their flashlights crossed like swords. She giggled, pushed him away, and escaped back to Tilroy. Skeeter ran after her, laughing, leaving Levona to stumble in the darkness over the rocks back to the fire ring. Tilroy had a flicker of flame going in the coals from our fire. Soon the room was bright with light, drawing in Petunia and Levona like moths.

A beer bottle hissed, then another. Petunia spread a blanket by the fire. Levona did the same. Skeeter went immediately to Petunia's blanket and lay down on his side. She frowned at him and sidestepped to Levona's blanket and sat down. "Tilroy, you sit here right by me," she said. Tilroy was putting more wood on the fire and knelt to blow into the core of the flame. Levona was a pillar, unsure what to do. Skeeter started to inch over to Petunia. "You go on and sit now, Levona," she said. Levona moved to sit next to her.

"Not here, you idiot!"

Levona flinched as if slapped and schlumped onto the blanket next to Skeeter, who groaned disapproval. Tilroy got up from the roaring fire pit, clearly proud of his pyrotechnic abilities, and hiked up his jeans, which had begun to sag to the level of an overbooked plumber.

Petunia put her legs out in front of her coquettishly, just like she had seen that girl do in *Flashdance*. Tilroy lumbered over and sat down heavily next to her. He reached into the bag and brought out a beer for Petunia and opened it. "Thank you, Tilroy," she said in her best Jennifer Beals imitation. Petunia leaned into him and put her arm behind his so they crossed. The contact made him jump. Levona waited for Skeeter to offer her a beer, but he just glared straight ahead at the shiny wall. Levona reached for one herself, mumbling about poor manners. There was a minute or so of awkward silence until Petunia said, "I don't think Icky Buckley's ever gonna get his Trans Am fixed."

"That car's a death trap, you ask me," Levona said. "What kinda car you got?"

"Uh, Camaro," Skeeter replied without a hint of enthusiasm.

"Camaro!" Levona exclaimed as if he had just told her he drove the USS *Enterprise*. "My uncle's got one a them. See, I knew we had somethin in common." She inched a little closer to Skeeter. "Is yours one a the ones with the stripe on the side?"

"Uh, no. Mine ain't got no stripe."

"My uncle, he's got the one with the stripe."

Petunia and Tilroy were oblivious to the patter as she took his hand in hers and moved even closer to him, until their legs were touching. Tilroy's mouth was hanging low and his arm was shaking, as if he was holding hands with the ghost of Rebah Deal.

"When'd you get that truck, Tilroy?"

"Month ago. My uncle got a new one an gave my daddy his."

"That's cool. Y'all gonna trick it?"

Tilroy relaxed a bit and nodded. "It's gonna be the shit when we're done."

They fell into another silence until Levona said, "Okay, now we all gotta give the Tellin Cave a secret."

"You don't believe that old fairy tale, do you?" Skeeter said. He was clearly resentful of his blanket partner and in no mood for jocularity. "I thought y'all was jus jokin in the truck."

"Ain't no fairy tale," Levona said. "We all gotta tell else who knows what's gonna happen."

Tilroy, whose confidence had been building with the new truck talk, said, "Y'all know my secret, so I ain't gotta tell nuthin to no cave." He folded his hands behind his head and leaned back on the blanket. He figured bravado in the face of the fifty-year curse would surely get around town.

Levona turned to him, pleading now. "You gotta tell—I tole you in the car. This ain't no time to be foolin with it. Not on no Rebah Deal night."

Tilroy turned to Petunia. "You go first."

She sat straight up on the blanket, perfect posture just like Mr. Paul had taught her.

"Okay, you know I live next door to the Bluelys. Well, me an him did it in the shed behind his house."

Skeeter looked over at her with a mixture of disgust and amusement. "That's fucked-up, girl. The Bluely boy's only twelve."

"Not the boy, you fool. Me an his daddy. Right there in his toolshed while his wife was cookin dinner—that's my secret."

"Did she catch you?" Tilroy asked.

"Mrs. Bluely? Naw, but I started howlin real loud, an Mr. Bluely, he tries to put his hand over my mouth, so I bit him, then he starts howlin, but he surely dint stop or nuthin. I can't believe she dint hear nuthin, but she dint." She paused and looked from Skeeter's open mouth to Levona's smirk to Tilroy's quivering lips and was satisfied her revelation had produced the desired effect. "Your turn, Tilroy."

He gathered back most of his earlier bravado along with a smug smile. "Tole you, I ain't tellin. Y'all already know what I done."

"What's it feel like, then?" Petunia asked and lay down next to him. "You know, killin someone."

Tilroy sniffed and closed one eye, as if paging through his many killing episodes the way folks flipped a jukebox menu. And amid the posturing he stumbled onto a simple truth that he had been puzzling over since that night. He finally understood what he was feeling inside and spoke of it softly, reverently. "It's like you own the universe."

Skeeter was looking over at his friend with a mixture of awe and jealousy. He was getting tired of the way everybody was treating Tilroy now, like he was some badass heavy metal rock star, but he also enjoyed the reflected glory, even from the likes of Levona Stiles. Levona reached for another beer.

"I got me a secret," Skeeter said. "Got me a good one." He went from face to face to ensure he had the group's full attention. Petunia looked bored and Tilroy was off somewhere in his own universe, reveling in his sudden understanding of homicide.

"Go on, tell, Skeeter. Is that your real name? I bet it's a nickname," Levona said.

Petunia leaned over to Tilroy and said, "Let's go over there for some peace." She stood and began to pull him up.

"Uh, yeah, it's a nickname."

"What's your real name then?"

"Lawrence."

"Lawrence Bight. That ain't a bad name. Why they all call you Skeeter?"

"My momma started it on acounta me bein a small baby."

"What's that mean? Skeeter?"

"Mosquito, I guess."

Levona paused to think things through, then burst out laughing. "I get it—Skeeter Bight." She laughed some more until she saw that Skeeter was stone-faced. She choked her cackle into a cough and inched even closer to him to show she didn't think it was a very funny name either, secretly pleased with her ability to puzzle out the shades of nickname giving.

Petunia ignored her and pulled on Tilroy again. This time he got up. He reached in the bag for two more beers and followed her over toward our hiding place in the crag hole.

"What bout my secret?" Skeeter complained. "I ain't tole yet."

"I know all your secrets, Skeeter *Bight*," Petunia dismissed as she laid out the blanket on a filthy old mattress ten feet in front of us. Buzzy and I took a step back into the darkness.

"I gotta tell my secret, y'all know that," Skeeter complained.

"So tell your damn secret, then," Petunia said. She and Tilroy were sitting on the mattress now, leaning against the cave wall. She was so close I could smell her perfume and watched, entranced, as the flame from the fire danced over the contours of her body.

"How long you an Cleo Fink been friends?"

"Me an Cleo been best friends since kids. I played on his hundert-pound team. Blocked for him."

Petunia was even more impressed. Not only was she about to rut with a man killer, but a man killer who hung out with the cool seniors. Kendra and them were gonna completely freak. And with Levona as her witness, they couldn't say a damn thing.

Levona was watching Petunia with one eye and keeping up nervous conversation with Skeeter. "So you gonna tell?" she asked.

"All right but you gotta swear you ain't tellin nobody. Got that?"

"I ain't tellin."

Skeeter seemed satisfied. "You know when someone stole my momma's car last year?"

"Yeah, I remember that."

"Well, it warn't stole. Me an Til wrecked it an made like it got stole. It's in a ditch over to Big Spoon all covered up."

Levona's face squinted up. "What kind a secret is that?"

"That's my secret."

"That ain't no proper secret."

"Is too. You dint know it, did you?"

"It's gotta be bout sex. Like the first time you done it or somethin like that."

"No, it don't."

While Levona and Skeeter argued, Petunia leaned over and kissed Tilroy on the lips. He kissed her back, awkward and hard, like he was trying to strip her lipstick with mouth suction.

"Take it easy," she said and shoved him backward. She leaned forward and kissed him softly. I looked over at Buzzy, whose eyes were cue balls.

"Ain't that right, Petunia?" Levona called over to seek support for her argument with Skeeter.

"Hmmm," Petunia answered onto Tilroy's slavering tongue.

"Skeeter's secret's gotta be bout sex, don't it?"

"Hmmmmmmm."

"Right. Petunia... *Petunia*!"

"What, girl?" Petunia shouted back.

"Skeeter's secret gotta be bout sex, don't it?"

"Right, now will you shut up for once?" she said and went back to Tilroy's quivering, drizzled lips.

"Tole you," she said and laid a hand on Skeeter's leg. Being right seemed to put her in a lascivious mood.

Buzzy and I were focused on the wondrous show on the mattress in front of us—Petunia Wickle and Tilroy Budget locked in a furious embrace. She pushed him back on the mattress and straddled him, pinning his arms above his head.

"You're crazy, girl," he said, losing whatever stickle of confidence was left in him.

"You don't even know," she said and ran her hand through her hair, raised her arms toward the ceiling to stretch, then pulled her T-shirt over her head, revealing a bright white bra one size too small. The edges of the bra were frayed; a safety pin connected a broken strap to the bra body.

Despite its age, the whiteness of Petunia's bra made it look like she was wearing two full moons. She reached behind herself with one hand. The bursting bra came loose and she slowly pulled it away. Her grapefruit breasts jiggled at their newfound freedom. I couldn't tell who was happier: Petunia's breasts or me.

She leaned down to kiss him again, detoured to his neck, and slowly made her way over his big belly. I looked at Buzzy, who gave me two thumbs up. Tilroy's face was shut tight, like he was about to undergo a painful medical procedure.

Petunia was at his crotch now. She unloosened his belt buckle, unzipped his pants, and slid them down. Tilroy was wearing white brief underwear pulled high to his navel and tight across his belly.

"You ain't even hard yet, Tilroy," Petunia said, looking up in frustration.

"You gotta touch it some," he replied, voice coming out as a guttural panic.

She pulled his underwear down and her face disappeared in his crotch, hidden by her long black hair, which draped across his belly. We could see her head bobbing up and down ever so slightly. On the other side of the cave Levona and Skeeter were entwined on the blanket, perilously close to the fire.

After a minute or so, Petunia looked up from his crotch. "It ain't…"

Suddenly Levona screamed. "Ahhhhhhhhhhhhhhhhhhhhhhh-hhhhhhhh!!" The fire, which had died to coals, was flaring now. Once we adjusted to the new light, we realized it wasn't the fire that was blazing; it was Levona's hair. It crackled like burning pine needles, and her screams punctured the cave. Skeeter picked up the blanket and whacked Levona's head to quell the flames.

She rolled on the floor screaming, "Ah! Ah! Ah! Ah! Ah! Ah! Ah! Ah! Ah! Ah! Ah! Ah! Ah! Ah!"

Petunia grabbed her top and rushed over as Skeeter finally extinguished the last of Levona's flames.

"Whud you do to her?" she screamed. Tilroy pulled his underwear back up to his belly button and zipped his pants.

"I dint do nuthin!" Skeeter shouted. "We was jus messin round an she laid back in the fire an her hair starts flamin. I dint do nuthin!"

Levona's screams had quieted, muffled by the blanket that Petunia had wrapped around her head. Tilroy threw wood on the fire for better light. "Way to go, fuckwad," he breathed. "I was jus bout to do her."

"I dint do nuthin!" Skeeter insisted. Petunia knelt to Levona, who was curled in the fetal position on the floor, whimpering in pain. She carefully removed the blanket to inspect her smoldering, nearly hairless head. A wisp of smoke rose from her singed hair as if from a snubbed candle.

"Are you hurt, baby?" Petunia asked.

"Uh, uh, uh, uh, uh."

"We gotta get her to the hospital. Her head's all red an burned up," Petunia said to Tilroy.

"You sure bout that?" he replied. "Looks like a bad sunburn to me. Mostly jus the hair what went."

Petunia stood up and faced him with hands on hips. "We . . . are . . . takin . . . her . . . to . . . the . . . *hospital*," she said with increasing emphasis on each word so that the last came out as a scream.

Tilroy and Skeeter grabbed the other blanket and the remaining beer and hustled out of the cave after Petunia and the whimpering Levona.

"It her fault; she laid in the fire," Skeeter whined to Tilroy at the cave mouth.

"Shut up, fuckwad."

It was the smell that brought everything back. It didn't reach me until they had left the cave and Buzzy and I climbed from the crag hole. The smell of burning hair, acrid and sickly sweet, hung in the air on an inversion of smothered memories.

As I stood and considered the fire, the true and absolute horror of that day came streaming back in a single razor-wire vision. I knew that if I closed my eyes, the sequence of it, like the film loop of a bad dream, would start again.

Buzzy added more wood and we laid out our sleeping bags again. I was dark and silent and brought my knees to my chest, continued to stare into the flames.

"You know, you ain't tole the cave nuthin," he whispered. "You should do that now, fore we forget."

"I don't want to tell the cave anything. I don't even want to sleep here tonight. That smell is gonna make me puke."

"We can go sleep up the tree house then."

"I'd rather just go home. I don't want to be a wimp, but I really think I'm going to puke."

"But you seen what happens when you don't tell. Just tell a little an we'll go."

I shifted on my sleeping bag and gathered up the rememberings. I had kept the truth hidden for so long that the lies were rooted in me like weeds. "My brother wasn't hit by a car like I told you," I said.

"My momma said she heard that," he admitted and looked

down into his hands. "Why ain't you tole the truth?" The fire popped and issued an arching cinder that landed near my foot. It glowed for a moment, then went dark.

"Because the truth is what's making my mom crazy. I guess my dad thinks if we all lie long enough, the lie will eventually become the truth."

"You don't gotta tell if you don't want to. Let's jus forget the Tellin Cave an go home."

But the memory had already shifted forward, and there was no possible way of sending it back. Like water overtopping a dam, it had to alight somewhere. I shook the ghosts out of my head and began.

Chapter 22

THE TELLING

Every Saturday back in Redhill I used to cut the grass. That was my chore, every Saturday." My voice cracked as the sequence of images aligned in their proper order. "I cut the grass." I paused and shifted my legs in the ash. "We had this brand-new riding mower. Used to take me only about twenty minutes to cut it all. I had band practice that day and I was late, but my father said I had to cut the grass before I left.

"I told him I would do it when I got back, but he made me do it then, even though he knew I'd be late for my practice. I could have easily cut it when I got back, but he made me—easily could have cut it after band." I brought my knees up and put my jaw in the space between them. "So I backed the mower out of the garage, filled up the gas tank, and started cutting. Usually when I do it I put the blade on medium and go slow so it cuts everything nice and even. But I was pissed, so I put it on high and floored it. I shouldn't have done it, but I was gonna miss my band practice. I could've cut the grass when I got back, you know. Could have cut it easy." I was suffused with a bitterness and regret that seemed to be corroding me from the inside out. The fire had died a bit, and Buzzy was stirring the coals with a stick. I watched how they danced and pulsed at the attention.

"My mom came out with Josh to weed the garden and plant some stuff. Josh was three then and was into everything. I mean everything. One time Mom even found him curled up asleep in the dryer. He was into absolutely everything. And he was fast, too. Man, you had to watch him or he'd be gone like a shot," I said and paused, remembering how Josh used to race across the lawn toward the street and how my mother finally had to get one of those kiddie harnesses with an extra-long leash to keep him in her sights.

"Anyway, I cut the backyard first. It was all uneven but I didn't even care, I was so late for practice by then. I cut the side yard, then came around the corner to the front faster than I should have, and Josh was digging in the front flower beds with my mom and he just ran out in front of the tractor. Just ran right in front of it. I slammed on the brakes and swerved and just missed him. I mean, I *just* missed him. Mom didn't see any of it, but I was shaking from it all and Josh was just laughing like he was at the circus or something.

"So I get off the tractor and take him over to Mom and tell her that I almost ran over him and I was late for band and that she should keep him off the grass until I was done. I swear I could have killed him if he'd got caught under those blades. I mean, it was that close."

I looked over at Buzzy, who was staring at a spot in the coals.

"It was good you put them brakes on when you did."

"Mom told me she had to finish the weeding, so she got out Josh's harness and put him in it and tied the leash to the bumper of my dad's car, since it was the only thing in the yard to tie him to. She got him his red dump truck to play with and went back to her weeding. And Josh was happy just playing with his truck on the driveway; he probably didn't even know he was tied to the bumper. I started cutting the grass again, only I put the blades on medium and cut it slow like I should. I went back and forth across the front yard, and Josh was playing with his truck in the driveway. You know those tractors, they're so loud when you're on them it's like everything else in the world is silent. Know what I mean?"

"Yeah, I seen em."

"Well I was going back and forth across the front, being really careful this time, and Josh was playing with his red truck, like I said. He was being a good kid like he's supposed to be. Just playing with his truck like a little boy. I cut one way and turned and started cutting the other way, going toward him, and saw that he was standing up now, just standing up holding his truck over his head and watching me. Just standing there holding up the truck. Only as I got closer I could see that it wasn't the truck he was holding; it was the old red gas can I'd left out on the driveway—I'd forgotten to put it back in the garage. He was just standing there looking at me and holding up that red gas can. He must have thought it was water, because he turns it upside down and the gas pours out all over him. He must have thought it was water the way he looked at me...questioning, sort of. Then he starts crying...I guess it must have stung his eyes or something. He was soaked from the gas, just standing there holding the gas can up over his head and crying."

I stopped and looked over at the undulating wall of the cave. The light from the fire and the shadows from the light made the curves and bumps of the wall come alive into seven stern old faces watching my every move. Seven elders sitting in judgment over my telling—all of them nodding with the pulsing fire, as if they understood perfectly but intended to pass judgment nonetheless.

"You don't have to tell me the rest. We can jus go if you want."

But I knew I couldn't stop. I had to get it out of me. "He was holding up that gas can, the dummy, because he thought it might have been water or something. I yelled to Mom, but she couldn't hear because the mower was so loud, and Josh, he just dropped the can like it was some poisoned toy or something, just dropped it right on the driveway. That's when she looked up."

I stopped and swallowed on that Saturday afternoon memory as it rushed in from the edges of my mind. As it is rushing into me now, so many years later.

"You know how when sunlight is really bright sometimes you can't even see flames? Like the sun won't let anything burn brighter than itself."

Buzzy nodded.

"That's what Josh was like. When he dropped the can it sparked and set all that gas on fire. The sun was so bright I couldn't even tell that he was burning at first, except for his hair. His hair just shriveled up like it was being pulled back inside his head. He opened his mouth to scream, but he couldn't. He just looked at me all confused. Mom couldn't see the flames either. Just his hair shriveling and Josh not even crying or anything, just standing there. After a second his clothes caught fire, and that's when the flames came. They shot up in a whoosh about six feet in the air and became like a cocoon around him, and he was still just standing there with his mouth open, just looking at me all puzzled as he burned." I took up Buzzy's stick and pushed the coals around some more.

"Everything moved in slow motion after that. I know I was on him in a second, but it seemed like the faster I ran, the farther away he got. I finally reached him, knocked him down in the grass, and smothered him until the flames went out. My father came out cause he heard my mom screaming. And man, was she screaming. She couldn't even move, just stood there screaming as if she was the one burning. My dad knew it was bad and laid Josh in the backseat of the car and we took off for the hospital. I rode in the back with him the whole way there. And poor Josh wasn't even crying. He was just looking up at me with his face all red and burned and he was shaking all over like the flames had taken all the heat out of him. He was so brave, he didn't even cry. Didn't even cry." I paused and swallowed again to keep my own tears down.

"Josh lived for three days in the hospital; then he died. That's my secret."

We negotiated our way back to the tree house in the nearly full moon. At the great oak we stopped and leaned against the tree under light diffused by the branches. I felt as if my soul, scarred and leaden from lies and bitter truths, had been finally turned loose. It seemed even breathing was easier after the telling.

"I'm gonna sleep up here tonight. You goin home still?" Buzzy asked.

I nodded.

"I'm sorry what happened to your brother, Kevin," he said quietly.

"I'm sorry about your brother too."

"What do you mean? He ain't dead."

"Yeah, but now he's got to figure out how to live with it."

Buzzy didn't say anything. He just looked at me, unblinking.

I continued, "Buzz, sometimes telling's not a bad thing, you know."

"I know," he said. Then after a few seconds, "You sure you don't wanna sleep up here tonight?"

"Naw, I'm going home."

"I'm gonna sleep up here tonight."

"All right, man. Later."

"Later," he said and was halfway up the tree before the echo died in the night.

The moon gave me enough light in which to walk back home. The town was quiet. In the distance I could see 22 Chisold looming iceberglike in the dark. The sky was pilloried in stucco clouds that occasionally blocked the stars. I eased up the front porch steps and opened the screen door. The front door was unlocked and the hallway table lamp was on. It worried me because Pops was always careful about locking down and turning things off at night. On the table under the lamp was a note: *Kevin, I left the door open in case Rebah Deal chases you boys out of the Telling Cave. Please lock the door and turn off the light.—Pops.*

I did both and quieted to the second floor, pausing on every creaking step. I slid into my darkened bedroom. The smell of campfire on my clothes. The smell of burning hair in my head.

Chapter 23

THE AIR AROUND AN EMPTY PEDESTAL

I stayed in bed most of the next day; the tellings pulled at me from so many different directions, I needed time to brood it all out. Finally talking about Josh's death seemed to ease my mind in ways I could not have imagined. It was as if admitting it all opened a pressure valve in my head to bleed off much of the guilt and sorrow I'd been carrying for so many months. Not all of it, but just enough so I could actually imagine a future without the smother of what happened. My telling seemed to give me a new outlook on my prospects, but the revelation that it was Tilroy who killed Mr. Paul chipped at me. I just couldn't understand how someone could turn on a friend so quickly, so viciously. Maybe Tilroy really was crazy. I feigned illness through dinner and took potato soup in my room to further ponder Tilroy and Cleo and the burden Buzzy carried. I fell asleep still pondering.

The following day, Pops had office hours in the morning, so I walked with him from Chisold down Main Street to his clinic across from Biddle's. After a quiet morning of filing and book-keeping, we went over to Hivey's for coffee and conversation. Since Paul's funeral, the town seemed to be in a state of absolute denial, talking awkwardly about feed prices, corn crops, tractor wheels, anything but the horror of Paul Pierce's murder.

Bump, Bobby, Lo, and several others were by the old wood-stove at the back. Grubby Mitchell was standing outside the circle, waiting for an excuse to join the group.

"Who else was Cleo waitin on? I heard Tide an Gators were takin a good look," Bump said, broom in hand, foot up on the seat of a wooden stool.

"Them two, plus Dogs an Michigan, I think," Grubby replied. "Paitsel would know." He took two tentative steps into the group and sat down quickly before anyone could object.

At the mention of Paitsel, everyone went quiet. It was generally acknowledged that he had "discovered" Cleo Fink when the boy had distinguished himself in a snowball fight at the 1978 Christmas tree lighting ceremony in downtown Medgar. Four inches of early snow hit the Saturday after Thanksgiving and Paitsel spotted Cleo whipping snowballs at the heads of other boys with dangerous speed and uncommon accuracy. Paitsel saw it as his duty to be vigilant in spotting middle school football and baseball talent. "Fink boy can throw a snowball," he said to the boys at the back of Hivey's a few days after the tree lighting. "Gonna call Ned for a look."

Ned Pike, the high school's athletic director; basketball, football, and baseball coach; and history, social studies, and gym teacher drove with him and Jesper to Fink's Hollow on a warming Saturday. The Finks didn't have a football in the hollow (or many balls of any kind), so Ned brought his own. He tossed it to Cleo, who caught it easily but held it in his hands like an unfamiliar rock. His throw back was wobbly but blew through Ned's open hands, hitting him square in the chest. He smiled at Paitsel and rubbed at the pain.

Ned came out to the hollow every Saturday thereafter to work with Cleo on passing mechanics, arm strength, and footwork. Two years later, by eighth grade, Cleo was practicing with Ned's varsity squad and set the Kentucky single-season high school passing record his freshman year. Sophomore year brought another record and the Class 1A state championship; by junior year he had broken every passing and scoring record on the Kentucky books.

"He was never serious bout Michigan," Bump sniffed. "Wrong offense for him is what Paitsel says."

"Do we know if he's gonna sign with Notre Dame? Once the others hear he got an offer, theys all gonna come courtin," Lo said. "I think signin early is a mistake."

Bump cut in. "I think it's decided. Esmer was in yesterday—man was cock walkin. 'My granson's goin to Notre Dame,' he tells me. Showed me the letter an everthin. I think he's gonna sign."

"Already did," said Jesper, who had just come in the front door. "Talked to Esmer this morning. Folks from the Indiana papers comin down tomorra. Lexington, Louisville too."

I wanted to blurt out what I knew about Cleo, about Mr. Paul, but held my tongue out of respect for Buzzy. The obvious pain he was feeling from carrying the secret around these past weeks was palpable, and I didn't want to add to his burden.

We filled our coffee cups, then went over to the back stove.

Pops cleared his throat and the men all looked over at once, then went silent in the face of complicit guilt and assumed reproach. Bump began to sweep at the immaculate floor; Jesper started working at a piece of breakfast bacon that had lodged in his teeth; Bobby Clinch tested the play of the blade on his utility knife.

"Morning, boys," Pops said in a tone as ordinary as the circumstances allowed. There were muted "mornin's" back, then awkward silence. "Sounds like Cleo has signed with the Irish. That's a piece of good news for this town."

"That's right," said Jesper. "We was jus talkin bout that. Great day for this town, I say." Nods all around.

"Great day," Bump agreed.

"Certainly is," Bobby Clinch said. "Banner day for Medgar."

"'Tis," someone else added.

"I think we should all plan a big ole party for him," Pops said. "Lord knows we need a reason to celebrate, don't you think?"

"Celebration is a great idea," Jesper replied with unnecessary enthusiasm. He was just happy not to be talking about the Paul Pierce tragedy.

"We're gonna need someone to honcho the project. Someone with planning experience...Jesper, I think you should head up the planning committee," Pops said with a slight smile.

Jesper puffed up, nodded, and leaned back, self-satisfied. "Well, I did help Paitsel discover the boy, after all."

"That you did. You have an eye for football talent."

"Well, it ain't an easy thing," he admitted. "Lots a kids got it raw. Did I ever tell you boys bout when I first saw Cleo?"

"Tell it again, Jesper," someone said.

"It's a fine story."

"Tis a good story. Go on an tell, Jesp."

"Well, it was a terribly cold November that year..."

Pops put his hand on the back of my neck and steered me toward the door. "That'll keep em busy for the next few weeks," he whispered.

"Okay if I walk over to Buzzy's house? I want to see what's going on with his brother."

"Just be back in time for supper." Pops turned and stepped into the street for the cross over to his office. I raced down Green Street and up the trail to the tree house. It was empty, so I walked down the hill and into Fink's Hollow, which was abuzz with activity. A white van with *WGZ TV12* emblazoned on the side was parked in the circle. Cleo was standing on the Giggins Hoo porch flanked by his parents and a toothless, smiling Esmer Fink. A TV lady had thrust a microphone in Cleo's face as he described the college selection process in copious detail. Clumps of Finks and other kin were watching from the gravel driveway. Buzzy was off to the side, picking up stones and throwing them at a plastic pail.

"Heard about Cleo and Notre Dame," I whispered, but didn't know what else to say.

"Yep, he finally got what he wanted. Been his dream to play there, an ain't nuthin gonna stop him."

"Did you tell him you know?"

A flash of anger came to him. "Don't be talkin bout that round here. Don't want none a that trouble." He picked up another stone, went to throw it, then dropped it on the driveway. "Come on," he said, and ran up the hill to the barn. We went inside and settled on two hay bales by the half-open sliding wood door.

"Man, I jus don't know what to do. I jus can't screw this up for him."

"Buzzy, you gotta tell him you know. You gotta try to get him to go to the sheriff on his own."

"You think he's gonna confess with Notre Dame wantin him? No fuckin way, Kevin. He ain't confessin to nothin."

"From what you said, he didn't do anything."

"It don't matter. Him an his friends is what caused it."

"I thought you said Tilroy did it."

"He did, but Tilroy warn't even with them when they walked into town. It was Cleo, Donnie, and Wiltry. With me followin them."

"Who are they?"

"Football friends."

"Where was Tilroy?"

"Tilroy was visitin Mr. Paul when them three went by an saw him an Mr. Paul sittin in Miss Janey's waitin room. Place was closed, but Tilroy was there, sittin down blubbering to Mr. Paul bout somethin, and Mr. Paul was holdin his hand. So Donnie starts to laugh an says somethin like, 'The old fag tryin to teach the young fag his bidness.' An he bangs open the door and starts teasin Tilroy an Mr. Paul, callin them all kinds a queer names. Then Tilroy jumps up an says he ain't no faggot, then starts callin Mr. Paul a fudgepacker an homo an jus goes apeshit on him. Jus starts hittin him hard. An Mr. Paul runs to the back of the place, but Tilroy follows him and pushes him out the back door. You know the rest."

"So Cleo never hit Mr. Paul or teased Tilroy."

Buzzy shook his head.

"Well, you gotta tell him you know everything. You can't be carrying this around with you. It's killing you. Plus he didn't do anything."

"I jus don't know what to do. I jus don't. I know it's wrong not to tell, but he's my brother." His voice broke.

The barn door slid open and Cleo walked in. "What are you homos doin in here?" he said and smiled.

Buzzy suddenly went cold. "We're talkin bout what happened to Mr. Paul. An don't ever be callin us homos again."

The smile left Cleo's face. "Easy, Buzz, it's jus talk is all. Hey, I put a plug in for you on TV. Thanked you for being my faithful trainin partner." There was an awkward silence before Cleo spoke again. "So what about Mr. Paul?"

"We're talkin bout who done him."

"Heard the Company's men done him on acounta him tryin to shut Mr. Boyd down."

Buzzy looked up from the floor hard into Cleo. "That ain't what happened, Cle."

Cleo regarded him. "How do you know what happened?"

"Because I seen it."

"What did you see?"

"Everthin."

"What's everthin? What did you see?"

"I seen you an Donnie an Wiltry go into Miss Janey's an I seen Tilroy beatin on Mr. Paul in the alley an I seen you standin there watchin while he kicked his teeth in."

Cleo's Adam's apple bobbed on a hard swallow. He sat down slowly on a hay bale and put his head into his hands. "Ohhhh, man," he said. "I think I'm gonna puke." He stood up, took two quick steps to the door, then sat back down quickly. He got up again and walked unsteadily into the dark and threw up. He retched for a minute, stood in the darkness for a minute more, then came back to the hay bales relatively composed.

"Who you tole this to?"

"Jus Kevin. I tole the sheriff I dint see nothing."

"Who you tole it to?"

"Nobody," I said.

Cleo assessed the situation for a few seconds, then sat down on the third hay bale and motioned us in, huddle-like. "Okay, here's the plan. If the sheriff comes back to you, don't say nothin more. Hear? Don't change your story in any way. We got two-a-days startin August first. Don't want nothin distractin me."

"You think you can jus quarterback this all away?" Buzzy said. "Life don't work like that. Folks is gonna find out. Tilroy's already tole people."

Cleo cursed to himself. "Who'd he tell?"

"Petunia an them. Cle, you gotta go to the sheriff," Buzzy implored. "You didn't do nothing! It was all Tilroy."

"Buzzy's right," I said. "It's all going to come out, and when it does you'll look guilty. You go to the sheriff now, you'll look like you did nothing wrong."

Cleo thought for a moment, then shook his head; his face went dark. "I worked too hard to get where I got, an I ain't throwin it all away cause Tilroy beat up some old fag."

"He wasn't just some old fag," I said, anger boiling inside me.

Cleo stood up now and pointed menacingly at Buzzy. "I ain't goin to the sheriff an you don't say no word to no one. You hear?" He poked Buzzy hard in the chest.

"But you gotta go see the sheriff, Cle. I can't be carryin this around."

He came up close to Buzzy and grabbed his collar. "Listen, you little shit, you fuck my ride up I'm gonna beat your ass so badly it'll make what Tilroy done look like a fuckin birthday party. You got that?"

Buzzy nodded. A tear came down each cheek.

"What if I tell the sheriff?" I whispered. "You going to beat me too?" A curious calm had come over me as I faced up to this much larger boy, knowing that I had rightness on my side. It gave me a bravery I'd never felt before and made the embarrassment of a beating at the hands of Cleo seem irrelevant.

He brought his nose to mine. "I will kick your fuckin ass all the way back to Redfuck, Indiana, or wherever the fuck you're from."

Normally such a confrontation would leave me shaking, but for some strange reason I wasn't scared. "Fuck...you!" I said calmly, looking squarely into his eyes.

He flinched as if slapped, then pushed me hard. I fell back across the hay bale and hit my head sharply on the plank floor, seeing stars. Buzzy lunged at Cleo, who simply grabbed him one-handed by the throat and pushed him back across the other hay bale so that we were lying next to each other, staring at the barn ceiling. He stood over us and glared.

"Fuck you, Cleo," Buzzy said through tears.

"You remember what I said, boy." He shot out of the barn, finger still pointing.

Tears were flowing freely down Buzzy's face now, and he made no attempt to hide them. "Fuck you, Cleo," he said as a whisper.

"I'm not going to tell, Buzzy. Unless you want me to."

He wrapped his arms around his chest, holding himself so tightly it looked like he was trying to cling to the remains of an older brother who had suddenly shape-shifted into something unrecognizable. He seemed to be clinging to the old reality because this new bend of things left little for him to grasp, left no one for him to look up to. He just kept staring at the beams in the barn ceiling and at the air in between and at the floating dust specks in the air, caught for us by the sword of light slashing through a dislodged plank high on the barn wall.

Chapter 24

JUKES HOLLOW

The key to packing for the Tramp, if rain is likely, is to seal your clothes in ziplock bags. Keeps em dry and compressed. Last thing you want up there is wet clothing."

The remnant of a slow-moving hurricane had dropped four days of heavy rain on eastern Kentucky, with more forecast over the next week, and we were prepping for the marginal weather.

I was giddy at the idea of hiking up into the mountains with Pops and living off the land mountain man–style. Almost two months in the cotton embrace of 22 Chisold Street combined with finally telling the truth about Josh had broken a sluice of dammed-up emotion in me. I was actually starting to feel a new way of being, as if I had finally hit on the hint of a trail leading out from the dark forest.

Pops placed his folded boxer shorts in a two-gallon ziplock bag, pushed out the air, and sealed the bag. He tossed it to me.

"Looks like freeze-dried underwear," I said and laughed.

"You laugh now, but when I'm high and dry and you're soaking wet for not taking an old man's advice, I'll be the one laughing."

"You mean you wouldn't lend me your freeze-dried boxers?"

"Nope."

"You are a nasty old coot."

He pulled out five or six bags and gave them to me. "Go ahead and try it. Works a charm."

I took the bags and did as he suggested, taking my clothes out of the backpack and repacking them compressed and sealed in the ziplock bags. The new technique allowed the same amount of clothes in half as much space.

"We can use the rest of your pack space for my mash supply," he said with a chuckle when he saw my progress. He picked up the old aluminum-framed canvas backpack and assessed its condition. "This was your mom's, you know. I first took her on the Tramp when she was about ten. She used this every year until college. After that, tramping with her daddy stopped being quite so appealing. She found other interests, like tramping with your daddy." He chuckled. "Held up pretty well, I think."

The pack was faded green and smelled of mushrooms and mold. Mom's earlier use of it gave the rucksack a special meaning for me. It was as if I could see her as a teen, hiking up the mountain with Pops, the many pockets filled with live-off-the-land gear, the straps wearing runnels into her shoulders from the weight of it all. I imagined them sitting side by side at the lake in a silence brought by simpler times, white-and-red fishing bobs floating on the water, shifting with the light breeze. "She became quite good at setting snares, you know," Pops finally said, as if he had secretly read my thoughts.

"Can you teach me how to do that?"

"Most certainly. It's a skill that will serve you well as a starving college student."

I smiled and unpacked my rucksack again to try and make

even more space. Pops sat in the chair in the corner of my room chewing on his pipe end and watching me with a wistful smile.

"You haven't mentioned Buzzy much lately. What's he been up to?"

"I'm worried about him," I admitted. "He hasn't been up to the tree house for two weeks, and when I walked down to his house they said they hadn't seen him around."

"He's probably off on a tramp of his own. We holler kids do enjoy our tramps."

But I knew better. I knew that the secret Buzzy was carrying had millstoned him. "When I asked his grandfather where he was, he didn't even seem to care. He just said, 'He'll turn up . . . always does.' I really think he may have run away or something. The whole Mr. Paul thing has him really upset."

Pops chewed on his pipe end, thinking. After a while he stood and said, "Let's finish up packing and get a good night's sleep."

We brought all of his camping equipment down from the attic into the living room—sleeping bags, fishing gear, tent, cooking utensils, hammocks—and laid it out along with our packs. Audy Rae was in the kitchen with Mom preparing food for our journey.

"We should be able to make it to Glaston in two days. It's only about twelve miles a day, but it's a hard twelve. When I was a kid . . ." His voice trailed and I looked up at him. His eyes were fixed intently on the doorway. I turned. Mom was standing in the arch, cupping her elbows with the opposite hands. The edges of her mouth turned up almost imperceptibly.

"Annie, you remember your first Tramp?"

The upturned edges became more pronounced. "I do," as a whisper.

"You caught the grandaddy of muskies, as I recall—must have weighed as much as you."

She smiled in full now. "I remember."

"You had it on the line for, what, about a half hour? You just were *not* gonna give up, no matter what shenanigans it tried. You had more fight in you than that dang fish—and muskie are known fighters."

She stayed in the doorway, smiling faintly, saying nothing, just watching me as I checked supplies.

"We'll bring two weeks of coffee and cooking spices," Pops continued as he loaded up a box full of fixings. "And just enough food to get us up there. Then we are on our own."

"What if we can't find any food?"

"Then we go hungry. Maybe eat bugs and roots."

"Have you ever had to do that?"

"Never. Food is abundant up there. I doubt we'll have much trouble, but I do make a tasty grub-and-dandelion salad."

I laughed, then realized he wasn't joking.

As we stowed all the gear in the packs, I could feel her gaze on me and on her old rucksack. I didn't look up for fear of pulling apart the moment, but instead watched her from the corners as she went to a time when love was unconditional, loss was unknown, and she had more fight in her than a monster fish.

The storm slashed and the wind howled and I fell asleep to horizontal rain pelting the old house like a thousand miniature drummers working out a beat on the siding. I woke just as the first flush of morning began to fill the dark spaces of my room. There was a gray form on the floor in the middle of the rug. It looked as if Pops had brought the packs upstairs and covered them in a blanket. It made no sense. I put both feet on the floor to investigate. The boards creaked and the packs moved. I pulled off the blanket.

It was Buzzy Fink, soaking wet and filthy and looking as if he hadn't eaten in a week. A purple-and-yellow bruise spread from his left eye down to his cheek—a half-healed scab on his lower lip. He was shivering.

"What are you doing here?" I threw the blanket back to him. He yawned, sat up, and wrapped it around himself. "How did you get in?"

"This is Medgar. Nobody locks doors here."

"Pops does, every night."

"Well, he dint last night."

"Where have you been? I've been looking all over the mountains for you."

"Tellin Cave. Then Tilroy came, so I left."

"Tilroy? Did he see you?"

"Yup. Saw me as I ran outta there."

"Why didn't you just sleep at the tree house?"

"That's the first place Cleo would look."

"You mean Tilroy?"

Buzzy shook his head. "I ain't afraid a Tilroy; it's Cleo who's after me. Tole everyone in the holler that I'm jealous a him so I accused him a beatin up Mr. Paul."

"Is that how you got those bruises?"

He nodded but didn't look at me. "Cle caught me in the barn an jus pounded on me. I got away an tole him I was goin to the sheriff. Then I grabbed some stuff an jus lit."

"Did you tell the sheriff?"

"Naw, I jus said that cause the beatin."

"Look, me and Pops are leaving this morning to go up to that lake he likes. Up in the mountains. You gotta come with us."

"I don't know, man. I may jus head south. Maybe go to Florida."

"That's bullshit. You can't just run away like that."

"Ain't got a better option."

"Come with us. We'll be gone two weeks. All this crap will blow over by then."

"I don't know. I think I better jus head out." He stood up and collected his saturated pack. There was a light tap at the door; it opened slowly. Pops was standing with a steaming coffee cup.

"Looks like you've been living rough, son," he said softly.

Buzzy looked out the window at the coming blue sky and the first glint of sun in a week coloring the valley. "It ain't rough, really. Jus a little wet."

Pops studied Buzzy for a few moments and took a sip of coffee. "Why don't we all go down to the kitchen and drink something warm?"

We followed him down the steps and into the kitchen, where he had a pot of coffee at the ready. He poured two cups, refilled his, and joined us at the table. Buzzy fidgeted with his drink. Pops said nothing, just watched him intently with his wise old eyes. More silence and fidgeting.

Finally Buzzy spoke. "He dint do nuthin."

"Tell me what you saw, son."

"You gotta swear you ain't gonna tell no one."

"Buzzy, I can't make that promise. A man has been beaten to death."

"I'll deny everthin."

"Lying is no way to go through life. I'd rather you not tell me, then."

Buzzy looked into his coffee and rubbed the side of the cup. Pops continued to fix into him, his forehead creases deepening as the silence stretched seconds to minutes.

"It was Tilroy what done it," Buzzy said without looking up from the black coffee.

"What?" Pops sat back, as if pushed there by the rapid acceleration of a car. "Tilroy's just a kid. He and Paul were friends. You sure it was Tilroy?"

Buzzy nodded quickly. "Cleo was there too . . . an some others. He tried to stop it all. I seen him try to stop it." He was pleading to his cup now. "It ain't like theys gonna take away his ride for this. He tried to stop it all."

Pops raised his chin slowly on the understanding of things. He rubbed his neck with his hand. "And that's why you've been staying up in the mountains this past week. So you wouldn't have to deal with any of this at home."

"I think Buzzy should come on the Tramp with us. Give all this time to blow over," I interjected.

Pops put a hand up to quiet me and just kept looking at Buzzy. "First thing we need to do is call your parents to let them know you're okay. Then we'll see what our options are."

Pops excused himself, went into his den, and closed the door. Five minutes later he came out and sat back down at the table. "Your mom was starting to worry over you."

"Did you tell her bout Cleo?"

Pops shook his head. "We need to think this all through first. One thing is for sure: you are gonna have to talk to Sheriff Binner."

Buzzy finally looked up from his drink and grimaced as if the brew was poisoning him. He nodded and whispered, "I know."

"But maybe not right away," Pops said. "Who else knows about this?"

"Petunia Wickle, Skeeter Bight, Levona Stiles. Tilroy's been big talkin round town, actin like a regular man-killer."

"Boy might as well put an ad in the newspaper. Sheriff Binner is competent law. I suspect he'll have Tilroy in for a talk in the next few days." Pops thought for a moment more. "Let's all head out on the Tramp, relax up at Glaston, and reevaluate when we return. I think this whole business will come out while we are gone. Secrets this big don't stay kept."

I smiled at Buzzy. He managed a slight grin.

"Let's go put your clothes in the dryer," I said. "You don't want wet clothes up there."

We threw our packs into the back of Pops' truck and piled into the cab. Pops pulled out to Chisold and turned onto Watford, then Main. "Need to get a couple pounds of fatback from Hivey's. When you're tramping, nothing beats crispy fatback with strong coffee in the morning."

"Hey, I thought we were living off the land," I said with mock disappointment.

"We are. I just fry it up for the smell. Call it redneck aromatherapy." He pulled into an empty parking spot in front of Hivey's. Inside, Jesper, Lo, Bobby Clinch, and Grubby Mitchell were at first coffee by the woodstove. Pops went to the freezer and pulled out a white-wrapped parcel of fatback, then walked toward them. "Morning, ladies."

There were replies all around.

"We was jus arguin bout you, Arthur. An now you walk in to settle it," Lo said.

"Make it quick, boys. We are off on the Tramp and two hours behind schedule."

Jesper spoke first. "Heard you sold Jukes to Bubba for two hundred thousand dollars cash money."

"Who told you that?"

"Bubba's permit man, Wall Fratz, was up Glassville applyin to widen Jukes Holler Road so they can get the big stuff up there."

Pops froze and looked at Jesper hard. His scowl unnerved the man. "I'm only sayin what Clarice tole Alison."

"What part of Jukes did he apply for? The front part or the hollow part?"

"Not sure. I can ask Alison to ask Clarice."

"I'd appreciate that. And to settle the argument, I'm not selling Jukes for two hundred or two million. I will see you gentlemen week after next." He nodded, turned, and walked down the aisle to the cash register. At the counter he patted his pants pocket. "Kevin, I left my wallet in the truck. Can you run out and get it? It's on the dash."

I hurried out the front just as a blue late-model Ford pickup jerked and heaved into the parking spot next to Pops.

"Don't be pumpin the brakes when you're turnin. Just push down on em easy." It was Sen Budget instructing the newly licensed Tilroy in the finer points of pickup-truck driving. They exited the cab. Tilroy seemed to have grown a few inches in the last weeks. He moved easily to the sidewalk, chin in the air, chest pushed out in front of him. A slight grin as if he was sporting expensive new clothes. He looked over at me. "What are you doin here, faggot?" His father guffawed and kept walking to the door.

"Buzzy and I are going up to Glaston Lake with my grandfather." I scowled inside myself at the solicitous tone, but the last thing I wanted was a run-in with crazy Tilroy. I opened Pops' truck door and grabbed his wallet from the dash. At the mention of Buzzy Fink, Tilroy pulled up and peered anxiously into the front window. His face went white. "Daddy, you go on in. I'm gonna check the oil."

Sen grunted and opened the door. I followed him inside. He brushed past Pops without a word. "Tilroy's outside," I whispered to Buzzy as Pops paid for the fatback. Buzzy shrugged and we followed Pops out into the late morning. The sidewalk and parking lot were empty of people. Buzzy and I scanned the area for Tilroy, but he was nowhere around. "Let's go, boys. Ten cents holding up a dollar."

We scrambled into the cab and Pops pulled out into the empty street and turned toward Route 32. As we passed the side of the building, we saw Tilroy crouched behind a Dumpster watching us. "That is one messed-up mutha," Buzzy said under his breath.

"Does he know you know?"

Pops looked over at us. "Who are you talking about?"

"Tilroy. I saw him outside, and as soon as I mentioned Buzzy he got all freaked and went and hid."

"He don't know that I know. Less Cleo tole him, but I doubt he'd do that. Cle's gonna pretend Tilroy never even existed. You watch."

"Why is Tilroy so freaked-out by you?"

Buzzy went silent.

We rode that way out to Route 32. As we pulled up to the stop sign, Cleo Fink, on his daily road-work routine, jogged in front of the truck. He waved at Pops, then pulled up suddenly when he saw his brother in the cab. "Oh, man," Buzzy said and slunk in his seat. Cleo stood at the bumper, hands on hips, staring in at Buzzy.

Pops put his head out the window. "Cle, you're holding up our Tramp. You're in danger of getting run over."

He stepped to the passenger side and Pops waved as we passed. Buzzy tried to slide even lower as Cleo locked on him. He stood there for a moment more, watching us pull away, then turned and headed back toward town.

Buzzy stayed slunked, staring into the dashboard for a mile down 32. Pops looked over at him. "It's all gonna pass, son."

We were quiet for the next few miles until Pops spoke. "We're going to take the old Jukes Hollow Road up the hollow, then park. The trailhead is on top of the plateau above Jukes. We follow that up over Bridger Mountain, across Six Hollow Ridge to Sadler Mountain, or what's left of it after Bubba Boyd got to it, then down Prettyman Hollow to the back of Old Blue National Forest. From there things get interesting. Blue is one of the last truly wild places left in the Appalachians, and help is far away, so we'll all need to keep our wits about us." He looked over at Buzzy and me with a seldom-seen seriousness. "There's an old game trail that runs up Prettyman Hollow to Irish Ridge. We follow the Irish Ridge Trail for about eight miles, then camp. Tomorrow we'll get down to the Blackball River and follow that for another eight miles or so, then cross over for the trail up to the summit of Old Blue. Glaston is on the other side of the mountain. It's hard to get to, and that's what makes it so special."

"Aint there an old loggin road up the back way? My grandaddy's been up there," Buzzy said, taking back his usual demeanor.

"There is. You gotta drive forty miles into Blue, then walk the last three to get to the lake. No disrespect to your grandaddy, but that way is a cheat. If you're gonna tramp properly, it requires you to strap forty pounds of gear to your back and walk for at least two days in the woods."

After a few miles Pops began to slow down, even though there was no detectable break in the thick forest. Suddenly an old road materialized, like a secret passageway, from the solid block of trees and undergrowth. Thick kudzu hung down from heavy limbs; hip-high thistle and horseweed labored to meet it in the middle. Pops stopped and turned slowly into the dark tunnel. It took a few seconds to adjust to the dim. A heavy canopy of leaves and overgrowth blocked out most of the light, leaving the road in perpetual twilight. The forest floor was peopled with huge ferns that sent their arms invitingly up and out. The road was hard-packed dirt with traces of old gravel and rock in the wheel ruts. Monumental trees, the largest I'd ever seen, covered in thick green moss on one side.

We followed the road in the murky light for about a mile until the hills began to close in and the pitch of the track pointed up, taking us onto the shoulder of a steep, rocky rise. We kept on the narrow course for a half mile more along the north shoulder of a sheer mountain. Knee-high loosestrife and jimson scraped the undercarriage; overhanging pipevine slapped the side-view mirror. Buzzy took his arm off the windowsill. Pops said that he was going to get a man up to clear the road next spring.

We drove across a ridge overlooking Beaver Hollow. I recognized Tilroy's house and the barn in the back where Sen Budget shot the family mule.

"I didn't know you lived near the Budgets growing up,"

"A few hollows over, thank goodness," Pops said with a half smile.

We descended into a heavily wooded valley of even larger

trees—old, majestic oaks, sycamores, and hickories—then forded a swollen stream that sometime past had been bridged, for the rottings of a wood foundation fell about both sides. The road flattened, following the valley floor deeper into the hollow. The mountain closed in until we were squeezed in a narrow cut no more than fifty feet across. Up ahead a huge sycamore had fallen across the road. "Looks like our Tramp is gonna start a few miles early," Pops said and pulled right up to the tree, shut off the engine, and exited the truck. We followed. The constant rain had given the woods steaming, rain-forest air. We pulled our packs out of the back and affixed them. Pops took up an old burled and polished walking stick with intricate carvings on the handle. I asked him about it and he held it up to the light and smiled, regarding the stick as if fond reminiscences were stored somewhere in the wood. "My father took this out of the core of a lightning-struck tree. The heat from the lightning made it as strong as steel. Gave it to me on my thirteenth birthday a few years before he died. Now I use it to beat back bears." He laughed and swung it like a baseball bat.

We followed the huge tree trunk to where we could slip under and over the spread of upper branches, then walked back up to the old road to begin the Tramp. Pops first, me, then Buzzy single file in one of the wheel ruts. The road curved around the steep side of a hill, then straightened out as the valley narrowed even more. A creek rushed down the middle, overflowing from the recent rains. As we rounded another sharp turn, two bus-size boulders bulged into either side of the road, leaving a gap just wide enough for a single car. "When I was a kid, I named these two boulders Ahab and Moby Dick." He reached over and gave Ahab an affectionate pat. "They are my sentries."

Once we were through Ahab and Moby Dick, the mountain walls gave way and the valley opened to a wide half-hourglass hollow, three hundred yards across and five hundred yards deep. A sheer rock wall eighty feet high at the far end with a full waterfall cascading to a broad pool on a rise. From there the water spilled down the hill and became the rushing creek we had crossed minutes before. The fields had gone fallow years ago, and saplings grew in them like giant corn.

The road hugged the edge of the valley and ended abruptly at a cul-de-sac of ruins. Straight ahead, a jumble of old logs from an ancient cabin splayed like pick-up sticks. To my right, a single cinder-block chimney competed with young trees for prominence. A thick oak door, weathered gray and long off its hinges, rested sideways against a rusted woodstove. Up the hill, several more foundations watched us through the underbrush.

But to my left, on the end of the slight ledge that led down to the fields and the creek, was a perfectly ordered stone-and-log cabin, preserved like a slip-covered antique.

It was small. A low roof sloped up slightly from a porch that ran along the entire front. Four thick knotted wood posts, polished from the years, held the porch ceiling upright. The door was solid and dark and cracked in places where the wood grain weakened—bright, modern lockage as out of place as chrome on a Model T. Two large windows on either side of the door traded sunlight for warmth in winter.

"Who lives here?" I asked.

"Nobody now," Pops said. We stepped onto the porch, took off our packs, and laid them down with a thud. Some early fallen leaves collected in the corner. Pops pulled keys from his pocket and fiddled them until the correct one untangled. "This is where

I was born," he said and turned the key in the lock. "This is Jukes Hollow." He pushed the door open and I stepped into another time.

The first room was the kitchen: sixties-era plates, cups, flatware, took dust in an oak cupboard against the far wall. Pine floor planks announced our every step. To my left, a large cast-iron cookstove sat in perfect repair waiting for a chance to fire again. The floor in front of it worn a half inch into itself. A small table with six chairs was pushed near the stove as if to covet its remaining warmth.

In the adjoining living room, a smaller woodstove sat against the wall in the space where most families now put televisions. Two chairs, separated by a simple table, faced the stove as if entertainment had been sought in the way that wood burns. The interior walls were whitewashed log, the thin paint giving the grain extra emphasis. An old stuffed bobcat head hung on the wall over an empty shelf.

At the back of the cabin were two bedrooms. The first was tiny, even smaller than my room at Chisold Street. I couldn't imagine three boys sharing such a space. A miniature window cut into the logs let in a slash of the world. Triple bunk beds hewn from local oak attached to the walls like shelves.

The other bedroom was twice its size. It was empty except for a huge four-poster bed, stripped of its mattress. The wood was honey-colored hickory; its posts, like small trees, almost touched the ceiling. The headboard was intricately carved with a strong woman sidesaddle on a majestic plumed horse held by an attending young man. At the footboard, two broadswords crossed over a flying bird. An eagle or maybe a hawk.

"My father's brother made that bed for him as a wedding present," Pops said, standing behind me. "Copied the carving from a woodcut of Queen Victoria's seal that a traveling stove salesman gave him. My mother wasn't an ostentatious woman, but she loved that bed." We stood there for a moment, regarding the workmanship. "Come on, I want to show you boys something," he said.

We walked outside to the fields. Pops had cut the saplings back ten feet from the cabin and maintained a path through them to the stream. On the right were the ruins of an old barn; left was a collection of abandoned farm equipment—plows, harnesses, some hand tools—under a collapsed shed. A tractor wheel with three trees growing through it.

We stopped at a crumbled stone fence that long ago demarcated the crops from the cows. It was just noon and the sun had attained Brice Mountain and was shining brightly into us. With the sunlight and the waterfall and the steep rock walls, Jukes Hollow was one of the most beautiful places I had ever seen.

Pops put his foot up on a rock. "You know, my brothers and I couldn't wait to leave this place. The Company offered free housing in town, so just about everyone left. Only my mother stayed—died in that cabin seven years ago."

"Where is everybody now?" Buzzy asked.

"Spread out all over. Hersh and Katie Mae have four children; three are married with kids of their own. Patsy lives in Florida, Glenda near Pittsburgh, and Dibley lives in Lexington, runs an auto-glass business."

"What about the fourth?" I asked.

"Den? We lost him in the Vietnam War," Pops answered. "Let's see, Jeb's kids are all over the place too. He had seven and I couldn't even begin to track them. Except Dealy, who runs the farm over by Big Spoon. I'll take you there sometime—he has a boy about your age."

We paused for a minute as packets of memories flooded back to him.

"Come on," he finally said and stepped over the pile of stones. We continued down toward the creek, where thick flat rocks had been placed in the water for crossing purposes. Once on the other side, we walked toward the waterfall, where the ground rose slightly, bracing the sides of the pool, which gathered the water before running it down through the rest of the hollow. The waterfall cooled the air and the constant rushing sound made it easy to think.

Thirty yards back from the pool, at the start of the Brice Mountain incline, was a tiny cemetery. Twenty wooden posts outlined its authority, their connecting fence pieces long since lost. The grass in the cemetery was low-cut and weed-free, as if they knew not to bespoil such hallowed ground. The front headstones, overtaken by rich moss, jutted from the earth at odd angles. The slope of the hill made the other markers seem like seatbacks in a movie theater. Despite the lack of fencing, Pops and I walked through what used to be the entrance gate. Buzzy stayed a few feet outside the perimeter watching us.

I drifted among the headstones, working my way up the small hill, reading my history in the granite chiselings. Pops had told me all the stories, and finally, I was attaching something tangible to my ancestors.

George Cranmore Peebles, my great-great-great-grandfather, who first staked claim to Jukes Hollow with his wife, Carlotta, and his brother Morley in 1849, had left Pembroke in Wales two years earlier and after a stint on the docks in Baltimore, set off for the west country. They were buried in the near corner of the grave-yard, marked by three flat pieces of jagged slate pounded into the ground, the crude inscriptions long since taken by the elements.

Sadie Peebles Kinneycut Johnson Jar Bean, one of George and Carlotta's five children, who outlived four husbands (none of whom rated burial in Jukes Hollow) and eight children and finally died at eighty-three of an infected thumb she received from a dogwood splinter while chopping wood with a hand ax.

Bradley Wilson Peebles, Sadie's little brother, who fought for the Confederacy in the last years of the war at the tender age of fourteen because some home guardsmen thought him fit and snatched poor Bradley from the hollow despite Carlotta's attempts to hide him in the smokehouse. He returned at sixteen with killing eyes and sent himself off west without a word. He reappeared in Jukes Hollow eighteen years later, a German wife and a young son in tow. The boy had been born in a soddy during a scrap with a handful of renegade Kiowas. They named him Franklin Cranmore Peebles—Pops' grandfather.

In the row behind was the stone of Oriel Peebles, Pops' father. I lingered by his headstone and remembered the stories Pops had told me of my great-grandfather's efforts to organize the mines and his murder at the hands of the Company's detectives, on order from Bubba Boyd's father. Next to him was Pops' mother. A simple headstone as befit her nature:

EMILY LITTLETON PEEBLES
BORN AUGUST 26, 1894, DIED JUNE 1, 1978

Next to her was a small marker; light-green lichen obliterated some of the lettering.

HELEN BRAN   EEBLES, BORN JAN 3, 914
DIED OF CONSUM FEB ARY 18, 1917

KATHER LI   EBLES, BOR   AY 22, 18
DIED MAY 23, 1918

WINNEFRED   STON PEEBLES BO JANU 7, 1921
DI APRI 1, 1924

BEL   DAUGHTERS OF EMIL AN ORIEL PEEBL

Pops was at the top edge of the cemetery, kneeling down, pulling young weeds from around a headstone, talking to someone in the air. I walked up behind him quietly.

"I brought Kevin up, like I said I would," he whispered between the waterfall sounds. "I wanted to wait until the time was right."

A crack of twig announced my presence. He stood with a handful of chickweed, letting most of it fall absently into the wind. The marker by his feet was clean and moss-free, the ground around it trim and perfect, like the yard at Chisold Street.

SARAH WINTHORPE PEEBLES
BORN APRIL 19, 1920
DIED IN LABOR DECEMBER 1, 1949

A VOICE LESS LOUD, THROUGH ITS JOYS AND FEARS

Pops knelt again and pulled at nonexistent weeds.

"She loved this place," he said, looking up at the ridge above us where the trees were holding summer green. "Loved the way the waterfall had an answer for everything." He stood and turned toward it. "We used to picnic on the other side there." He pointed to a flat spot by the water where a magnolia shaded that part of the pool. "I must have played there a thousand times when I was growing up and thought nothing of it. Then she comes and makes it the most important place in the universe to me."

We stood on the hill, Pops and me, looking over Jukes Hollow: the creek, the fields, the cabin, the rocks. I saw in my mind how it must have looked then. The barn and the other houses crowded around the circle. Children raised in a pack, infused with laughter and purpose and a desire to rise above.

And how it was now, empty and unused, the lives and laughter long moved on, leaving just remembrances and the roots attached to them. I started to understand why Pops could never sell Jukes Hollow. The idea of Bubba Boyd and his tractors filling everything in with Bridger Mountain overburden infuriated me. "How could they even think of destroying this place? I just don't get it."

"Men like Bubba Boyd think the earth owes them a living. They take whatever wealth they can from the mountains and move on. I actually feel sorry for him, I really do. He can't for the life of him see the simple beauty in a waterfall or understand the importance of history and place. If I have one hope for you, Kevin, it's that you never become one of those men."

The mountains have their own memories.

Rooted in marrow rock, hard set to the crests, fused in the folds and braes where the white water races. Their earliest recollections manifested to primordial, wild and feral, then became tamed with the people. Cheek Mountain and the Pierce boys grappling and shredding each other over Docey Eberhild—she chose Strom, which made Quillar flee west; Goat Leg Hollow and Wilmer Gilvens, two months off a coffin ship, sinking cabin piers into her flat shoulder and the cabin shaping up week to week with a front-porch view of Indian Head; Corbin Hollow and Bertum Skill courting, then marrying a half-wild Melugeon girl named Hetta Goins despite banishment threats from his father; Sadler Mountain and Nevis Jensen teaching his son Jesper how to read the dullings for turkey sign on an autumn dawn. They all remember Bobby Clinch and the orphan bear cub he raised to adult on saved meat scraps and deer killings; and years later when Bobby came upon it over by Indian Head, the bear on hinds, taking in man scent, head cocked in recognition. All these old memories rooted in the earth, now pulled out and piled in cairns of spoil or pushed down the hollows to level the land.

Chapter 25

THE TWICE-TOOK MOUNTAINS

We ate cold ham sandwiches slathered with Audy Rae's home-made mustard by the waterfall where Pops and Sarah Winthorpe used to picnic. "When I brought her up here, all my kin could do was gawp. It was like an alien goddess had landed in Jukes. She had this flowing chestnut hair halfway down her back." He shook his head. "They had never seen anyone so beautiful. But they soon found out that her true beauty came from here," he said and tapped at my heart.

Pops smiled at the recollection and folded the plastic sandwich baggies and put them in his pack and stood and slung it on his shoulders. Buzzy and I did the same. We were at the base of the sheer rock wall that ran the western end of the hollow. We walked over to the circle of ruins where the wall face eased and allowed for climbing.

"We're gonna have to climb up to get to the trailhead. My brothers and I never got around to cutting stairs into the rock. There are some well-placed vines as ropes if needed. Follow me rock for rock, boys." He reached and pulled himself up to the first rock, then put his foot into a crevice and pushed up to the next toehold, then again to the next one. I followed and Buzzy came after. About halfway up, ledges jutted out, which made the ascent much easier, like a set of steep basement steps.

Near the top he took his pack off and threw it over the edge of the wall, then jumped up and grabbed the root of a sapling that had grown out of the rock. He pulled himself up and over the edge. After a minute, Buzzy and I reached the final ledge. I looked down over the hollow, at Pops' birth cabin, over at the cemetery, and back to Ahab and Moby Dick, faithfully guarding the entrance to Jukes Hollow. It was a hard life then, but the simple dignity with which they lived it made me proud. We took off our packs, threw them up to the ledge, then scrambled over the rimrock.

The bracing creek ran straight down the middle of a bowl-shaped valley that ascended to a peak eight hundred feet above us. A thin dirt and rock trail at creek side snaked up the mountain. We affixed our packs and followed Pops on the trail to the rushing water sounds. The pack was heavy on the incline and the straps dug into my shoulders. I could hear Buzzy huffing behind me. Pops' gait was long and certain, and soon he was a hundred feet ahead, navigating the awkward course and jutting rocks with an ease and grace I didn't know was in him. I looked back at Buzzy, red-faced and sweating. He was focused on his feet, watching one go in front of the other. "We gotta catch up." I breathed and expanded my step to narrow the difference. Buzzy grunted and matched me. Pops had paused on a flat rock overlooking a three-stage waterfall, leaning on his walking stick, drinking from his canteen.

"This rock here marks the top of Jukes. It's about a hundred seventy acres up either side of this bowl and fifty acres below the waterfall where the cabin is. Everything above us is Bridger Mountain, which is now owned by the Company. Their plan is to blow the top off the mountain and push everything into Jukes. That ain't gonna happen, least as long as I have a breath in me." He paused and looked over the beautiful hollow of his childhood. "My brother and I own Jukes together; when one of us goes, the other owns it outright. Hersh would sell out in a Memphis down-beat. Quite an incentive to stay healthy, don't you think?"

"How come you can't give your share to Mom?"

"I can if Hersh dies first. Like I said, the last living brother owns Jukes. Until then he and I have to agree on everything. That's just the way my mother wanted it. Guess she figured deci-sions about the place were best made by the folks who grew up here. Wise woman." He turned and headed up the trail, his walk-ing stick working like a third leg, pushing off the dirt and stones to propel him forward. Soon he was a distant speck on the trail face.

Buzzy and I rested a moment more, then clambered after him. He continued to shrink in the distance despite our efforts to keep up. "Man, he's haulin ass."

"Come on," I urged and double-timed it, grabbing the back of my pack to hoist the weight off my shoulders. We scampered up the steep trail, hunched over, me staring at my feet as they made like two horses in a neck-and-neck race. After a half hour, we reached the ridgetop. Pops was sitting under an ash tree with his hiking hat low over his face, sleeping. We threw our packs down, huffing and blowing.

"Lord help us, it's as if you boys have never hiked up a moun-tain before," he said without looking out from under his hat. We collapsed next to our packs, against the wide tree trunk. I looked over at Buzzy, who was breathing out of an O-shaped mouth.

"Why are you going so fast, Pops?"

"When you see Glaston, you'll know. Besides, I gotta show up you striplings, don't I?" He stood and sniffed at the mountain air, hands on hips. We were at the top of Six Hollow Ridge, which ran across the crest of Beaver, Pine, Jukes, Slow, and what was left of Corbin and Wilmer Hollows. We picked up our packs and headed north on an old logging road that ran the ridgetop. The route was truck wide and accorded easy passage across the rolling shoulder of mountain, giving good time for the next three miles over a series of minor hillocks and shallow dints. The trees were lush and large, with holly, mountain laurel, and dogwood filling in the forest floor. As we came over a gentle rise, the trees ended abruptly. What lay before us was a scene of unimaginable devastation.

⌇

We stood on the edge of a flat, gray moonscape two miles across and dotted with pooling water of a color unknown to the natural order of things—orange, red, purple, bright green. It looked like a rainbow had fallen out of the sky and each hue had gathered into its own pond. Pops stopped and leaned on his walking stick.

"We are at what used to be the top of Corbin Hollow." Pops pointed to a slight indentation in the landscape between two gray plateaus. "They blew the tops off Indian Head on the left here and Sadler there in the middle and pushed all of it into Corbin. When they were done, they covered the whole area with that green spray-grass stuff that will grow anywhere. Last summer, when I hiked through here, grass was growing everywhere, even on the rock. It looked like a massive Chia Pet."

Now it was nothing but gray and a hint of straw where the spray grass had died. "None of it took," he added, though he didn't need to.

From our vantage point two hundred feet above it all, we could see across the dead land to the far tree line. From here to there were three long flattop plateaus where Indian Head, Sadler, and Cheek Mountains had been. Between them, where the Company pushed the overburden, were shallow valleys filled up with the rock and soil taken from the mountains. A series of roads rutted over the flat tops and through the valley fill. Rock piles twenty feet high dotted the plateaus in between the rainbow ponds. And on the middle table, checked by a wide oval berm, was a lake brimming with black coal sludge—not normal black, but a darker, ominous alchemy of black that seemed to have been contrived by the devil himself.

The mine operation was completely barren of trees, grass, or any vegetation. The huge oaks and rich green of Jukes and the surrounding mountains made this place seem like a wholly different planet, one that had its normal color bled out.

In the valley beyond the far trees, I recognized the twisting road that ran through the middle of the Mitchell farm. The fields were empty now, and I traced the line up to the cul-de-sac. Two of the barns had been carted away, leaving flat concrete. The third was a pile of beams and boards splayed like pick-up sticks. The old Mitchell house was nothing but a single sidewall, chimney rising above the fist of brick like a middle finger raised to rebuke

The trail from the woods disappeared, so we picked our way over rocks and gray mud down to a roadway of gravel and more mud. Huge tire tracks were filled with rainbow water from the recent rains. We followed the rutted way that ran on the valley fill around the curve of the first flattop. The road rose and merged with the plateau that had once been Indian Head. We walked among the rock piles—rock that had been hidden underground for millennia—now exposed and stacked like displaced corpses.

Pops' face was a twist of anger. "Indian Head was not a large mountain, but notable for a huge rock formation at its summit. When you saw it from the south, it looked exactly like an Indian warrior in profile." He turned halfway around to orient himself to the history. "It was about sixty feet high and just an amazing sight—you could see it for miles. Folks around here called the Indian face Red Cloud because the rocks had a reddish tint to them, but the legend goes back hundreds of years to the Shawnee who lived in these mountains before the white man. It was said that any brave who could scale the face would be able to steal some of the warrior spirit's bravery and would be protected by the gods in battle. No one ever achieved it and many braves died trying, until a white hunter, captured by the Shawnee and sentenced to a torturous death by the Shawnee chief Blackfish, negotiated a reprieve if he could scale it. He did and was adopted by Blackfish himself as his son. The Shawnee called him Sheltowee, but we know him as Daniel Boone.

"Since then, generations of Missi County boys tried to prove their courage climbing up the face of Red Cloud—only thirteen actually made it."

"Did you ever climb it?"

Pops smiled. "I did. But not until my third try." He looked up at a place in the air where Red Cloud had been. "That's a story for another day. Let's get on down the road." Pops moved out with dispatch, his pace quickening to escape the tortured landscape. We were able to keep pace on the flat land, down into a slight depression that was once Corbin Hollow. On the side of the track was the rusted boom of an abandoned dragline, its broken cable curled like a waiting snake.

The road thrust upward sharply to the next plateau. Pops' pace gave him separation and he achieved the top a minute before us. He stood there on the edge and surveyed the rubble as Buzzy and I scrambled up the slope. "This used to be Sadler Mountain. In front of us was Wilmer Hollow, where the Kracken family lived." He waved his hand at the filled-in valley below us. "Sold it all to the Company for thirty-five thousand dollars and moved to a trailer park somewhere in central Florida." He shook his head at the inequity of the math.

"Kevin, I told you about the Sadler Mountain War, and, Buzzy, I know your grandfather has told you about it. My father and your grandfather led the efforts to unionize the mines in the thirties. Then Bubba Boyd's father had my dad killed and your grandfather led a revolt against the Company. They were life-long friends, my dad and your grandfather. He and about thirty miners holed up on this mountain for three months, launching a series of guerrilla raids against the Company. The Boyds imported 'peace officers,' who were nothing more than hired guns, and sent twenty up to root the miners out. Not a single one came back. Then they sent up sixty to try and flush em out; they retreated after a day. Your grandfather was a handful as a guerrilla fighter. He and his Sadler Mountain boys brought the mines to a standstill. Finally, Washington, D.C., sent down the federal marshals to get everything running again. The union prevailed, and life for the miners started getting better after that, thanks to your great-grandfather, Kevin, and Buzzy's grandfather. They were true men—something for you both to live up to."

"My grandaddy tole me stories. I always thought it was him tellin porky pies."

"You need to pay attention to your grandfather and show him the respect he's earned. Those stories he tells you are all true."

"Yes, sir," Buzzy said, chastened.

We walked up the fifteen-foot berm to the top of the slurry pond. It was the size of two football fields end to end. The first few inches of water were clear, casing the obsidian ooze like window glaze. And below it, the infinite black maw of slurry, murky and foul, as if everything malevolent in Medgar was spawn of this disconsolate brew. We stood on the edge, silently watching the span of black lap the berm top. Buzzy took up a softball rock and tossed it into the muck. It hung in the air for a moment, then hit the surface with a dull plonk, disappearing under the effluent. The lake surface smoothed itself, removing all evidence of disorder.

"Let's get off this dump and into the trees. We can pick up the trail over that way." Pops pointed with his walking stick and moved out. The top of the Sadler Mountain ruins were criss-crossed with ruts and berms, and it was a difficult hike to the edge of the trees. "It's an old game trail that leads down into Prettyman Hollow, so it's gonna be tough to spot."

"What about that third mountain? What happened there?" I asked.

Pops looked sadly over to the gray scar that was once Cheek Mountain. "That's where Paul Pierce grew up. Now you know why he tried so hard to shut Bubba Boyd down."

"Why did he sell to Mr. Boyd in the first place?"

"He didn't. Years ago his grandaddy sold the mineral rights on Cheek Mountain to William Beecher Boyd. Folks didn't think much of it since coal was mined underground. But the law also allows companies with mineral rights to kick off the surface owners and dig at the coal from the top. So Bubba moved on in and just took the mountain. Paul had no legal way to stop him."

"How much did Mr. Paul's grandaddy sell the rights for?"

"Four hundred and seventy-five dollars."

The dust and rocks from the dig had spilled into the forest, creating a collar around the mine that was caught somewhere between death and verdant life. We walked along the edge of the clearing, trying to scout the trail, trees and undergrowth yellow and dying as if a cancer was trying to invade the forest.

Pops paused at the edge of the Sadler Mountain remains. "I've been in these mountains for sixty years, and it's all a foreign country to me now. I don't recognize any of this anymore. I'm guessing we go in here." He pushed off the edge of the plateau, down a steep gravel embankment to the beginning of the forest. First the yellow-and-gray-dusted mountain laurel toiling through the overburden, then a few dying pines, a line of oaks and poplars, stripped of leaves. Farther in, the gravel gave way to the forest floor, but the undergrowth was still yellowed and dying. We hiked through the stand of struggling trees, deeper into the forest until we crossed the old road that had once led up to the top of Sadler Mountain.

Up ahead was a cemetery of twenty or so headstones. The marble and sandstone markers were fairly new, but all of the lettering had been etched away. It looked like a tombstone store had set out samples for prospective diers. I paused and stood in front of the stones. Buzzy came up next to me. "Is that creepy or what… bunch a tombstones with no writin on em. It's like the family never even existed or nuthin."

Pops had kept walking but turned and noticed us looking over the stones. He walked back and stood with us. "This is the Prettyman family plot."

"How come none of the headstones have writing on them? It just seems really weird."

"Coal dust has a high sulfur content. When they blast up the mountain, it all settles on everything. Then it rains and becomes sulfuric acid and erodes things like headstones."

Pops and Buzzy moved on ahead, but I stood there for a few moments more, looking over the blank headstones and thinking of the Jukes Hollow markers, which carried my history on them; thinking of the people and the place that was being systematically dug up, hauled off, eroded away. It was as if Bubba Boyd had taken the mountains and now he wanted to take all the memories.

Chapter 26

NIGHT VISITOR

⌇

I caught up with Pops and Buzzy just as they found the old trail down the side of Sadler Mountain into Prettyman Hollow. We followed the trail for about a mile, then took a right at what Pops said used to be a rushing creek. It was now a trickle of fetid brown metallic sludge, discoloring the rocks like a giant swath of burnt sienna paint. The trail crossed what was left of the creek and followed a shoulder that ran away from the broken earth. Pops paused at a large rock on the side of the trail. "This marks the entrance to Old Blue National Forest... one of the last truly wild places east of the Mississippi."

"I'm glad we're away from there," I said to no one in particular. "They've ruined everything."

"I thought it was important for you boys to see that," Pops replied and started up the trail. The land before us was lush again, with hills that pushed up from green valleys, some with immense rock cliffs, some with granite knobs dotting the foliage. "We follow this trail up to Irish Ridge, stay on the ridge for about eight miles, and camp up there tonight. There's a nice protected spot in the rocks. It's my usual stopping point for the Tramp."

The afternoon was getting on, so we picked up the pace. We hiked for an hour down another hollow, then up to Irish Ridge. The ridge ran southeast to northwest into the heart of the national forest. Occasionally we broke out onto a treeless patch with views that went into forever. The far mountains faded to a deeper green all the way to the horizon, which merged with one of the bluest skies I had ever seen. Finally, up ahead in the sweep of evening, we saw a formation of car-size boulders strewn in a semicircle. Smaller rocks formed a fire pit in the middle. We took our packs off and leaned them against the big rocks. Next to the fire circle was a neatly stacked pile of wood for a fire.

"Someone left us some wood."

"It's a courtesy pile," Pops said and passed me his canteen. "One of the unwritten laws of the mountain. Every time you break camp, leave a woodpile for the next guy. If you've ever come into a camp in the cold dark, it's a welcome thing."

"But what if other people don't do that? It's not really fair unless everybody is doing a courtesy pile."

"Well, somebody's gotta be first, don't you think? Just imagine what would happen if we all left a place a little better than we found it?"

"My grandaddy says that too," Buzzy piped up.

"Your grandfather has the right perspective on life, Buzzy. You boys go on and set up the tent while I get a fire going."

We laid the tent out on the only piece of flat, clear ground. At Buzzy's suggestion we piled up pine needles for bedding and staked the tent on top of them. The fire was crackling to life and Pops began unpacking utensils and food for dinner.

"Man, I'm beat," I whispered to Buzzy. "I've never hiked like that in my life."

"Your Pops goes at it. I think he wanted to show us up."

"It wasn't hard," I said and laughed.

The camp was on the highest part of the ridge, rocky and thin of trees as exposure over time had worn away the dirt and most of the vegetation. What remained were weathered white pines, gnarled and twisted, clinging to the stony soil with determination.

The hot August sun was making its way to the far west; Buzzy and I climbed up the largest of the boulders so we could look out over the mountains. We picked up some broken rock pieces and threw them one by one as far as we could down the ridge side, listening to the sound they made as they pinged off trees or flushed last fall's leaves.

I turned to him. "You know what we should do for the next two weeks?"

"What?"

"Just live."

He looked at me, interested but skeptical. "I ain't plannin on dyin up here."

"Yeah, but you are planning on thinking. Let's just live without thinking about anything. Put all this bullshit with Cleo and Josh out of our minds."

Buzzy looked back out to the sun-basted mountains. We were silent for a time. Finally he said, "You can see a little piece a Glaston Lake from here." He pointed to a sliver of blue in the shadows between two mountaintops. It looked far.

Before I could answer, the smell of cooking hamburgers hit us both. The dull hunger we had been feeling flared on the aroma of the grilled meat. We looked at each other, smiled, and raced back to camp.

Pops had three huge hamburgers sizzling on a griddle next to a pot of Audy Rae's special molasses beans. "Thought you boys got et by a bear." He flipped a burger to the sound of popping and spitting grease. We sat on rocks around the fire eating the burgers and beans with no ketchup or mustard. I never knew that a simple hamburger could taste so good.

We cleaned up from dinner, washing pots and dishes in a spring a few hundred feet down the ridge side. Pops tied our food bag to a rope and slung it over a branch outside the rock circle. We turned in soon after sunset, and within minutes Pops was snoring lightly. Buzzy and I lay on our sleeping bags, staring at the tent ceiling and listening to the syncopation of Pops' breathing and matching it to our own.

I bolted awake instantly on the sound. Heavy footsteps and the sharp snap of a twig. Buzzy was upright next to me, eyes white and wide. We both looked over at Pops, who was snoring contentedly.

"What was that?" he hissed. I shook my head. More footsteps. Buzzy reached under his sleeping bag and pulled out the crossbow pistol, already loaded and cocked. The steps came closer. I nudged Pops, but he just grunted and rolled on his side. Two more steps toward the tent, another twig snap. A three-quarter moon was washing the inside of the tent with diffused light, and as the intruder came closer, his bulk obscured the moon and cast a shadow over us. Buzzy clicked the safety off the crossbow and raised it to the tent door, hand shaking. I nudged Pops' shoulder to roust him awake, but all I got was sleep talk. The shadow lingered for a moment, then moved swiftly away, making no attempt at stealth.

We stayed upright, motionless, listening to the sound of retreating footsteps bothering the night. Soon it was quiet again except for a few crickets and Pops' light breathing.

"What the fuck was that?" I hissed. "Was it a bear?"

"Warn't no bear," Buzzy replied.

"How do you know?

"I don't know. But I don't think those were bear footsteps. Sounded like boots to me."

"Who would be up here this time of night? Maybe a hiker or somebody."

Buzzy kept looking at the zippered flap of the tent. "Maybe."

We sat up for another hour not saying a word, just listening to the night sounds in the woods—the hooting of an owl, the hissing of a distant cougar, crickets. After a while we lay back on top of our sleeping bags and eventually found restless sleep.

⌇

"Likely a bear," Pops said, seeming unconcerned about our camp intruder. "He probably smelled our food bag and wanted a taste. Most of the bears up here are harmless; there's plenty for them to eat. So as long as you don't startle a mother with cubs, they'll give you a wide berth." He was cutting thin strips of fatback into the skillet. "You boys go get canteen water to boil, then scout some wood for a courtesy pile. Let's leave it bigger than we found it."

We walked to the edge of the clearing and down the ridge into the forest toward the spring. "You think Pops is right about the bear?"

"I got no idea, but I don't know which'd be worse, a bear or some creepy mountain man stalkin us."

"Whatever it was, I don't want to be meeting it again. Sooner we get out of here the better."

We made it down to the spring, which spewed out of two rocks pushed together against the ridge face. It ran to a shallow pool ringed in mud. In the soft ground near the water was a clear, fresh boot print. Buzzy saw it first. "Look at this. You see it? Tole you it warn't no bear."

The boot print was so clear we could read the make and size—Timberland, eleven. "It could be an old one," I offered. Buzzy said nothing. I filled the canteens and we dragged fallen branches back into camp for the courtesy pile. "Pops, we saw a man's footprint in the mud down by the spring. Buzzy doesn't think it was a bear last night. He thinks it could have been a man."

"Well, this is a popular camping spot, what with the spring and the protection of the boulders." He turned a piece of fatback with a fork. "Could've been a hiker or a poacher." His confidence gave me comfort. If Pops, with all his wisdom, experience, and courage, wasn't concerned, then neither was I.

We wolfed instant oatmeal and coffee and a few strips of the fatback, then packed up the tent, overfilled the courtesy pile, and broke camp, careful to haul out all our trash. It was eight thirty and the sky was bright blue, with a few billowing clouds to the south. "We've got thirteen hard miles to do today if we're going to make Glaston Lake by nightfall. Kevin, why don't you lead us?"

"Do I get the walking stick?" I put out my hand and smiled.

He picked it up and appraised it with obvious affection. "This is one you have to earn, son." He turned his palm up in an "after you" motion, and I took off down the trail, Buzzy behind me, Pops bringing up the rear.

We followed the trail for another few miles across the ridgetop, then down into a beautiful wooded valley, stopping halfway in to snack at the Pancakes, an outcropping of four flat table-size rocks nature had stacked on each other.

The trail took us to the edge of a raging river, mud infused and swollen to flood from the weeks of rain. The jet roar of white water as it crashed down a thirty-foot cliff to rocks below.

We stood on the bank, watching the powerful torrent throw itself over the edge. "This is the Blackball River," Pops said, as if reading my mind. "Very dangerous water, especially now. There's a footbridge about eight miles up for crossing." We followed the trail riverside for most of the afternoon, past screaming rapids at first, then miles of lazy curves, until the trail ended abruptly at the bank, then continued ninety feet across the other side, the rope tatterings of the old footbridge streaming into the water like abandoned fishing lines.

Pops stood on the edge, hands on hips. "This is an unhappy complication." We looked up and down the stream for a narrowing or a fallen tree to help us cross, but there was none. "All this water's coming off Glaston—unlikely it'll let up anytime soon. Looks like we're gonna have to get wet."

"Yahoo! I could use a swim," I said with mock levity.

Pops took his pack off and dug into it. "Kevin, I appreciate the humor, but this is a dangerous situation. This river is full of boulders and undercuts that can suck you down and not spit you back for days. Frankly, I've half a mind to turn back rather than risk it."

"Sorry, Pops," I said sheepishly. It was the first time he had ever admonished me, and it stung.

He put his hand on my shoulder and gave me a thin smile. "We're fifteen miles into the wilderness with no chance of help. Don't be sorry; be vigilant."

Just then, the carcass of a drowned deer raced past us as if to punctuate Pops' warning. Its head was submerged, its belly down, with hind legs pointing to the sky. It looked like an outsize duck diving for fish. We watched it pass and continue down the creek, turning belly up on the turbulent edge of an eddy. It circled, as if two-stepping with the current, then disappeared under the surface. We all stared at the space where the dead animal had been.

"Let's not be that deer," Pops said.

Chapter 27

THE CROSSING

⎯⎯⎯⎯

Buzzy and I shook off our packs and Pops brought out a long measure of nylon cord. "We're gonna work this just like a clothesline with a pulley on each end—only the pulleys are us." He unfurled the rope and tied the two ends together with a square knot, testing it twice. He tied a loop in the middle, then put it over his head and under his arms.

"I'm gonna swim across with my end of the rope; then we'll work this loop back clothesline-style. Send the packs over one at a time, then the first boy puts the loop under his arms and swims it while we hold the ends and feed him across. The last boy loops in and swims while we two pull him as fast as we can from the other side. You got that?"

We nodded solemnly and moved upstream about a hundred feet. I looped the rope around a boulder.

"Good thinking, Kevin. How else can we cut our risk in this operation?"

I thought for a moment. "Don't fight the current so much. Swim diagonally with it."

"That's exactly correct. What else?"

"Swim like you got prahanas bitin at your ass," Buzzy said to break the tension. Even Pops laughed at that.

"It'll be easier for us because you'll be on the other side pulling," I offered. "We just can't get loose of the rope."

"Under no circumstances can you get loose of the rope. At all costs, don't get loose of the rope."

Pops took off his hiking boots and shirt and put them in the top of his pack. We did the same. He stepped off the bank, letting out a yell about the cold water. The current took him immediately ten yards downstream. He quickly recovered and cut across the water with powerful strokes.

The current kept pushing him downstream, but with each stroke he made good headway. He was three-quarters across just as the rope lost the last of its play. He reached up and grabbed an overhanging limb and pulled himself half out of the water, then jungle-gymmed to the far bank. He scrambled onto the shore, dog-shook the water off, then walked back to the crossing point. "Go on and send the packs over," he shouted above the racing-water sounds.

Buzzy picked up Pops' pack. "This sucker ain't gonna float. Weighs a frickin ton." He tied the rope to the aluminum frame.

"Wait just a second." I opened the pack and pulled out the cooking supplies and Pops' clothes, which were encased in extra-large plastic ziplock bags. I opened the first just a crack and blew air into the top. It expanded like a balloon. I sealed it and did the same with the four other bags and repacked everything, barely fitting it all into the space. "Great thinking, Kevin," Pops shouted. Buzzy eased the pack into the maelstrom. It went under for a moment, then bobbed on the top. I held the rope, feeding it as Pops pulled the pack across quickly. He grabbed it from the river and shook the water off. I pumped up the clothes bags in our packs. Buzzy tied each to the rope and Pops pulled them one by one to the other side.

"You want me to go first?" Buzzy asked.

"I think I should, since I'm lighter. I'm gonna need you holding that rope hard. When you get in, bring the line with you and we'll pull you across, like Pops said. The current will swing you most of the way, I think."

Buzzy nodded. "All right, let's go." I put the loop over my head and secured it under my arms. Buzzy braced himself against a rock. I stepped off the bank into cold river water.

The force of the current immediately knocked my feet out from under me. I regained footing and moved off the sandy bottom into the deep water. The rush of it pushed me downstream until the rope tightened. Buzzy braced against the pull and fed the line to Pops, who was pulling hard and fast. I swam as best I could, but most of my progress was due to him.

I was halfway across when I heard Buzzy yell above the din. "Tree comin!" I looked upstream and saw a huge tree stump with a ten-foot root spread, half submerged and bearing down on me from fifty yards away. Buzzy hesitated for a moment, then took a running dive into the water. The rope went slack and Pops turned, slung it over his shoulder, and pushed away from the bank like a draft horse. I reached the overhanging tree and grabbed the branch, slipping the loop off my shoulders. Buzzy was still in the middle, swimming hard, but the giant stump was nearly on him. I scrambled up the bank, grabbed the rope, and pulled with Pops.

Buzzy's head kept bobbing in and out of the water as he tried to swim and watch the stump at once. As it came near, he flipped over to fend it off with his feet. The stump parried and the sharp roots turned to him. Pops and I heaved once more and pulled him clear just as the stump rushed past. A few more pulls and he was up on the bank, on hands and knees, heaving for air. Pops and I collapsed on the ground.

We stayed catching our breath for a few more minutes. Finally, Pops stood. "Buzzy, that was quick thinking. No way we could have held on if that stump had hit." He walked over and put a hand on his back. "You okay, son?"

Buzzy nodded and coughed.

"We all best get on the trail," Pops said. "The hardest part of the hike is still to come." We put on dry clothes and affixed the wet packs to our backs. The woods were in the first brush of evening as Pops took off up the trail.

"You saved my ass!" I said to Buzzy. "Thanks."

"You tole me this was gonna be a vacation. That was no fuckin vacation."

"Look, man, from here on out it's gonna be great. Pops said Glaston Lake is unbelievable."

"Then let's jus get our asses there." A tired smile flashed the gap in his two front teeth.

We hiked a few hundred yards through the trees, then paused at the base of a huge mountain. Its foundation shot up sharply from the valley, as if it had been driven out of the earth by some cataclysm deep in the core. Its sides were thick with pine and oak and ash that caressed the rise like a thick green beard. And rocks. Strewn rock bowling balls, beach balls, VW Bugs, sedans, trucks, trailers, houses, that all seemed to have been tossed casually from the granite top to alight at the pleasure of gravity. I could see a twisting murmur of trail drawn brown on the green and gray, snaking the face like a scar.

"This is Old Blue, one of the highest mountains in Kentucky and the hardest part of the hike. Three miles of uphill switchbacks, but once you see the lake, you'll know it was worth it." We stood with our packs, looking up the long, steep climb. "Buzzy, why don't you lead this last leg?"

The trail wound back and forth up the base of the mountain. Buzzy grabbed the straps of his pack, leaned forward, and pulled it higher on his back for leverage. I was three steps behind him, and Pops was following close after. We traversed the slope of the hill, then across the face of the next mountain, then back on Old Blue. Buzzy was huffing, I was sweating, even Pops was red-faced. "The good news is we've got this downhill on the way back," he said between breaths. After two more switchbacks he called for Buzzy to rest. Buzzy stopped at the elbow of the trail and bent over with hands on his knees. I did the same, while Pops leaned on his walking stick. The sun had sunk below the mountaintop, and it was cool in the shade. Despite that we were sweating with effort.

"I reckon we're two hours out with about four hours of light left, so we need to keep the pace. Once we're on top, it's all downhill to the lake. Buzz, let's take a quick rest every third switchback."

Buzzy nodded, took a deep breath like he was diving into a pool, and started up the trail. Pops and I followed like lemmings, back and forth up the steep slope.

We paused by a spring that Pops said was clear to drink and cupped our hands to catch the water. It was cold and flinty.

Pops dug into his pack and pulled out three oranges, throwing one to each of us. "How did Grandma ever get up here?" I asked, orange juice and pulp running down my chin.

Pops laughed. "What are you talking about? I struggled to keep up with her."

"Yeah, but weren't you carrying all the gear?" I spat an orange seed.

Pops spat a seed and shook his head. "She carried her share. More than, if you factor it by body weight. She was a thin girl but strong."

"My grandma's thin too," Buzzy said, spitting three seeds at once. "But I doubt she could get up this mountain."

"Think we'll have orange trees here when we come back next year?"

"Now, that would just make it perfect, wouldn't it?" Pops said. "Pick our own oranges as we slog up this mountain." We laughed at the notion.

After another half hour of switchbacks and rests, the top of the mountain came into view through the trees. "We're almost there," I said, as much to urge myself as to encourage Buzzy, who was slowing noticeably.

"I see it," he said. "Let's keep goin til we hit the top." It was past time for a break, but there was no argument from Pops or me. The switchbacks began to get shorter as the mountain narrowed near the summit; however, with each turn the trail became steeper, until, finally, we were crawling up a forty-five-degree angle, trying for footholds and handholds to give us purchase. Fifty feet from the summit our pace quickened to a mad scramble over rocks and dirt—gnarled roots propelling us to the apogee of Old Blue.

Buzzy was first over the top. He threw his pack off and stood in the sunshine, hands on knees, catching his breath. "Mutha."

I grabbed a rock on the summit lip and pushed off another

into the light. I sloughed my pack next to his and joined him gasp for gasp. We both looked back at Pops, whose head top was just above the lip. In an easy movement he was up and over, standing next to us.

The summit of Old Blue was stocked with ragged juniper, windswept and stunted by the altitude, sneaking up through the rock and the moss. Behind us, through the thin brush, I could see the land we had just traversed, the rain-swollen river snaking the valley and the long signature of Irish Ridge. In the distance, the wound of mountaintop removal looked like a cancer on otherwise exquisite skin. Next to it, the few twinkling lights of Medgar.

We turned, and before us, in a valley bounded by Old Blue, Little Big Top, and Harker Mountain, was the most beautiful lake I had ever seen. It was a mile long, almost perfectly oval, with dark-blue water ringed on one side by a sandy beach and on the other by granite sheer. At either end and in the middle next to the beach were huge outcroppings of rock thirty or forty feet off the surface of the lake—the water was like a layer of just-laid glass. A fish broke the surface and sent out rings of tiny waves. It felt as if we were settlers making first way west and coming upon a place that had never known man.

"Isn't it something, Buzzy?" was all I could think of to say.

"Ain't it just," was all he could think of to reply.

⸺

We stayed on the top of Old Blue for ten minutes more, taking in the extraordinary splendor of the valley. The sun had just slipped behind the farthest mountains and turned the summit to dusk.

"Boys, let's get on down to camp. We're losing daylight fast.

It'll be slap dark before we get set up." We took our packs and followed Pops over the edge of the mountain. The trail down to Glaston Lake was even steeper than the ascent, zigzagging sharply through more boulders and jutted rocks. At times we had to turn sideways and half slide down the gravelly trail, bodies nearly parallel to the slope. "Mind your step. You don't want to be tripping on this hardscape."

Glaston was tucked into a high mountain valley, so the descent on the back side of Old Blue was much shorter than the ascent, and as the trail moved to switchbacks we made quick work of it. The air was rich gloam when the course leveled and we could see the blackness of the lake water in front of us.

The path circled halfway around the lake, following the sandy beach through a stand of trees. The air was cool and the sound of the peepers and crickets echoed over the still water. Pops stopped at a group of large pine trees and rocks, a fire ring in the middle. He slung his pack down. "You boys get the tent up while I work on a fire," he said and moved to a huge courtesy pile next to the fire ring.

We set up the tent on a sandy space between two trees a few hundred feet back from the water. Pops had the early flare of a fire, feeding twigs and pinecones for the stoke.

"Man, I'm beat," Buzzy said as we connected tent poles and nylon.

"I just want to eat and sleep," I said.

Pops had the fire going and put on a pot of water to boil. We threw up the tent as he added freeze-dried beef stroganoff to the water. We sat around the fire, eating the piping-hot meal and saying nothing. I felt a fatigue in my bones that I'd never before experienced—a noble exhaustion born of accomplishment and extreme effort.

We ate the entire pot of noodles, each going back for thirds. It was only ten o'clock, but my body felt like it had been working itself for days. Despite the threat of bears, we left the dirty dishes and crawled into bed and fell immediately asleep to the sound of a frog calling a mate across the cool black of Glaston Lake.

Chapter 28

THE WHITE STAG

It rained most of the night, and I rose just as first light was coloring up the morning. Pops and Buzzy were asleep on top of their bedrolls in the tent. I quietly unzipped the flap and stealthed out to take in the lake and the mountains. Workings from last night's dinner were piled in the ashes of the fire ring. I collected them and walked down to the water's edge.

Verdant hills, topped in granite, hugged the lake on three sides. At each end and next to our camp, huge rock outcroppings formed cliffs that ran straight down into the water. The lake was a blue mirror and a hawk flew from above and dove low over it before rising and winging out to the trees. There were a few stars in the brightening sky, but not a wisp of rain cloud. After the tornado of life in Redhill, it was the first moment of absolute calm I had ever experienced. I quietly laid the dinner accessories down on the soft sand so as not to alter the fabric of the morning.

I heard a slight rustling of leaves behind me and turned to the woods. A huge, blizzard-white deer was standing still in the old-growth pines—an albino buck with a gigantic rack of antlers. We were both statues, assessing each other in the new light. The stag shook its head and neck, as a lion tosses his mane, then walked slowly to the water. As he bent to drink and his muzzle touched the water, it sent out rivulets on the perfect plane.

I was fifty feet away and took a small step toward him; his head immediately jerked up, regarded me. I took another small step forward. He went back to the water with one eye watching. I slid silently his way, taking short, careful steps. We were twenty feet apart when he brought his head up and squared his body to me. I stopped and we gazed at each other for half a minute.

The stag's chest was high and strong, its shoulders and thighs rippling with sinew. I stepped toward him. The buck didn't move. The base of his antlers was thick as my wrist, and the rack, splayed into eight branches on either side, was covered in soft brown velvet that rounded the tips and made him seem much younger than his years. I took another step and put my hand out. He sniffed at the air and stepped to me. My heart pounded as I moved ahead slowly.

We were ten feet apart now. I took a tentative step forward, then another. He brought his chin up and appraised me, raised his left hoof for a moment, then stomped it down.

When I was two feet from the stag, I slowly reached my hand out to touch his powerful neck. His fur seemed to stand on end, inviting my fingers closer. I expected his eyes to dart wildly as I came so near, like a stallion's, but instead he locked his with mine. They were moist and pink, which gave them a strangely intelligent mien—kind, sad eyes that seemed to carry with them the secret wisdom of the earth. Just as my hand brushed his fur, stirring in the tent and the rip of a zipper on the door flap. Buzzy popped his head out and blinked bleary-eyed at our surroundings.

The stag jerked away and bounded off into the undergrowth. He stopped at a safe distance and turned to look at me. We stared at each other again for a few seconds; then he spun and disappeared into the woods.

I ran up to Buzzy. "Did you see him? A *huge* white deer with antlers like tree branches! And he let me walk right up to him. Did you see him?"

Buzzy blinked in disbelief. "I dint see him. All I saw was you lookin at the woods."

I took him down to the water to show him the place where the buck drank and pointed to the spot in the pines where the animal had gone.

"He let you get that close?"

"Yeah," I said smiling. "It was seriously cool."

"Damn, I wish I'd had my crossbow ready."

"Why? You wouldn't shoot something like that."

"Hell I wouldn't. How cool would it be hangin *that* on my wall. Cleo would go nuts."

"Buzzy, there is no way you are shooting the white deer. No fucking way." I squared to him the way the deer squared to me.

He went silent and looked at me quizzically and a little hurt, unable to parse my meaning.

I softened. "Look, man, there are some things in this world that just are not meant to be killed. I think that white stag is one of them."

Buzzy looked out at the space where the deer had been and nodded as a gradual seep of understanding made its way into him.

───

We scrubbed the dishes in the lake water, scouring them with sand to remove last night's meal. Pops was just waking as we got back to camp. I made a fire and had the coffee water at a boil when he exited the tent, stretching.

"Kevin saw a white buck," Buzzy blurted before I could. "He almost let him touch him. Says the sucker was huge—at least sixteen points." Buzzy spread his arms wide for the dimension.

"The White Stag?" Pops asked, clearly surprised. "You saw him? How close did you get?"

I told him.

"Son, you have seen a rare sight indeed. I've been tramping in these woods all my life, and I've *never* seen the White Stag—heard tell, but have never seen him. And you got that close?"

I nodded and he regarded me proudly. "It's all that vet training I've been giving you. Animals can sense that." He winked and put the never-lit pipe to his lips.

"It was so cool, Pops. It was like he knew I wasn't going to hurt him."

Pops nodded. "That stag is the stuff of legend. Folks have been seeing him or his kin for years... but only in glimpses."

I brought him coffee in an old dented aluminium cup. We sat around the fire while I recounted the White Stag for the third time and we swapped stories of momentous animal sightings while fatback fried in the skillet. Buzzy told of a black fox he had seen on Skull Mountain. Pops talked of two-headed lizards and Siamese sheep from his veterinary school days. We ate the fatback with hot oatmeal, then cleaned the dishes down by the lake.

Back at camp, Pops was relacing his hiking boot. "That was the last of our food, boys. This morning let's get a game plan for victuals. We can't live on fatback alone. Buzzy, did your grandfather ever teach you how to set snares?"

"He taught me how to set a rat trap."

"Well, that's a start. Do you understand the concept of bait and trigger?"

"I think so."

"Good. Now, I'm partial to spring snares, so we'll need to carve some triggers. Drag snares are easier to deploy but tend to lose game. A good spring snare will catch a rabbit almost every time."

Pops chopped half a dozen three-foot-long staves from several straight branches around camp. He took one up. "First thing is to strip the bark, then carve one end into a point. That's what we'll drive into the ground." When all the branches were debarked and sharpened, he chopped off the top eight inches of each stake. "These will be the triggers. We carve a notch into the stake and a matching notch into the trigger, and we're halfway home." He quickly cut the stake and the trigger and showed how they fit into each other. "The key to good trapping is to find the trails that the varmints use and set the snare right where they walk. You use a thin wire for the noose and prop it up with sticks about four inches off the ground." He drew the mechanics of a spring snare in the dirt.

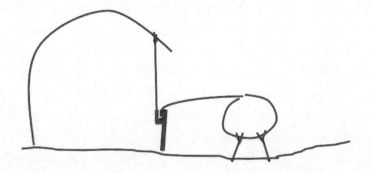

We carved the triggers and fashioned six nooses from a spool of thin wire Pops had in his pack. "There's a field of underbrush on the other side of the cliff that's full of rabbits." He pointed to the rock face that jutted out into the water. "We'll get them coming to drink at the lake."

We followed Pops over the cliff hill and into a wide thicket of saplings and mountain laurel and briar. He showed us the tamped switch grass that marked the animal trail. "Here's some fresh rabbit turd—always a good sign." He chose a ten-foot sapling and stripped it of branches. He pulled the sapling down, set the trigger, and propped the wire noose up with two Y-shaped sticks. "Now we add some brush on either side of the trail to funnel them into the snare, and soon we'll be eating rabbit stew."

He handed me a snare fixing. "Now you two make one."

Buzzy and I chose a trail that came out of a coppice of holly bushes. He stripped a sapling with Pops' bowie knife while I pounded the stake into the ground. We set the snare and Pops nodded approval.

We set four more, then started our walk back to camp. "We'll need to check the snares often, so anything we catch doesn't suffer unnecessarily." As we neared our tent Pops detoured to an old poplar tree and a faded green tarp held down by rocks. Underneath the tarp was a long handmade dugout canoe and two wooden paddles. "Made this on a Tramp in the midsixties—held up pretty well, I think. Help me with the back end, boys; she's a heavy one." Buzzy and I picked up the back and followed Pops to camp. "Now, who wants to learn how to fish?" he asked and pulled two collapsible fishing rods out of his pack.

"I already know how to fish," Buzzy protested. "Since, like, age three!"

"I do too. Mom took me once."

Pops dismissed us with a wave. "You may have *been* fishing, but that's very different from *knowing* how to fish. To really know how to fish you need to understand how fish behave. Just throwing worms on a hook with a float may get you lucky, but it won't get you good. I, on the other hand, will teach you boys to think like a fish."

"Can you teach me to swim like a fish? That strikes me as more useful," I said, hand on mouth to hide my grin. Buzzy wiped a smile.

"Dang ungrateful pilgrims. I've a mind to leave you up here for a few days and see how Buzzy's rat-trapping experience feeds you." He threw us each a rod.

I purposely held the wrong end and mocked a cast to Buzzy. "I got a big one Pops, what do I do?"

Buzzy dropped to the ground and began fish flopping.

Pops walked over and peered at my catch. "All you got is a holler fish...better throw that one back." He took our rods and walked off, satisfied at having got the better of the exchange. He turned at the water's edge. "You striplings coming?"

We laughed and ran after him. "Aren't we taking the canoe?"

He stood at the rock outcropping next to camp, a daypack slung over his shoulders. "Not today. I'm going to take you to the best honey hole in Kentucky, where we will hunt the smartest, most intuitive freshwater fish in this or any other lake: *Micropterus salmoides*."

"Salmon?"

"Largemouth bass."

The cliff jutted out thirty feet into the lake. A narrow shelf, just wide enough for a sideways foot, ran from the beach to the end of the rock. "A few years back I found a spot where the real lunkers like to parley. It ain't easy to get to but worth the effort."

We tightroped out to the end of the cliff, then climbed up ten feet to another ledge, then down again to an undercut alcove two feet off the water. The recess ran sixty feet across the face of the cliff.

Pops took off the daypack and removed a rectangular canvas folder. He unzipped it and spread it on the rocks. Inside were rows of colored worms, silver lures, gleaming hooks, furry flies, wooden grasshoppers, plastic crawfish, lead weights, extra line.

"Bass are curious fish by nature, so it's easy to catch a yearling—they'll strike on anything that moves. However, the smartest ones learn from their mistakes and become skittish and mistrusting...and big! Catching lunkers is an art, and knowing where they congregate is only half of it. They don't like the light, so they tend to lurk in the deep or around structure: under ledges, around fallen trees, under piers, in weeds. Under this here ledge is where they lounge during the day.

"Every time I come up to Glaston with Chester and Lo, I outfish them ten to one—drives em nuts. And here's why." He pulled a dark purple rubber worm from one of the pockets in his canvas tackle holder and held it up to the sunlight. "A black grape worm on a Texas rig." He turned the worm in his fingers to show us the delight of its workmanship, its exquisite coloring. "Don't tell Chester or Lo, but I'm a weightless wormer. I let the worm drift down slowly right in front of the bass's nose; then I read the line with my fingers."

He tied the hook to the line and set the barb inside the worm. "We'll each take a turn at it. We don't want too many lures hitting the water at once. Watch and learn, pilgrims." He plopped the worm into the water in front of the ledge and let it slowly sink. After a half a minute it had sunk out of sight. Pops let out the line by hand, holding it between his thumb and forefinger. His head twitched to the left as if he had heard a sound. Then he jerked the rod up and quickly reeled, jerked again and reeled some more. The rod bent on the weight of the fish. With a few more turns of the reel, a huge bass was flopping on the ledge. "Whoa, that's big," I said in a near whisper.

"At least a twelve pounder." He removed the hook and laced a keeper cord through the bass's gill and out its mouth and put the fish back in the water at the end of the undercut. "Let's change worms and you try it."

"Can't I use the purple one?"

"You can, but the other lunkers down there have already seen it. I change worm color every cast just so the fish don't get used to seeing the same lure." He peered over his sunglasses at us. "That's one of my fishing secrets I expect you boys to keep to yourselves." We nodded.

He affixed the bright-yellow striped worm to the line and hid the barb inside it and gave me the rod. "Just plop the worm into the water; the fish will hear the sound and it will get their attention; then just let the goby sink down past them."

I did and watched the yellow worm disappear in the clear water. I slowly unspooled the line just like Pops, until the line went slack. "I think I'm on the bottom," I whispered.

"Okay, jiggle the rod to make the worm move just like a live worm. They may be looking at it right now." I did as Pops said, then again. Nothing.

"Okay. Pull it to the end of the ledge there and slowly reel it up. We'll let you try the Black Grape on your next cast." He set a Lemon Zinger for Buzzy and coached him as he sent the worm into the depths. Same result.

We fished for an hour in the morning sunlight. Pops caught four more large fish, and Buzzy and I hooked some yearlings, only one of which was worth keeping.

"We've got lunch and dinner, so you boys ready for some cliff diving?"

I looked at Pops curiously.

Buzzy grinned. "Sure!"

"Follow me, then."

We balance-beamed back across the ledge. Pops put the string of fish in the water by the beach and we climbed the hill above the secret fishing spot, coming out of the woods onto the sunny top of the face forty feet above the water's surface. My stomach tingled as I approached the edge and looked down.

"We call this Jumping Rock—creative, don't you think? I was about your age when I did my first dive. It was a way to show my brothers I had sand. But I was terrified—almost wet myself."

"It's a far way down," I said.

"Long as you push off from the ledge, you'll be fine. Just don't dive close to the wall." He took his shirt off and stood on the edge, toes curled under. He was ramrod straight; arms leveled out front. He brought them out to his sides, then parallel to his body. He crouched slightly and pushed hard up and out, arching his back, throwing arms out like angel wings into a perfect swan dive to the clear water below. Buzzy and I exchanged impressed eyebrows.

He peered over the edge. "You ready?"

"No, you go first."

"Naw, I'll follow you."

"You're older; you should go first."

"You're a guest in my state. Guests always go first."

"You're bigger."

"You got brown hair."

"What, are you scared?"

"Hell yeah!"

"But you dove into a raging creek to save my butt. This is nothing."

"Then you go."

"Can't."

"Why not?"

"Because I think I might wet myself." We laughed.

"Screw it. Let's go together."

I nodded and we moved near the edge, took running steps, and leaped off the rocks together, yelling all the way to the water. We splashed in with surprising force. I opened my eyes in the clear; Buzzy gave me a thumbs-up and we kicked to the surface, breaking the water as one. We high-fived and whooped our way to the shore. Pops did a few more dives, then took the fish back to camp.

Buzzy and I cliff-jumped all morning, each leap giving us the confidence to try a few awkward dives. By early afternoon we were swan-diving like Pops.

After a few more dives we walked back to camp. Pops had gathered various herbs and tubers to pan-fry the bass in a mixture of wood sorrel, wild onions, ramps, and watercress. We ate, changed clothes, and lazed in our hammocks for an hour until he roused us to check the snares.

We took the trail up to Jumping Rock, pausing at the top to look over the clear, uncorrupted lake. We both saw him at once, on the cliff across the water, prone on a flat rock, the distance obscuring his features. "Who the hell is that?"

"Gotta be the guy from two nights ago. He must've followed us or something."

"What are we to him?"

I shrugged. "Let's check the snares and tell Pops." We hurried over the hill to the snare field. One snare was tripped and empty, the others still set. We reloaded the one and ran back to camp.

"Do you think it's the man from the other night?" I asked Pops.

"Boys, there was no man from the other night. He probably just came up here for peace and fishing and didn't count on noisy teenagers disturbing his quiet."

I smirked at Buzzy but let the matter drop.

After a dinner of bass and the mountain gather, we sat around the fire, listening to the thunder of a burgeoning storm and to Pops telling stories of his time in the war.

"The Japanese were ferocious fighters. On Saipan we came upon a field hospital and captured it. We had the enemy doctors tied up to a palm tree and our corpsman was tending their wounded. One of their wounded soldiers, man with an arm and half his face blown off, grabs the medic's pistol and shoots him, then turns it on us. Fought like a wounded cat to the end."

"Did you ever kill a man?" Buzzy asked.

"I did. I killed men who were trying to kill me."

"What's it like? Killin someone. Tilroy tole Petunia it felt like he owned the universe."

Pops smirked. "It's a sight less attractive than that. However, when you prevail in mortal battle there is a euphoria you feel having not died. There is also inherent respect that you owe the vanquished. But what Tilroy did was just sick. Him deriving any feeling of pleasure from it makes me despair for the boy."

We were silent for a time, watching the fire have its way with the wood. I took up my old copy of *The Call of the Wild* and started reading by flashlight. Pops poked at the coals with a stick, sending sparks flying like lightning bugs. A single meteor ran a line across the Milky Way. "Shooting star," Buzzy called. "Make a wish."

"There'll be plenty of wishing tomorrow night. That's when the Perseids will be at peak."

"What are they?"

"Every summer around this time the earth passes near the tail of the Swift-Tuttle comet and it causes a meteor shower—some years are better than others. This year we're going right through the tail, so it's supposed to be quite a show."

"Will we be able to see it from here? There are a lot of trees."

Pops shook his head. "We're gonna climb to the top of Old Blue. I watch em there most years." He stirred the fire again.

"You never told us the story of you climbing Red Cloud."

"Ahh...yes." He put the smoking stick aside and scratched his growing stubble. "Both of my brothers tried to climb the face on their sixteenth birthdays, and they made it—barely, but they made it. As a result, it became a serious rite of passage among our kin; many tried, but no one else in the family could do it. On my first attempt, I got halfway up and just couldn't get higher. It was a sheer face up the neck, then jutted out at Red Cloud's chin. When I quit, my brothers let me have it. It was like I dishonored the family name, and it rode heavy on me, I have to admit. Second time I tried was six months later, alone at night so no one could watch me. I guess seeing Red Cloud every day reminded me of my failure. I wanted to prove to myself that I could do it. This time I got as far as Red Cloud's nostril." Pops laughed and stirred the fire again.

"When did you finally do it?" Buzzy asked.

"It was the evening before Chester, Bump, and I shipped off to the war. Those boys didn't even attempt it; they just climbed the back way. But I guess I was determined to win some of that Red Cloud protection before going off to fight, or maybe just to show up my brothers. Regardless, this time I made it to the top. It was a feeling I will never forget—felt like I could do anything, after that."

"So you think Red Cloud really had special powers?" Buzzy asked.

"I do."

"Wait a second, Pops. You mean like *magic* power?"

He looked at me with a wry smile. "I mean the power to inspire a bookish kid to think he could accomplish anything in the world. If that ain't magic, I don't know what is."

"But that's really just you believing in yourself."

"Maybe, but I think it was Red Cloud who gave me that belief." He shifted on the rock and took a sip of mash. "Let me ask you both something. What did it feel like when you first made the top of Old Blue?"

"Amazing."

"Yeah, amazin."

"Like you were invincible?"

"Yeah, sort of. Yesterday was the hardest thing I've ever done in my life. The whole day was a test. I know I can do harder things now."

"Me too. I feel like this is jus the beginnin of what we can do."

Pops sat back, satisfied. "I knew there was a little bit of Buck in you boys."

"Who's that?" Buzzy asked. "I don't know him."

"He's the hero of a book I'm just finishing." I held it up. "He goes from civilized to wild in Alaska."

"What makes him go wild?"

"Well, he's a dog and falls in with a pack of wolves and ends up head of the pack."

"So he kinda goes back to what he was meant to be."

"Uh...yeah. That's a good way to put it. His instincts just take over and he survives. You should read it."

"Maybe I will."

We went silent again. After a while Pops said, "You know, *Call of the Wild* was Ray Mitchell Jr.'s favorite book."

"How did he die anyway? You never told me."

Pops topped up the mash in his tin cup. "Ray Junior wasn't like his daddy. He was a bright boy from the start. Mayna taught him to read early and he took to it like a Lab to water. When he was about ten he used to walk into town to borrow books from me. All those books you're reading now, Kevin. He'd take one back every Sunday to read for the week. Had to hide them from Grubby."

"Why did he have to hide them?"

"Grubby's expectations for Ray didn't extend past the farm. He regarded things like reading and education as superfluous to Ray's destiny, which was to run steer like his daddy, his daddy's daddy and his daddy before him. And young Ray wanted nothing more than to please Grubby, but farming just wasn't in him. He had a hunger to learn that burned in him like a coke fire. We would sit on the porch at Chisold each Sunday afternoon and talk about what he read that week.

"One day Grubby caught him reading when he was supposed to be working and whipped him raw. Came storming into my office saying I was trying to get his boy to 'deny his place.'" Pops shook his head and took a sip of mash.

"He was a great student, Ray was. A born writer—used to write the most incredible short stories and poems. Couple months before high school graduation, I convinced him to apply to the University of Kentucky. They had this new writing program. Didn't tell Grubby. Figured if he got in we'd find the money and somehow get Grubby to agree.

"Come June we heard from Kentucky; Ray was accepted into the program. That same summer he got his draft notice. I met with Grubby and Mayna about him going to college, but Grubby wouldn't have it. And Ray wanted to please his daddy more than anything, so he turned down college and went into the army. After basic training he came back up to Medgar on a three-day pass before shipping out to Vietnam. I'll never forget the sight of him walking up my porch steps with his head just about shaved and his starched army uniform. He looked about fifteen years old."

Pops looked off into the night as he continued the story. "Ray said he just wanted to thank me for lending him all those books and helping him with his writing all these years. I told him when he came back safe and sound from the war, I would convince Grubby to let him go to college. He just smiled and said nothing—he just knew it wasn't going to happen."

"How did he get killed?" Buzzy asked. "I heard it was in one a them enemy tunnels."

"What were the tunnels?" I asked.

Pops continued, "The Vietcong were guerrilla fighters and had spent years digging tunnels throughout South Vietnam. They used to live in them by day and attack at night. Because Ray was small, almost jockey size, he was the one who had the job of rooting in the tunnels they found for any VC. One tunnel turned out to be a division command post. He surprised a whole room full of VC colonels and generals. Then the VC attacked and his platoon was driven off and Ray was captured. Rather than kill him immediately, the VC tortured him to see what he knew."

I went cold. "What did they do to him?"

"What they did to him isn't important."

"Oh, come on, Pops, we gotta know what they did to him to make the story. Come on, we're old enough to know this stuff."

Pops declined. I kept pestering him for the next five minutes to tell us. Finally, he lost patience with my badgering.

"You really want to know what they did to Ray Mitchell?" he said with a stripe of anger. It was one of the few times Pops had been visibly irritated with me. I knew I should retreat, but I had to know how they tortured Ray.

"Okay." He put his sour mash tin down and leaned forward, looking straight at us. "They brought him into a room in one of the tunnels. First they beat him to a pulp...broke his jaw in twelve places. Then they hammered bamboo slivers under his fingernails and pulled them off, one by one. They beat the bottom of his feet with clubs until his feet were ruined. They punctured both eardrums with sharpened chopsticks. Then they cut off his thumbs and were working on his fingers when they were overrun by the army. They strangled him and retreated. That's what they did to young Ray Mitchell. You boys satisfied?"

Buzzy and I swallowed in unison. "I'm sorry, Pops, we didn't mean to make you angry. We were just wondering."

"I know you were just wondering, but sometimes wondering is better than knowing."

We were all silent for a while. I helped Buzzy watch the campfire embers; Pops was considering the cooler air that collected off the lake. Finally he spoke. "I didn't mean to snap at you, boys. It's just that I hadn't thought about Ray in a while and maybe I felt guilty about that."

"Did he make it up the top a Red Cloud? "

"No, son. He didn't."

Pops stood and went off to bed and left Buzzy and me at the embers.

"Man…what do you think he was thinking when they were torturing him like that?" I asked, not really expecting an answer. I was overtaken with thoughts of young Ray Mitchell and how, the week he was held captive, the soft life in Medgar continued unabridged. Smith's was open to brisk hot-weather business when they brought Ray to the underground room and shattered his jaw with an iron stave. Miss Janey's was crowded that Saturday, with still-shiny mirrors and fewer clippings in the corners when they broke the bones in his feet for the first time. Biddle's had just reopened after the expansion with new red vinyl seats and shiny chrome about the time they pried off the first of his fingernails. Jesper Jensen was the newly crowned Hivey's pinochle champion when they burst Ray's eardrums with a sharpened chopstick. Everyone in Medgar went about their business that week. Pops waited anxiously for his daughter to come home from her third year of college as Ray lost his right thumb. Lo was packing powder at Juliet Seven when they cut off the left one. Grubby was tending his growing stock, trying to raise a grand champion steer while his only son, tortured, then garrotted, was left naked by the retreating Vietcong.

"I bet he was thinkin he shouldn'tve tried to please his daddy so much," Buzzy said after a while.

Chapter 29

THE HUNDRED-YEAR STORM

Pops was already at the fire frying fatback and boiling coffee water when we woke the next morning. He cooked four bass filets in the fatback grease with wild garlic and black trumpet and bear's head tooth.

After breakfast Buzzy and I hiked off to check the snares. At the top of Jumping Rock we scanned the lakeside for the strange visitor, but he was nowhere around. Then through the trees to the snare field.

The first snare was tripped but empty. The next had caught a huge brown rabbit, which was hanging upside down, eyes closed, body still, noose around its thigh. I reached to take it down and its eyes shot open. It shook frantically, writhing in abject terror for twenty seconds, then went still, chest heaving. I grabbed the line and the rabbit shuddered and quivered again until I let go. "How are we gonna get him back to camp?"

"We're gonna chop his head off." He pulled Pops' hatchet out of the large pocket in his pant leg.

"Oh man, I don't think I want to see that."

"Don't look then." He grabbed the rabbit's hind legs and

slipped off the snare. The rabbit fought ferociously, twisting and shaking in Buzzy's grip. He slammed its head on a rock, stunning it to quiet, then laid it across a fallen tree and lopped off its head in a quick motion of the ax. He strung the rabbit up on a tree branch for blood draining. The animal's hind legs moved rhythmically, as if it was blindly hopping around in search of its severed head.

We caught two more smaller rabbits, which Buzzy dispatched with a quick flick of the ax. The fourth snare was tripped but empty, the others intact. We reset the triggered snares and carried the headless rabbits back to camp.

"We will make quite a stew for lunch," Pops said when he saw our haul. "Let me show you boys how to field dress a rabbit." We followed him down to the water. He took the bowie and pressed the tip into the rabbit's back, then peeled off its fur like he was skinning a banana. He chopped off its four feet, then slit its belly. "You want to tease out the entrails so the intestines don't break open. Then remove the heart, liver, lungs, and other organs." He gathered up the rabbit guts and flung them into the lake. "Always wash the game thoroughly so no bacteria remains." He rubbed the carcass vigorously in the water, then held up the rabbit by its leg stubs. "You are going in the stew," he said to the varmint. "You boys dress the others while I ready the pot." He handed me the knife and walked back to camp.

I shook my head and passed it to Buzzy. "Come on," he said, clearly perturbed. "I'm only doin one." He cut the fur, then quickly stripped and gutted the animal, washing it in the lake. He gave me the bowie. "Your turn, Indiana."

I hesitated.

"What? Don't they got dead rabbits where you come from?"

"Only roadkill."

I held the headless rabbit. Its fur was warm and downy. I made a two-inch cut in the nape of its neck and pulled the skin away from its back. It came off easily, as if I was pulling rabbit-fur gloves off a delicate hand. I cut off its feet and pulled the skin free. The rabbit was scrawny without its fir, glistening like a newborn.

"Now for the gross part." I cut into the underside and opened its belly. I considered the entrails, unsure exactly how one is supposed to "tease out" guts.

"Reach in an pull the intestine out gentle; then the rest'll come."

I did and the guts spilled like colander-poured spaghetti.

"Now cut the organs out."

I scraped out the heart, lungs, and everything else.

"I'll do the gut chuckin for you." Buzzy picked up the innards and cast them into the lake. "Go on an wash it good."

I briskly rubbed the rabbit inside and out; then we walked up to camp. Pops had gathered a half bucket of hopniss and some chanterelle and shaggymane. He added water and more wild watercress and cut the rabbit carcasses into thirds and threw them into the pot, bones and all. In an hour we were eating one of the best stews I had ever tasted.

Then to our hammocks, digesting wild everything and watching the clouds morph across the splendid sky.

Around three o'clock Buzzy and I rousted from our lay-about and decided to explore the other side of the lake and try to scout the mystery camper. We hiked up Jumping Rock hill, past the snare field, and over the larger cliffs at the north end.

We watched Pops go lakeside to check the fishing rods—it was then we saw him again, the strange man dressed in black, standing on the rock cliff at the south end of the lake, watching the camp with binoculars. From a distance it was difficult to make out any features—just a dark shape on the granite.

"I swear that's the man from the other night," I said, a pitch of fear in my throat.

"Don't know, but he's takin a long look at Pops."

We watched him watch the far shore until Pops went into the trees and the man left the cliff. We crept a half mile through the woods, quiet as Shawnee sneaking up on an enemy camp, tiptoeing around fallen twigs, leaf piles.

At the back side of the cliff we came upon the intruder's campsite—a smoking fire, a simple sleeping bag under a blue tarp strung between trees, a small daypack against a rock. Buzzy stood.

"Where are you going?"

"Gonna see who it is. You keep lookout. Gimme a bird whistle if he comes."

"No, I'll just yell."

"Don't be yellin. He'll know we're here. Just give a whistle."

"I can't whistle."

"What do you mean you can't whistle?"

"I mean I can't whistle."

"Why not?"

"Never learned how."

Buzzy looked at me with a pitiful gaze, as if my suburban upbringing left me severely wanting in the ways of boy.

"I'll give you a woo-woop if I hear him coming back. I'll make it sound like an owl or something."

Buzzy seemed dumbfounded by my lack of whistling ability. "I guess that'll have to do."

He quietly stepped through the trees to the stalker's camp. I spun which ways, looking for movement, listening for approaching steps. Buzzy poked through the pack, scouted the camp for clues. He came back and motioned me to follow. We worked quickly through the woods, around the corner of the lake to the start of the flat beach, and sat by the water on a rock.

"Find anything?"

"Nuthin to tell me who it is."

"What was in the bag?"

"Jus food an some clothes. No fishin rod. Coulda took it with him, though."

"No, we'd see him on the lake fishing. Maybe he's a hunter."

"Maybe he's huntin that White Stag."

"He'll never find it."

"How do you know? He could be an expert hunter come up jus to kill it."

"The White Stag is too smart. That's how he got to be so old. People have been probably trying to kill him for years. He's not gonna be fooled by a single hunter."

Buzzy thought about it. "Maybe you're right about it all."

"About what?"

"About how some things jus ain't meant to be killed."

"Maybe."

We hiked the trail that ran through the woods back to camp. Halfway there Buzzy pulled me behind a rock.

"What? Is it him?"

He shook his head and shushed me. I stuck my head around the boulder. Three turkey hens and a huge tom turkey were wending down the trail—hens flashing tail and the tom following scent like a bum to whiskey.

"I never got this close to a turkey...hardest animal to hunt. The tom is ruttin, so he ain't payin attention to nuthin but the girls." Buzzy peeked around the rock, then took the safety off the crossbow pistol. The hens left the trail, promenading off into the woods. The tom stopped, smelled the air, then turned to follow. Buzzy leapt from behind the rock, knelt, aimed, and squeezed the trigger. The bolt whooshed from the pistol and buried in the shoulder of the turkey. The hens scattered and the tom took to the trees. We ran after him, thrashing through the woods down a long hill. We followed him for a half hour to a clearing in the middle of an unknown valley floor. In a hundred-by-hundred-foot space were rows of what looked like bamboo. The tom took a step out of the woods and into the field. A shotgun blast pierced the quiet of the meadow, and turkey feathers flew into the air, floating like the flotsam of a pillow fight.

We looked for the shooter but saw no one. The feathers were still drifting down as we crept toward the flopping bird. The tom's head and neck were completely blown off. Buzzy reached over and grabbed its twitching claw and the thin wire caught around its leg. He removed it and followed the wire over to a sapling with a shotgun lashed to it. The wire connected to the trigger through an eye hook screwed into the wooden butt of the gun. "It's a booby trap," he breathed.

I faced the plot of bamboo, neatly rowed and well tended. "Why would anyone booby-trap a bamboo farm?"

"Cause that ain't bamboo," he said. "Let's get outta here!" He grabbed the turkey by the feet and carefully walked through the trees, as if navigating a minefield. When we were a safe distance up the slope, we turned and looked over the clearing. "What was all that?" I asked, heart pounding.

"Pot field."

"You mean marijuana?"

Buzzy nodded.

"How do you know?"

"Seen it before. People grow it up here."

"What's with the booby trap? We coulda been killed."

"That I never seen before. Frickin scary."

We hiked up the incline back to the lake and followed the trail to camp. The turkey was heavy—about twenty pounds—and Buzzy kept shifting it from hand to hand. Pops was at the lake edge fishing when we walked into camp.

"Whoa-ho! Look what the hunters brought back. That's an impressive piece of shooting. Wild turkeys are a hard get."

"We found a pot field that's booby-trapped. Shotgun blew its head off."

Pops stopped midcast. "What kind of booby trap?"

We told him.

Pops frowned. "There are folks growing crop out here, but I've never heard of anybody booby-trapping; that's just idiotic. Where's the field?"

We described the location, then told him about the man spying again from the far cliff.

"He was probably checking to see if I was DEA. The feds have come down here a few times rooting out growers and methamphetamine labs. You boys stay around the lake from now on. No more wandering in the woods. Any man dumb enough to set a booby trap is capable of anything. As long as we don't go near his field, we'll be fine."

Buzzy handed the bloody turkey over to Pops, who felt its weight and smiled. "Heck of a shot, son."

"He was ruttin, not payin attention."

"Females have that effect on toms . . . and on men." He regarded the fowl. "We are going to be eating fine tonight!"

Pops dressed the bird and stuffed it with several huge king bolete mushrooms, a mass of wild onions, garlic, rosemary, and goatsbeard root. We roasted the turkey on a spit carved from green ash limbs, each of us taking a go at turning. It tasted nothing like Thanksgiving turkey—each bite seemed to melt on my tongue into an explosion of flavors: goose, chicken, steak, and several I couldn't recognize.

We lay around the fire, gorging on wild tom turkey and watching the sun move behind Harker Mountain.

"Tonight we should see quite a show in the sky. It's the peak night and astronomers are forecasting a heavy dose of shooting stars; could be one every few seconds."

"What time does it start?"

"About midnight. Let's try and get some sleep before then."

We lingered at the fire, then drifted to our hammocks and eventually found sleep.

"It's time, boys," Pops said, shining a flashlight to spur us awake. He had prepared a light pack for each of us and pulled the bedrolls from the tent. He gave us both flashlights and we followed him on the trail in the dark, bobbing slashes of light exposing the rocks and stumps. The trail inclined on the face of Old Blue and we labored up the switchbacks to the hardscape near the summit. Our progress slowed as we neared the top, steps narrowing on the vertical. We picked our way through the rocks and finally clamored over the lip of the mountaintop. We followed Pops to a rock outcropping that faced north and afforded a full view of the valleys and hollows below and the night sky above.

We put our sleeping bags out on the rock and lay on top of them, facing skyward, hands behind our heads.

After a while Buzzy spoke. "I wonder if Cle went to the sheriff."

"I hope so. Once the sheriff comes to him, his window for a good outcome is likely closed," Pops replied. We were all silent for a time as we pondered Cleo and Tilroy and how the death of Paul would most certainly change their lives.

The stars were set in swaths of white, so bright they almost cast shadow. Soon Buzzy's breathing became rhythmic as he surrendered to sleep. Off in the distance, we heard the growl of a very large cat. "There are a few big cougars in these hills," Pops said before I could comment. "You definitely want to give them a wide birth."

"Have you ever seen one?"

"A few times, but only from a distance. They hunt at night and sleep most of the day, so they're tough to spot. Nasty critters."

Finally I put Tilroy out of my head and asked a question that had been on my mind since I arrived in Medgar. "Do you ever wonder what things would be like if Grandma hadn't died?"

We both sat up on the import of the question. He looked at me with a sad smile and put a hand to my shoulder. "Every single day of my life." His voice trailed off into the memories of his brief moment in the orbit of Sarah Winthorpe. We went quiet again. I kept stealing glances at him, watching the stars reflect in his moist eyes, watching his Adam's apple bob on every hard swallow as the projection of what might have been writhed inside him.

Finally he spoke. "You know, I used to take your mom up here to watch the Perseids when we were tramping together."

I made no reply at first, then asked, "Do you think she's ever gonna be like she used to?"

Pops gave his temples an index finger massage. "Kevin, you're old enough to understand this, so I'm going to tell you straight. Your mom will always carry Josh's death heavy in her heart, and because of that she may never be like she was. That doesn't mean she won't heal, but it's going to take a very long time."

"I feel like I didn't even know Josh." I examined the frayed end of my belt.

"Go on, son."

"When he died, everyone was coming up to me and saying how sorry they were and how sad I must be. I miss him, but I'm not sure what I'm supposed to feel; and now that he's gone I can't even remember what he looked like. I have to keep looking at the pictures to remember. It's like he was never even there."

"That's a perfectly normal feeling. Don't feel guilty about it." He had his hand on my shoulder again. "Do you understand?"

"I think."

He continued to look at me. I looked at my hands. Suddenly a white light streaked from the corner of the sky, across the heavens, disappearing over Bother Mountain.

"What was that?" I asked.

"I believe that was the first meteor of the night." Thirty seconds later another one, brighter than the first, shot from the same direction. "The show is starting—let's lay back and watch."

I tried to shake Buzzy awake, but it was like rousting deadwood. He mumbled something and turned on his side.

Two meteors at once flashed across the compliment of stars; one burning out halfway home, the other flaming well past Mingo County. Then a single shooting star and another double following close behind.

"That was a good one," Pops assessed. "They say this will be the best shower in the last hundred years. The earth is passing directly into the comet's tail this time. I think we're in for quite a show."

The next one was a double, then another single right behind like a two-stage rocket with a chaser.

"Cool!"

"I make a point of watching the Perseids every summer. It makes me feel small—not a bad thing occasionally." Pops winked.

The stars seemed to pulse now, as if any one of them could break out and hurtle to earth, as if they had all marshaled to watch the best and brightest on parade. The valley was dark and quiet; even the crickets were silent in deference to the show unfolding above our heads.

They came in a rush then. A flood of shooting stars like nothing I could have imagined. From the northeast corner of the sky, they rained on us like flaming hail, two to three a second.

Four came at once, all orange; then a small yellow one leaving a fire trail; then two bright white ones; more threes, fours, all streaking across the sky in an endless machine-gun flurry of excellence and wonder.

"I've never seen it like this," Pops said in awe.

And they kept coming and coming. A huge red one with no tail; five small ones in formation, tails twined; two bright big ones followed by a slow yellow one with a green tail; another double, then a triple. Barraging punches of fire that took my breath, my speech, and everything else. Each meteor demanding my full attention and none of them getting it. It continued like that for ten minutes, then gradually subsided to a regular pace. One or two every ten seconds, one every half minute, one every two minutes.

Suddenly a huge fireball, by far the brightest of the night, burst across the now quiet sky. A white center and a yellow and green double tail that hung in the air like jet stream. It streaked above us, this final meteor, and disappeared behind Bother Mountain as if it was crashing to earth, obliterating half of Missiwatchiwie County. Somehow we knew it was the last shooting star of the night, but neither of us could move. We just stayed on the rock, silent and still.

I knew that I would never be able to look at the sky the same way again. And everything else I've seen since that early morning so many years ago—every waterfall, every canyon, every mountain—is judged by the watermark of what we witnessed that night.

We lay there in silence, Pops and I, on top of Old Blue, the two of us just watching the tired stars. Watching the hint of light blue to the east. Watching the hollows below us draw and swell toward morning.

Chapter 30

THE MOUTH-HOOKED LURE AND THE QUEEN BEE

We walked down from Old Blue in the assembling dawn and collapsed in our hammocks. At about noon we began to stir—Pops at last night's coals, me at lakeside to fill the pot.

"It was like the stars were all falling from the sky at once," I told Buzzy after we had eaten lunch of last night's bird. "I tried to wake you up."

After the meal, we lay around camp for a few hours: Pops with his hiking hat over his eyes, Buzzy shading his with a T-shirt. I was exhausted but couldn't sleep for thinking of the last two days: the meteor storm, the mysterious visitor, and the White Stag.

Around three o'clock I hiked over Jumping Rock to check the snares. There were two sizable rabbits and a woodchuck caught up in them. The woodchuck had been strangled from the snare wire. I released it from the trap and threw the carcass into the woods. The rabbits were still alive but put up little fight as I dispatched them with the ax. I reset the snares and walked back to camp. They were both up when I returned—Pops sweeping out the tent, Buzzy poking at the coals. I hoisted the game and Pops smiled, then followed me down to the lakeside to help clean them. We roasted the rabbits and fried fatback and wild watercress for an early dinner. Afterward, I took the fry pan down to the waterside. As I scoured the pan with sand a strange sensation washed over me that I was being watched. My head jerked up and I saw him—directly across the lake, leaning on a rock, peering at me with binoculars. I quickly washed the pan and ran back up to camp.

"I saw him again. Across the lake looking at me."

"The pot guy?" Buzzy asked.

I nodded. Pops seemed unconcerned and kept banking the fire.

I stood with Buzzy, pointing out the rock that the stranger had used for leaning.

"Could you tell who it was?"

"Naw, he was too far."

"This is gettin kinda creepy."

"Getting?"

Pops came over to us. "Boys, instead of fretting over our mystery companion, let's go fishing for some muskie. They're not good eating but they're great fun to catch. Fight like swordfish. I know of a hole across the lake where they lurk."

Buzzy and I grabbed our rods and piled into the dugout, keeping an eye out for the menacing interloper.

I took up a paddle in the bow and Buzzy held the other in the stern while Pops navigated and readied the tackle in the middle. "The best lure in the entire world for muskie is the Lundberg Stalker; bought it special from Sweden. Walks the dog better than anything I've seen."

344 • Christopher Scotton

"But does it catch the fish?" I joked. "Another outing like the other day and I may take up needlepoint just for the thrill."

Buzzy guffawed and Pops smiled.

"I don't think they've invented a lure that can automatically boat a fish for you, although you and Chester would be enthusiastic customers."

With a few strokes we were away from shore, sliding through the water to the middle of the lake. The dugout was heavy, hard to maneuver, but stable. "Head on over to the cliffs that way," he said, looking up from lure tying. We angled the canoe toward the cliff where we had seen the intruder. "This is the deepest part of the lake. Muskie like the deep."

Pops had affixed three wooden lures, carved and painted like large minnows with a set of trihooks at the head and tail. "The key to muskie fishing is to jerk the rod so the lure moves like a real fish. Do that for about ten seconds, let the lure sink a little, then do it again." He cast out and demonstrated the technique.

We threw our lures across the water, plopping them in the lake like thrown stones. We mirrored Pops' reeling method and soon the lures were flashing fishless next to the boat. We cast again.

Then again.

And again—for ten minutes more.

"I don't think there's anything down there," I said after cast twenty.

"They're there. My father used to say, 'An impatient angler comes home with an empty creel.'"

On the next cast my line tugged hard, almost pulling the rod from my hands. "I got one."

"Pull it up to set the hook."

I did.

"Now jerk it again and reel in the slack."

I did. It felt like I had hooked a tractor tire. "I think the line's gonna break," I yelled.

"It won't."

Suddenly the fish started to run, turning the canoe around and pulling it forward. My feet braced the gunwales; I held the rod handle with both hands. The canoe pitched forward on another tug from the fish. I yanked up on the rod and the line went slack for a moment, which allowed me a cranking interval. Each time I pulled up, the line slacked and I spooled the fish in a bit more.

The fish moved from the front of the canoe to the side and I shifted with it. The line slacked; I stopped reeling. "I think I lost him."

"You didn't lose him," Pops shouted. "He's trying to make you think the line broke. Keep reeling."

I cranked even faster. Suddenly, the fish breeched, leaping full body out, shaking and twisting in the air to rid itself of the hook. It was huge, more than three feet long, with red-tinted fins and yellow-green body, spots like a leopard.

As it turned in the air, water sprayed off in a crown and the mouth-hooked lure flashed like a camera. The muskie splashed back to the water and dove, bending the rod straight down, almost capsizing the canoe.

"Pops, help me!"

"No, you can do it, son," he urged.

My spooling became jerky as the fish fought. The line slacked again and I reeled as fast as I could. The muskie rushed back to the top, this time just thrashing below the surface in the sun. I pulled in the rod again and cranked the line. Ten minutes later, after a series of dives and ascents, the huge fish was at the side of the canoe. I couldn't tell who was more exhausted, the muskie or me.

Pops reached over the side and pulled it into the boat. It flopped once, then was still, gills fanning. Its head was long and predator-ugly, with four large sharp teeth at top and bottom. The lure was hooked into his lower lip. Pops put on a glove and reached into the fish's mouth to remove it.

He picked the fish up and gently laid it back in the water. It floated for a moment just below the surface, side fins moving slightly, then with two quick tail flicks, it disappeared to the deep.

"Muskie are best caught and released. They are a boney eat."

We stayed out there for two hours, casting into the hole. Buzzy caught three smaller muskie; Pops hooked another monster and a small crappy through its tail fin. I landed two more muskies, none of which fought like the first, and a keeper bluegill.

The sun was a half hour from Harker Mountain when we drew up our lines. I was in the bow, Pops in the middle, and Buzzy in the stern. They dug their paddles into the water and the heavy canoe lumbered forward toward camp.

It came from behind us like a queen bee winging hard by our heads, then diving into the water. Phhhfffftttt. Splash. A half second later the report of a gun. Pops spun to the sound. The cliff face was empty.

Phhhfffftttt. Splash . . . Bang!

We all flinched.

Phhhfffftttt. Splash . . . Bang!

"Everybody down!" Pops shouted. I lay flat in the bottom of the canoe. He and Buzzy dug hard with their paddles.

Phhhfffftttt. Splash...Bang!

"Buzzy, *get down*!"

"No, sir!" he yelled back.

Pops thrust the paddle in again; Buzzy did the same.

Phhhfffftttt. Splash...Bang!

Chapter 31

Everything in Between

‿

I moved forward on my stomach, put my head on the bow, and dug my hands in the water as if piloting a surfboard. Phhhffffttt. Thunk...Bang! A bullet hit the side of the canoe. "Paddle, boys. We gotta get outta—" Phhhffffttt! Thump! "Uhhhhh, shi..."

"Pops is hit!"

I turned. Pops was slumped forward, a spreading bloom of red on his upper left chest. He was coughing, a dribble of blood on his lips. I moved to him.

"Get the fuckin paddle! We gotta get outta here!" Buzzy yelled.

"I need to help Pops," I screamed.

"Then paddle, mutherfucker!"

Pops lay back in the canoe, his head on Buzzy's lap, face ashen, eyes focused on a point somewhere in the sky.

Phhhffffttt. Thunk...Bang! Splinters flew.

I stood to go to Pops and almost toppled the canoe.

"*Paddle, mutherfucker!*"

I grabbed the paddle and thrust it hard into the water. "*Go!*" Buzzy yelled. We dug deep in unison, sending the ponderous boat forward. Three more shots sounded, but they fell short as we moved out of range.

"Come on! We gotta get him to camp," I yelled.

"I'm comin on," he yelled back.

We worked the paddles in a frantic rhythm and in two minutes came to the beach. I splashed out and pulled the canoe to shore.

We laid Pops in the bottom of the dugout. His breathing was thin, eyes fluttering. I bit on my knuckle until blood. Buzzy ripped open Pops' shirt; buttons flew. The exit wound in his chest was bleeding and bubbling on every exhale. Buzzy lifted up his shoulder to check the smooth entrance wound and the blood pooling in the bottom of the canoe.

"Boys, I—"

"Don't talk, Pops," Buzzy said softly.

I stood and wrapped my arms around myself, jumping up and down as if to counter a chill.

Buzzy hovered over him like an emergency room doctor. He took Pops' bowie knife from his hip sheath and cut shirt strips. He balled them up and plugged the entrance and exit holes.

"What are we gonna do? We can't let him die up here!" More jumping and stamping. Tears flooded, bile burned in my throat.

Phhhfffftttt. Bmmmmmp. A splash of sand. Bang!

I jumped on the sound, then dove onto Pops to protect him. Buzzy ducked behind the canoe.

Phhhfffftttt. Thunk. Splinters at Buzzy's head. Bang!

"Muthafucker!"

The shooter had moved from the cliff to directly across the lake. Buzzy ran up to camp and hid behind one of the big rocks. I lay on top of Pops, felt his breath on my cheek. I closed my eyes, expecting the queen bee wing and the bang and the impact of a bullet. A strange peace came over me as I shielded him from the sniper. It was as if a hit on me instead of Pops would somehow bleed out any lingering pain of Josh.

The gun went silent. After a minute, I picked my head up and saw movement across the lake. I looked back to camp. Buzzy was peeking from around the rock. "We gotta get him out of the boat," I yelled. "Help me lift him."

He nodded and ran toward us, bent low. Halfway across, the ground at his feet exploded and a rifle report echoed off the mountains. He dove down into the sand, spraying some of it into the canoe. He grabbed Pops' legs and I looped my hands under Pops' armpits and we lifted him out. He grunted in pain, blood pool smeared in a swath across the boat bottom.

He was lighter than I imagined; his warm blood soaked through my shirt. "Go!" I urged. Just as we took off, the sand in front of Buzzy jumped.

Bang!

We sprinted toward camp and made it just as the next round ricocheted off the rock. "Fuck. Shit! What are we gonna do?"

Buzzy said nothing. He just peered above the rock at a space across the lake. "I think he's shootin from those rocks across there, but I don't see nobody."

"He's gonna move again. We gotta get out of here. If we just get away from his pot field, he'll stop shooting."

"We can't go nowhere til we plug up them holes. You stay here an start packin. Take the tent, sleepin bags, rope, anythin else you think'll be useful. Leave everythin else. Also get a fire goin an some water boilin."

"What if he comes?"

"Shoot him with the crossbow."

He took up the big knife.

"Where are you going?"

"We gotta make a poultice to plug them holes. Gonna try an find some cranesbill an alumroot; maybe goldenseal an boxberry. My granma used to pack our cuts with it when we was kids. Stops bleedin and infections." He ran off.

I crawled to the tent and found Buzzy's crossbow pistol, which gave me little comfort. I rolled up the sleeping bags, removed some dirty clothes, and quickly collapsed the tent, stuffing it in its carry bag. I revived the fire with pinecones and sticks from the courtesy pile. The canteens were nearly empty, so I grabbed the cooking pot and ran down to the lake, zigzagging to avoid the bullets, but there were no shots. I ran back to the fire and set the pot to boil, then moved to Pops, who was lying on a bed of pine needles behind the safety of a large boulder. His lips were gray, his face white. His breathing was lean, and the hole in his chest bubbled and whistled on every exhale. The blue shirt pieces were soaked red. Dirt had collected above his eyebrow. I gently brushed it away. His eyes fluttered, then opened. "Bastard shot me," he said, then licked his lips. "Canteen, son."

I put my hand behind his head and gently raised it to bring his dried lips to the canteen. He took several large gulps. "Not much left. I'm boiling more now."

"Thanks, Kevin."

I opened his shirt to check the wound. Blood had coagulated in dark clumps around the hole, but the core remained raw and bleeding.

"You and Buzzy get the hell outta here," he breathed, then coughed. "Go get help."

"No way I'm leaving you up here with that psycho."

"You need to get to safety, son."

"I'm not leaving you. It's decided."

Pops closed his eyes, shook his head, and coughed again.

I brought the packs to the protection of the rock and laid the contents out in front of me. I grouped all the unnecessary items to the side—bathing suits, extra underwear, some books, extra shirts and shorts—and packed one change of clothes for Buzzy and me, several for Pops. All the camp hardware—ropes, lines, hatchet, saw, extra crossbow arrows, waterproof matches, rain gear, flashlights, leftover turkey and rabbit, lighter, pocket knives—went into the side pockets of Pops' backpack. The water came to a boil and I filled the canteens, then went back to the lake for more.

I heard footsteps in the woods and raised the crossbow. Buzzy stepped from behind a tree and rushed to me, hunched over.

"Did you see him anywhere?"

He shook his head. "You?"

"No. What did you find?"

He unwrapped a T-shirt and placed a pile of roots and leaves on a rock. "These two are the goldenseal; they'll help keep infection out. This one here is the cranesbill, which is for bleedin. The other is alumroot, which is also for bleedin. I couldn't find no boxberry."

"Your grandma taught you well," Pops said weakly. "Cranesbill and alumroot work better when used…" He coughed. "…together."

Buzzy had washed the dirt from the roots in a spring on the mountain and began peeling the outside layer with the bowie knife. I did the same with the pocket knife. We diced the roots and put them in the boiling water. "Jus til they're soft; then we mash em into a poultice an plug up them holes."

"Feel like I been hit by a dump truck," Pops whispered.

"Don't be talkin. You're lung shot. Save your breath for breathin."

"Why would they be shooting at us anyway? It's just a pot crop."

"It ain't the pot guy," Buzzy said.

"How do you know? Did you see him?"

"No, but it wasn't enough pot to shoot us over."

"What about the booby trap?"

"It was for animals, not humans; that's why he set it so low. If it was the pot guy, he woulda jus scared us off an missed. This mutha is tryin to kill us."

"Buzzy's right," Pops breathed. "It isn't the pot guy."

"Pops, don't be talkin."

Pops brought up a shaky hand and waved Buzzy's comment away.

"Who was it, then?" I asked.

"No earthly idea."

Buzzy tested one of the root cubes and pronounced it ready. He emptied most of the water into another pot and began mashing the roots with a fork.

"Take that extra water an clean out the wound. Make sure you get all the dirt out. Especially out the back where he's been layin in it. Put a clean shirt down there or somethin."

I opened Pops' shirt. He looked at me with a wan smile. I poured a little bit of the hot liquid into the wound. He jumped at the pain, grabbing my arm and squeezing.

"It's hurting him too much. I can't do It."

"You mash, then. We gotta get it cleaned out." He handed me the fork and I started breaking the roots down. Buzzy sponged the exit wound, then poured more solution into the hole; Pops' body tensed on the pain. The wound bubbled as he coughed.

"Stop it! You're hurting him!"

Buzzy ignored me.

"Pops, I'm gonna shift you on your side so's I can clean the back. It's gonna hurt." He rolled him over and Pops grimaced. He washed out the entry hole. "You got the poultice done?"

"I think so."

Buzzy washed his hands in the leftover root water, then began packing the entry wound with the poultice.

"It's a lung shot, so tape plastic over the exit hole," Pops whispered. "Tape it on three sides and leave one open so air can get in and out."

Buzzy packed the entry wound, then covered it with gauze and tape. We carefully eased Pops onto his back.

The exit wound was the size of two half dollars with tatters of flesh and lung and fractured bone. He carefully lifted bone splinters out of the wound with the blade of the pocket knife.

"Don't pack it too tight around my lung," Pops said. Buzzy carefully placed some mashed root into the wound. I took a ziplock from the pack and split it with the pocket knife and handed a plastic square to Buzzy. He taped it on three sides and wrapped gauze around it. He placed the unused poultice in a ziplock bag with a sprinkle of root water.

"How does that feel?"

"Like some bastard lung shot me then a coupla striplings decided to play witch doctor." He coughed.

I took Buzzy aside. "Is he gonna die?" My voice cracked as all the fear, guilt, sadness, of before came racing back, but doubled up because it was Pops.

"I dunno. The bullet went clean through an looks like it only took some lung with it. But we gotta get him to a hospital."

"I just can't be having him die on me, Buzzy. Promise me he isn't gonna die on me!"

He looked away. "We gotta make a stretcher or somethin. You stay with him while I go get some poles an stuff." He took Pops' ax and handsaw and disappeared into the woods.

With the wounds plugged and packaged, some of the color returned to Pops' face. His breathing became steady and deep. I knelt beside him and wiped his forehead with a wet T-shirt.

"Thank you, son." He sounded weak, but his voice had lost the desperate rasp of before.

I took a new shirt from his pack and helped him to a sitting position. I gingerly removed the bloody old shirt and threaded his arms through the clean one.

He grunted and huffed from the pain. "Kevin, hand me my jug and prop me against this rock."

More grunting and huffing as I moved him. He kept his left arm at his side and pulled the cork out with his teeth and took a sip of mash, then coughed. Something heavy bounded through the trees. I took up the crossbow and crouched in front of him, shielding an attack. Buzzy pushed out of the underbrush, dragging two stout pine saplings. He laid them parallel, then placed smaller limbs across the saplings like railroad ties. He lashed the crosspieces to the larger poles. We flipped it over, tied Pops' walking stick to the frame to strengthen it, then laid the bedrolls on top for padding and placed it next to Pops. We slowly eased him onto the pinewood stretcher, him grunting and blowing and grimacing.

"Let's do an equipment check," Buzzy said. We ran through the essentials. "Shit, we gotta go get the paddles. They're down by the canoe."

"No, we don't. Just leave them."

"We're gonna need em."

"No, we won't; let's just go."

"How we gonna cross the river?"

The river.

"Forget it. It's too dangerous. We can just do the rope thing."

"We used almost all the rope to make the stretcher."

"We'll find some other way across. You can't be running down there."

Suddenly Buzzy bolted for the canoe, zagging and juking to avoid a bullet. He grabbed the paddles, spun, and sprinted back to camp, two shots exploding at his feet. He threw the paddles to me and dove behind the rock. "Jesus Christ!"

We huddled in the shelter of the rock for five minutes. Finally Buzzy stood to hoist the pack and a bullet thunked into the tree next to him, then the rifle report. He jumped to the ground. "Shit!" The sun had already set behind Harker Mountain, but we were two hours from the cover of night.

"We'd better wait until dark."

"No way, Buzzy. We gotta get to help now."

He looked over the top of the rock, then quickly ducked his head down.

"How we gonna get outta here without gettin shot?"

"We can sprint to the trees over there. Once we're in the under-brush, he can't see us."

He nodded. I was at the front of the carrier, Buzzy at the rear wearing the pack. We picked up the stretcher, bending low to avoid the bullet plane.

"When I say go, we sprint for the woods. You ready?"

"Ready."

"One, two, three, *go!*" We ran hunched for the underbrush fifty yards away. Halfway there another shot hit at Buzzy's feet. Briar and mountain laurel ripped at our bare legs as we plunged in and drove through the undergrowth until the camp and the lake were out of sight.

We put Pops down on a clear flat spot. I knelt to him and brushed a mosquito away from his face. "How are you feeling?"

"Like a horse kicked me in the chest." He coughed.

"We're gonna get you out of here."

"Listen to me, son. Under no circumstances are you to put yourself in harm's way for me. Your mother needs you."

I sat down next to him and for the first time contemplated losing him. Tears slid. "But I need *you!*"

He reached up with a shaky hand and wiped them away. I took his hand and held it. Buzzy saw us and moved off to the side. Pops and I stayed like that for about five minutes.

Finally I said, "Does it hurt when we carry you?"

"Don't worry about what hurts; worry about getting us all home safely."

I nodded and stood.

"Best keep off the trail til dark."

"Good thinking, Buzz," Pops said.

"Stop talkin, Pops. It ain't helpin you."

He coughed.

We picked up the stretcher and slalomed through the trees and brush, out of sight from the lake. We worked our way to the slight valley between the lake and the rise of Old Blue. After an hour, with dark coming on, we crossed the trail down from the summit.

"You boys best prop me up on my side with my good lung above my shot one. And lash me in—I don't want to be falling out and rolling back down the mountain."

We secured Pops with the last of the rope, wrapping it tightly around him and the crosspieces, leaving his right arm free.

Buzzy and I switched places. It was lighter at Pops' feet, but the pack dug into my shoulders. Regardless of the weight I kept pushing, keeping Buzzy on pace from the back.

It was full dark, but there was enough light from an early moon to see the rocks and fallen limbs on the trail. We were halfway up the switchbacks, moving deliberately, when Buzzy slowed, then stopped. "Gotta rest."

"Can't rest. Come on, let's go. We'll rest at the top." He huffed, then stepped forward. My heart was thumping, sweat running out of me, but I pushed Buzzy on, setting our pace from the rear. The trail steepened and the switchbacks shortened as we neared the summit. Buzzy faltered and stumbled, losing his grip on the right-hand pole. Pops pitched sideways and grunted in pain. I pulled up to right the carry. Buzzy stopped.

"Keep going," I urged. "We're almost there."

"I can't do it."

"You gotta do it. Let's go." I pushed the carrier into his back. "Come on, man." He stepped forward onto the steepest part of the trail. Pops was forty-five-degreed, tied in like a mummy, as we slowly worked to the top. His eyes were closed, but I could tell he was awake.

We stepped, then stopped for a moment, stepped, then stopped, up the steeply angled trail. The moon was bright on the mountain face and the summit came into view. "We're almost there," I said between grunts. My shoulders were numb and my legs were quivering from the weight.

"I feel like a piece of furniture brought up from the basement by two underpaid moving men."

We were twenty feet from the top with Pops almost vertical. Buzzy slipped on the gravel and went down facefirst. "Ow, mutherfucker," he yelled, then apologized to Pops.

"No apology needed, son. Couldn't have said it better myself."

He turned to me, blood streaming from his nose and lip. "I can't get traction on the gravel. I need my hands to grab." We put down the stretcher, laying it sideways against a rock to keep it from sliding down the mountain.

"We could pull him up with ropes from the top."

"We used all the rope. All we got is like ten feet left."

"Why don't we tie the front end of the stretcher to the pack frame. You wear the straps, which will keep your hands free to help pull us up."

"That could work."

We untied the frame and set the pack against a rock. I took the last length of rope and lashed the frame to the first crossbar. I held it up while Buzzy brought his shoulders into the straps. I lifted the back and we started up the incline. He pulled from the front, hands free to grab roots and rock holds, and I pushed from the rear, on the last twenty feet to the summit. We came up to the edge of the top, which took Pops completely vertical. Buzzy grabbed a rock hold, put his leg over the ledge, and gripped the base of a young tree. I pushed with all my strength to help him achieve the summit. Once over, he sloughed the shoulder straps and turned to pull the litter over the rock ledge. He dragged Pops back off the face and collapsed. I climbed up and over and crawled to them.

Pops smiled at me weakly. "I haven't had this much fun since the Mingo County goat rope."

"I want to make sure you're not bleeding," I said and pulled back his shirt and gently unpeeled the bandages. The entry wound was still packed tightly and pus was beginning to ring the exit wound. I stood and looked down the mountain to see if the shooter was following us, but I saw no movement under the moonlight. Buzzy was still prostrate next to Pops. "It'll be easier on the way down," I said.

"Another hundert feet an I was a mind to ask the shooter to jus go ahead an shoot me!"

"Don't even joke about that—but I don't think he's following us. Maybe it was the pot guy, after all."

Buzzy didn't reply. I let him rest for another few minutes while I tended to Pops and went over the side to retrieve the pack. "It's time," I said on my return.

"That's what I know." He sat up, then stood. I reattached the frame and shoulder pads to the pack.

"I'll take the front this time," I said.

We picked up the stretcher and walked to the east side of the summit. I hopped down to the trail and Buzzy passed Pops down feet first. I steadied the spar on my chest and walked backwards slowly. Buzzy jumped off the rock, then eased the carrier off the summit, and we started slowly down the steep. I braced the stretcher against my lower back while Buzzy helped it down from above. I slipped on the gravel and hit my tailbone on a rock, screaming on the pain that shot up my spine. Two steps later Buzzy slipped.

"Do I need to escape this contraption to supervise you striplings?"

"I think my butt bone split in two," I said.

"You'll be the first in the family to fart in stereo," Pops retorted. His confidence and humor gave me comfort. After a few more slips and slides, the trail evened to switchbacks and we hurried down the face of Old Blue.

We came off the shoulder of the mountain to the flat valley that ran between Old Blue and Bother Mountain. After several hundred yards through the trees, we pulled up short at the flooded river. The downpour from the previous nights had swelled the water and pushed it even farther over the banks.

In the hard dark, with the moon hours taken by Old Blue, we stood staring at the unbridled movement of the water and the long, flat valley beyond; staring at the far bank and its broken bridge with rope tatters tailing in the river; staring at the near bank and its undercut earth and overspilled sides; staring at everything in between.

Chapter 32

IN THE WEAVE OF
TIME AND BEING

We placed Pops and the pack behind a large fallen tree, which shielded him in case the shooter came. Buzzy and I stood near the edge staring at the quickened current. "We best wait til first light. I can barely see the other side."

I started pacing in a circle. "We gotta try now. If he's following us, the more space we put between him and Pops, the better."

"So how we gonna get across? We used all our rope, the river is higher than last time, an we can't see shit."

"We gotta at least try. We can't just sit here."

"Buzzy's right, Kevin," Pops said from the tree. "River's gotten more dangerous, not less."

"We gotta get you to a hospital. Gotta get away from this guy."

"No doubt. But it's not gonna happen tonight. Let's camp well off the trail and rest up." He coughed. "We can try first light."

We moved two hundred yards downstream and set up the tent in a thicket of holly bushes. I untied Pops and we helped him into the tent onto a bed of the three sleeping bags. It began to rain and I sat in the open tent door watching it splash in pools on the saturated ground. Pops and Buzzy soon drifted off, but I couldn't sleep for the roiling worry. Every twig crack became the shooter creeping in to finish; every hooting owl became an approaching assassin, a hissing raccoon, an impending ambush.

As dawn neared, I lay next to Pops and put my hand across his chest, felt the rhythmic beating of his heart as it joined with mine in reassuring meter.

—————

I woke to saw sounds and the thwack of a hatchet on limb. I exited the tent and followed the noise. The rain had slacked to a steady drizzle as dawn added detail to our surroundings. Our frieze of holly was ringed by large ash and pine trees, which gave us protection from the sniper.

"We gotta make this thing float," Buzzy said when he noticed me standing. "Take the hatchet an chop these limbs off."

He went to another sapling, felled it, then brought it to me for pruning. We lashed the trees to the underside of the carrier with the rope we had used to tie in Pops. The five logs protruded three feet from either side of the litter, giving Buzzy and me an elevated perch from which to guide the raft. I tied the pack across the top to give Pops a cushion on which to prop himself. He was still asleep in the tent when I climbed in to ready him—soaked with sweat, mouth moving but no words. I took off my shirt, wiped his brow and neck. He woke to the touch, his face hot, his voice a weak whisper. "What's the plan for the river?" He shuddered as he spoke.

"We're making a raft to paddle across."

"The current . . ." He coughed. ". . . is deceptive."

"I know, Pops. How are you feeling?"

"Not great. I'm getting infected."

"What should I do? Should I clean the wound? Put on more poultice?"

"It's got to work through me."

"Do you want some water?"

"I want some mash...Did you bring my mash?"

"We did. We're going to move you to the raft now. You can have some then."

He nodded and tried to sit up, then coughed and lay back down. Buzzy came into the tent and we slid Pops to the door and lifted him up and carried him to the river's edge. I went back to break down the tent. I zipped the doors and windows, removed the poles, and started to fold it. The air stayed inside it like a balloon. "You gotta open the door and windows so the air gets out it," Buzzy said as he checked the buoyancy of the raft. It barely stayed on the surface. "We may have to add more logs," he said.

"Let's use the tent to float it." I picked it up and showed him its balloon qualities.

"What if the air leaks out?"

"We'll be across before that happens."

He nodded.

I opened the tent door to capture more air, then zipped it up. I placed it on the water and we laid the raft on top of it; the air in the tent lifted the litter off the water. We put one of the bedrolls on the crosspieces for padding and stowed the others in the pack to keep them dry. "Don't be tying me in, boys." Cough. "That's asking for...trouble on this boat."

"We used all the rope on the extra logs."

"That's a mercy. If this craft tips...I'll take my chances with the snakes."

We gently placed Pops in the middle on the bedroll. Buzzy climbed onto the front and I pushed us off from the bank into the rushing current. We immediately were pulled downstream. "Paddle!" I screamed, although Buzzy was already digging with fury. We were halfway across when the first shot hit the water and the rifle reported. "Shit!" We thrust even harder. The next shot splintered Buzzy's paddle and knocked him in the water. The raft spun as he hit the river. We were seized by the current and quickly separated from Buzzy, who was swimming hard after us. The water splashed near him, then another rifle shot echoed off the trees. He dove.

The river took us backward as Buzzy broke the surface gasping, twenty feet upstream. I thrust in my paddle to slow us. "I'm good. You get outta here," he yelled.

"No way. It's too dangerous to swim. Just grab on and ride it." We turned again, and in a few strokes he was at the back of the raft. I paddled as hard as I could and he kicked to reach the other side, but the river kept us centered. We rode downstream for a half mile, out of shooting range. The river took a hard left and the current swung us wide, close to the original bank.

"Let's rest here an get a plan. I'm touchin.'" He braced against the current in the chest-deep water and pushed the raft into calm under an overhanging willow. We tied off on the tree and lifted Pops to dry shade. His eyes were closed; sweat poured from his face and neck.

"I can't believe he's following us."

"He ain't followin us."

"Yeah, he is."

Buzzy shook his head. "He's followin me."

"What do you mean?"

"All them shots were at me. Evertime I put my head up or went down the beach, he shot. Evertime you did, he dint. Even jus now, when I was in the water, he was shootin at me, not Pops."

"But he *shot* Pops. You saying he was aiming for you?"

Buzzy nodded.

"Who would want to shoot you?"

He shrugged. "All I know is if we stay together he's gonna keep shootin at us. Eventually he'll get you, me, or both."

"What should we do?"

He pulled the crossbow pistol from the pack pocket. "I'm gonna go huntin him."

"Son, that's out of the question," Pops breathed, eyes wide-open now. "We are dealing with a . . . psychopath here. Best we stick together." Cough. "Float downriver to the trail. We can put some miles . . . between us and him."

"I disagree, sir. We're sittin ducks with a long way to home. He'll never expect a kid to come for him. Y'all get downriver. I'll meet you up the camp on Irish Ridge."

Pops shook his head.

Buzzy continued. "Look, we gotta do the exact opposite a what he thinks we'll do. If we're lucky, I'll be back before dark." He knelt to Pops, opened his shirt, and peeled back the bandage. "It's gettin all infected."

He went to the willow tree and carved two fists of bark and put them in the poultice bag. "When you get to camp, make a tea with the bark. It'll get his fever down." He took a few fingers of poultice from the bag and grabbed the extra bolts from the side pocket of Pops' pack, then handed me the big knife in its sheath. "You keep the bowie." We helped Pops onto the raft. "Keep him high on top; we don't want the river water gettin in there. An don't ride the raft too far downriver; you got that waterfall."

"Buzzy, I'm scared for you!"

He looked at me for the first time with the eyes of a child. "Me too."

"Let's just do what Pops says. He's always right."

He shook his head, looked down into the river swirl, then back up to me—child eyes traded for hard. "I gotta do this."

"But—"

"I gotta do this."

I reluctantly untied the raft from the tree and climbed onto the back and grabbed the paddle. Buzzy pushed us off with his feet.

"See you on Irish Ridge," he said. I turned sideways to reply, but couldn't find the words. He was standing on the bank, crossbow hanging by his side, eyes hooded with resolve. I swallowed hard on my dry tongue and felt the taste of vomit in my throat. He raised his hand slowly to wave good-bye. I did the same. He brought it down, watched us for a moment more, then turned and disappeared into the undergrowth.

As the river took the raft and we moved slowly away, I felt a strange sensation that I was stationary and it was Buzzy who was pulling away from me—Buzzy and the bank and the willow trees drifting off to some unfathomable point in the future; to some unknowable rank in the weave of time and being; to some place in the past that would cycle back on itself until the point and the rank and the brightest recollections of him were rendered to oblivion.

Chapter 33

THE RIVER

⌇

I paddled into the main current and felt its pull downstream. Pops was awake and propped good lung high, mash jug at the ready. "We've got six miles of easy river...til the first rapids," he said, coughing. "There's a hard double-S turn...right before... so we should put out there."

"Don't talk, Pops."

He waved me away.

The air in the tent kept us buoyant on water that swirled and spun in eddies and whirlpools. I sat astraddle the logs at the rear of the raft, legs trailing in the brown, ruddering with the paddle to keep the craft pointed downstream. The river swung in a few wide turns to the right and the left but mostly stayed true to the middle of the valley.

A half hour later from somewhere upstream, the sharp crack of a rifle shot echoed off the surrounding hills, hanging in the air like coming thunder. I jerked around to the river behind, trying to cipher some understanding in the echo. My throat tightened and a numbness spread over me; the trees and the sky seemed to close in like we were rafting a tunnel.

Pops' eyes bolted open. I looked at him, tears welling.

"We don't know that was Buzzy," he said.

I shook my head slowly and closed my eyes as tight as I could, hoping the darkness would blot out the reality of what we'd just heard. We listened for another shot, but the air was achingly silent. My tongue tasted of sour milk.

"Don't even know...that was the same shooter. Could have been...a poacher."

But we both had recognized the rifle report.

"Why would anyone want to shoot him?" I asked.

"I'm not buying...that the attacker was gunning for him... and not me." Cough. "With me gone...Bubba Boyd has a clear path...to Jukes." He coughed again.

"Why would anyone want to shoot him?" I asked the river and the full clouds and the limitless sky. A line of old willow trees leaned in over the bank on the expectation of an answer.

⌒

The valley leveled out and the river widened and meandered back and forth through the trees. We floated in sullen silence for most of the morning amid logs, dead animals, tree branches, and other debris from the storm. For a while we ran alongside a waterlogged chest of drawers with a snake swimming next to it, as if he was herding home a choice garage sale find.

I kept pressing us forward, digging the paddle deep into the water, switching sides and thrusting in again.

"Once you get to the double S...best head to the left bank... we don't want to be...running rapids."

After another hour, the slope of the valley dipped and the river paced. I kept paddling to increase our speed. Up ahead the first sharp turn to the left loomed. The current swung us wide to the right bank and pushed the raft sideways; I dug furiously to correct us, but the river had its own mind. We hit an eddy and turned completely around until we faced downstream again. I paddled hard for the middle. The current picked up and the river curved tightly to the right. I made for the far bank, to a group of willows on the river edge. The current turned us backward and swept the raft past the trees. I reached up to paddle hook one of the limbs, but it bent away. The push of water sent us back to the middle of the river. Next came another hard left turn. I thrust deeply to keep us centered so the turn after would sweep us to the far bank. Most of the air in the tent had leaked out and we were sagging low in the water. The current spurred and we went down, then up the first small rapid.

"How you doing, Pops?" I asked. He nodded, closed his eyes, and coughed.

As we came around the curve I drove the paddle into the water with all my strength to achieve the far bank. Two large boulders split that half of the river. We were turned sideways in a line for land but drifting into the path of the rock. I shoved the wood in hard, then again, but the current was too strong. The front of the raft bounced off the rock, spinning us back to the middle.

Pops grunted from the jolt. I backpaddled frantically to point us to shore, then forward as the current pulled us downstream. I made one more stout attempt to exit the main flow, but the river began to bend the other way and we were sucked back to the middle. A hundred yards ahead I could see white water bubbling and spewing into the air. Our pace accelerated and we were drawn into the rapids.

"Hold on, Pops!"

His eyelids flickered and he grabbed the rail of the raft as we careened into the first dip and back up to the top of the water. I ruddered with the paddle as we went down into another dip, up and down again, then up, this time with force. The front of the raft went airborne and came down with a splash. Another large rock loomed, cutting the river in two, eddies swirling on either side. I paddled hard to the left and pushed off it with my bare foot as we careened around the rock and down into a deep trough. We spun sideways at the bottom, then shot up and over, each of us coming off the raft into the air, then splashing back with it. Three more roller-coaster dips and catapults, then one hundred yards of relative calm.

Up ahead was an even larger series of rapids, then more calm followed by empty space where the water charged over the cliff to a jet engine roar—it was the huge waterfall that marked Irish Ridge Trail. We took the first large dip with ease, sliding down and back up the wave with practiced piloting. In the second trough, the raft spun sideways and the tent snagged on a submerged rock. The nylon pulled tight as it caught on one of the crosspieces, and the raft flipped over, dumping Pops and me into the raging river. The current sucked me down deep and scraped me across rocks and the gravel riverbed. I pushed off the bottom and broke the surface just as I rode down a trough and over a wave. I looked upstream and downstream for Pops, but the river was empty.

Suddenly, his blue shirt flashed to the surface as he turned in the water, gasping for air. His good arm reached up in a one-armed backstroke. Blood was pouring from a gash on his scalp. He turned on his stomach, then went under again.

I swam to the place in the water were he went down and dove, feeling frantically for him. I opened my eyes, but the brown offered nothing. I surfaced and spotted him struggling ten feet downstream. I reached him in three quick strokes, grabbed under his arms, and kicked with my legs to keep us both afloat. The overturned raft ran past and I grabbed it with my free arm, pulling Pops' head out of the water.

The river turned slightly to the right, just enough to give us some swing to the far bank, but I could feel the pull of the current taking us closer to the cliff. I spied three boulders jutting from the water downstream, twenty feet apart and each one a little closer to the bank. I kicked with all my strength to the first rock and made it around to its far side. I pushed off as hard as I could, toward the far bank, and swam with Pops and the raft to the next. The raft hit the middle of the boulder and spun toward the bank. I pushed off again, like a swimmer on the last lap of a world-record race; and again at the third boulder. The force of my legs brought us out of the main current and into the calm water. A tree had fallen into the river, and a pile of limbs had collected in its dam. I kicked into the quiet of the fallen tree, bumping it gently like a broken fighter jet touching runway.

I stood in waist-deep water and pulled Pops to his feet. He was semiconscious, the deep wound in his head streaming blood. I dragged him to the shore and up onto the bank and laid him on a bed of leaves in the shade. Despite the heat, he was shivering as if he had been lost in a blizzard. I went back into the water to the raft and struggled to flip it over. The pack was still tied to a crosspiece. I floated the raft over to the side and labored it up onto the bank. The first aid kit and the poultice were still sealed in plastic. I quickly spread out the pack's wet contents in the sun to dry and went to Pops.

His lips were gray, his face was bluish white, and his breathing was thin and raspy—whistling from his chest on the in and out. I opened his shirt. The wound was as gray as his lips. The poultice and plastic had washed away, leaving a film of dirty water in the angry tissue. I dried it with a clean shirt and repacked the entry hole with the poultice, then put the last of the root mash back in the bag. I taped plastic and gauze on the exit wound, then put a butterfly bandage on the laceration at his scalp line. One of the bedrolls was reasonably dry, so I wrapped him in it to ward off his chills, then went to the raft to assess the state of our equipment. The stretcher was in good shape; the ties had actually tightened in the water. I cut the knot on the raft logs and untied them from the carrier. I sawed the two end poles on the stretcher to make them even with the first crossbar. Then I hatcheted the other end poles at angles so they would glide over the ground. I removed the frame from the pack and lashed it to the first crosspiece, then tied the pack lengthwise as a prop to keep Pops' good lung elevated. I put my arms through the shoulder straps and started toward the trail to test the rig. It moved easily across the ground but was heavy on my shoulders even without him.

I laid it next to Pops. He was still shivering from a phantom chill. I left him in the sleeping bag and brought his legs onto the travois, then looped my arms through his and shifted him over. He didn't stir or make any sound. I quickly laid him on his side and tied him in, wrapping the rope around the edges of the spars and crisscrossing it across his body, trussing him up like a Shawnee infant.

I picked the travois up by the straps and rested the crosspiece on my knee and hooked my right shoulder into the strap, then the left. The frame had a padded belt, which helped balance the load. I tightened it and lifted the frame up to bear the weight on my hips. My legs wobbled; I took a shaky step forward, then another. Each step sent a jolt of pain up through my shins, which were scraped raw from the river bottom. I ignored the pain and bent over for pulling leverage, starting slowly toward the trail like a draft horse, pushing off each deliberate step with Pops' walking stick. Once at the trail, the going was easier as the travois poles slid across the wet ground. The valley dipped down and the roar from the waterfall took all the forest sounds.

Up ahead the trail forked in three directions. I stood at the confluence of the paths, unsure which was the correct choice. I gently laid my burden down. I could see the beginning of Irish Ridge in the distance, but none of the trails appeared to lead up to it. The path to my left backtracked across the valley. The middle trail seemed to meander along the valley floor, leading nowhere. The path on the right bypassed the end of the ridge and kept going south. Any one of these could be the right trail, but none seemed familiar.

I looked over at Pops, whose breathing was shallow and weak. Panic began to take me. I ran five minutes up the left hand trail, hoping to find the Pancakes or some other known marking. I came back at hiking speed, counting on it to spark a memory. It all seemed new. I did the same up the other two trails but saw nothing to help me decide.

I knelt next to Pops. He had the complexion of a man on a slow creep to death. "Pops, I need your help." Panic, exhaustion, hunger, stitching my voice. He stirred. "Pops, I need you." I shook his good arm.

His eyes shot open. "Sarah, are you home, love?" he said in a voice only half his. "I stopped at Riordan's and got those peaches you like. Sarah...are you home?"

I turned back to the trails, drew my knees up to my chest, and sobbed. Pops' life was in my hands and I couldn't even remember the right way home. It was the most hopeless I had ever felt. More helpless than in the car with Josh, his burned and blistered head in my lap. I wrapped my arms around my knees and buried my head in them. My only hope of ever actually having a father figure who cared about me was slipping away. With Buzzy gone, Pops going, and Mom out of her mind, I had no one left. Death would have been a welcome friend. At least in my life before this I had always had Pops.

I always had Pops.

Always had him.

I looked up from my knees and he was there. Standing in the middle of the trail watching me with curiosity and calm. I turned back to Pops, who had fallen unconscious. I was frozen as he moved toward me; three steps forward, then he stopped, lifting his head as if appraising all that was before him.

Chapter 34

THE WALKING-STICK SPEAR

He regarded me for a moment more, then turned and walked slowly to the middle trailhead. I stayed in front of Pops, squatting with hands on knees, blinking in disbelief. He took three steps down the trail, stopped again, and looked back at me, waiting. His coat shimmered in the afternoon sun, seemed almost transparent in the heat of it—antlers that looked to have grown and multiplied in the days since.

I stood and quickly shouldered the travois, shoving my arms into the straps. I secured the belt and followed. He stayed a few hundred feet ahead of me, never looking back, slowing down when I faltered, speeding up as I quickened my pace. His hooves seemed to be walking on a cushion of air. After fifteen minutes the White Stag stopped in the trail, shimmering still, and turned around to face me. I took another step, he took a step back. I stopped. He regarded me with old, sentient eyes that gave me a remarkable certainty about the trail choice. I took a step forward and he turned and dashed into the trees.

I dragged Pops as quickly as I could to the spot where the Stag had broken trail. I wanted to see him one last time, wanted to look in those wise old eyes to know that everything would turn out okay. The woods were clear of underbrush, but the deer had disappeared—no white tail retreating in the gloam; no hooves on last year's leaves. The trees were quiet; the only sound was the calling of a random bird. I stood staring at the place in the forest where the buck should have been, unsure of what I had just seen. Was I hallucinating from exhaustion, hunger, stress? Did I fall asleep on the trail and dream the animal? Or was he part of some unexplainable ordinance sent to shape an outcome? Regardless, I put my shoulder to the trail, plodding methodically step by arduous step.

At the crook of the first big incline, the four flat, stacked boulders of the Pancakes came into view. I laughed loudly. "They're here, Pops. You can't see them, but they're here!" A slash of excitement and energy cut through me as I hurried my pace and pushed on past the rocks. After two hours, the path began to level out as I neared the top of Irish Ridge.

The trail was narrow but just wide enough so we could pass unhindered by the rocks and boulders that were strewn on either side of the course. Giant cotton-brained thunderclouds stretched across the horizon and seemed to be creeping closer at each break in the trees. A thick understory of redbud, dogwood, and silver bell created a canopy on the crest of the ridge and narrowed my focus so that the two trail edges became tracks and me a singular, purposeful, lumbering train pulling my cargo forward, relentlessly forward, in a deliberate, unstoppable rhythm until the night drove the evening west and the thunderheads pushed the thick air east. The boulders from the campsite loomed ahead as night and storm collided on the ridge.

I brought the carrier to the cold fire ring and laid Pops next to it. I freed myself from the travois and immediately was taken by the weightlessness one feels on a falling roller coaster. It was as if the power of the White Stag could even conjure a breach of gravity.

I grabbed a handful of pinecones for tinder and created a kindling tent from courtesy-pile wood. In a minute the camp was bright with fire glow.

Pops was unconscious by the fire, each inhale a fray with his battered lung, each exhale a triumph of volition. I took the cooking pot and flashlight and plunged over the side of the ridge to the spring. As I approached the pool, a large animal growled and moved away into the woods. Around the water, in the rim of mud, were two huge paw prints. I knelt to examine them. They were the tracks of a large cat, each the size of my palm, water from the saturated ground just starting to seep into them. Too tired and too worried about Pops, I filled the pot and hurried back up the slope to the fire. Pops was stirring, pushing against the ropes of the travois. I untied him.

"Annie?"

"It's me. Kevin."

"Kevin?"

"Your grandson."

"What are you doing here?"

"I'm taking you home."

"Where are we?"

"Up on Irish Ridge."

His eyes darted to the unfamiliar. "Where's Annie?"

"She's home. We'll see her soon."

He laid his head back down and closed his eyes on the puzzlement of it all.

The water began to boil and I put a thumb-size portion of the poultice in the water and took it off the fire to cool. I put on a smaller pot with canteen water to make the willow tea. It came to a boil and I added a fistful of the bark and let it steep.

"I'm going to wash out the wound now. It's probably going to hurt."

He had fallen back to unconsciousness and didn't answer. I opened his shirt. Even in the weak firelight I could see the spreading flower of infection on his chest. I poured the hot liquid into the wound. He didn't flinch. I washed out the river scum, spread the exit wound with poultice, retaped the plastic on the chest wound, then dressed both holes in gauze.

By the time I was finished, the fire had burned low and a storm was filling the trees with bursting light. I fed the fire and wrapped Pops back up in the bedroll and sat looking into the flames. I thought about Buzzy and the certainty of that single rifle shot.

My mind pushed forward memories of my time with him: the first meeting under the tree house; the malevolence of Tilroy Budget; the easy friendship unburdened by the expectations of others; the Telling Cave and the horror of the burning hair and the beating and the burden Buzzy carried; our hike up to Glaston Lake and our too few days there, which gave me a first sweep of light for the future.

I jolted awake on a close shot of thunder. The fire had gone to embers, but the lightning storm was still sparking up the ridge.

"Are you back?" I called to the woods from wishful thinking. "Buzzy, is that you?" An intense bolt streaked the low sky, illuminating the camp and the ridgetop.

I saw him for only a second, then another second in afterimage, a huge mountain lion crouched between two boulders on springed haunches ready to leap at me. I took up a smoldering stick and flung it. "Get out of here!" He stayed for a moment, then turned and went down the side of the ridge.

In panic, I threw two arms of wood onto the coals and almost extinguished the fire. I pulled the bowie from the side pack pocket and unsheathed it. It was a full foot long; the bright blade reflected the moon and the storm clouds passing in front of it. It was razor sharp but too short for anything but close defense.

I took up the walking stick, felt its heft in my hand, tested its strength with my foot. I lashed the knife to the end of it, fashioning a formidable spear. I stood and jabbed at the air, slashed at an imaginary foe.

The fire finally began to catch the wood; I stacked on more to light up the camp. As the flame built, I sat next to it and Pops, spear ready, facing the steep side of the ridge, where the big cougar had retreated. The light of the fire made it impossible to see into the woods, so I just crouched, staring at the wall of dark, whirling with the spear on every night sound.

Pops stirred, then opened his eyes. "Kevin?"

"Yeah, Pops," I answered, not taking my guard off the darkness.

"I'd like my jug...please."

"I don't think it's a good time for mash."

"I got a hole...in my chest...size of a baseball. If I'm gonna die...want to die...with the taste of good mash...on my lips."

I heard an owl hoot on my left and spun to it. "I've got a better idea: don't die."

"That's my plan...but it's good to have...a backup. What are you doing...with the spear?"

"There's a big mountain lion out there. It was ready to strike when I threw a stick at it."

"Why didn't...you wake me?"

"Didn't want to worry you. Besides, you're shot and infected. You're not in great shape for lion slaying."

"I've got eyes and ears...another set...will be helpful."

"Not as helpful as that crossbow pistol."

Chapter 35

UNDER THE PROTECTION OF RED CLOUD

My recollections of that night on Irish Ridge so many summers ago often flash before me in the smallest of detail, as if it was all captured up in a documentary that my brain has stored in a vault all its own: the way the light of the fire gave color back to Pops' face and softened his lines to years younger; the way my sense of hearing became catlike, able to discern even the faintest of night sounds; the way the clouds passed over us, making it seem as if the moon was moving; the way Pops' eyes darted with fear I'd never seen.

It was the soft break of a twig behind us that made me whirl with spear ready. The big cat was sitting at the edge of firelight, only twenty feet away. I scrambled to my feet, grabbed the spear and a smoldering stick. "Hya!" I yelled. "Get out of here!" I jabbed the spear at him. The animal didn't move. I flung the stick at his head, missing by inches. He didn't flinch—just continued staring at me with quiet malevolence, tail flicking back and forth as if he was contemplating the fate of a wounded house mouse.

I stood over Pops, spear engaged.

"Try not to show any fear whatsoever," he hissed. "He can smell that I'm wounded."

But my hands were shaking and my knees felt ready to buckle. The cat continued to sit, watching us impassively. The fire was at embers and I moved carefully to the courtesy pile and threw wood on the coals, keeping one eye on the big cat.

"What's he doing now?" Pops asked.

"Same. Just watching us."

I waved the spear over my head and screamed, but the cat stood its ground. It was as if Pops and I were the occupants of a turned-around zoo, with the cat as a curious keeper observing our every movement. Or maybe we were in some protective cordon that the animal couldn't penetrate. Regardless, the cat stayed, watching and watching. Tail twitching.

After a half hour of locked eyes and tensed muscles, I realized Pops had fallen unconscious. My legs were on fire from the standing, from the journey, and my back and shoulders were aching for relief. I had to sit, had to ease the pain in my legs—but only for a moment; only for a moment. That was all—just to ease my legs; only for a second; a second or two...tops.

I slowly moved to the ground, sitting with my back to Pops' head, facing the mountain lion. Only for half a minute—that was all. I braced up the walking stick spear as a bulwark against an attack. Just until my legs were rested. The lion watched intently but made no movement toward me.

Rest for maybe a minute, no more.

Two minutes, tops.

A blur muddled my vision, inviting the darkness from the edges of the camp to creep in closer, closer, until my mind merged with the night and the woods and the black of it all.

It happened in slow motion: the splaying of the mountain lion's forelegs as it leapt at me; the cocking of its claws and the pink between its paw pads; the whiteness of its fangs and the four sharp teeth in between; the primordial hatred in its eyes and the vertical black slit of pupil at its core. I went for the spear, but it was somehow weighted down. I pulled up with all my strength, but it wouldn't move. The cat came down on me hard, claws digging deep into each shoulder. I could hear Pops yelling in the background, or maybe I was the one yelling as the lion's claws ripped at my flesh. I smelled the cat's hot, dead breath as his fangs closed around my throat.

I bolted awake on another thunderclap and brought up my hands to pull the cat's fangs from my neck, but they were gone. I jumped up easily and looked around for the spear. I grabbed it and turned back to where the lion had been. The ridgetop was totally empty except for Pops and me. I felt for claw marks and fang punctures, but my skin was clear. I blinked and whirled, but the cat was nowhere around. The fire had burned to coals and Pops was breathing quietly. I went to him and he stirred.

"How are you feeling?"

"Not good...Think the infection...is all through me...We better get to a hospital."

"We'll get going soon."

"When did you eat last?"

"Dunno."

"You need to eat. Gonna...need strength."

I built up the fire and put the willow tea on to warm.

Pops was taking in quick, short gasps as if he had sprinted up a flight of steps.

"I'm worried about your breathing," I said softly.

"Think I lost this lung... Just can't... get breath."

"Drink the willow tea. Buzzy said it will help your fever."

He sipped it slowly and coughed. I ate a piece of the leftover rabbit meat. It was chewy and slightly bitter, but I could feel the sustenance run through me with every bite.

"It was the White Stag," I said as much to myself as to Pops. "He was protecting me the way Red Cloud protected you."

"Kevin... there is a way... in these mountains... a chain of things that I don't fully understand... The White Stag chose you... Don't know why... but he did."

I thought about it as he drank tea, then drifted back to sleep. Just knowing I wasn't alone—knowing that I was guarded by something inexplicable and ecumenical—gave me energy and courage I had never felt before. At once the pain in my thighs became a dull annoyance, my cut shoulders irrelevant, my aching back a badge of honor. I filled the almost empty canteens at the spring, reserving one for the willow tea; took the extra rope and tied Pops into the carrier; then extinguished the fire with kicks of dirt. I picked up the end of the travois and put my arms into the straps and started down the Irish Ridge Trail toward extrication, atonement, deliverance.

The lightning storm passed and the moon shone through occasional clouds. The trail was flat and followed the crest for eight miles more before it dipped down into Prettyman Hollow, directly below the west side of the mining operation.

I leaned forward, took the brunt of weight on my shoulders, and started a pulling rhythm of exactly one hundred steps, then a minute rest. I counted the steps out loud to keep me anchored to an understood reality: one hundred steps, rest for sixty alligators; one hundred steps, sixty alligators. At every tenth stop, by finger reckoning, I laid the travois down, checked on Pops, cut a mark into the left litter pole, and gulped water. Every fifth notch I ate a strip of rabbit meat. By the time the sky started to lighten, I had notched the pole eighteen times. As the sun peeked over the eastern mountains, Pops woke and I put the carrier down.

"Where are we?"

"Up on Irish Ridge. You need to eat, Pops. I've got leftover meat."

"From the turkey?" His voice was barely a whisper.

"That and the rabbits we caught."

I cut a slice of the meat and put it in his good hand, then gave him the canteen with the willow bark tea. He chewed the meat and sipped the tea. I sat cross-legged in the trail next to him.

"Did the tea help you last night?"

"It helped me want to pee...and other things."

"Can you hold it? We need to keep moving. I want to get to the mines as soon as we can. There'll be help there."

"Better do it now...otherwise gonna soil myself...That's an indignity...I can't abide."

I untied the rope and brought him to his feet. He took a shaky step, then swooned into me. "I got you, Pops."

"Can't seem to find my feet."

"Don't worry, just lean on my shoulder." I wrapped my arm around his waist, took an uncertain step forward. His skin was strip-mine gray and seemed to hang off him in surrender. I helped him to a squat against a large tree. He exhaled with the effort and tried to unbutton his shorts, hands shaking so badly he couldn't finger the snap.

"Here, Pops." I undid his pants and pulled them and his boxers down to his ankles. He closed his eyes and laid his head back against the tree as if the bark had turned to goose down. The urine came as a yellow highlighter stream bubbling into the ground. At that moment the man who existed for me on a column of strength and courage had never seemed so old, never so shockingly frail. And yet, through this realization I felt a depth of love for him that I never knew existed—a new cut of the stuff born of mutual respect, not hero worship, squared shoulders and leveled eyes replacing adoration and servility.

As he defecated, I turned to the travois.

"Kevin, did you pack . . . toilet paper?"

"Didn't think we were going to need it."

"Hand me a shirt, then."

I walked over with my extra T-shirt. He tried to wipe himself but his good hand shook violently, other arm dead at his side. He tried again but gave up. "Let me, Pops." I took the shirt and wiped his bottom clean, then pulled up his boxers and shorts and snapped his pants. I looped my arm around him and nearly carried him to the stretcher. I laid him back on the travois, on top of the bedroll, and tied him in.

He motioned me to come closer. His eyes quavered. I leaned in.

"I wiped your ass . . . when you were a baby . . . Now we're even."

"Now we're even," I said and brushed a fly away from the bandage on his forehead.

Chapter 36

AT THE BOTTOM
OF PRETTYMAN

⌒

I balanced the crossbar on my knee, looped my arm through the strap, and hoisted the litter end onto my shoulders. The sun had just achieved the eastern mountains, turning the cloud base between to a ferment of purple, red, orange, and blue. Even the scar of the mountaintop mine acquired passable shadings under the color.

It had to be Tuesday or Wednesday morning, and soon the mine would burgeon with workers. We were seven miles away with many hills and hollows to travel, so I lowered my shoulder to the trail.

"One."

⌒

By noon the course began its slow descent into Prettyman Hollow. An explosion from the mine echoed through the trees. It was the most encouraging sound I had heard in days. I hurried my pace down the hill, drawn to the blast like penitent to preacher.

Every half hour or so another explosion thundered over the mountains, each a little louder than before.

A sign up ahead marked the end of Old Blue National Forest. The path curved around the ridge end and down to the bottom of Prettyman. It was early afternoon when we reached the hollow bottom. I stopped for the first time in hours, unwrapping the last of the meat for the final push up the long hill to the mine.

"Pops, I'd like you to eat and drink something."

He didn't stir. I gently shook his good arm.

"Wake up, Pops. We need to eat before this last hill."

He was still.

"We're at the bottom of Prettyman."

No movement.

"Not much farther to go now," I announced loudly.

I shook his arm, harder this time; his head went side to side, as if answering.

"Pops?"

Nothing. I knew that I was losing him. I put my cheek to his mouth and felt the faintest of breaths, put my hand on his heart to detect its fragile rhythm. For a moment the trees and the mountains and the sky, everything in the natural world, seemed to close down around me.

I took his good hand in mine and squeezed. "Pops, please! We are so close. I'm going as fast as I can." Several tears splashed onto his forearm. "Just stay with me."

⚊⚊⚊

The trail narrowed, with jagged boulders crowding the way. By two o'clock we had advanced less than a quarter mile up the slope. Another explosion rocked the air; the ground rumbled as if from the stub end of an earthquake.

My mouth was a desert and my head was pounding and spinning as I pulled him toward the top of the hill. As afternoon slid on, I could see the first hints of the mine in the yellowing tree leaves and gray dust on the undergrowth. I limped past the abandoned cemetery and its collection of soulless headstones.

The sound of a massive truck engine gave me hope. I slowly pulled Pops up the overburden to the top of the plateau that was once Sadler Mountain. In the distance, about a half mile east, four pickups were dwarfed next to the gargantuan haul truck I had seen coming through town—its left rear tire twice as tall as the men gathered around it. One of them waved to the others and climbed into his cab and drove off.

I put down the travois and ran toward them, half skipping on shin pain. Two other men shook hands; one patted the other on the back as they walked to their trucks. They waved to the last man and went.

I hobbled toward him, calling out and waving my arms. He checked a tire on the haul truck. I was about a quarter mile away, screaming for his attention. He went to the back of the big rig. I could see cigarette smoke curling around his head. "Help!" I shouted. He exhaled, flicked the cigarette into a puddle, and climbed into his truck. "Hey, *help me!*" I ignored the shin pain and ran toward him. I came to the edge of the plateau and stumbled down the gray gravel to the road. He started the truck and backed into the course.

I was a hundred yards behind him now, waving my arms and trying to occupy his rearview mirror. He started to pull away; then brake lights flashed. He stopped. I was catching up, sweeping the walking stick in the air as I ran. He reached over and rolled down the passenger window. I yelled to him as loud as I could. Country music blared from the cab—something about prison. The brake lights doused and the truck's rear tires spun on the loose gravel. They found purchase and the truck peeled off, exhaust still fogging the air when I arrived at the spot.

"Fuck you. Fuck you. Fuck you. Fuck you." My shouts echoed off the hills for several more rounds, then died.

"Fuck," I whispered, hands on knees as I fought for breath.

It was all down to Jukes.

The White Stag had constructed a rampart of confidence inside me that I had never felt before. I couldn't quit on him now, wouldn't let him die.

I went to Pops and took up the travois to start across the ruins of Sadler Mountain, picking through the rock piles and the rainbow pools of poisoned water. I dragged the carrier down the ramp off Sadler to the road that ran over the Corbin Hollow valley fill. The gravel had been compacted and pulverized by the weight of the dragline and the haul trucks, so it was easy passage to the next ramp, a forty-degree angle up to the plateau that was once Indian Head. This and the hill up to Six Hollow Ridge was the last difficult ground to cover. Once I got to the ridge, it was four miles to Jukes, to the truck, and to help. I paused at the bottom of the ramp and took a drink from the canteen. My head was a dull throb; my legs hurt at the slightest movement; my shoulders pulsed with every beat of my heart; but none of it mattered.

I took my first step up the steep ramp, using the walking stick for push. In a half hour we were at the Indian Head remains. I stopped for water, scanned the rest of the mine, which was empty and quiet.

There wasn't a trail up the hill to the ridge, but I recognized a lightning-struck tree at the top. I kept pushing up the hillside, over the broken rocks and damaged landscape toward the split tree. I took more water at the trailhead, then pushed through the deadfall to Six Hollow Trail—still good light as we left the broken mountains behind us.

Six Hollow Trail was an old logging road that ran across the tops of Beaver, Pine, Jukes, Slow, and what was left of Corbin and Wilmer Hollows. The way was wide and flat, and we made good time despite my total exhaustion.

Jukes was a magnet for me now; each step closer increased the strength of its pull. I paused every ten minutes to check on Pops—my cheek to his mouth to verify breath—but the closer we got to Jukes, the worse he seemed to be.

We passed over Slow Hollow as the trail ran up and over a slight hill. Ahead I could see the big ash tree that marked the beginning of the Jukes Hollow trail. I bustled my pace and reached it as twilight was settling over the woods. I took a gulp of water from the canteen without breaking stride. The trail down into Jukes was narrow and rocky, jostling Pops as the travois poles recorded the uneven ground. He moaned on a particularly rough drop.

"You okay, Pops?" He didn't answer and I wasn't expecting one. "We're almost home," I added, though I knew he was unconscious.

We came to the flat rock that marked the beginning of Jukes

Hollow. I cruised past it without pausing. The creek on my right picked up speed as it gathered water from various springs on the downslope. In the fading light I could see the top of the waterfall, could hear the splay of the water hitting rocks below.

We pulled up to the edge of the cliff overlooking the old cabin. I laid Pops gently on the ground. His breathing was infant-like, faint, short breaths as if his one good lung had shrunk to newborn. I jostled his arm to wake him, but he didn't stir. I was running out of time.

Both sides of the precipice ran to sheer rock. The best option seemed to be lowering Pops down the face by the waterfall. I untied him and carefully pulled the bedroll off the travois. I removed the rope from the crosspieces and unlooped the webbing. My plan was to tie him tightly into the bedroll, lower him to the ground, then reassemble the carrier for the last mile to the truck.

I readjusted Pops inside his bedroll and tied the rope tight, crisscrossing him to a mummy. I wrapped the extra line around a sapling on the edge of the cliff, then around my waist, with the other bedroll between my skin and the rope. I tied double knots every five feet for gripping, then brought Pops to the edge. I braced against a rock and slowly began to lower him down, taking the pull of the rope onto my hips and arms. I let the rope slide slowly through my hands, protected by the sleeping bag cushion. The edge protruded two feet, so there was no danger of him hitting the rocks as he lowered. Pops' head lolled on his neck as he descended, his body turning several times on the drop.

My counterweight and the twist around the tree gave the rope sufficient purchase to check his descent. His feet touched and he gently lay down in the grass at Sarah's picnic spot.

I gathered the makings of the travois and tied them as a bundle and lowered them down with the rest of the rope. When the bundle made ground, I threw the line next to Pops, then went to the far side of the cliff.

I lowered the pack to the first ledge and slowly climbed down, taking hold of a trumpet vine that was growing out of the rock, using it to rappel ledge to ledge, then jumping to the hollow floor, wincing from the pain in my shins.

I limped over to Pops, who was lying peacefully in the middle of the picnic spot. I went to hands and knees and brushed my cheek to his mouth. A feather of breath. I reassembled the travois as quickly as I could, leaving out several crosspieces. I gently pulled him onto the carrier, shouldered it, and raced up the slight hill toward the road.

I rounded the corner of the cabin and saw a shadowy figure coming out of the woods in the dusk. As he came closer, I could see the black line of a rifle barrel cradled in the bend of his arm.

Chapter 37

WHAT NEIGHBORS DO

The rifleman saw us and accelerated, slipping the gun from his arm to his right side. A dog barked in the distance. I looked around frantically for a place to hide. The hill to our left was too steep for the travois; behind us the rock face prevented any escape. I made for the cabin door, throwing off the shoulder straps and pushing Pops into the porch corner. I fished his pockets for keys while the rifleman advanced, gun ready.

Pops' key chain was a fist of unknowns. I shoved keys into the cabin door lock—a large silver key stopped half in; a green one slid in but wouldn't turn; a brass key wouldn't go past the tip. I shook the key circle, hoping to light on the correct one. I tried a slim gold key with a blue cover on the fingerhold; it slid in but the lock stayed fast.

"Hey!" he called, striding purposefully. I went to the pack, pulled the bowie out of its sheath, and whirled. I recognized him from the meeting at Hivey's—it was Gov Budget. At a hundred feet he switched the rifle to his left hand and started a half run.

I went at him, covering the space between us easily, fear and rage balming my exhausted body. "Nooooooooooooooooo!" I shouted and lunged with the knife. He stepped aside with surprising grace and grabbed my arm at the wrist and twisted it. With the same hand he seized the hilt of the knife, disarmed me, kicked me to the ground, and tossed the knife aside. I landed on my wrist; the pain almost made me pass out.

"What the hell you doin, boy?"

I gathered, stood, and ran at him again.

He was a matador now, and I was a bull, charging on fury, pain, and hatred. He slipped me, still casually holding the rifle, and seized my collar with his free hand. He held me at arm's length while I launched windmills. "You best settle down, tiger, or I'm gonna womp ya."

"You killed Buzzy and tried to kill Pops."

"What the hell you talkin bout? Where's your grandaddy?"

"You're the one that shot him."

"Boy, I ain't even shot a coon tonight." He looked to the porch where Pops was lying, squinted in the marginal light, then dropped me to the ground and ran to him. I picked myself up and followed.

"Where's he shot?"

"In the chest."

He knelt, opened Pops' shirt, took his pulse. "When this all happen?"

"Two days ago up at Glaston Lake. Someone also shot Buzzy Fink." I knelt next to him.

"Shot the Fink boy?" He looked at me in disbelief.

I nodded.

"Where's he at?"

"Still up there."

"We gotta get him to Glassville."

I stood, unsure and immobile.

"Come on, boy!" He shouted and picked up the front end of the stretcher. I took up the back. "I seen his truck by the felled tree."

We jogged down the Jukes Hollow Road, jostling Pops when our steps got out of sync. We passed Moby and Ahab and climbed over the fallen tree to the truck. He opened the gate on the bed and I slid the travois into it, pushing from the end until the front poles banged the back of the cab. "I'm going to ride with Pops," I said. He nodded and climbed into the front seat, pulling the ignition key from the mass. He backed up, inching the vehicle around until we were turned, and headed down the road, ash limbs slapping the truck sides like baseball cards on bike spokes.

We carried Pops through the automatic door at Glassville General. "Got a man been lung shot!" Gov Budget shouted. "We got a man needs help!"

The admitting nurse bolted around the counter; a young doctor pushed through the silver metal trauma room doors, stethoscope draped around his neck. Two more nurses appeared with a gurney. We set the travois onto the white specked linoleum and untied him.

"Let's get em up and into the back," the doctor said. They squatted, each took a piece of Pops. "On my count—one... two... three." They lifted him together onto the gurney and slid the bedroll off him. A red-haired nurse placed an oxygen mask over his mouth and forced air into him by squeezing a rubber ball on a mask. Another took his blood pressure. "Eighty-three over forty an fallin," she said. The doctor examined the wound for a moment, then said, "Okay, let's go!"

They whisked him through the silver double doors to the back room. I followed.

"You best wait out here," the blood pressure nurse said to me. "If you're kin, check in with Nurse Karpo." She disappeared down the hall.

Nurse Karpo was occupied with paperwork, so I waited for a moment, then opened the doors slightly and slipped into the corridor that held the trauma rooms. The place was quiet except for voices three rooms down. I followed the sounds to an old man slabbed and gray on a table, stripped to the waist, an oxygen mask covering his face. A team of doctors and nurses hovered; a doctor, up to his wrists in a gaping chest incision, shouted orders to everybody. Plastic bags, one with blood, one clear, hung from a stand.

It took me several seconds to realize the man on the table was Pops. A nurse called blood pressure every fifteen seconds, while two others attended the doctors.

"Seventy-five over forty an fallin."

"We've got a bad pneumo in the left lung, maybe a simple in the right. Gotta get a tube in there."

The second doctor probed deeper into the wound. "Plus, this infection's gone systemic. Jerry, retract the lung a bit more. And get those bone pieces out of there."

"Seventy over thirty-eight; still fallin."

"Damn…let's get this tube in there." A nurse passed him a scalpel. He made an incision in Pops' side and snaked a tube into him. "Come on, where are you?" he said to the tube end as if querying lost keys. "Judith, how much O negative do we have?"

"Just eight more units, Dr. Taber."

"Well, get it up here and call Johnson City," he replied curtly.

"Sixty-eight over thirty-five, fallin."

Suddenly the heart monitor went into hysterics. "He's fibbin," a nurse said urgently.

"Shit."

I couldn't contain myself any longer. "What's wrong? You gotta do something," I yelled. Everyone at the table looked over to me, surprised I was in the room.

"Judith," Dr. Taber said quickly, and one of the nurses rushed over.

"You can't be in here, young man. Come with me."

"What's wrong? I want to know what's going on!"

Another nurse whisked over a cart and gave Dr. Taber two defibrillator paddles.

"Two-twenty," he said, then placed one paddle above Pops' heart and the other at his side.

"Clear."

Pops' body tensed as two hundred and twenty volts surged through him; bits of dirt fell from his boots to the trauma room floor. The nurse pushed me out of the room, took my hand, and closed the door.

"Three hundred...clear."

I heard the clumpf of another shock.

"They're doin the best they can on your daddy. Come on over to Nurse Karpo." To Nurse Karpo she said, "Jobeth, can you see to this young man?"

"He's my grandfather," I corrected in a whisper.

"What, honey?"

"He's my grandfather."

"Well, they're doin the best they can with your grandaddy." She directed me through the doors to the waiting room.

I gave Nurse Karpo all the details of family and the journey.

"Let's take you back and get you all checked out."

"Just a second." I turned to the waiting room, where Gov Budget was hanging back by the entrance, cooning hat in his hands, black hair plastered to his head. I went to him.

Gone was the menace I had seen at Hivey's. He looked at me with sunken eyes, unburdened by any great curiosity and ringed in gray and dark-blue shadows that logged his hard living like tree rings.

"Thank you for helping me bring him here."

He nodded. "It's what neighbors do."

"I'm sorry I ran at you like that. When I saw your rifle, I thought maybe it was you shooting at us."

"Don't worry bout it. I mighta thought the same." We were silent for a while, trying to find some common conversation.

"Well...thanks, Mr. Budget."

He nodded and looked straight ahead at the picture on the wall of an English garden with two lines of boxwood leading to a teeming fountain.

Chapter 38

RECOVERY

⁓

I need to see my son. Where do you have my son?" I could hear her frantic voice through the admitting station window. I was in exam room one, bandages on scrapes and an IV in my arm.

"Calm down, ma'am. What's your son's name?

"Gillooly... Kevin Gillooly."

"Oh yes, right this way."

Mom burst through the open door with Audy Rae close behind. She pulled me up into an encompassing hug, careful not to pull out the drip needle from the glucose bag pumping fluids into me.

"I love you so much." It was the first time she had said those words since Josh. The joy I felt finally hearing them made me almost float out of the bed.

"They won't tell me how Pops is. Can you find out?"

"I'll go get Dr. Killen," Audy Rae said and left.

Mom looked at me with worn-out eyes that were still focused on a place in the near past.

"It's going to be okay," I said.

I don't know if I meant Pops, all of us, or just me.

It didn't matter.

Audy Rae walked in with the doctor. He managed a grim smile, nodded to us. "Annie, we should probably go out in the hall to discuss this."

Audy Rae put her hand on my shoulder. "Dr. Killen, Kevin carried Dr. Peebles twenty-five miles through the mountains to save him. I think he's earned the right to hear what you have to say."

Dr. Killen looked at me. "Heard the story. That was a brave thing you did."

I nodded.

He looked at Mom. "Your father lost half his left lung and will probably lose the rest. I think we can save the right, but he's got advanced blood poisoning and his liver and kidneys are shutting down. We're giving him a transfusion now, but it's gonna be touch and go all night."

"What are his chances?" Mom asked.

"I can't really say. It depends on his kidneys and—"

"Just give me a number." She closed her eyes and brought fingers to her temple as if just saying the words caused her head to hurt.

The doctor paused, regarded her for a moment. "Fifty-fifty."

She took a half step back, as if the news was attached to a strong headwind. She put her hand on the table to steady herself.

"It's going be okay."

I don't know if I meant Pops, all of us, or just her.

It didn't matter.

The crackle of Sheriff Binner's walkie-talkie woke me from a sleep so sound that for a moment I had forgotten where I was, what had happened. After a few seconds it all came to me with the clarity of new glasses. "Is he...?"

The sheriff spun, quicker than I imagined he could, and smiled. "He ain't out the woods, but looks like he's gonna make it."

I closed my eyes, said a silent thank-you.

"How about Buzzy? We've got to go find him."

"We'll find him. That's why I'm here. I wanna know everthin that's happened. Jus start from the beginnin. From when you left your grandaddy's house."

I recounted the hike up to the mountaintop mine, the intruder that first night, our idyllic days at the lake, the man spying from the rock, the booby-trapped field, the shooting, and the journey back.

He made notes in a palm-size book. When I finished he flipped it closed, put it back in his front shirt pocket, and regarded me as if sizing up a new recruit. "That was quite a feat, son. Scarin off that lion an carryin your grandaddy back twenty-hump miles."

He looked at me for a moment, as if trying to summon a more accurate assessment. His hands were on his knees; his chin rose to me. "Quite a feat indeed."

"Can I come with you to help find Buzzy? I think I know where he is."

"Help would be much appreciated if you feel up to it and it's okay with your momma. The state boys were scouring the lake last night but couldn't find nuthin. I'm gonna call em right now to meet us up there. You an me can drive the back way."

⸻

Andy Rae, Mom, and I stopped by Pops' room to check on him. The color had returned to his face and he was shaved and freshly washed—a ventilator moved his chest up and down, shoulder trussed in a bulky bandage. Several tubes snaked into his arm from hanging drip bags. A nurse came in for a blood pressure check. "When's he going to wake up?" I asked.

"Not for a while, honey. We've got him induced to help clear out the infection."

Audy Rae put her arm around my shoulder and kissed it. Mom just watched Pops, the back of her hand pressed hard to her lips.

Sheriff Binner poked his head into the room. "We best get on the road. We're meetin the state boys at noon."

~

"Roy, we're on our way. Call Lexington an have them put a bird on standby."

"*Thought you said it was a recovery, not a rescue?*"

"We don't know what we're gonna find up there. Jus get a bird ready for me."

"*Ten-four.*"

Sheriff Binner put the radio transmitter back into its cradle and adjusted the seat belt on his massive belly.

"Your grandaddy an me go way back, you know. What you done is big."

"I was just trying to save him."

"Well, you certainly done that. But you also done a great service to the county. Folks here are starvin for heroes, an your grandaddy is one a the only ones we got—him an Cleo Fink." He looked over at me. I nodded and looked out the window, unable to focus on anything but the feel of my heart rending over what awaited us on the Old Blue trail by the Blackball River.

"Not many folks can say they faced down a mountain lion with jus a bowie knife."

"I made a spear out of it."

"It was a brave thing, regardless."

I looked back out the window, tried to put Buzzy out of my mind. "Pops said brave is when you have time to think and still act at risk to yourself. I was just trying to save him."

"I don't care what you call it . . . took guts."

"I think what Mr. Paul did took guts."

"That sounds like somethin your Pops would say."

"Do you know who killed him?"

"I do." He looked over at me. "So do you."

I nodded, swallowed. "Did Tilroy confess?"

He shook his head. "Cleo come to me. Tole everthin."

"Did you arrest Tilroy?"

"Aint been out to the holler. That's tommora's bidness."

"Who do you think was shooting at us?"

"In my line a work, you learn not to specalate."

"Buzzy thought they were shooting at him, not Pops."

"Murder is all about motive, Kevin, an I jus don't see one for shootin Buzzy Fink. Your grandaddy? Now, that's a different matter."

"You think it was the man that owns the mines, Mr. Boyd?"

"Well, he wouldn't a pulled the trigger, but he's got men who would. We gotta get more data fore we go too far down that path."

We were speeding north on Highway 70 toward Lexington, lights flashing, no siren. Cars in the left lane shifted over as we came up to them, drivers checking seat belts and speedometers.

After twenty miles we took a left onto Route 5, a narrow, cracked road that wound between a series of abandoned coal tipples. In a while, the sheriff slowed and pulled into a dirt track, which immediately went to an incline.

The road narrowed and we cut through a stand of white oak and sweet gum that closed in and created bark walls up the first hill. We rolled down into a clear-cut valley, then up onto a ledge that twisted deep into the sea of timber. After ten miles of bumps and turns, we cut into Harker Mountain and wound around the base, then down into a shallow dell, then up to the high valley that held Glaston Lake. The sheriff slowed as we came to the end of the road, which widened to accommodate parking for three cars. A blue Ford pickup filled one of the spots. We parked next to it and exited the patrol car. The truck looked familiar, but I couldn't place its owner.

Sheriff Binner went to it, placed his hand on the hood, opened it, and felt the engine.

"Cold."

"I think I recognize the truck," I said.

"I know I recognize it. It's Sen Budget's."

"You think he was the shooter?"

"Don't know. Did he have a motive?"

"Maybe the mine guy was paying him."

"Or maybe he's up here fishin."

A patrol car pulled up, followed by a state police van. Two men in tan uniforms exited the van and opened the rear door. They pulled out a collapsible aluminum stretcher and a brown backpack, red first aid cross on it. Two others climbed out of the patrol car.

"Boys, come on over," Sherriff Binner said. He waved everyone in. "This is Kevin Gillooly, Art Peebles' grandson. He thinks the Fink boy is shot on the other side a Old Blue by Blackball. Let's hike up an over, then fan out along the bank. Yell if you find him."

We started up in single file with the state police team in the lead and Sheriff Binner at the rear. The path snaked around the end of Glaston Lake, where the shooter had camped, then joined up with the Old Blue trail.

Through the trees I could see to the beach with the dugout canoe. Although it had been only two days, the idyll of Glaston Lake seemed like two lifetimes ago, the beauty of the place carried off by my thoughts of what we would find on the banks of the Blackball.

As the path ascended, Sheriff Binner fell behind. I hung back with him for a while, but the urgency I felt to find Buzzy kept pushing me forward. I stopped and waited for him a third time.

"You run on ahead, Kevin. I'll make it quick as I can."

I double-timed up the switchbacks and caught the others as they were starting on the steep to the summit. We reached the top and the men pulled themselves up and over the ledge. One of the sheriff's deputies reached a hand down; I grabbed it and he lifted me over the rimrock.

We stood and rested at the top, peering down at Sheriff Binner, who was laboring up the slope.

I moved to the flat where we had watched the meteor storm and looked down at Glaston Lake, its stillness sitting in ignorant silence to the tragedy that unfolded there. The state police paramedic with the backpack sidled up to me. "Heard you took on a cougar with a knife and lived to tell the tale."

"It was going to attack us. I just scared it away."

"Name's Skill. Wayson Skill." He put his hand out and I took it.

"Are you related to Mr. Skill who runs the newspaper?"

"He's my uncle."

"He and my grandfather are friends."

"I know," he said with a slight smile. "It ain't a large town."

The other paramedic came over, then the deputies. "What did it feel like? Once you knew you'd beat it," the one with the fold-up stretcher asked. His name was Kimpton Silkwater.

"I didn't beat it. It just went away after a while." I told them the whole story from the time of the shots to rushing at Gov Budget with the knife. When I was finished, they looked at each other, then me.

"You got balls, Kevin," Wayson Skill said.

"I just did for him what he would've done for me."

"You did a sight more than that, I think," Kimpton replied.

Sheriff Binner was nearly at the top, taking one step, stopping to blow out a breath, then taking another.

"I think we're gonna need to help the sheriff up over the lip," I said.

He came to the top and put both palms on the ledge, which was at his breastbone. "How's this gonna work?"

The two deputies, Roy Marker and Bud Jennings, jumped down and positioned on either side of his tree-trunk legs. Skill and Silkwater each grabbed a hand. The deputies laced their fingers and lowered them to knee height. Sheriff Binner stepped into Deputy Marker's joined palms; Marker grunted and swayed on the weight. Binner put his right foot onto Deputy Jennings' hands, and together the men slowly stood, raising the sheriff's body above the ledge as if he was being levitated by some unseen magician. The paramedics grabbed him under the arms and pulled while the deputies pushed his feet up so they were equal to the summit. He stepped off like he was exiting an escalator, momentum taking him forward three steps. He turned to offer a hand to his deputies and easily pulled them to the summit.

We all stood while Sheriff Binner caught his breath. "Ain't been up here in eighty pounds," he said with a chuckle. He moved to a rock and sat down. "Boys, I go down that back side, you'll be callin the state bird to airlift *me* out. I'm gonna stay up here an supervise. Y'all head down an check in time to time on the radio."

They nodded and we dropped over the edge and slid down the embankment to the beginning of the switchbacks. In a half hour we rounded the last elbow of trail and started on the slight slope that ran through the trees to the river. I was in the lead, with the paramedics behind me and the deputies behind them.

As we came through the trees, I recognized him immediately and broke into a run. A group of black buzzards was walking his perimeter. "Get away from there," I screamed. The men ran after me. "Don't touch anything," someone yelled from the back.

Chapter 39

THE CROSSBOW BOLT

The crossbow bolt had entered Tilroy Budget's throat below his Adam's apple in the hard-cut cleft above his breastbone.

His eyes, or what was left of them, were half-open, and his mouth was slack-jawed. He had fallen back against a rock and died in a sitting position, with one leg straight in front and the other bent back like he was stretching before a run.

A rifle with a black scope was at his side, finger curled around the trigger. A single dark line of blood ran from the entry wound to the neck of his black Def Leppard T-shirt.

I was transfixed on the dead boy, stunned that Tilroy was the shooter. He had taken Mr. Paul's life in senseless rage, but what he did to Pops and Buzzy was calculated.

A chill took me as I stared at him—stared at his empty eye sockets, his bloated body, and the still-curled trigger finger. The buzzard-plucked sockets and the bloat made him seem like a giant discarded rag doll, rejected, abused, and thrown down from above. I felt a stark lack of empathy as I gaped at his distended body, and it scared me. I quickly looked around for Buzzy, but the trail was empty.

The deputies and paramedics fanned out, hunting signs. "I got blood," one of them called. The others went over, careful of where they stepped. "It's pooled here, then looks like he dragged himself into the bushes there." The deputy hounded the blood trail through the mountain laurel and holly. I followed.

I recognized the rippled black soles of his old army surplus boots through the hanging willow branches that screened him like hippy beads dangling from an open door. I ran forward, pushing down the urge to vomit.

Buzzy had pulled himself through the brush to a shaded spot under a large willow tree. He was propped against the trunk as he would be if lazing under the tree after a river swim. His eyes were closed in soft sleep, and his mouth was turned up slightly on its ends as if he was entertaining a dream.

The bullet had hit him in the left thigh and traveled out his side. He had slit his shorts with a pocket knife and had stuffed the wounds with leftover poultice, then bandaged them with strips of T-shirt. I stood and felt bile choke out my throat.

Wayson Skill leaned into him, put a hand on his chest. "I got a heartbeat," he yelled. "Ain't much of one, but it's there."

I started toward him, but Deputy Marker held me back. "Let em do their job."

"I'll do Ringer's, you do BP."

Kimp Silkwater pulled a plastic bag out of the rucksack, unwound the tubing, and handed the needle to Wayson Skill. He turned Buzzy's forearm up, slapped it to raise a vein, then slid the needle into him. He opened a knife and cut away Buzzy's shorts. "He's got all kinds a crap in here," Wayson said, examining the packed wound.

"That's a poultice he made for my grandfather when he got shot."

"Let's truss him with it in. I don't want to start him bleeding down here."

He turned to Deputy Marker. "Tell the sheriff to call for the medevac."

The deputy pulled the walkie-talkie from his holster and brought it to his mouth. "Sheriff Binner?"

Crackle. *"Binner."*

"Fly the bird, we got us a live one." Crackle.

"Who is it?"

"Fink boy."

"Roger that. Best bring him up here. Canopy's too thick down there."

"Ten-four."

The deputies broke out the stretcher, unfolded the aluminum poles, and locked the crosspieces in place.

"Is he gonna make it?" I asked.

They ignored me and kept working on Buzzy, wrapping the wound for the trip to the top of Old Blue.

"Let's get him on and go. Bird'll be here in a half hour."

They lifted Buzzy onto the carrier and tied him in with five straps that rolled out from the left side of the stretcher and clipped into the right side. The paramedics each took an end and pushed through the underbrush to the trail where Tilroy Budget lay. They ran past him without notice, but I paused and stood over the boy. I wanted to feel something—wanted to find some understanding in his actions; some empathy in his upbringing; at least a fragment of sympathy for the secret he carried.

I stayed for just a moment more and thought about my own father, how I still wanted his approval, still craved his love, still drank up drops of attention. I considered the shell of Tilroy one last time and pondered the certainty of rearing; the inevitability of desire; and the turn life takes when the two are set hard against. I turned back to the trail and ran to catch the paramedics and Buzzy Fink.

The far-off beating of the blades came to us just as we left the switchbacks and started on the steep. The paramedics easily handled Buzzy's weight up the incline. The drum of the helicopter came closer as each minute passed. By the time we reached the top it was circling overhead.

The men lifted him to the summit and slid the stretcher onto the rock ledge, then climbed after him. Sheriff Binner pulled Buzzy free of the edge.

"Nowhere to land up here so they're gonna send a basket down. How is he?"

"Lost a lotta blood. Surprised he lasted this long out here. Seems like a tough kid. Filled up the wound with a poultice he made for Dr. Peebles. That probably saved him."

The helicopter downdraft created a dust storm that sent dirt scurrying away in rivulets that turned back on themselves into miniature tornados. A large basket big enough for two lowered from the side. Sheriff Binner reached up and guided it to the ground. They quickly unstrapped Buzzy and moved him to the carrier. The basket wasn't long enough to lay him out so they sat him up against the wall, legs splayed to the other side. Wayson Skill jumped in with him and his partner gave an up thumb to the pilot.

The basket lifted off the ground and did a slow pirouette in the air as it rose. A man leaned out of the helicopter with a hand on the winch line, guiding it up into the bay door. He swung the basket into the bird and closed the hatch. After a few moments it banked away from us, the immaculate blue of the sky replacing the crisp shadow of the undercarriage.

Chapter 40

LEAVINGS OF THE SOUL

After two weeks they moved Buzzy down to Glassville General from Louisville Trauma. The bullet shattered his femur but missed an artery by millimeters. The doctors pinned and plated the bone back together and he was bed-bound in a hip-to-ankle cast while bones knitted. On the morning of his arrival, I stopped in to see him on my daily visit to Pops.

"I was comin round the corner a the trail an he was comin the other way. We saw each other at exactly the same time. He raised up the rifle an I went down on one knee an we both shot."

"What did it feel like when you shot him? Was it like Pops said?"

"I was jus happy to not be kilt an all, but I ain't feelin no respect for that fucker."

"Why was he trying to kill you? Because you saw him kill Mr. Paul?"

Buzzy shook his head.

"Why then? I don't get it."

"On account a I seen him doin stuff with another boy."

"What do you mean?"

"Fag stuff...you know."

"What!" I nearly shouted. "Where was this?"

"In the woods after I ran away. I was hunting with the crossbow pistol up on Round Rock—that's the mountain with all the big rocks on it. So I'm huntin and I hear noises on the other side of a rock; I think it's a deer or something, so I sneak around it all quiet, an there's Tilroy with some boy from Knuckle leanin against the rock with their pants dropped down jus wackin each other off. I mean, I'm like five feet from them an they're goin at it on each other an don't even notice me. So I start to back up an accidentally step on a twig or somethin. Tilroy opens his eyes and looks straight at me. I mean straight frickin at me. I jus turned an ran."

"You mean Tilroy is a homo? I don't get it." I shrugged my shoulders with frustration, confusion.

"All the older kids at school kinda thought he was, an when Cleo an his friends started teasin him about bein a fag at Mr. Paul's, I guess he wanted to show them how much he wasn't."

"And he was trying to kill you for that?"

"For a kid like him, from a family like that, me sayin what I saw woulda been the worst possible thing."

I paused for a moment and thought about this new revelation and the sad wisdom in Buzzy's words. Finally the pieces started to make sense and I began to feel a pensive awareness of circumstances other than my own; a knowing that brings with it a kind of stillness that I didn't quite understand but accepted it for its own.

"Cleo told everything," I said after a few more minutes with the still.

"He tole me. Says he don't know what Notre Dame's gonna do."

"You two okay?"

"Yeah, we're good. He pologized for bein a dick."

"That's good."

More stillness.

"What did it feel like, getting shot?"

"Like someone stuck me with a red-hot poker—hurt like a mutha. But the worst part was the dyin part."

"You didn't die."

"But I dint know that. I plugged the hole up best I could, but I kept bleedin an gettin weaker. Right before I passed out, I figured I was a goner."

"Were you scared?"

"Hell yeah I was scared. But then it went all weird when I got weaker. The pain stopped an I felt kinda peaceful. Like my body was ready to give it up."

We were silent for a while more. A comfortable silence built on shared accomplishment and the confidence of courage earned.

"Heard you faced down a cougar."

I nodded and recounted the whole story, from river to hollow. "I swear it was just like Pops and Red Cloud—like the White Stag was protecting me, giving me strength to keep going."

Buzzy nodded, thinking on it. More comfortable silence.

"So why did you drag yourself through the bushes? We almost couldn't find you."

"After bout a day, them buzzards come an started pickin at him. I tried to throw sticks to shoo em off, but they jus ignored me after a while." He paused and swallowed. "I seen one pull his eye out an fly off with it." His voice cracked. "I couldn't stay there an watch."

I couldn't think of a single thing to say.

"What the hell took you so long, anyway?"

"I had to carry Pops back by myself twenty miles. That's what took me so long." I paused and tried to remove the image of Tilroy's empty eye sockets. Tried to get back to the still.

"How's your momma doin? Bet she's glad you an Pops ain't hurt."

"She seems a little better, but Pops says she may never be like she was. Says losing a kid is like a piece of your soul dying. Says it's different from a wife dying or a brother dying."

"I think they all suck."

"I guess when terrible crap happens, how much of your soul that's left behind is how much you can heal. I think losing Josh and watching it happen the way it did took most of hers with it."

He turned toward the window and was silent.

"Hey, look, I'm going to go visit Pops. I told him I'd bring him his mail." I held up a bundle of envelopes.

"When are you comin back?"

"Tomorrow. I see Pops every day."

"I mean when are you comin back here?" He looked out the window again as he said it.

"Tomorrow, dumbass. After I check in on Pops."

He nodded but kept his eyes fixed on a birdbath in the garden in the middle of the courtyard where two blue jays were fighting over water rights.

～

Pops' room was at the other end of the corridor. The second bed was occupied by a thin, gray-lipped man with sinkhole cheeks and an oxygen tube snapped to his nostrils. The infection had taken a week to fully flush; then the doctors grafted skin from Pops' posterior to cover the wound.

"I'm wearing my ass on my chest," he had said and chuckled. "Chester's gonna have a field day with that." He would be hospital-bound for one more week to allow the skin to take, then home for a month of recovery. Audy Rae was already planning a party.

"Here's Cougar Man, come to bust me outta here," he said when I walked into the room. "I'll take another bullet before I eat any more of this hospital slop."

Lo and Paitsel were standing by the bed—they both nodded on my entrance. Pops had yesterday's copy of the *Missiwatchiwie County Register* on his lap with my picture filling half the top fold.

Register Exclusive: Kevin Gillooly's Amazing Journey

Several editions of the *Register* from previous days were on the side table.

One Dead, Two Critically Injured in Glaston Lake Shooting
Teen Shooter Tied to Pierce Slaying
Fink Out of ICU

"Our run-in with Tilroy is giving Chester a bountiful harvest of news," he said. "After you read this latest piece, they're gonna have to move me to a bigger room just to fit your ego."

"Already read it." I grinned. "I went into Hivey's this morning and all the men had it. When they saw me they went all weird, whispering and pointing. Finally Mr. Jensen came up and just shook my hand and said, 'You done a good thing.'"

"Jesper always gets tongue-tied around celebrity," Paitsel said. He tried to smile, but his face was pulled down from poor sleep, grief still collecting in bags above his cheeks.

"But it's not just them. Everybody's been looking at me different, like I'm an alien or something."

"What you done is big-time, son."

"Lo's right, Kevin. What you did is the stuff of legend. People will be talking about it for years."

"I was just trying to save you. I don't know what I would have done if you'd died."

"I know it would have ruined *my* weekend," he said, eyes twinkling.

Lo shook out car keys. "We'll leave you two for private. You ready, Pait?"

Paitsel nodded. "Need to stop by Hivey's. Wanna thank the boys for everthin."

Lo patted Pops' leg. "You take care a yourself, Arthur."

"I'll come up Wednesday with Audy Rae," Paitsel added.

As they went, Lo slapped Paitsel's back. "We might wanna get a game up with Jesper an Bobby while we're there."

"That'd be good."

"What are you reading, Kevin?" Mom asked through the porch screen.

I showed her. She smiled and came out onto the porch. "One of my favorites. Medgar isn't so different from Maycomb, is it?"

"At least Maycomb didn't have a huge strip mine hanging over it."

She nodded and sat next to me on the wicker sofa. She opened her mouth to speak; then her mind seemed to wander back to familiar black, taking her silent. It was like that with her in the first few weeks after the shooting—bursts of engagement, filaments of conversation, then hours of silence.

The shooting seemed to have reanimated parts of the old Mom that were now desperately trying to climb out of the bleak hole of heartbreak, only to be pulled back into the void by the immensity of loss.

But the bursts still came. Tuesday at dinner she snorted when Audy Rae did a lip-licking Bubba Boyd impression. Thursday she asked me not to slam the front screen door quite so much. Friday she suggested I wipe my muddy feet on the doormat. It wasn't much, but it was enough for me to construct footings of hope.

Every afternoon we would drive to the hospital to see Pops and Buzzy, who were now sharing a room at Pops' insistence. They were at cards when we arrived—Pops in a chair by Buzzy's bed, Buzzy still immobile for leg healing.

"You just missed Paitsel and Chester. They would have liked to see you."

"Me too. Next time tell them the porch is open for business. They can come by anytime."

"Ha, that's a lot of conversation for a fourteen-year-old to hold up. Think you can handle it?"

"I don't know, let me try. 'Alexander the Great was no late bloomer...won his first battle at sixteen, you know,'" I said in my best Pops imitation.

He laughed and flicked a four of diamonds at me; it whizzed past my head. "You may think life is one long punch line, but Paitsel is heart-attack serious about trying to shut Bubba Boyd down. Guess he sees it as his mission for the honor of Paul's memory."

I nodded and Pops continued. "Says he found some documents in Paul's papers that can prove Bubba's pumping slurry underground without a permit. Says he's got a friend outside Washington, D.C., who knows someone who knows someone in the Office of Surface Mining."

"But it ain't gonna bring the mountains back," Buzzy replied.

"It ain't gonna bring em back, but it might prevent others from being taken. Look, I know it's a long shot, but at least someone's doing something."

We brought Pops home the following week, ambulance lights spinning in a three-car convoy. Paitsel and Lo had built a temporary ramp up the front porch steps, and we installed him and his wheelchair on the porch, with mash on ice in an *SWP* glass. Mom had painted a welcome-home banner and strung it across the front porch sash. The boys at Hivey's arrived as a crew, walking up from the woodstove, Grubby Mitchell trailing behind them like an orphaned calf. Then came Lo, Chester, Paitsel, and some neighbors I'd not yet met, filling the porch and spilling into the living room.

"Pait, what's the latest on the OSM inspector?" Pops asked once the conversation settled.

"Comin in two weeks, he says. Meetin up with Bubba an his site team to see for himself."

"Who's he bringin? I heard one a them fancy lawyers is comin," Jesper asked.

Paitsel shook his head. "He's a fed boy—them lawyers work for the Appalachian Project. Apparently he's got the power to slap a CO on Bubba that'll shut the whole thing down."

"I thought they gave owners time to fix things. You sure he can issue a CO?"

"The feds got special powers. It's the state that gotta give abatement."

"An Bubba gots the state boys bought here to Frankfort. What makes you think he ain't gonna buy thisn?"

Paitsel shrugged. "I don't, Bobby. But the state boys is definitely bought, so we ain't got many other options, do we?"

Everyone nodded and sipped, then went silent. No one tried to find deeper meaning in the horror of Paul's death and the equal horror of how quickly Tilroy had turned. For the simple empirical was so terribly self-evident for all—a good man was beaten to death by a boy with promise. Trying to parse anything existential out of it or pontificate on the certainties of nurture just left a silent hole in the conversation until the awkward quiet got the better of someone.

"Paitsel, you done real good with this," Jesper said.

"Umm-hmmm," Andy Teel agreed.

"This is a top job, Pait," Bobby Clinch added.

"Tis," Chester agreed.

Chapter 41

THE CALLING IN

$\backsim$

Bubba Boyd's black Cadillac came slowly up the access road, as it always did when the demo team set up for a big blast. The car parked next to another new haul truck, three days deployed, and seemed remoralike against the massive yellow beast.

Bubba fingered the slurry pond report from Silas McCherry, his chief engineer, and pondered options. Paitsel's mischief-making was an unwelcome complication, but manageable. This new protest group he organized was going to fizzle just like the others. But now, with the petition logged, the Mitchell farm permit would have to go through regular channels. Could be months. "Goddamn Paitsel," he breathed.

"Yes, Mr. Boyd?" his driver said.

"Nuthin, Harlan."

For two years, now, Silas had been naysaying the Cheek Mountain dig—telling him the void underneath was too unstable; complaining they should have used a centerline dam for containment. And now he said they couldn't keep pumping into the Hogsback on the risk of a catastrophic collapse. Said the only option was to shut down until the permit came through and they could build more containment down mountain. But Wednesday shipped 270 tons—best day tally ever. *Shut down, my ass.*

It was Billy come up with the answer, he laughed to himself—simple, cheap, problem solved: make the dang crest ten, twelve foot higher with overburden. But Silas tried to kill that one too, until Bubba put his foot down.

McCherry was conferring with another hard hat when Bubba exited his car and walked toward them.

"Hey, Silas. Blaine. How you boys doin today?"

"Been better, Mr. Boyd," Silas said and glanced over at the digger truck piling gravel and riprap on the dam crest. "Did you read my report?"

"I did. Seems like a jumble a mights an maybes."

"Well, one thing I know for certain, just riprapping the crest ain't gonna work. Every foot of slurry is gonna add about two thousand tons pushing down on the upstream toe. I didn't build it for that kind of pressure. It may not fail right way, but it's gonna fail."

"In your opinion."

"Yes, sir."

Bubba smiled, patted him on the back. "Silas, let's walk on up an watch this big-ass blow. I swear I never get tired a seein it."

"I don't think that's a good idea, Mr. Boyd. All the new crest rock is too unstable."

Bubba blew a breath out his nose. "Up the dam's the best place to watch a blow, son. You know that." He started on the berm and after a few steps turned to Silas. "You comin?"

Together they slowly made their way up the dam face, Bubba pushing off his knees to facilitate each laborious step. At the crest, Silas stood hands on hips, assessing the overfilled lake of slurry. He pointed to where the black water lapped at the crest rock. "You see, sir. We've got no freeboard left. You just can't add height to the wall without reinforcing the downstream face and toe. And we got no room to bolster downstream. All the weight of the new slurry is going to push on the base of the dam."

"In your opinion."

"Gravity ain't my opinion, Mr. Boyd."

The digger crew went off to gather more overburden and Bubba regarded the twelve feet of rock and gravel they had just added to the southern crest of the dam. "We jus need it to hold for a few months while we get Mitchell's permitted."

A piercing horn clanged across the site, silencing the tractors, idling the draglines, and stilling the haul trucks. Men exited their vehicles and turned to a vast shelf of carved-out mountain a hundred yards across and fifty yards high—the last shoulder of what had been Cheek Mountain. A single stand of orphaned trees stood at the top of the hill, their understory bushwacked away so that now they seemed like naked prisoners paraded out for public humiliation.

"Looks like the boys have set the blow," Bubba said. "Gonna be our biggest one yet." He rubbed his hands together excitedly. "Come on, Silas. Let's climb on up an watch from the new top." He was giddy now, like a boy readying to launch his first model rocket.

"Sir, I wouldn't test the stability of the new riprap just yet. Give it a few days to settle."

"I always like watchin from the top—where we're at ain't the top no more."

"And, sir, blast this big, you really need to get your hard hat."

He ignored Silas and started up the newly laid gravel to reach the upper crest of the dam, and once so achieved he stood, legs wide for the steady, and overlooked his domain. Two hundred and seventy thousand square feet of the black lake—seventy million gallons of slurry—then the wide, gray guts of Cheek Mountain.

The blast holes had been drilled at twenty-foot intervals in four lines across the top of the ridge, charged with ammonium nitrate, filled with number four fuel oil, then capped and wired.

Every time Bubba watched a blow, it brought him back to his youth, to the Fourth of July celebrations his daddy used to orchestrate in town. He'd bring in massive fireworks from New York and a few Italians to dig and set the mortars. Daddy always let him light the fuse in those days, and that initial feeling of dominion, peculiar and comforting, spread its warmth within him like first liquor.

The trigger man looked up at the lone figure, high atop the riprap, to make sure he was ready, for he knew better than to detonate when Mr. Boyd was distracted. A flag man gave Bubba the signal, and the trigger man focused his binoculars on the crest. Bubba raised a hand from his side languidly, then slowly, purposefully turned his thumb up. A second horn sounded.

"I named it Mountain Heritage Action Network to attract all them former hippies an radicals up north." Paitsel chuckled. "It worked. We got a busload comin in for the rally." He passed Pops the flyer he had mailed to Jonathan Pendrick at the Appalachian Project in Washington, D.C.

We were on the porch at Chisold with him and Chester just as the sun started to fall. "This is good work, Pait," Pops said, clearly impressed. "You're doing Paul proud."

Paitsel nodded sadly. "Yeah, I think so."

"I'm running it free for the next week in the *Register*, plus doing a feature," Chester said.

Pops pointed his pipe end to Paitsel. "How the heck you get Ralph Stanley and the Osborne Brothers to play?"

"Baseball buddy knows their manager. They'll draw some folks."

"You got that right. What kind of pushback are you getting from Bubba?"

"Nuthin yet. Other than he made sure we couldn't have it in town. Jesper's place is better anyway. The Company is organizing a counterrally in town, so having it on private land means less potential for trouble."

"You watch yourself, Paitsel. Bubba Boyd is a ruthless son of a bitch with money and power behind him. You are nothing to him."

"Yeah, but sometimes nuthin ain't a bad hand."

As soon as the trigger went, smoke from the firing explosives blew out of the holes in a right-to-left rhythm like some old phantom train, invisible but for its billowing shoots of white, erupting silent at first, then giving to staccato booms as the sound arrived. The concussion traveled the length of the escarpment, and Cheek Mountain seemed to shudder and swell as would a lumbering mastodon, surprised and indignant at the many spears of man. The mountain gathered itself for a moment, then collapsed at once in a great rumbling sigh as the hard rock shattered, the subsoil liquefied, and the orphan trees rode the rubble down to oblivion.

On the settle, a great gray cloud of dust pushed out and

rolled across the lake toward Bubba, washing over him, washing through him as he stood spread legged and steadfast to the bulwark. As the dust cloud continued down mountain, he made no move to slough it from his sleeves, made no attempt to shake it from his pants, and indeed he wore the smithereens of Cheek Mountain proudly, a further stamp of his complete and total dominion.

As the explosion's echo was fading, there began a low trembling from the bowels of the newly shorn earth, which many took for the settling of Cheek. It grew in pitch and violence, sending some men to the ground and causing the thick, black slurry to overslap its walls.

Bubba Boyd bent his knees and pushed his arms out to the side in an attempt to steady himself on the roiling crest. A particularly strong sway loosened the riprap, and the lot of it began to slide into the slurry with Bubba on the top, riding it down like a surfer. As he neared the lake, he began to backpedal, arms twirling in a vain play for balance and purchase. When the last of the riprap slid into the lake, Bubba pitched in with it, entering the slurry chin first, like a child taking a maiden poolside dive.

Silas would later testify that as Bubba flew through the air, the slurry lake opened up to receive him; he swore that the slurry parted prior to Bubba hitting the surface as if it was calling in one of its own. None of it can be verified, and it was likely just the action of the undulating water that Silas saw.

After a few seconds, Bubba's head bobbed up, minstreled black, and he started backstroking to the shore, flailing both arms at once. The movement seemed only to draw Bubba deeper into the slurry. Silas rushed up the riprap, got down on his knees, reached out an arm.

"Grab my hand," he implored.

Bubba moved a little closer.

"Grab my hand."

But the slurry had other ideas. Bubba shimmied his body around so his right hand could grab McCherry's. The movement pushed him well out of reach, and the pull of the slurry began to prevail. It was as if an ocean undertow had somehow found its way into the lake and was slowly drawing him down, drawing him under. The slurry was chin level now, then in his mouth. He spit out the black water, then bubbles as his mouth succumbed. He gave one final blow out when his nose went under, and he continued a slow sink until it was just his popping eye whites against the black of everything—surprised and indignant at the audacity of earth.

Seven hundred and fifty people packed into the Jensen farm for the rally. A banner strung between two poplars read:

Stop Mountaintop Removal Now!
Join the Mountain Heritage Action Network

The Osborne Brothers played first, then Ralph Stanley, then both bands together for a final rendition of "Paradise." In between were speeches from Paitsel, Chester, and Jonathan Pendrick, and a moving tribute from Betty Dodger about Simp's love for the wild places. Pops, only a week out of the hospital, watched from Jesper's back porch with a satisfied grin.

The counterprotest in the parking lot off Main Street drew three hundred surface miners from across the county and their families, an impressive turnout considering there was only free barbecue and beer. Hand-painted signs sprinkled the crowd:

These Are Our Mountains!
Coal Is Good

A clown roamed the coal party making balloon animals for the kids. Someone else was painting faces.

Bubba's death and the manner in which it befell him dominated the talk at the protest and counterprotest. At one they spoke of a celestial reckoning, an overdue comeuppance; at the other talk was of bad luck, unclear futures, and a family's grief.

All their lives they had taken bearings on the certainty of his pres-
ence; some found freedom in abdicating authority; others hackled at
his dominion over their lives. For them there was confederacy in a
common enemy; others took ease in determined prospects. But all felt
comfort of the familiar.

And now, with him gone and the draglines idled, uncertainty was
their new incumbent, accountability a sudden, unwelcome com-
punion. They took up their lives like the newly paroled, gingering
these found freedoms and secretly dreading their ambiguity. He was
a common adversary to rally opposition, a tangible benefactor with
whom to unite. Whether set hard for or against, now their notion
and understanding of things hung on abstraction. Now they had to
fathom out an uncertain future. Had to disentangle the unknown.

Chapter 42

NEEDFULS

When the OSM inspector finally came and saw the filled-up slurry pond, he immediately halted the Cheek Mountain dig. The state regulators scheduled a hearing in Frankfort the next week to fast-track the new containment pond on the Mitchell farm.

I brought Pops out to the porch later that week with morning coffee and the paper. I locked his wheels and adjusted the light blanket in his lap. "Thank you, son. Your superior nursing is tempting me to remain a permanent invalid."

"Don't get too used to it; after next week you are on your own." Mom pushed out the front door with coffee and sat next to him.

"Well, we wanted to talk to you about that. We think it would be best if you and your mom stayed here for a while longer."

"I've got school. What about Dad? What about my friends?"

"Not sure about any of that, but let's talk it through. On school, you could enroll in Missi High School with Buzzy. Try it for a semester, and if you don't like it, switch back to Redhill for second semester."

"Do you want to stay, Mom?"

She rubbed her arms as if a sudden chill had taken her. "I don't think I can ever go back to that house. At least not anytime soon."

"What about Dad?"

"I don't know."

It took me a nanosecond to weigh my options. "I'm not leaving you."

She held out a hand. I took it.

"All right, it's settled. I'll call Edward tonight and the school tomorrow. Better alert the sheriff too; the girls at Missi High are liable to riot on first day."

Mom smiled. I rolled my eyes.

Audy Rae pulled up in her car. Today was her day off and she usually used it to deliver canned goods, clothing, and other items to the county's poorest. Sometimes Mom came along if she felt up to it.

"Got the Budgets on my list this week," she said to Pops. "I don't know what the Lord is trying to tell me with that one."

"He's trying to tell you that Darwin was right."

Audy Rae shook her head. "Something." She turned to Mom. "You up for a ride out to Beaver Holler, Annie? You and Lucille knew each other from high school."

"I'd like that," she said softly. "Maybe there's some comfort I can offer."

"That's a kind thing, honey. I think she would appreciate the thought."

"Can I go too?" I asked. "I can help carry stuff." Since Tilroy's death three weeks ago, the Budget clan had not come into town, talked to the *Register*, or emerged from their cloistered hollow. I was curious about how they were managing their grief and wanted to try to thank Gov Budget again for helping Pops. We took the truck, three across the front bench, through town and out Route 17 to Beaver Hollow Road.

We arrived at the cul-de-sac to a yapping dog and bleatings from the two goats the Budget clan had acquired over the summer. Lucille Budget was sitting on her front porch in an aluminum lawn chair, watching her ten-year-old son throw stones at the barking hound tied to a tree in the front yard.

"Hey, you, come over here," she yelled to Audy Rae as we got out of the car. I was carrying a paper bag that contained an assortment of canned goods and secondhand clothing. Audy Rae had even cleaned out Pops' disused clothing closet and added some of her family's old wearables.

She stopped, smiled wanly at Lucille, and walked to the bottom of the porch steps.

"What can I do for you, Lucille?"

"You can do for me to say what the hell you're doin here."

"I'm doing the delivering for social services this week."

"Lemme see what you got. Get on up here."

I walked up the steps behind Audy Rae and Mom and set the bag at Lucille's feet. She had one arm raised and tucked behind her head. Her armpit hair was slicked flat from sweat, giving it the appearance of a dirt stain. She began rummaging through the bag and pulled out a can of creamed corn and put it on the side table. Next came two cans of pumpkin pie filling, then a jar of pickles and two boxes of Tuna Helper. She removed a man's white dress shirt and held it up by the shoulders, examining the workmanship like a master seamstress. Cigarette dangling from her mouth, a ten minute ash dangling from the cigarette.

"Hello, Lucille, do you remember me? It's Annie Peebles," Mom said to her. "We went to high school together."

Lucille kept at the shirt. "Yeah, I remember," she said. The cigarette ash tumbled to her chest, mixing with flecks of morning scrapple.

"Well...I just wanted to say hello and tell you how sorry I am to hear about Tilroy."

She checked the size of a child's winter coat. "Well, now you done it."

"Yes, I guess I have, haven't I," Mom replied. I watched her watch Lucille Budget sort through the clothing. Mom smiled but said nothing else.

After a minute I drifted over to Lucille's son by the tree. He had exhausted his supply of dog stones and picked up a whippy green stick. The dog saw the boy approaching and ran to the other side of the tree. The boy chased it around the poplar until the leash was wound up and the hound immobilized. He raised the stick and the dog blenched. He brought it down hard on the dog's snout to a piercing yelp from the animal and a frantic scramble to escape the beating. The boy raised his arm again and the dog hunkered for impact. He held the stick in the air, laughing as the dog cowered with eye whites watching the boy's arm for any movement. He started to bring it down hard and I caught it in midair. The dog yelped on the expectation. The boy whirled to me with crazy eyes. "Give it."

I took the switch from him and broke it.

Lucille was holding up a pair of polyester slacks, wondering if her sister Betty would fit into them. She heard the dog's yelp and yelled through the slack assessment, "Rayful! Don't be hittin on George no more; he's gonna bite your ass again."

Rayful pulled free and ran toward the barn at the back of the house. "An leave them goats be!" she yelled after him. I went to the dog, who was still cowering in the dirt. I stroked his head, then went to the porch.

"What else you got in the car?" Lucille asked Audy Rae.

"In the car? Oh, we have about three more parcels to deliver," she replied pleasantly. "We're heading up to Bonny Holler next, then over to the O'Shea place. The O'Shea brothers were both struck with the lung, as you know. Ernestine and Kendra are having a bad time of it."

"Well, don't jus stand here jowlin...go get what else you got."

"Excuse me?"

Lucille noticed me kneeling next to George. "Hey," she said to Mom. "Tell your boy don't be pettin on someone else's dog without permission." Then she yelled over to me, "Hey, boy, don't be pettin on that dog. He's a known biter."

I jerked away from the animal. At my sudden movement, George winced, steeling for a blow.

Lucille turned her attention back to Audy Rae. "Well, what you waitin on?...Go get the other stuff," she said and held up a pair of men's trousers for a quick look. "I can't be usin no Tuna Helper if I ain't got no tuna, now, can I?"

Audy Rae's forehead crimped. She folded her arms against her chest but kept smiling. "I'm sorry, Lucille, but I can't give you more...The O'Shea brothers are in a bad way and the Sletts up in Bonny are counting on this food to carry them til month end. I can't be giving you their needfuls."

Lucille put the pants back in the bag. "Let's you an me get somethin straight right now. *You* ain't givin me a goddamn thing. This is giveaway stuff. The O'Sheas or the Sletts ain't claimed it. Now, go on an bring that other stuff up here."

Audy Rae didn't move.

"Come on!" Lucille yelled and clapped her hands together. "I can't be waitin all day."

"Let's go get in the car," Audy Rae said to us and turned to walk off the porch.

Just then, a brown El Camino pulled into the driveway behind Pops' truck. Sen Budget got out and walked toward the house, eyeing the truck in his driveway. My mind immediately went to the cold killing of the family mule six weeks ago. I swallowed. He sauntered up the steps, looked to Mom and Audy Rae. "What the hell are *they* doin here?" he said to Lucille under his breath.

The skin on my neck went to goose bumps as he said it, and I found myself clenching fists.

Lucille was solicitous. "Nothin, Sen, honey; she was jus droppin off some needfuls."

"Where's Daddy's medicine?"

"Right here, Bunny." She held up a medicine bottle.

He looked down at the bag of clothes at her feet. "What's all this stuff?"

"Just some extra clothes from my family and social services," Audy Rae said. "I thought you could use them."

Sen smiled at her from a canted facade. "*You* thought *I* could use them?" He slowly took the food from the bag and placed it on the side table and walked over to Audy Rae and held out the bag. He was standing as tall as he could, which was only eye to eye with Audy Rae, his thin frame blown up like a puffer fish. Audy Rae took the bag.

"The day I take charity from a nigger is the day I put a bullet in my brain."

Audy Rae said nothing but kept her gaze locked onto his.

"I beg your pardon...what did you call her?" came an incredulous voice from Mom. She stormed up to Sen Budget and stood a half head taller in front of him. "How dare you speak to her that way." She jabbed a finger into his chest. "Came all the way out here to help you. You've got a lot of nerve." I was taken aback at the fury in her voice. Her face was flushed and her left hand was planted on her hip—finger still in the air.

Sen stood with his mouth agape. Lucille was hiding her thoughts somewhere behind all that flesh. My goose bumps became the size of ball bearings. Rayful and the girls were shrubbed together on the other side of the screen door, displaying a rare solidarity that only an outside threat could convey.

Sen looked at the ground and smiled, then opened his mouth to reply, but Lucille beat him to it. "Who the hell you think you are, comin into a body's porch an tellin them how to behave? Y'all take your bag a shit an git the hell off our propty, you hear?" She pushed up from the chair and lurched forward so the heaving appendage that was her belly touched Mom, adding an exclamation point to the command.

Mom took the bag from Audy Rae and we marched off the porch and into the truck. Sen's El Camino had blocked our exit, so Audy Rae drove off the driveway onto the dirt yard and up to the road. George regained a jot of confidence and offered a decisive yap.

Chapter 43

JUKES HOLLOW

Each day the next week Pops became stronger, moved around better. On the Friday before school started, we walked down to Biddle's for lunch. He was on a cane now, moving slowly, arm and chest still trussed. We stopped into Hivey's to say hello before the meal. Paitsel, Jesper, Bobby, Grubby, and the rest of the crew were loafing earnestly at the back by the cold woodstove.

"Mornin, ladies," Pops said.

"Look who's found his legs," Paitsel said.

"You goin to the big meetin tonight, Arthur?" Jesper asked.

"Don't know anything about it. Is it yours, Paitsel?"

"Not one a my meetins. Billy Boyd called it. Says he wants to lay out his plans for the Company. Says when the Mitchell farm permit goes through he's gonna need eighty more workers. Plus about forty temps for the construction."

Pops shook his head.

Paitsel took a sip of coffee. "Wars ain't won on a single battle, Arthur. We gotta take the long view. Mitchell's gonna happen. We gotta focus on preventing future permits."

"How do they know Mose Bleeker actually ate human flesh?" I asked Buzzy later that afternoon, referring to the likely source of his prized toenail.

"He spent three weeks down the mine with nothin but a canteen a water an come out fatter than when he went in. They found three a the bodies unspoilt, but they never found the other two."

"That doesn't prove he ate them."

It was his first day in a wheelchair and he was testing its workings back and forth across the hospital room. He stopped and spun to me. "They asked him how he stayed alive down there, an he jus smiled crazy an said over and over, 'Ain't kilt nothin, won't nothin die; ain't kilt nothin, won't nothin die.' Mr. Mose couldn't walk the streets without people starin an kids throwin stones. They all took him for a man-eater, so he started drinkin and become the town drunk. My grandaddy says he was a terrible miner, but he was a first-rate town drunk."

"I think I'd let myself starve before I'd eat human flesh."

"Not me. I'd cut a chunk a leg meat an roast it whole over an open flame an make me a sauce outta blood an kidney. That's the best part, the kidney."

"I thought the best part is the liver—baked in a piecrust."

We both laughed.

Buzzy thought about that for a moment, then said, "What if you got your arm chopped off an it was the only thing left to eat; would you eat it?"

"I'd probably bleed to death."

"Naw, you tied the blood off with your shoelace an lived."

"I guess I'd rather eat my own arm than someone else's."

"Druther lose an arm than a leg."

"I'd rather lose neither." I gripped them both.

"Suppose you was a prisoner a war and they was gonna chop off an arm or a leg but they was gonna let you choose; which would you choose?"

"They couldn't do that; it's against the Geneva Convention. I saw it on an old movie."

"Okay, you was stolen by aliens; they ain't got no conventions...which would you choose?"

"Where on the leg would they chop it?"

"At the knee."

"Definitely the leg then."

"Not me."

"Imagine having to scratch with no arms."

"Or havin to pick your nose." He did.

"Back in the Middle Ages in Persia they used to chop off people's hands for stealing—Pops told me."

"What'd they chop off if you lied?"

"Dunno, your tongue, I guess."

"I'd like to be a king back then. Wouldn't have to listen to nobody. What would you want to be?"

"What do you mean?"

"If you could go back in time an be someone else anywhere, what would you want to be?"

"Maybe a pirate on a ship in the 1600s, exploring the islands and plundering stuff."

"I'd like that too. I'm gonna change my time to that time."

We talked for hours that day of the ships we would skipper and storms we would breach; the sails we would unfurl and the crews we would captain. The precise place on the horizon where the ocean becomes the sky; the exact spot on the chest to run through a rival with a sword; the configuration of the southern stars. We talked of the islands we would visit and the suns we would set; the mountains we would scale and the beaches we would take; the pillage we would covet and the beautiful girls who would fall in love; the hearts we would break.

That night, the last hot of August air settled onto the porch despite the darkness. Lo and Chester were at the town hall meeting Billy Boyd had called, and Paitsel was in Frankfort lobbying mining regulators.

I poured Pops mash on ice and settled into the wicker chair next to him.

"You know, Thomas Edison only had three months of formal education—made his way on hard work."

And so it began.

"What are you gonna do on your last weekend of freedom?"

"Dunno. I'm thinking about going up to Jukes. Maybe spend the night up there."

"Good idea. You're rooted deep in that hollow."

"I'm thinking about clearing out all those little trees around the cabin. Maybe get rid of some of the junk in the ruins. Clean the place up a bit."

"That's a great respect, son. See if Audy Rae can drive you—I'm not ready for the highway just yet."

"I think I'm going to ask Mom."

Pops began to spin his mash slowly. He nodded and gave me the satisfied look of a man cataloging the well-completed segments of a work in progress.

Mom stared down at the car keys as if they were found pieces from a forgotten puzzle. "Audy Rae can take you, or Pops," she said quietly.

"Pops can't drive and Audy Rae is shopping in Glassville. I need you to take me."

"No, I can't. My mind sometimes . . . sometimes it . . ."

"I'll keep you focused."

"We'll get into an accident. If you got hurt I couldn't forgive myself."

"You'll drive slow."

"Pops has to come."

"He can't. He's resting."

She exhaled. "I don't even think I can remember how."

"I'll show you."

"How do you know?"

"Pops taught me."

She backed slowly out of the driveway onto Chisold, then took an arcing, deliberate turn onto Watford. Once on Main, we picked up speed to low double digits and crept to the stoplight at Green. The streets were nearly empty of cars, which made for easy passage through town—we crawled past Biddle's, Hivey's, Smith's. The lights were on at Miss Janey's; a cheery *Come In! We're Open!* in the door glass. I looked into the big front window at the barren cutting stations, then through to the empty washing department, then over to the reception area.

And there he was, leaning against the desk, arms crossed, smiling proudly from his bright-blue eyes, head cocked slightly to the right, a set of black combs in his white barber's jacket pocket. Tilroy's deft pencil and pastel strokes forming a precise rendering of the blade thin and the posture perfect—glassed and framed and hanging in reception as promised.

We turned onto Route 32, the urinal-mint factory dark and empty on the hill cut-in. Mom seemed to be gaining confidence now, speed increasing to thirty, me pulling threads of conversation from everything that had happened.

"Buzzy seems lonely in the hospital. I don't think he gets many visitors."

"His family doesn't come out of the hollow much."

"He just looks so sad in there."

"He's been through a lot."

"We've *all* been through a lot," I said with a tired laugh.

"But we've got each other."

"He's got his family," I protested.

"True. But those kids are expected to make their own way in the world. They don't get much support."

"That sucks for him."

"It's just their way. The kids do okay, so maybe there's a wisdom to it."

It was the longest and most lucid conversation I'd had with my mother since Josh.

I stowed the saw and hatchet in the porch corner, next to Pops' walking stick, left behind in the rush to the hospital, then went down to the waterfall. Grass had grown shin tall at his and Sarah's picnic spot, so I found a rusted scythe from the old shed, sharpened it, then took the long off the grass. I finished the job with the old push mower, cutting it close the way it was kept back then.

After raking the clippings, I cut saplings near the cabin, sawing them out one by one at grass level. By the time evening spread, I had cleared the entire side yard of trees.

At full dark I gathered the tools, laid them on the porch, and took a meatball sandwich and a Mountain Dew from the cooler Audy Rae had packed. I lit the kerosene lamp and sat on the porch, back against the cabin wall, walking stick across my legs, just listening to the night sounds—the same night sounds Pops heard as a boy so many years ago.

After an hour of night listening, I took the pack and the cooler and the lantern inside to the second bedroom with the triple bunks cut into the wall.

I put my sleeping bag on the top bunk, Pops' bunk, and climbed up the ladder and settled into his old bed.

Buzzy and I are working beaverlike to dam up a creek. He lays the fresh-cut bamboo measuring rod down on a fallen log and notches two cuts to mark the measure. We're at a two-handled saw, pulling and pushing the blade in opposition across the face of the tree. We cut through the base and hoist the log onto our shoulders—me at the front, him at the rear. This should be the last; then we'll be swimming, he says. We place it on top of the logs already in the creek and fit it to the notches we had dug into the bank. A cliff materializes on the edge of the dream. I'm first, he says and climbs the rocks. It's too shallow, I yell. But he ignores me and dives off. Don't, I yell as he floats in the air. He spreads his arms and executes a perfect swan dive into the water. After a few seconds, he breaks the surface as a wholly different boy—a smaller, thin boy with brown hair. His face is deeply familiar, but I just can't place him. This new boy exits the water and smiles to me. Jeb taught me that, you gonna go? I shake my head and he climbs to the top of the rocks. He dives again, another perfect swan, and comes to the surface as a young man. He cuts through the water with powerful, efficient strokes and climbs out to a waiting towel held by a beautiful woman with long chestnut hair. "You gonna go?" he says to her. She smiles, kisses him, then shakes her head. He climbs back up the cliff and dives in again, this time surfacing as the Pops I know. The beautiful woman on the bank has disappeared. Pops winks at me and climbs the rock for a fourth try. Arms out in front, then at the side to steady himself. He does a perfect swan dive into clear water. I wait for a moment, but he doesn't surface. I call out over the water but get no response. Panicking, I strip to my shorts and dive under, but he's already slipped away from me.

Chapter 44

JULY 2014

~~

We slide the burled casket carefully from the dark-blue hearse. The handles feel cool despite the stifling heat scalding eastern Kentucky this July. It is much lighter than I expect and we hoist it hip high as if empty. After three or four awkward steps, our walkings join to an intended cadence, and once so aligned, our pace is slow and purposeful, off the road, onto the grass, and down the hill toward the crossing.

The mourners file behind us as we move slowly toward the burial site on the hill. The sun, which shied all morning behind low clouds, swaddles us now in warm light. At the graveside, dirt from the hole is piled to the side, covered with an Astroturf carpet. Flowers everywhere. We cortege the casket to the grave and set it on the platform. We all gather around the coffin in a semicircle, clasping hands in front and behind for lack of purposeful utility.

"Dear friends," Pastor Barnes begins. "Let us pray..."

I scan the crowd for familiar faces, recognizing many through the application of years. They are stooped and creased now, some attended by grown children, others on their own.

He is standing by himself, off to the side. The tall man with beamed shoulders and a thick neck. His blond hair is cut short at the front, not quite a crew, and the back tails his shoulders. His dense beard is two shades darker than his hair. With hints of red.

He moves closer to the casket. Despite the beard I recognize him instantly. Recognize the three-piece suit he wore to Pops' brother's funeral ten years ago, now tight across him.

I smile and Buzzy Fink smiles back.

In 2002 Billy Boyd's Monongahela Energy traded the reclaimed plateau that was once Sadler, Cheek, and Indian Head to the commonwealth in exchange for mineral rights on a string of mountains north of Medgar up toward Big Spoon. Within two years a new supermax prison sprouted on the barren site with lights that Christmas-treed the stub of Sadler and washed all the luminance from the stars.

The Company took Floss Mountain first, then Limber, then Kinny and Chute—eight hundred acres clear-cut and ready for blasting, hauling, and filling. The jobs soon followed—dragliners, blasters, haulers, and supervisors—and outrage after that: anger at each new hollow fill, umbrage on every rust-running creek, rage with each new cancer diagnosis.

Paitsel organized protests, wrote letters, made phone calls, and cajoled B-list celebrities, but as always, the money was on the side of the mines. Each year the lines were drawn deeper and to ever more acute angles as cousins stopped speaking, kin became estranged, liquored friends fist-fought over draglines instead of women.

Katherine Marie Sloane was born on December 14, 1979, in the Subic Bay Naval Hospital while her father was on maneuvers in the South China Sea. After the Philippines came a fickle of postings around the world—Pensacola for first and second grade; then four years in San Diego; Dubai for junior high; senior year at the American School in London while her father taught at Greenwich.

She chose the University of Kentucky for their premed program and because she liked the brochure. After that, Emory for medical school.

She first saw him coming from a lecture on Merton. She was on her way to the chem lab with some friends when their sidewalks wove into one. He was by himself and walked as if he didn't mind being alone.

She chanced upon him again the following week when she was buying new running shoes for the cystic fibrosis 10-K. He was working at Foot Locker on weekends for walking-around money. She asked him the difference between the Advantra and the Road Warrior. He mumbled something about vacuum-molded soles. She could tell he was nervous, could feel his eyes on her as she examined the instep of the Jog Master. She wasn't surprised when he turned up at the race, and his attempts to keep up with her were valiant.

They went for coffee afterward and she caught him twice looking at her. Watching the tiny hairs that covered her earlobes and the space of skin at the end of her eyebrow. Watching the way the light overhead gave her chestnut hair a reddish tinge when she cocked her head a certain way.

She was a first-year med, she told him. He told her he was getting his masters in fine arts and wanted to write. She wanted to specialize in pediatric surgery, she said.

They talked of their parents. He hadn't seen his father in five years. Hers was teaching at the Naval Academy in Annapolis before retirement. She told him how it was to never have a home for more than a few years.

They discussed Nietzsche and cognitive dissonance in children. They argued architecture and whether Jan Brady was prettier than Marcia; if Gilligan really wanted to be rescued; if the Grateful Dead were any good.

She rubbed her coffee mug when thinking and tossed her hair to the side when she laughed.

They each told a dirty joke. Neither had any bumper stickers.

He tried to compliment her. She turned red and remarked on the coffee. He liked that she didn't wear bangle earrings—liked that she wasn't afraid to wear a cappuccino-froth mustache.

They each recited Shakespeare. She was Lady Macbeth spurring him to murder. He was Henry urging her at Agincourt. She was in love by the end of his mangled St. Crispin's Day speech.

She told him of her volunteer work at a children's clinic in town and about the time she berated a man in Safeway for hitting his own boy. They agreed that the animal rights people go overboard. Neither had seen a UFO.

They stayed until five p.m., examining each other's lives and discovering empathies in their opposite experiences. They parted, promising to meet for Italian the following Friday. She wrote her number on the back of the coffee-shop bill.

They married nineteen months later at the Naval Academy Chapel. His father came but left the reception early; his mother and grandfather danced all night with total abandon. She began her residency at Emory and he took an assistant professorship in the English department. Within a year she was pregnant and the trouble started. A difficult carry became a disastrous birth. Kate's uterus ruptured and she began hemorrhaging. The doctors saved her with an emergency Cesarean and amid the blood and building expectations came a little girl on air and light named Sarah Ryder Gillooly. My daughter.

Pastor Barnes' benediction speaks of renewal and a life to celebrate. Mom thanks the assembled for coming and tells a few anecdotes from Pops' life, then asks everyone back to Chisold Street for food. She jokes that she laid in extra Clinch Mountain sour mash on his specific instructions.

Kate squeezes my hand. "You sure you want to stay up here by yourself tonight? Mom can take Sarah."

I brush away a gnat cloud and kiss her. "I'm sure. I'll come by and get some stuff."

She smiles sadly, touches my cheek, and walks with Mom, Audy Rae, and the rest of them to the waiting cars at the cul-de-sac. I watch as they trace the trail down the hill, across the creek, and through the old field, now fully taken by trees.

It was Audy Rae who found Pops, sitting in the green wicker chair where she left him the evening before. Mom was down in Atlanta at an exhibition of her paintings and Audy Rae agreed to take care of him for the weekend. She knew he had passed as soon as she rounded Watford and saw him in last night's clothes. He looked asleep, but she knew otherwise. She closed his eyes all the way, brushed his hair with her hand, and went into the kitchen to call Dr. Killen.

After a while I walk down the trail, across the creek, through the young woods to the cabin. Before the baby, Kate and I would sometimes drive up from Atlanta for secret weekends in Jukes Hollow. I'd work on my thesis, she would study for her boards, and we would zip two sleeping bags together and entwine ourselves on the pine floor.

I linger on the cabin porch for a while, recalling those times, then head to Pops' old truck, still serving faithfully after all these years, and drive toward town to pick up my old camping gear from 22 Chisold. At Route 32, on impulse, I take a left instead of a right and after a few minutes turn into Fink's Hollow Road. Buzzy and I had not really spoken since I arrived, what with the funeral arrangements and other death duties. I drive up the hill to the houses, with Giggins Hoo sitting proudly in the middle of it all.

I see someone in the shadows of the porch and walk toward the house. In the darkened corner, sitting on the old La-Z-Boy recliner, is Buzzy's uncle Elwin, now patriarch of the hollow.

Buzzy's mother doesn't see much of Buzzy nowadays. He comes around once a month to take her to lunch at Sizzler, but because she and Crystal don't get along (fight like rabid cats, actually) they stopped visiting as a family around the time Tanner was born. Now, except for the lunches, it's only Christmas and the boys' birthdays.

I walk between Giggins Hoo and Buzzy's old house, now occupied by strangers, past the barn and up the trail to the tree house. I find the rock that marks the path to the old oak. The course is overgrown and underbrushed, but I can still read a faint gesture of trail and follow it along the shelf. After five minutes I tip the slight crest and the huge tree is before me. Buzzy is by the base, as I expected, smoking a cigarette and looking up at the remains of the tree house. He hears the crackle of leaves and turns around.

Shortly after high school started, Mom and my father separated. With everything she had endured in the preceding years, the divorce came as a relief, in some way providing passage on that cut of her life.

Buzzy and I entered tenth grade in September, him in a wheelchair for first semester. Our Glaston Lake adventure and the attending publicity made us local celebrities, and kids in school competed for our friendship. But we stuck together for the next three years as we grew through adolescence.

Cleo's senior season was another record breaker, but Isak Fink passed in his sleep shortly after Cleo left the hollow for Notre Dame. Buzzy and I watched his father's slow slide that second summer, never really talking about it, never really needing to.

With no charges filed, Notre Dame quickly forgot the inconvenient circumstances of Cleo's involvement in the beating death of Paul Pierce. Second string as a freshman behind Tony Rice, then midway through their march to the national championship, Cleo's throwing shoulder separated during a dorm roughhouse.

Surgery, another separation, and he was back in the bedroom he shared with Buzzy, apprenticing at Wickle's Hauling.

By our own senior year we had abandoned the tree house for more adult pursuits. We secretly bought his cousin Licky's Dodge Dart for four hundred dollars saved from chopping firewood and selling it out of Pops' truck in the suburbs of Lexington. The car was registered to Buzzy and we kept it on an old mining road since he never told his grandfather. We hardly ever drove it, but it made us feel emancipated nonetheless.

At homecoming that year we had full rein of Twyla Buford's sister's trailer with Twyla and me in one room and Buzzy and Crystal Smith in the other.

For spring break we told everyone we were going camping up at Glaston and instead drove the secret car all the way to Panama City.

The rest of the spring was parties and the run-up to graduation. The excitement of applying to colleges and the quiet that came over Buzzy when I talked about it. Driving all night after prom to Hilton Head, then laughing as Crystal and Twyla got their prom dresses soaked by a big wave. Graduation in the tent on the football field and the look on Pops' face as I stood to give the valedictory address.

After another summer chopping wood, I went off to Columbia. Buzzy's uncle got him a job building wood forms for Clemet Construction in Glassville.

We saw each other whenever I was home from school, but gradually, as we put years and divergent experiences between us, we found less reason to meet. During those few awkward visits we always regressed to retelling that first summer together.

Crystal got pregnant when they were twenty, and Buzzy married her in a courthouse ceremony. He bought a suit for the occasion, honeymooned her on a four-day weekend in Myrtle Beach, then moved into Crystal's mother's trailer in downtown Medgar.

Once Tanner was born, they rented their own place at the Dew Meadow Park (next to the new Walmart outside Glassville). Even though it was only a single-wide, Crystal was boastful of the trailer because it had one of those retractable awnings that came only with the top-of-the-line double-wides.

The old oak hasn't changed at all. The years since my last visit growing on it in indiscernible fractions. The tree house is gone, except for a few pieces of the platform. The ruins look like a hunter's tree stand, alone in the nest of the big branches. Around the base are a few ebbed fragments of the old house; a fleck of a wall; some shingles half buried under the leaves; the arm of a red rocker over by a stump.

Buzzy's tie is loosened and his jacket is draped over his arm, a sweat blossom across his back.

"Hey, Indiana," he says.

"I thought you might be up here," I say.

He turns back to the tree.

"I tried to climb it but couldn't get much past two foot. Gettin old an fat, I guess."

"I'm not even going to try," I say.

"Sorry I wasn't able to come to Tingley's. I been workin a double shift last two weeks. We been so busy we had to turn away some jobs."

"Don't worry about it."

We are silent for a minute, trying to rediscover the easy conversation of our youth.

Finally he says, "I never tole you this before, but I used to wish your grandaddy was my grandaddy, too. That we were brothers." He pauses, then continues. "I used to wonder what it would be like, havin him to look up to."

"But you looked up to your grandfather. He was a good man."

"I looked up to him, all right. I just dint have to be lookin up very far."

I open my mouth to comment but let the thought fade in me instead.

Buzzy breaks the silence.

"You know, I used to envy you, Kevin. You were my best friend, but, man, I used to envy you."

"Envy me? I'm the one who envied you. You were the most popular kid in school. I was happy just to get your castoffs."

"Yeah, an look at us now." He gazes up into the broad branches of the oak. "You see, I knew that summer, when the Glaston story got out an we had all them reporters callin after us. All them people wantin to know us—bein on TV an in the newspapers an stuff. I knew that my life was never gonna get better than right then. We was fourteen years old an in the fuckin *Lexington Herald*, for Christsake."

We are silent again, standing under the arch of the oak, pretending to be fascinated with what is left of the tree house. I finally bring the conversation back to a tested topic.

"Remember when Levona Stiles' hair caught on fire that time? When she and Petunia came up to the Telling Cave with Tilroy and Skeeter?"

He brightens and laughs. "I swear I thought you were gonna wet yourself when she took off her top."

He shakes his head and kneels to pick up a quarter-size piece of tree-house wall.

We are awkward again, searching our catalog of experiences for common conversation.

"How's your baby?" he asks. "Heard you had a girl."

"Not much of a baby anymore; she's almost three. How are your boys?"

"Great."

"What are they, seventeen and twenty?"

"Nineteen an twenty-two."

"Twenty-two! He's a grown man. How's Crystal doing?"

He pauses.

"We've separated."

"Sorry to hear that. When did this happen?"

"Last week," he says, then hesitates again. "It's been comin."

The conversation tails. I look up at the sky and see nothing but blue.

"They say it's going to be a really hot summer. Probably from all that global warming stuff."

"I heard that," he says, then pulls a thread of conversation from the comment. "Do you ever watch the Weather Channel?"

I shake my head.

"Oh man, the Weather Channel is great. I watch it all the time. I love watchin what the weather is like in places like Africa or China someplace. Drives Crystal nuts."

"We don't have cable," I add, as if some justification is required for my lack of interest in third world weather.

"No cable?"

"I mean, we can get it if we want. But we decided we wouldn't really use it."

"What do you do for sports?"

"I don't have time to watch it anyway. I never knew how hard teachers worked until I became one."

We are silent until finally he says, "Well, I'm gonna head on back. I'm takin my momma out to lunch. I try to do that once a month."

"That's a good thing."

We walk silently back down the trail to Fink's Hollow. He smiles at the sight of the old truck and puts his hand on the hood as if to draw out more memories from that magical time in our lives. Finally he sticks out his hand and I take it. "It's good seein you, Kevin. I jus wish it was for better reasons."

"Yeah, it was good to see you, too. And thanks for coming out to the hollow. I appreciate it."

He nods, then says, "Next time you're in town, give me a call. I'll be in my new place by then. You can come over or somethin."

"Yeah, I'll do that," I say. "I'll definitely do that."

He turns and walks off toward Giggins Hoo. I follow the road out of the hollow and back to town.

Medgar is alive with activity now, with the mines heaving and the prison nearing capacity. I drive through the west side to Main Street. The place is a puzzle with familiar pieces cut to a new picture, for all the old Main Street stores are gone. Dempsey's closed in 2001 after a Food Lion opened at the old urinal-mint factory. It is now an antique store. Miss Janey's shut that same year after Miss Janey suffered a stroke and lost the use of her right arm. It's a quilt shop.

Smith's is long gone, out of business soon after 2003. It reopened as a 7-Eleven. The movie theater is a movie theater again, offering first-run films. Bank of America took over the Monongahela Bank and Trust in 2005, people two deep at the ATM.

A McDonald's gilds the corner of Watford and Main. The coming of the arches was a bitter blow for Hank Biddle, and he sold out soon after to an Indian family who turned the place into a Sizzler franchise.

Perhaps the most jarring casualty on Main Street is Hivey's Farm Supply. Shortly after the new century, a modern farm store opened in the Walmart complex in Glassville, and Hivey's business dropped precipitously. Bump Hivey finally closed the store on Christmas Eve 2006 and moved his family to Johnson City. The place idled for eight years until it reopened four months ago as an overpriced coffee shop.

I push through the front door, half expecting Jesper Jensen, Bobby Clinch, and Grubby Mitchell to be sipping Venti Skinny Lattes at the back by the plastic woodstove built into the coffee bean display.

Unfortunately, Jesper died of a heart attack in 1999 during a round of Auction Pinochle with Lo Gilvens, who went undefeated in ten straight games. With Jesper gone, the loafing at Hivey's just wasn't the same and the group gradually disbanded. Bobby took over booth six at Sizzler, and Grubby drifted through make-work, then down to Florida after Mayna passed.

Several young couples are at tables by the coffee-shop window, reading the Saturday paper. Two people in line at the counter face smiling baristas. I take away a black coffee and walk around the corner to the alley on Green Street.

Although the signs out front have been swapped out, the alley and the attending memories remain as before—I try to shift them toward the positive; toward Paul happening upon a flat-tired Paitsel or wearing level-five hazmat gear to a gutter cleaning; toward the hair ribbon and the rifle-shot slap. But they drift back to the beating and the boy and the curious paradox of it all. I've thought about it often in the years since that first summer in Medgar, and I'm no closer to understanding how evil can be both numbingly complex and so astonishingly simple at once. I linger a while longer, then go back to the truck and drive up Watford.

I turn onto Chisold and Pops' old house comes into view. Wise and experienced next to the new houses crocusing the neighborhood. A crowd is gathered on the porch. An elderly man sits in the old green wicker chair. In the heat I think for a moment that it is Pops, but as I come closer I see it's Chester Skill. Mom is next to him, holding a pitcher of iced tea and pouring it into passing half-empty glasses.

Audy Rae comes out the front door with a tray of brownies, and several of the children line up reverently for one before escaping into the yard, the way a puppy jiggers off with a treat. The new neighbors are there, mostly young couples.

I park and walk into the yard, pausing by the big hickory to watch Pops' old and new friends chat, drink tea, sip sour mash, and tell stories about his life. Kate takes the iced tea pitcher from Mom and goes into the house to refill it. Chester tells about the time Pops drove Sarah Winthorpe's father's car into the reservoir in Lexington because he was too proud to admit to her that he didn't know how to drive. Several people throw their heads back in laughter. Paitsel tells of the turkeys and toys Pops delivered secretly every Christmas. Most nod their heads, smiling sadly.

Sarah sidles to Mom's legs and raises her arms to be picked up. Mom bends and sweeps her from the porch. She sees me standing by the hickory and wiggles back to the floor.

"Daddy!" she squeals and bounds the steps toward me, her chestnut hair giving itself to the sun.

The last of friends leave the porch and I pile the old camping gear in the back of Pops' truck, kiss Kate and Sarah, then head through town to Jukes Hollow Road.

I park at the huge rocks by the entrance and stand next to Ahab, running my hand along its cool, dark length. As I do, an image comes to me of a boy striding up Jukes Hollow Road, leather-bound book tucked under his arm, walking stick pushing off the hardpack. He passes me, passes through me, running his hand along Ahab in the exact path of mine.

I follow him on the road to the half circle of cabins, each busy with activity—folks working a cornfield, others hauling wood. A thin woman, aged beyond her years, is sweeping off the cabin porch with a home-tied broom. "Arthur, don't you be readin til chores."

"Done em," he says and races off to the waterfall before she can protest.

I walk down the hill, across the creek to the wounded ground where Pops has been laid. It was spade and shovel work since Tingley's couldn't get a backhoe across the creek, and they packed it as best they could, spreading excess in the woods, then scattering flowers over the bruised earth.

I notice stray chickweed around my grandmother's headstone and kneel to pull it. I take two steps back and look at them together. Side by side, as if sleeping in on Saturday morning.

SARAH WINTHORPE PEEBLES

BORN APRIL 19, 1920

DIED IN LABOR
DECEMBER 1, 1949

A VOICE LESS LOUD, THROUGH
ITS JOYS AND FEARS

ARTHUR BRADLEY PEEBLES

BORN JANUARY 3, 1919

DIED JULY 3, 2014

THAN THE TWO HEARTS
BEATING EACH TO EACH

I let the chickweed fall from my hand to follow the wind.

I walk over to the waterfall, to my grandparents' picnic spot under the magnolia, and sit on the bench as evening comes, just listening to his voice in the action of the water. I reach into the pack and pull out a half bottle of Clinch Mountain sour mash and a glass with *SWP* etched fancy into it. A light pour and spinning ice as I contemplate the man who shaped my life so expertly. I raise the glass and tip it toward him. "You know, if Hannibal had used mountain goats instead of elephants, he might've conquered Rome."

I stay on the bench by the picnic spot, feeling the mash and the memories and the last of the afternoon air as it is pushed out by the settling night. After a while I walk up to the cabin, light the kerosene lamp, and follow the flickering yellow into Pops' childhood room. Up onto the top bunk and under my old sleeping bag—the attic smell of the bedroll mixing with the faint scent of wood pulled from the ancient pine along with a century of living that resides there. They are a comfort as I drift off with Pops and Buzzy and that singular summer when we left the coverings of boy behind.

The next morning I wake with the cabin still jacketed in dark and stay there listening to the old sounds from his youth. After a while I climb down and walk out to the porch as morning breaks over the hollow. I stand on the hill by the cabin side, looking out at the creek, the field, the rocks, the waterfall, and the fresh scar in the graveyard.

I see in my mind how it must have looked when Pops was a boy. The rocky soil and sometimes sun yielding the best corn it could. I go back to the porch and linger, imagining a morning coffee gathering of weather predictors, crop forecasters, and coal pundits. I push open the front door and walk inside, feeling the history of the place rush to me. I amble through the kitchen to the doorway of the big bedroom, my footsteps submitting closed-museum echoes in the morning still.

The bed is mattressed and quilted now, and the boys have run from their room to their parents' bed and dove under the covers, kicking each other and pushing for position until their father tells them to quit. There's a chill this morning, so they lay together under the warm quilts, three boys in the middle, the parents touching feet to feet in an unspoken embrace. They have a full day of work before them, she to the morning milking, then a day in the corn rows, picking the early ears before the crows; he to the Hogsback seam.

But it's Saturday. So they lie together five minutes more, just touching feet, floating on the quiet as the boys drift back off. Finally, she slips out of bed and into the kitchen to fire the stove for the beginnings of breakfast.

ACKNOWLEDGMENTS

Several folks within Hachette created a swell of early enthusiasm for the novel and this initial momentum was critical for a complete unknown like me, with absolutely no writing credentials, to get noticed among the many fine writers on the company's list. Chris Murphy, Rick Cobban, Karen Torres, Lily Goldman, Erica Hohos, Steve Marz, John Lefler—thank you for reading *Secret Wisdom* ... for loving it, backing it, and pitching it throughout 237 Park Avenue. Thanks also to the rest of the Hachette sales team for your passionate support of the novel—you are the essential unsungs in this industry!

My editor, Deb Futter, is an absolute joy to work with—her instincts are spot-on and her edits made this a much richer, more focused story. Thanks to the rest of the Grand Central team: Dianne Choie and Kim Escobar, who kept me on task with patience and grace; Brian McLendon, a man of a thousand ideas and the tactical chops to make them happen; and Sonya Cheuse, yin to Brian's yang—I don't think I could have a better marketing and publicity team.

Thanks to my agent, Stephanie Cabot, whose deft mingling of encouragement and reality kept me grounded through this exhilarating, wrenching, incredibly fun process. To the fantastic

Gernert team: Anna Worrall, Ellen Goodson, Chris Paris-Lamb, Rebecca Gardner, Will Roberts, and the rest of the crew—to the balcony all!

A special thank-you to a young man who probably had more to do with getting this novel published than most, Andy Kifer— long-distance runner and reciter of perfect St. Crispin's Day speeches. He was the first in the industry to read *Secret Wisdom*, plucked fresh from the Gernert slush pile, stayed up all night on a weekend to finish it, then raved about it on a Monday to his colleagues throughout the eighteenth floor. Andy, I owe you a huge debt and some Shakespeare mangling lessons.

To my family: Michael, Connor, and Janice—your love, support, patience, ideas, and encouragement made the journey possible and the destination achievable.

And to God, from whom all wisdom comes...secret or otherwise.

Reading Group Guide

DISCUSSION QUESTIONS

1. How did your view of what happened to Joshua (and, subsequently, what happened to Kevin and the rest of his family) change as it was gradually revealed exactly how he died and how his death affected each member of the family?

2. Kevin is withdrawn, angry, and wracked with guilt when he arrives in Medgar. How does Pops make Kevin feel comfortable in his home away from home? How does Pops' influence in particular change Kevin as a person?

3. Describe Buzzy's relationship with Cleo. How does each brother view the other? What were the different ways that each of them was tested, and how do they each end up ultimately?

4. Pops works with animals and grew up on the land he continued to live on, while Buzzy knows all about the forest and the ways its inhabitants can help humans. How are their relationships with nature different from Kevin's? How is Kevin's understanding of land and nature changed by the end?

5. Is it possible for Joshua's accident to have been Kevin's fault, even partially? How would you feel in Kevin's place? In his parents' place?

6. How did Kevin's grandmother Sarah affect Medgar? Pops? Kevin?

7. Why was Paul's reveal of his homosexuality—a fact that almost everyone knew—such a shock at the town meeting?

8. Pops describes the Budget family as "different." What role do they play in the community of Medgar? How does Tilroy fit in with his family at the beginning of the novel, and how does his death change the family in the end?

9. How do class and financial status shape the different inhabitants of Medgar? Discuss the meaning of quotes such as the following one from Pops about Buzzy's family: "The Finks are poor, but they're proud poor. Esmer runs the Hollow hard. Kids stay in school, they truck their garbage out once a week. These are solid people."

10. Compare the attitude toward Paul and Paitsel at the meeting the night before Paul's beating ("We can't be havin this kinda sick, Satan devil cancer in our town") and the conversations Kevin heard from all different townspeople regarding Paul days later ("Uncommon generous. No better man in town, I say"). How do those two different

perspectives get pulled back and forth, both in the town and in Kevin's mind?

11. Pops physically punished Bubba Boyd for speaking ill of Sarah: "The fury that exploded and the speed with which it arrived frightened me—it was as if a raging magma, held down for so long by rearing and position, ruptured its vessel and spewed forth in an overpowering surge." How does this capacity to become enraged fit with the rest of Pops' character?

12. Describe the turmoil that Buzzy suffered between when he witnessed the attack on Paul and when he finally confessed to Kevin. What would you have done in his place?

13. When Buzzy got an A in school, his father's reaction was surprising to Kevin: "Buzzy the Brain, gonna live above his rearin." Why would a parent react like that? What did that statement make Kevin realize about the truth of living in the hollow?

14. "It's like you own the universe." Why did Tilroy attack Paul?

15. Pops tells the boys about the magic and power he felt after climbing Red Cloud, a feeling he compares to theirs upon climbing Old Blue on their tramp, and Kevin feels he understands the new knowledge: "Yesterday was the hardest thing I've ever done in my life. The whole day was a test. I know I can do harder things, now." What other experiences in the

story brought out similar reactions in Kevin and Buzzy? Do you think the "magic" of Red Cloud or the white stag can really exist?

16. How did the difficult and daring rescue of Pops help Kevin (and Buzzy) complete his summer transformation from boy to man?

17. Kevin finds a moment of connection and empathy when he considers Tilroy's body for a final time: "I stayed for just a moment more and thought about my own father; how I still wanted his approval, still craved his love, still drank up drops of attention. I considered the shell of Tilroy one last time and pondered the certainty of rearing; the inevitability of desire; and the turn life takes when the two are set hard against." How was he able to call up understanding for this troubled young man who violently killed a good man and shot Kevin's own grandfather and friend? How would you have felt in Kevin's place?

18. Considering what happened by the end of the summer to all the different characters—Kevin and his family, Buzzy and his, Tilroy and his, Paul and Paitsel—do you find everyone's transformations (or lack thereof) satisfying? Why or why not?

19. Kevin and Buzzy have changed since they became fast friends the summer that Kevin moved to Medgar. Buzzy expresses his envy of Kevin and the life he always knew Kevin would have, even when they were young. What kept the boys so

close together during their teenage years, and why have they grown up to have such dissimilar lives? Do you think either of them could have done anything to maintain their close relationship?

20. The lingering effects of violence are an important theme in the novel. How does the violence done to the mountains serve as an allegory for the violence perpetrated by and done to characters in the novel?

A CONVERSATION WITH
CHRISTOPHER SCOTTON

Q: Why did you choose eastern Kentucky as the setting for the novel?
A: That area of Appalachia is such a beautiful setting with incredibly unique, interesting people...but it's also a tragic and quite sad place where the people have been forced into this Faustian bargain with coal. That paradox seemed to be a fascinating and rich backdrop for Kevin's story.

Q: Setting is such a critical part of the novel, almost a character itself, yet you've never lived in Appalachia—was that a hindrance in writing the novel?
A: I think any capable writer can create an authentic setting with a reasonable amount of research and location work. I spent a good bit of time down in West Virginia and Kentucky, up in the hollows and in the small towns, meeting folks and just listening to their stories. The key is to let the marrow of a place sear into your consciousness so that when you are writing, you can transport yourself there.

Q: Why did you choose to set the book in 1985? How did the events going on in Appalachia and in America as a whole at that time affect the characters in the novel?

A: I thought it was important for the reader to understand and experience the complete arc of Kevin and Buzzy's friendship. Here are two kids from completely different backgrounds who come together at a critical time in their lives and forge such an important bond. Yet, as so often happens, both kids were already set on a certain life path defined by rearing and place, background and expectations. It's a sad reality that early friendships sometime don't survive the life we find ourselves in. So by setting the novel back in 1985, I could bring the reader to the present day at the end of the story so they can see how Buzzy and Kevin have changed as adults, bittersweet as it is.

Nineteen eighty-five was also an important time in the region as mountaintop removal started to expand rapidly without much regulation. The analog today is the headlong rush to fracking without nearly enough data on aquifer contamination. I think it's an interesting comparison.

Q: *You speak of a Faustian bargain the people of eastern Kentucky have made with big coal—is the book anti-coal?*
A: I don't see it as anti-coal and I hope it's not perceived that way. I certainly didn't set out write a polemic about the evils of big coal because I think the issues are far more complicated and nuanced. But the reality is that the economy in this region is shackled to coal. The land is difficult to farm, access in and out is limited, so there is little scope to break the addiction, if you will, to the money coal brings. Now, back when the coal was extracted from underground mines, that Faustian bargain was somewhat hidden from public view—miners died underground or in the quiet of their homes. However, mountaintop removal has really laid it bare and exposed the great inequity of the deal. But without many

economic alternatives, the people of Kentucky and West Virginia need to make some really hard choices about their economic future. They are loyal, hard-working folk who deserve much better, in my opinion.

Q: *Love and loss are powerful themes in the novel—how are they important to Kevin's redemption?*

A: Loss is obviously a universal experience and is essential for any kind of redemption. Loss can take many forms: loss of innocence, loss of integrity, or in the case of Kevin, loss of a loved one. His loss is greatly compounded, though, by the loss of his mother, who's folded into herself after witnessing the tragic death of her youngest son. Kevin also must deal with the loss of the relationship with his father, who has stacked Kevin with blame and guilt. Here's this fourteen-year-old kid whose world has just been torn apart. But out of the wreckage, Kevin finds a faltering path to redemption.

Q: *Joshua's death is a gripping, horrifying, and much anticipated (and dreaded) part of the story, particularly since it is referenced several times before the reader finds out what happened. Just as that was a catalyst for Kevin's guilt, his mother's shutting down, and their move to Medgar, was that a starting point of the story for you, or did it come later?*

A: It actually was the starting point. A number of years ago, I met a good friend's mother for the first time—she was an incredibly beautiful woman who seemed to carry with her a deep-set sadness that only showed itself in her unguarded moments. I asked my friend about it and she told me the story of how her older brother died before she was born—it was Joshua's story. I was horrified, of course—it's an experience well past any parent's nightmare—but from it I began to build Kevin's story.

Q: *Who or what event in your life inspired the characters of Kevin, Buzzy, and Pops?*
A: I think every writer mines characters and plot from their own experiences and certainly Kevin, Buzzy, and Pops have parts of me in each of them. I grew up about thirty miles outside of Washington, D.C., in country that very quickly became suburbs, so Kevin and Buzzy are an amalgamation of that childhood. I never really knew my grandfathers and I guess Pops is the grandfather I wish I'd had—I suspect he's the grandfather a lot of us wish we'd had.

Q: *Kevin's rescue of Pops—much of it by himself—is harrowing and both emotionally and physically wrenching. How were you able to put such a difficult but believable journey together? Did you hear any stories about similar experiences?*
A: I've always been fascinated with how people behave in highly stressful, life-threatening situations—some rise to the moment, others curl up and go fetal. These situations strip away the façade of the persona we've tried to construct and lay bare the person we really are. In Kevin's case, his father has layered on so much self-doubt, guilt, and anger that it takes this difficult journey to awaken the strong, righteous, caring person he really is. Pops is his last, best hope for a normal life and Kevin knows it, owns it, and delivers.

Q: *The earth's healing power seems to be an important motif in the novel—you call it a madstone. What is a madstone and why is it important to the story?*

A: A madstone is an old folk remedy to cure snake bites and fevers. It's a calcified hairball-like thing from the intestine of a cud-chewing animal—you're probably thinking, "Cool, where can I get one?" If someone is bitten by a copperhead or a rabid dog, the madstone would be applied to the bite and the poisons would be drawn out of the bite. Madstones vary in strength and effectiveness—a madstone from a cow is only mildly effective; a madstone from a deer is considered quite powerful. However, the madstone from a white deer is the most powerful of all and unicorn-like in its scarcity. Interestingly, madstones can't be bought or sold or they'll lose their power; they must be found or given.

In the novel, the earth becomes a madstone for several of the characters, drawing out the pain and poison from the losses they suffer.

Q: *Do you believe in the magic or spiritual significance of symbols like the white stag?*
A: Very much so. We only understand a sliver of the known world, let alone this mysterious, magical, spiritual unknown world that seems to exist in the ether around us. We've all had those "white stag" moments where we come upon the unexplainable or magical or spiritual. I think it's the height of human arrogance to believe that existence ends at the observed world. Call them guardian angels, malaaika, fravashi, or spirit guides, the inhabitants of this possible netherworld populate nearly every culture—they are difficult to explain, impossible to prove, but a comfort if you believe in them.

Q: *There is a recurrence of both physical and emotional violence in* The Secret Wisdom of the Earth—*to the land, within the commu-*

nity, and within Kevin's own family. How does violence impact us as we grow up and shape the adults we eventually become?

A: There are two kinds of violence in the world: intended and unintended. Both leave a mark, but the scar of intended violence is quite deep and often slow to heal. It's a scar that can debilitate and reshape lives in tragic ways. But through fortitude and resilience one can rise above. Paul is a great example of that. He suffers terrible beatings at the hands of his father, but through sheer will patches together a good life with Paitsel. The violence done to the mountains is obviously intended and serves as an allegory for Paul's pain and for others who have suffered similar violence.

Q: Can you talk about your writing process—how do you work?

A: My writing process is all about stealing moments. I wrote the bulk of the novel while working in London and helping raise my sons. I'd get up at five a.m. and write for two hours, then head off to work. Come home and put the kids to bed, then revise what I wrote in the morning. Then I returned to the States and founded a search engine company (unfortunately not named Google). That job was twelve- to eighteen-hour days and I didn't write a single word for seven years—the job was just too demanding. The company was a spectacular failure and was one of many that became Google roadkill. When that company failed, I joined a VC firm for a few years and went back to my five a.m./eight p.m. writing/revising cycle. That allowed me to finish *Secret Wisdom*.

Q: You've rendered the characters in Secret Wisdom *so vividly— what's your process for bringing them alive on the page?*

A: I do a pretty deep character outline in my head—I get to know absolutely everything about them, understand their behavior and motivations completely. Then I let them loose in the setting and just see what happens. I don't really work off an outline; rather, I let the fully-formed characters drive the action.

The old writing chestnut "show, don't tell" is probably the single most important technique in creating vivid characters. Place them in situations that reveal themselves to the reader... however, that reveal must also advance the plot.

Q: *How has your experience running technology companies informed your writing?*

A: Not at all; in fact the two are quite antithetical and take completely different skill sets. Writing by its very nature is an interior activity—you go on these internal journeys to the far neighborhoods of your brain, rattle some doors, and write about the people who answer. Being a good CEO requires a wholly different set of capabilities—exterior skills such as leading teams, communicating effectively to groups, having an unflaggingly positive attitude, decisiveness, reading people, hiring well, firing well. So no, running companies hasn't helped my writing at all, although one or two of my past investors would argue that some of my business plans qualified as fiction.

I think where it has helped me is in understanding the business of publishing. Finding an agent is actually a lot like finding venture capital—many of the same tenets apply...stuff like doing your homework to find the right agent, making a professional approach, selling an idea. I was surprised how similar they actually are.

Q: *What's next? Are you working on a second novel?*

A: I am. It's a completely different story—different time period, different setting. I don't want to give too much away, but I'm looking forward to sharing it.